*Acclaim for*
Virginia Bedfellows

"American history was never like this in high school! Filled with period detail, *Virginia Bedfellows* relates the randy adventures of two male indentured servants in Colonial Virginia. Lance, an apprentice cordwainer, or shoemaker, and Adam, who assists the plantation's manager, experience sexual passion, fall in love, and even contemplate marriage in this tale, which blows open the myth that gay men did not participate in the settling of the Americas."

Neil S. Plakcy, author of *Mahu*

"Who knew Colonial Virginia was this hot? Morris delivers a heartfelt story of love and loss amidst the historical landscape of mid-1700s Williamsburg where two boys, thrust from their upbringing in England, are forced to fight for new lives and the love they find in each other. This is a stirring, sexually charged tale that reminds us that gay love has ever been an inevitable part of history—even when its discovery meted out punishment and death—and has emotionally equaled the passions and pathos of its heterosexual counterparts in every age."

David Foucher, Publisher, EDGEboston.com,
EDGE Publications, Inc.

"In this thick and juicy eighteenth-century saga, Gavin Morris celebrates the 'his' in history. No, make that the 'ours' in history. What a great idea to set a hot-and-bothered man-on-man romance in pre-Revolution America . . . . Of course we were there! Here's a hearty salute to Morris and his dashing cast of wild colonial boys."

Jim Gladstone, Author of *The Big Book of Misunderstanding;*
Editor of *Skin & Ink: Hot Tatoo Tales*

"Gavin Morris's historical novel, *Virginia Bedfellows,* deals with a subject that has rarely been written about: indentured servants shipped from England to her colonies in America. It describes the men, often (but not always) felons, condemned to seven years of servitude in the colonies, in lieu of a lengthy prison term in England. Like slaves, they would be auctioned off upon arrival, and could be sold by one master to another. They were marginal characters in their new surroundings, and therefore less beholden to traditional sexual roles and mores. The man-to-man sexual scenes are pretty explicit, more stirring than modern such descriptions, since the death penalty was meted out to anyone caught performing an 'unnatural act.' This novel is an entertaining read as well as an instructive lesson in American history."

Joseph Itiel, Author of *Escort Tales: The Trophy Boy and Other Stories*

## NOTES FOR PROFESSIONAL LIBRARIANS AND LIBRARY USERS

This is an original book title published by Southern Tier Editions™, Harrington Park Press®, an imprint of The Haworth Press, Inc. Unless otherwise noted in specific chapters with attribution, materials in this book have not been previously published elsewhere in any format or language.

### CONSERVATION AND PRESERVATION NOTES

All books published by The Haworth Press, Inc., and its imprints are printed on certified pH neutral, acid-free book grade paper. This paper meets the minimum requirements of American National Standard for Information Sciences-Permanence of Paper for Printed Material, ANSI Z39.48-1984.

### DIGITAL OBJECT IDENTIFIER (DOI) LINKING

The Haworth Press is participating in reference linking for elements of our original books. (For more information on reference linking initiatives, please consult the CrossRef Web site at www.crossref.org.) When citing an element of this book such as a chapter, include the element's Digital Object Identifier (DOI) as the last item of the reference. A Digital Object Identifier is a persistent, authoritative, and unique identifier that a publisher assigns to each element of a book. Because of its persistence, DOIs will enable The Haworth Press and other publishers to link to the element referenced, and the link will not break over time. This will be a great resource in scholarly research.

# Virginia Bedfellows

# HARRINGTON PARK PRESS®
## *Southern Tier Editions*™
## Gay Men's Fiction

*Elf Child* by David M. Pierce

*Huddle* by Dan Boyle

*The Man Pilot* by James W. Ridout IV

*Shadows of the Night: Queer Tales of the Uncanny and Unusual* edited by Greg Herren

*Van Allen's Ecstasy* by Jim Tushinski

*Beyond the Wind* by Rob N. Hood

*The Handsomest Man in the World* by David Leddick

*The Song of a Manchild* by Durrell Owens

*The Ice Sculptures: A Novel of Hollywood* by Michael D. Craig

*Between the Palms: A Collection of Gay Travel Erotica* edited by Michael T. Luongo

*Aura* by Gary Glickman

*Love Under Foot: An Erotic Celebration of Feet* edited by Greg Wharton
  and M. Christian

*The Tenth Man* by E. William Podojil

*Upon a Midnight Clear: Queer Christmas Tales* edited by Greg Herren

*Dryland's End* by Felice Picano

*Whose Eye Is on Which Sparrow?* by Robert Taylor

*Deep Water: A Sailor's Passage* by E. M. Kahn

*The Boys in the Brownstone* by Kevin Scott

*The Best of Both Worlds: Bisexual Erotica* edited by Sage Vivant and M. Christian

*Tales from the Levee* by Martha Miller

*Some Dance to Remember: A Memoir-Novel of San Francisco, 1970-1982* by Jack Fritscher

*Confessions of a Male Nurse* by Richard S. Ferri

*The Millionaire of Love* by David Leddick

*Transgender Erotica: Trans Figures* edited by M. Christian

*Skip Macalester* by J. E. Robinson

*Chemistry* by Lewis DeSimone

*Friends, Lovers, and Roses* by Vernon Clay

*Beyond Machu* by William Maltese

*Virginia Bedfellows* by Gavin Morris

*Seventy Times Seven* by Salvatore Sapienza

*Going Down in La-La Land* by Andy Zeffer

*Planting Eli* by Jeff Black

# Virginia Bedfellows

Gavin Morris

Southern Tier Editions™
Harrington Park Press®
An Imprint of The Haworth Press, Inc.
New York • London • Oxford

For more information on this book or to order, visit
http://www.haworthpress.com/store/product.asp?sku=5623

or call 1-800-HAWORTH (800-429-6784) in the United States and Canada
or (607) 722-5857 outside the United States and Canada

or contact orders@HaworthPress.com


Published by

Southern Tier Editions™, Harrington Park Press®, an imprint of The Haworth Press, Inc., 10 Alice Street, Binghamton, NY 13904-1580.

PUBLISHER'S NOTES

The development, preparation, and publication of this work has been undertaken with great care. However, the Publisher, employees, editors, and agents of The Haworth Press are not responsible for any errors contained herein or for consequences that may ensue from use of materials or information contained in this work. The Haworth Press is committed to the dissemination of ideas and information according to the highest standards of intellectual freedom and the free exchange of ideas. Statements made and opinions expressed in this publication do not necessarily reflect the views of the Publisher, Directors, management, or staff of The Haworth Press, Inc., or an endorsement by them.

This is a work of fiction. Names, characters, places, and incidents either are the products of the author's imagination or are used fictitiously, and any resemblance to actual persons, living or dead, business establishments, events, or locales is entirely coincidental.

Cover design by Lora Wiggins.

### Library of Congress Cataloging-in-Publication Data

Morris, Gavin.
    Virginia bedfellows / Gavin Morris.
        p. cm.
    ISBN-13: 978-1-56023-588-0 (pbk. : alk. paper)
    ISBN-10: 1-56023-588-8 (pbk. : alk. paper)
    1. Gay men—Fiction. 2. Indentured servants—Fiction. 3. Virginia—History—Colonial period, ca. 1600-1775—Fiction. 4. Williamsburg (Va.)—Fiction. I. Title.
PS3613.O77234V57 2006
813'.6—dc22
                                                                                        2005027585

# CONTENTS

༚❧

1747: Aboard Ship    1

1747-1748: Cromley Hall    21

1747-1750: Williamsburg    40

1748-1750: Ashley Landing    66

1750: After a Hunting Trip in the Woods    88

1751-1752: New Good Names and an Ugly Old One    102

1753: Williamsburg    122

1753-1754: Ashley Landing—Letters    164

1754: Ashley Landing: A Winter Visitor    190

1755: Williamsburg and Ashley Landing    211

1755: The Cemetery at Ashley Landing    241

Late 1755: In a Thicket of Bushes    265

If a man also lie with mankind, as he lieth with a woman, both of them have committed an abomination: they shall surely be put to death: their blood *shall be* upon them.

Leviticus 20:13 (King James Version)

*Crimen inter Christianos non nominandum*
"It is a Crime not to be named among Christians"

9th Provision of the Virginia legal code of 1610: "No man shall commit the horrible and detestable sins of Sodomie upon pain of death."

1624-25: Execution by hanging of Richard Cornish: In testimony sworn in court, William Crouse, 29, said that on "the 27th of August last," Richard Cornish, Captain of the good ship *Ambrose,* "being then in drink" did cut his cod piece and "made him go into bed and then the said Cornish went into bed with him, and there lay upon him, and kissed him and hugged him," and by force turned him "upon his belly" and put him "to pain in the fundament, and did wet him."

*Minutes of the Council and General Court of Colonial Virginia*

A Man who is so Lascivious in his Temper, that his Desires and Inclinations are almost insuperably heightened by a Bed-fellow of his own sex, is in a dangerous Condition, and ought to make use of the most effectual means to mortify it, before he can without Folly or Impudence hope for the assistance of Divine Grace.

*Onania, or The Heinous Sin of Self-Pollution*

Anonymous. London, 1723, and Boston, 1724

Cornholing: An eighteenth-century American term for anal intercourse.

# 1747: Aboard Ship

"It's dirty work selling men—even if we call it 'setting off,'" Captain Henry said to himself. "But damn, it is profitable."

He stood at the open window in his cabin at the prow of his ship and stared out at the smooth Atlantic Ocean. The nine-week voyage was almost over. His 250-ton ship was two days out of the busy harbor of Hampton in the Colony of Virginia.

The sailing across the ocean from his native England to the new country had gone well. Only one major storm had disrupted the daily routine. Although food supplies and drinking water were now running low, there was enough of both for the time remaining before they reached the harbor. Captain Henry ran his hand over his face and smiled. With his two officers, he had toasted his thirty-second birthday on the voyage. The officers had wished him many more smooth and prosperous sailings. He had been at sea for over twenty years now in one capacity or another, from cabin boy to captain. He loved the sea, but he was always glad to have a voyage near its end. Especially when it promised to be a profitable one.

The cargo aboard the *St. George* was 283 head of human freight. All of these men were the legal property of Captain Henry. A small handful of them were already spoken for. Acting as the agent for several wealthy Virginia families, the captain had located three tutors, two architectural draftsmen, and a furniture maker. These men would be turned over as indentured servants to their new masters shortly after arrival.

The rest of the men would be sold, or "set off" as the authorities preferred to call it, aboard ship to the highest bidder. Over half of these men had signed indenture papers with the captain in England.

doi:10.1300/5623_01

In return for their passage, food and drink during the voyage, and, upon leaving ship, a large bundle of clothes and bedding, these men had voluntarily bound themselves to five years of "good and faithful service" under a colonial master. After the auction, they would leave the ship with their indenture papers and a dated bill of sale to their new master.

Virginia planters were badly in need of men with skills such as carpentry and masonry, and Captain Henry had been fortunate in finding a large number of skilled artisans to sign indenture papers. They would bring a good price, up to 30 pounds sterling or 600 pounds of tobacco. Actually the captain preferred the raw cargo of "weed." It brought an excellent price back in England, and an even higher one if he exported it from England over to Amsterdam. Since Captain Henry had kept his expenses on each indentured servant's food and clothing at less than four pounds sterling, he would make a handsome profit.

The rest of the cargo were king's prisoners. They were hardly volunteer passengers. They had been released from London's Newgate prison to earn a pardon through a seven-year indenture forced upon them. His majesty's government had contracted for their transport to the new world. The king was glad to be rid of them and their care, and Captain Henry was willing to take on that care—for profit. The prisoners were all felons. However, the legal definition of what constituted a felony in Britain stretched broadly from the theft of a loaf of bread to feed a starving family to murder and rape. Captain Henry's convicts were, therefore, a motley mixture of men.

Captain Henry often wondered what was the worse fate for these felons. Conditions at Newgate were filthy and crowded. Unless an outside friend could pay the prison keepers, food was scarce and bad. Since the death penalty applied to more than a hundred felonies, most of them trivial offenses, many prisoners faced execution. However, prison sicknesses often exacted payment first. It was easy to get thrown into Newgate, but hard if not impossible to get out.

Life below deck on the ship was hardly any better. Four prisoners were crammed together in a six-foot-square space. Chained throughout the voyage, they were not, like the indentured servants, allowed to go on deck for a few hours daily. Although they wore the same clothes during the entire voyage, Captain Henry saw to it that they were not underfed. It was to his advantage to have healthy convicts on the auction block. Still some often died, especially from typhus. Fortunately only three had been buried at sea this voyage.

The tall, handsome captain shuddered when he imagined what life was to be in the new country once a convict was sold. Lucky was the one with a skill. He would sell for a high price; like the skilled indentured servant, he would live better than the common laborer. However, most of the prisoners were destined to become common laborers to work in the wilderness. There they would suffer from the rough life in the wilderness as it was cleared into farmland and from the even rougher treatment of overseers.

"Almost better to die here on ship than to labor in the wilds," the captain said to himself. Then, aloud to no one, he exclaimed, "I'm a lucky devil." And, as a sea captain and businessman, he was a lucky man.

Captain Henry's abilities and demeanor had won him respect aboard ship. There had never been even the threat of a mutiny among his ship's crew. He expected hard work from them, but he treated and fed them well, although he never allowed anyone to exceed his daily portion of rum. The officers and mates liked to work under the captain. With neither of his officers did the captain have a close friendship, yet neither considered him aloof and unapproachable. All of this meant that Captain Henry ran an efficient ship.

The captain did not spend much time in London. However, the respect he had aboard ship carried over among those business associates he had in the city. He was known as a shrewd bargainer, but not a cheat, when it came to supplying his ship and buying the necessities for the indentured servants and the convicts. The London agents who worked for him locating the men willing to sign indenture papers and who arranged the contracts for the prisoners would never have dared to trick the captain. They often laughed among themselves and said that even when Captain Henry was at sea he still kept an eye and an ear on their transactions. All of this meant that Captain Henry ran a profitable business.

He was indeed a lucky man in many ways—ways that counted in the public world. But Captain Henry barely had a life beyond that. At twenty-one, when he was second mate aboard ship, he did what was expected of him. He married. Although he had a strong affection for his young wife, he realized later that he was never really in love with her. At her death, six months after the birth of their baby daughter, he felt a release, a kind of freedom from a bond that was not natural for him.

Occasionally now, as he lay alone in his bed aboard ship, he recalled a particular brief conversation with his late wife. They had finished their intercourse on the first night of his return from a voyage. The captain sighed as he turned from her and lay on his side.

His wife waited a moment and then asked, "Was I pleasing to you?"

"Why, yes, of course." His member was becoming limp. He turned to her and said, "Why do you ask?"

"You seemed so far away at times," she replied. "Almost as if you were thinking of something—or someone—else."

"No, love," he assured her. "I must still be a bit at sea."

"I wonder if I am who you need," his wife said in a low voice.

"Hush such talk," the captain said as he turned for sleep.

Now, he knew. She had been right.

Captain Henry placed his baby daughter in the care of his sister, who welcomed the baby to her own large family. Three times a year Captain Henry saw his daughter, now ten years old. The young girl always delighted in her "uncle's" visits.

His sister's house in the fashionable area near St. James Park was not, however, where Captain Henry was this late August afternoon. He was aboard the *St. George.* On his writing table lay the unopened ledger listing the names of the prisoners. Within the next few hours he wanted to read through the list and arrange the order of sale on the days of the auction. Usually on the first day he auctioned off the older men without any special skill; they were generally sold as common laborers. Then, on the second day, came the younger men who would leave the ship destined for the job of clearing the wilderness. He saved for the last day those men with some special skill. The youngest men with a skill were always the last to stand on the auction block. They brought the highest prices at the close of the setting off.

Reading through the list of prisoners was a necessity that Captain Henry never liked to perform. Not that he had more moral qualms about selling off prisoners than he did in auctioning the indentured servants. Dirty work, yes, but an intrinsic part of every sailing to the colonies. It was that every time he read through the list he realized just how lucky he was. For a minute or two an overpowering fear caused a cold sweat to run down from his armpits and stain his shirt. He well knew that his own name could be followed by the word *felon*. Only as the sweat dried did the captain's fear lessen and his breathing return to something close to normal.

His undetected felony was that detestable crime not to be named among God-fearing people. Before a court of law he would be condemned as a "sodomite." In the everyday parlance of the streets his crime was "buggery." For those more in the know of the slang of the day, Captain Henry would have been known as a "molly." Of course, in the mouth of a man who did not like to lie with other men, this was a term of ridicule. But for those who enjoyed the pleasures of another man's body and for whom such pleasures, whatever form they took, were neither crime nor sin, "molly" was a term of affection. Since the term swept across and obliterated social classes, it bonded a large group of men in London.

Less than a year after the death of his wife, Captain Henry discovered that he liked sex with other men. His first experience was with a young man who picked him out of the crowd outside St. Paul's and propositioned him. At first the captain had been angry, fighting to deny that he found the young man attractive. But the young man was persistent. What the captain learned in that dark alley near the cathedral was that he enjoyed spilling his seed into the young man's warm mouth. As he withdrew, however, the captain promised himself, "This won't happen again." He paid the young man the pence he demanded.

As Captain Henry walked briskly out of the alley into the crowd of people, he made sure that the flaps on his codpiece were properly buttoned. Conflicting emotions crowded his mind. He was surprised at how quickly he had submitted his member to the young man's mouth. But he felt no shame in what had happened. In fact, it was as if something natural had happened, as if something buried within him had been released. He knew that there were frightening consequences had he been caught in the act. At the least, fines and the pillory, and, of course, death if convicted of performing an unnatural act. However, he had not been caught, and the warm, half-erect member in his breeches made him delight in his sudden surrender in the dark alley.

Captain Henry knew that his promise not to let another man touch his sex was a hollow one. However, he never paid another man for sexual favors. There was no need. Captain Henry was more at sea than in London. But, whenever he was there, he returned to St. Paul's. Through one of the young men he met and took into the alley, he learned about the molly houses scattered north of the Thames, both inside and outside the city. After that, he abandoned St Paul's. The molly houses were safer and more pleasant. There was singing, dancing, and drinking. Best of all were the private rooms where two men could "marry," as they liked to call it. However, something better happened. To his amazement and delight, he discovered while on a walk from his sister's house a whole new world at the far south end of St. James Park where men of his bent met, talked, and made arrangements. Many an evening Captain Henry and a new companion walked back to the Red Oak Tavern at the corner of St. James Square overlooking the park to pay for a room for the night. There the captain learned pleasures that went far beyond what had happened during that initiation in the alley with the young man.

It was a double life, and the captain did not hide that fact from himself. At sea, his life was one of controlled energy. Against the worst kind of storm, the captain's forceful determination kept his ship under control. But in London his energy broke loose into uncontrollable streams of passion. After such outbursts of sexual pleasure, Captain Henry suffered no remorse. He knew though that something was missing in these pleasures that was there in his work aboard ship. The demands upon him at sea were often harsh, but there was always an intimacy between him and his responsibilities—a melding into one.

In the private room at Red Oak Tavern there were pleasures aplenty but never the intimacy the captain longed for. Spent, the captain and his companion of the night kissed and dressed. Then they walked their separate ways. Seldom did they see each other again. The captain was lonely after such sexual encounters in a way he never felt at the end of a sea voyage.

Captain Henry did not believe that his lying with men was either a crime or a sin. He felt neither shame nor guilt after spilling his seed in the body of another man. Hell was a place he did not believe in, so he had no fear of eternal damnation. Besides the lack of intimacy in his sexual encounters, the only other thing that marred his London experiences was their furtive nature. As a sexual partner, he longed for the openness he had as captain on his ship. But he realized that it was foolishness on his part to expect the public world to accept his sexual preference as a natural one. So better the bit of hiding, even pretense, than finding his name marked as a "sodomite" on a list of prisoners.

As he looked down at the unopened prison ledger, Captain Henry found his hand rubbing his codpiece. Nine weeks was a long time without exploring another man's body. On occasion the captain wondered if any men on board felt as he did. Surely in the crowded quarters where the crew slept, usually naked, two to a bunk, hands must have reached across thighs to another man's crotch. Surely some mornings a man must have awakened to feel a hard rod pressing against his buttocks. But even if there were crew members responsive to such overtures, they would not have been welcome in the captain's quarters, simply because of the threat to the captain's discipline. Even more impossible was any intimate sexual contact with his mates or officers. So Captain Henry slept alone. His only sexual release during a voyage was that provided by his own hand.

As he was about to unbutton the flap of his codpiece, the captain stopped himself. "No time for that now," he said in a low, sharp voice. His hand moved away from his crotch. He paused. Then he slapped open the ledger. Sighing deeply, he forced his mind to try to move from his half-erect member to the business at hand. "Get on with it," he reprimanded himself. "You can pleasure yourself later tonight."

Looking down at the ledger, he ran his finger down the pages, taking note of the ages of the prisoners. He wanted first to cull out the men he would put last on the auction block. He was searching for young men between sixteen and twenty-one years of age with a skill in high demand in the colonies. Although he discovered well over a score of such men, he did not find as many as he had hoped for.

"Damn my luck," he cried out. But no sooner had he cursed than a name and age sprang out at him. "Lance Morley, seventeen," he read. But what most caught his eye was another bit of information about the young man: "Apprentice cordwainer."

Captain Henry arose from the table and went to his cabinet. He took out a bottle of brandy and poured himself a generous tumbler full. "Damn my luck, indeed!" he shouted and smiled. He took a large sip of the brandy and set his tumbler down next to the ledger. Rubbing his hands together, he whispered, "Let's hope it turns out like I want." He picked up the tumbler and went to the window of his ship. It was starting to grow dark, and a few stars were visible. As he stared out of the cabin window, his mind raced ahead to Williamsburg, the new capital of the colony. After the ship's business was taken care of, Captain Henry would treat himself, as he always did, to a few days of relaxation in Williamsburg before the return voyage.

On his most recent visit there, he had promised a friend that he would keep an eye out for a young indentured servant suitable to serve as an apprentice shoemaker. His friend, John Thomas, was the only cordwainer in that growing town, and he badly needed a third apprentice in his shop. American lads were too busy trying to make a fortune in the raising of tobacco or rice to take up the trade of shoemaking, Thomas had complained to Captain Henry.

Three years ago the captain had first met Thomas at the gaming table in the popular Raleigh Tavern. Although there was a sour quality in Thomas's disposition that the captain disliked, he still considered Thomas his closest friend in the colony, and he gladly accepted the cordwainer's invitation to the hospitality of his house and dinner table. Occasionally Captain Henry laughed to himself as he had to admit that perhaps it was Mistress Thomas's good table which provided the real basis of his friendship with Thomas. After the weeks of ship's fare, his mouth watered at the imagined taste of fresh meat and fish. Even more he savored the aroma from Mistress Thomas's chess pies.

Actually Captain Henry had almost forgotten his promise to Thomas until he saw "Lance Morley, 17, Apprentice cordwainer" in the ledger of prisoners.

"Don't you ever have a boot and shoe man among your indentured servants?" Thomas had asked Captain Henry during his last visit. Their card game was finished. Thomas was pouting about his loss. The tapster set two mugs of dark ale before them.

"Not that I recollect," the captain admitted.

"Pity. I need one desperately. I have two apprentices, one of them hardly worth his keep. My own sons have another six or eight years before I can begin to teach them the trade."

"Cordwainers must love their home country too much to try to live here," the captain mused.

"That may be. Be attentive though. My shop thrives. I can pay you well for the right fellow. I might even toss you a new pair of boots," Thomas said.

"That will be the day hell freezes over," the captain said to himself, knowing how reluctantly the cordwainer honored his debts at the gaming table.

"I want a man who already knows how to cut and stitch after a fitting," Thomas said, unaware of the captain's amusement over the offer of the boots. "I have no time these days to teach a green hand."

"I'll try," the captain said. He turned to his ale, thinking more about the chess pie at the table that night than the promise he made.

Yet now, eight months later, perhaps here was the man. "Yes, this chap Morley may be what I promised Thomas I'd look for," the captain told himself. Thomas might balk at having a felon in his shop, but the seven years of bound service instead of the usual five for an indentured servant would quickly do away with that objection. Also, a seventeen-year-old must have been an apprentice of several years. Thomas would not be buying a green hand, but a worker in need of supervision, not instruction.

"I'll demand at least twenty-five pounds sterling from friend Thomas for this lad," the captain said to himself. "But hold a minute. I ought to make certain that Morley has four sound limbs and a rational mind. I see Thomas only twice a year. Still I don't wish to taint my brief visits with him and his family by offering him a poor servant. He complains about one apprentice not being worth his keep. I should not like to add another. I would miss his wife's chess pies. Yes, I'd best have a look at Morley."

Captain Henry left his cabin and went topside. He found a second mate enjoying his pipe at the ship's railing. "Mate Adams," the captain said, "when you have finished your pipe, I wish you to go below to the prisoners. Locate the young man Lance Morley among them. Unshackle him, and bring him to my cabin. I have questions I need to ask him about his apprenticeship in London. He may be of special use to me at the auction."

"Aye, Captain," Mate Adams replied. He was a bit puzzled by the captain's request. Usually such questioning, if any were needed, was left to one of the officers. *This Lance Morley must truly be a special person among the prisoners*, the mate thought to himself, *but that is no affair of mine.* Soon the mate finished his pipe and went below.

Captain Henry remained on deck for a time to speak to several of the crew members. He asked them if they, too, would be happy to have their feet on land again. Their answers hardly surprised him. It was dark when the captain returned to his quarters. He lit a lamp and once again ran his finger down the list of prisoners in the ledger. This time he needed to select the prisoners to join with the indentured servants as the first group of men for the auction block. He had almost half of his list when the task was interrupted by a knock on the cabin door.

The captain answered the knock with a brisk "Enter."

The door opened, and Mate Adams pushed a dirty but handsome young man into the room.

"Lance Morley, sir," the second mate announced.

The young man stumbled as he walked into the room, still uncertain of newly freed feet. The captain waited until the prisoner seemed to secure his balance.

"You're Lance Morley?" the captain asked.

"Yes" was the reply.

"Yes, sir, to Captain Henry," the second mate barked and struck Lance in the ribs. The blow was not a hard one, yet it sent the young man to the floor. Like all prisoners, Lance wore only a shirt. Lance lay on the floor with his shirt well above his navel.

"Get up," the second mate snarled and yanked Lance to his feet.

Lance steadied himself as best he could and turned to look at the captain. "Yes, sir," he said in a low voice.

The glance at Lance's thick, stubby sex briefly shifted the captain's mind from the present questioning to any one of several anxious pairings between him and a young man at the south portico of St. Paul's. He closed his eyes and quickly he forced himself back to the ship.

"That will be all for now," the captain told his second mate.

"Aye, sir," the mate replied and left the cabin.

The captain and the young prisoner stood without moving and stared at each other. Although he was frightened and puzzled as to why he had been brought here, Lance did not blink or take his eyes off the captain. The captain stared all the harder. "He's got spunk," Captain Henry said to himself. Finally the captain spoke. "Have you complaints about your treatment below?"

Lance hesitated. The question was absurd. He wondered if it were only a trick question. However, his mother had taught him at an early age that lying often brought more serious consequences than telling the truth, no matter how painful it might be.

"Sir, men are not born to lie chained close together and lie in stench."

The captain made no reply.

"Men, sir, were created to stand upright and to walk about. Below we can only lie down or sit up and squat for the chamber pot when it is passed around."

"Aren't your hands unlocked every other day so that you can stand up?" the captain replied to Lance.

"For only a brief time, sir," Lance retorted with a tinge of bitterness now in his voice.

"Your food?" the captain asked.

"No better than what I ate in Newgate," Lance answered. He did not understand the reasons for this questioning. The bitterness inflamed him.

"Your other complaints?" the captain said.

The ache in his side from the second mate's blow prompted only the first word of Lance's reply. The rest came from deep within him. "Sir. I watched the man next to me starve himself to death. For two weeks he cried out the names of his wife and children and prayed for their protection. Then, in the third week as I reckoned the passage of time, he refused to eat or drink. One of the other prisoners gladly took it from him. My ears will always hear the echo of his cries and then the death rattle in his throat. It took him so long to die that I thought I would go mad."

Lance turned his eyes away from Captain Henry. A quiver ran through his body, and Lance hugged himself, his chains across his chest. It hurt. But the louder he heard the echoes in his mind, the harder he pressed the chains. His head down and his eyes closed, Lance stood that way for a long time.

Lance's compassion touched Captain Henry. Here was a man before him with four sound limbs and a rational mind. He knew that Lance's complaints were an honest description of a prisoner's life below deck, but he also knew that nothing could be changed.

Finally Captain Henry broke the silence in the cabin. "When were you committed to Newgate, Morley?"

"Early this year, just after my birthday."

"And what was the charge against you?"

"A false one."

The captain laughed and said, "No doubt most of the felons below would give that very answer."

Lance looked at the captain and in a firm voice replied, "Sir, I cannot account for those men. But the charge against me was a false one."

"And on what false charge were you convicted?" the captain asked and laughed again.

"Attempt to murder," Lance replied. "But that is a false charge."

"Whom were you not going to murder?" Again the captain laughed, wondering if the young man would ever tell his story.

"I hit a drunken constable. I did not mean to kill him. I meant only to bloody his nose."

"A foolish action on your part. What provoked you?"

"The bastard called my master's young daughter a slut."

Captain Henry nodded. He waited for Lance to continue.

"My master's wife had asked me to take Angelica with me to the pastry shop. She wanted us to buy sweet rolls. As Angelica and I were walking near Covent Garden, the constable and two other drunken men came out of a tavern. The constable looked at us. Then he threw his hands up into the air and shouted, 'Now there's a pretty little slut.'"

Lance paused. Then he continued, "Angelica is not a slut. She does not even know the meaning of that word. She is like her name, a little angel. For his insulting lie, I hit the man. I would do it again." Lance dropped his shoulders and his chained hands. He was exhausted. The long voyage had been its own kind of torment, but worse now was that clash between his hatred of the drunken constable and his terror of what lay ahead for him.

Captain Henry believed Lance's story. The charge against him was, as Lance claimed, a false one. The captain would need to make clear to his friend Thomas that the young man he was buying was not really a felon. Also, he liked the young man before him. He responded to Lance's quickness of mind and his integrity. But the captain fought back another kind of response to the handsome youth.

"In Virginia you will need to be more careful, Morley. Your new master and the magistrate there will be quick to add extra years to your indenture for any misconduct, even if you consider your action justified. If you strike a constable there you may well find yourself a bound servant for the rest of your life. A pardon for your crime will come after seven years of service only if you control your temper and your fists."

Throughout the voyage Lance had tried desperately to push from his mind any thoughts about what was going to happen to him in the new country. The prisoners did not talk among themselves about their lives after the auction block. However, the remarks and jests from the ship's crew were a daily reminder of their future. "That one will die in the wilderness." "Here's a man who will be beat to death by his new master." "Skinny bastard, you'll weigh even less after starving on Virginia mush." Looking down at Lance as he was using the chamber pot one day, a passing crewmember had joked, "It's a pity a young lad like you won't be able to use that tool between your legs for seven years, except to piss." Survival, however, was more on Lance's mind than sex.

"Sir, what will happen to me once we are there?" Lance asked.

"That will depend."

"On what, sir?" Lance pursued.

The captain shrugged his shoulders as if he did not hear the question. Instead he asked, "How long were you an apprentice, Morley?"

"Almost four years, sir. My father paid my master five pounds to teach me shoe making. I was twelve then. In two more years I would have been a journeyman. Already my master was speaking to me about staying with him in the shop for wages."

"Was he a good master?"

"Like a father to me, sir," Lance replied.

Captain Henry doubted that John Thomas would prove to be like a father. He asked, "Are you a good cordwainer?"

"My master said I was the best apprentice he ever had. He said I had a natural talent for making excellent shoes and boots."

"Your skill may be useful to you in Virginia, Morley," the captain said.

Lance looked at the captain, hesitated, and then burst out, "Let me stay on the ship, sir. I don't want to go to Virginia. I am afraid. I don't want to die in the wilderness, or be beaten or starved to death. Please, sir, let me stay on the ship. I'm strong. I'm a good learner. I could become a good seaman. Sir, I'll do anything for you."

The outburst surprised Captain Henry, but he understood the urgency of the passionate plea. He walked up to Lance and put his hands on Lance's shoulders. He smiled at Lance as he shook his head and said, "Morley, I bought you from His Majesty. I don't want to lose money on you. Also, my contract with the king says that I will leave you in the colonies. There you must stay in bound service for seven years until you have earned your freedom papers and a pardon for your crime. I intend to make a profit on you. I intend to honor my contract with His Majesty. No more talk of staying aboard ship."

Although disappointed, Lance was not surprised by the captain's refusal. He had expected it. He sighed deeply and told himself he must accept whatever was going to happen. No matter how right he knew he was in bloodying the constable's nose, he knew his quick temper was his own responsibility. He looked up at the captain and nodded.

"Take heart, Morley," the captain said. "I doubt you will starve, and, if you obey orders, you will not be thrashed. You won't labor in the wilderness either. In fact, what would say to being sold as an indentured servant to a Williamsburg cordwainer?"

For the first time since he had entered the captain's quarters, Lance's eyes brightened, and he smiled. "I should like that very much, sir."

"I think it very likely that is what will happen," the captain replied. He said to himself that, yes, he had found a good man for John Thomas.

"Tell me, Morley, how long does it take to make a shoe?"

"My master could do it in one day. It took me a bit longer because I still needed to be very careful at every step."

"And how is a shoe made?" the captain asked, more anxious to keep Lance with him in the room than to learn about shoe making.

Lance's spirits lifted. He trusted the captain's word that he would probably be indentured to a cordwainer. Now he was being asked to talk about something he loved doing. "First, sir, it's a matter of selecting the leather," he began and launched into a flood of details.

Captain Henry only half listened to what Lance was saying. He went to the open window of the cabin and looked out at the ocean. The full moon was reflected in the water. The presence of the near-naked Lance had carried him back to his encounters with young men in London. He ached as he remembered the pleasures of their bodies. Now, he wanted Lance.

When the captain returned to where Lance was standing, still talking about the making of shoes, Lance was surprised at the look in the captain's eyes. There he saw a longing that he had seen before. He suspected that he knew what the captain wanted from him.

Nearly eighteen, Lance was no beginner when it came to sexual experiences. He had lost his virginity to a baker's wife who had invited him into a storeroom and then lifted her skirts. He lost another kind of virginity to an older apprentice with whom he shared a bed. Hal had rolled him over on his back one night, kissed him, and then taken his body. Lance enjoyed this second loss of virginity much more than the first. Frequently thereafter the two young men made the leather mattress of their bed creak. Hal also introduced Lance to St. Paul's where Lance found other young men his age as well as older men who in parting slipped a coin in Lance's hand. It was there at St. Paul's that Lance learned about the urgent looks in the eyes of men. Now he saw it in Captain Henry's eyes.

For the first time in over nine weeks his sex swelled slightly.

The two men stood without moving. Each stared hard at the other. Finally Lance said, "I'll tumble in bed with you, if you wish." He moved toward Captain Henry, stretching out his chained hands. The startled captain moved back several steps. Then, he hurried past Lance toward the door of the cabin.

"No," Lance cried out as he dropped to his knees.

The captain turned toward Lance. "Quiet," he commanded. Lance collapsed on the floor. The captain stared down briefly at Lance and then left the cabin.

"What have I done!" Lance exclaimed aloud. He buried his head in his chained hands. As he started to cry, he reproached himself for the sexual overture. Why had he ruined his chance to go to Williamsburg? Now, he told himself, he would be sold as a common laborer to work in the wilderness. In his delirium he wished he had died aboard ship and been buried at sea. That would have been better than dying in the wilderness. Lance did not know how long he lay there, his tears wetting his face and the floor. It was far worse than lying with the other chained prisoners below.

After what seemed an eternity to Lance, Captain Henry returned. With him was Mate Adams. The two men looked down at Lance, his knees drawn up into his chest, his shirt above his bare butt. Lance did not dare look up at the captain.

"Mate Adams," he heard the captain say, "I have struck this prisoner to the floor. He uttered a rude and offensive remark to me. He must be punished."

When the second mate started to pull Lance to his feet, the captain stopped him. "No, leave him there. I will take personal charge of the prisoner now, since I have special plans for his indenture. I will also mete out his punishment."

"Aye, sir," said the mate.

"Get me chains for his feet. As punishment, he shall stand, naked and chained, in my closet for the remainder of the voyage and, upon arrival, until all the other men are sold at the block. He shall have no food, except a crust of bread, and only a draught of water each day."

"Aye, sir," the mate said again.

"I do not wish, however, to inhale his sour smell from my closet. Tell my cabin boy to bring two pails of hot water."

"Aye, sir. Is that all?"

"Only this, Mate Adams. Do not let this matter go beyond you."

"No, captain," the mate promised.

"Your word then," the captain said.

"Upon my word, sir." Captain Henry knew that he could trust his second mate.

The mate glared at the huddled prisoner. "When you offend a good man like Captain Henry, you deserve worse punishment than he has devised for you. You should be beat until you are dead," he snarled. "Thank the captain for his kindness in sparing you that." Then turning to the captain, he said, "Good night, sir."

"Good night, Mate Adams. But do not forget the chains for his feet."

"I'll fetch them immediately," the mate said and left the room.

After the mate had gone, Lance stirred and looked up. However, the captain said nothing. Again he went to the open window. He stood there, his back to Lance. Lance was afraid to speak. His offensive remark, he supposed, was his overture to bed with the captain. But what Lance did not understand was why the captain had told the mate that he had knocked Lance to the floor. That was a lie. Lance knew it, and he knew the captain must know it.

Shortly, a light knock on the door broke the silence of the cabin. "Enter," the captain called. A very young boy, struggling with two large pails of water, entered the room, followed by Mate Adams with the foot chains.

"Help the lad with his pails, Mate Adams, and then get my bathing tub from the closet. Leave the chains by the prisoner," the captain said.

Bewildered and frightened, Lance heard the iron chains drop at his feet. He watched as the mate brought out a large bathing tub and poured one pail of water into it. The mate roughed the lad's curly hair and told him, "Let us leave the captain." Again the two men bade each other good night. The captain gave the cabin boy a gentle pat on his head. The door closed. The captain went to latch the bolt. Captain Henry and Lance were now locked alone in the cabin.

Captain Henry stared hard at the trembling Lance but said nothing. He went to his safety cabinet, unlocked it, and got out a key. "Hold out your hands, Morley," he said. Lance obeyed, and the captain quickly freed his hands from the chains. The captain let the chains drop at Lance's feet. Lance vigorously rubbed his wrists. "Now get off that filthy rag of a shirt and get into the tub and wash yourself," the captain told Lance. He got a bar of gray soap from his medicine cabinet and tossed it into the tub of hot water.

Lance raised his shirt over head and stood naked. He had not bathed since his arrest and detention at Newgate. Lance wondered if he were awake or dreaming. Perhaps his terror had reduced him to a mad man! The street near Covent Garden, Newgate, the stench of the ship's prison quarter, and now this small room with a tub of hot water. Where would it all end? But, for now, damn what was to come next, Lance knew what he wanted—to be clean.

Lance stepped into the tub and sat down. He rested his back against the upright at one end of the tub. He sat like that for a long time, cupping water in his hands and drenching his body. He ran water through his shoulder-length wavy auburn hair. Then he ran the soap over his body and through his hair. He drank in the clean smell of the soapy water.

While Lance bathed, Captain Henry assiduously avoided looking at the tub. Instead he concentrated on the list of prisoners. He wanted to complete his task soon. Lance heard nothing from the captain except the scratching of his pen and the occasional turning of pages. When the captain had all but finished the desired arrangement of men on auction days, he loudly cleared his throat. That noise startled Lance. He took it as a wordless signal from the captain to hurry his bathing. Since he did not want to further anger the captain, Lance quickly stood up and reached for the other pail of water. Slowly he poured it over his head and body.

Only when Lance stood up, fully exposing his naked body, did Captain Henry look at him. Slowly he let his eyes take in every part of the young man's nakedness. Lance was not as tall or as muscled as the captain, but he had a sturdy build. His chest was covered with a rich mass of reddish-brown curls, matching the hair in his armpits and surrounding his sex. A stubble of a short reddish beard covered his lower cheeks and chin. Lance was not at all certain as to what he was supposed to do next.

Still keeping his eyes on Lance's body, Captain Henry went to his chest of drawers and pulled out a large soft cloth. "Here, Morley, dry yourself," he said. Lance took the cloth and ran it over his body.

"Sir," he began.

"No, Morley, be quiet," the captain broke in with a firm voice.

Captain Henry went once more to the open window. This time though he looked out for only a few seconds. He pulled the exterior shutters together and latched them, then the interior windows. He closed the several ledgers on his desk and stacked a sheaf of papers neatly. He took off his coat and vest and hung them on a chair.

Dry, Lance hugged the cloth against his chest. He shut his eyes. Although his body was cleaner than it had been for months, his mind trembled with fear again. His bare foot touched the iron chains, and he shrank back from them. Why had he spoken as he did? Why had he ruined any chance for a decent life in the new country? The questions seemed to curse him. His head drooped momentarily, but he quickly raised it. *Once again I am responsible for what has happened to me,* he said to himself. *Accept it, and don't whine.* He must wait now for the chains around his hands and feet.

Finally Lance opened his eyes and looked toward Captain Henry. He gasped aloud. The captain stood naked, his large sex erect.

The captain held out his arms and came to Lance. He gathered Lance into a tight embrace. The lips of the two men met. They kissed passionately.

When the captain pulled away from Lance, he whispered to him, "Come to bed, Lance."

# 1747-1748: Cromley Hall

When he was five years old, Adam Bradley was brought by his aunt to live at the estate of Lord Cromley near Tunbridge Wells in Kent.

"Are you certain that you will not marry and have your own children?" Lady Cromley had asked her favorite maid, Sarah.

"Yes, your ladyship, I am certain. Although I am still young and not past the age of childbearing, I have not the desire to marry and leave my service at Cromley Hall. I want to raise my sister's youngest child," Adam's aunt replied.

"Nor would I like to lose your service," Lady Cromley nodded. "If you will delight in raising your nephew, then the little lad is welcome at Cromley Hall."

"Thank you, your ladyship," the maid said.

Adam was the eleventh and youngest child of parents slowly being devoured by too many children and too little money to care for them. His father was one of several assistants to a butcher. What scraps of meat Adam's family had on the table were bits stolen from the butcher shop. His father worked hard, trying to support his family. But he worked harder in bed, giving his wife a child each year.

Fortune had dealt a better hand to Adam's spinster aunt, Sarah Mann. She was as familiar with London court life as she was with that at the country estate. She had tasted the leftovers from many a party either at the country estate or at the London townhouse—even some at the royal palace. "Why I truly believe," she once had exclaimed, "that His Majesty King George left this tart especially for me." The kitchen staff cheered and bowed to her.

When his aunt left with Adam, she was surprised at how easily his mother gave up her child. "He is only a burden to us here," Adam's mother said. "And now he is that to you."

doi:10.1300/5623_02

"If he is a burden, he is a welcome one to me," his aunt replied, looking down at the small boy grasping her gloved hand. Although a bit puzzled and frightened, Adam shed no tears about leaving his parents. Never in his life had he felt anything so smooth and soft as the glove holding his hand.

With the move from his parents' hovel in Dover to Lord Cromley's late sixteenth-century castle with its several recent additions, Adam believed he was in Paradise. His cubicle of a room on the top floor of the servants' wing offered the young boy a private view that extended for miles. Below his window were the formal gardens with their boxwood mazes and numerous topiaries. Beyond the gardens lay the meadows, and beyond that the forests. Adam shouted with delight the first time he saw deer emerge from the woods to graze in the meadows. He was even more fascinated by the red fox that boldly ran into the formal gardens.

Young Adam quickly became a familiar figure at Cromley Hall. Although he never entered the private or great rooms of the castle, he freely roamed alone in the public rooms. On chilly afternoons he raced endlessly up and down the long gallery. He made up stories about the richly dressed people whose large portraits hung on the east wall of the gallery. When he was old enough to be of help, he was the frequent companion of the cleaning servants. His favorite tasks, however, were those in the large kitchen. There, between chores, he could pinch off a piece of pastry with only a minor scolding.

By the time Adam was fourteen, he had an education that far exceeded one usually given a young boy of the servant class. True, it lacked the rigorous discipline of the Charity School in Dover. But, under his several teachers, Adam was blessed with a far greater range of information and experience.

Adam learned to read and write under the instruction of the tutor to Lord Cromley's children. Adam often accompanied the older Cromley children on their walks with the tutor. His special charge was to keep an eye and a hand on the young lord. The tutor became fond of Adam and one day asked him if he, too, would like lessons. "I should like that very much," Adam replied, wondering if he were responding to a question that had actually been asked. Daily lessons soon took place in Adam's room during the Cromley children's nap time. To the delight of the tutor, Adam's quick wit made him a good student. "You can read as well as any London schoolboy," the tutor told him. "And you write a neater hand than many a fashionable gentleman." Such praise made Adam work all the harder.

Adam learned his third R under the guidance of the steward of the estate. Like the tutor, the steward liked Adam for his good nature and native intelligence. The skill with which Adam did his figures amazed the steward, and under him Adam became acquainted with the ways of managing a large estate. At fourteen, Adam was no longer cleaning floors and furniture or tending to the fires in the kitchen. He was the youngest of the assistants to the steward. "Perhaps you will replace me one day, Adam," the steward had told him.

"That will not be for many years, sir," Adam replied modestly, but still basking under the steward's compliment.

Not all of Adam's education took place inside the castle. Lord Cromley had a large stable, and he prided himself on his horses. His hunters had a reputation for being the best in Kent and in the neighboring districts. Like the tutor and the steward, the stable master also took a liking to Adam. As a young boy, Adam helped clean the stables. Later he learned to groom the horses. His touch calmed even the wildest stallion. He proved a good rider, and the stable master allowed the fourteen-year-old Adam to exercise the most prized horses.

Adam thoroughly enjoyed working with his three teachers. Each had something different to give him. Adam liked to think that he had all the knowledge of the world. There was, however, one R, a fourth, that of religion, which held no special attraction for him. Dutifully Adam learned his catechism and could repeat his responses without hesitating or stumbling. But he did not see how his answers about either the creation or the afterlife supplied any useful information for his life at Cromley Hall. The clergyman's explanation about Adam's soul meant little to the young boy. Especially confusing, however, was a warning given by the clergyman when Adam was twelve. "You must never touch yourself," Adam had been told. He thought such advice nonsense. How could he eat without touching himself? How could he piss without touching himself? How could he do almost anything without touching himself?

When Adam asked both the stable master and the steward for an explanation, both men had burst out laughing and told the young boy "to wait and see." Hurt, Adam turned to the tutor, a younger man than the other two. Although the tutor's response left Adam still puzzled, at least he did not laugh at Adam's question. Carefully choosing his words, the tutor slowly said, "When you are several years older, Adam, you will find that you have longings that are new and strange to you. You will feel them in your member, which will be larger than it is now. Your member will sometimes be hard. Don't be afraid of these new longings. If you want to touch your member to relieve yourself of these longings, do so."

"But what if I . . . ," Adam began.

"No. I have said enough. When the time comes, you will understand what I have told you without further need to ask anyone."

Sometime before his fifteenth birthday, Adam understood. He awoke one morning with his hand grasping a large, hard cock. For all of his supposed worldly knowledge Adam had only recently learned and started to use the vocabulary of the stable yard. He rubbed his foreskin vigorously. Soon his hand was sticky with thick, creamy liquid. "So that's what the good fellow meant!" Adam exclaimed. Relaxing and smoothing the cream over his stomach, Adam told himself, "To hell with 'Don't touch yourself.'" He liked the tutor's "Do so" much better.

A year later Adam got another lesson in sex. This time Betty, a kitchen maid much older than Adam, persuaded him to come to the storeroom with her. She promised that she had a warm spot which Adam had never been in before. Adam knew she was not talking about the storeroom. Frightened but curious and anxious, he went with her. "Be damned," she exclaimed when she had his breeches off him, "you're hung like a horse." Panting, she helped Adam guide his hard tool into her nest of hair. Once there Adam quickly sensed what to do next. He was surprised at how quickly he finished his business.

As he adjusted his breeches, Betty asked, "That was a first time for you, wasn't it?"

"Yes," Adam admitted without blushing.

"We must go at it again another evening. Perhaps you will tarry in me longer next time."

During the next month Adam returned twice to the storeroom. Each time he was reluctant to go. He realized after that first afternoon that he had given much more pleasure than he had received. He wanted something more. He did not know what. Also there was a bit of hurt pride. Adam learned through talk he overheard in the stable yard that he was not the only one to enjoy Betty's favors. She bestowed them liberally. "I don't want anymore with her," Adam told himself after his third visit. He was certain that Betty had read his mind since he had been far from energetic while lying with her. Betty had grunted, "What's wrong, Adam. Been handling and wasting yourself in bed too much?" Adam did not respond. He was glad to have the afternoon at an end.

Adam was surprised, then, two weeks later when he passed by Betty in the yard outside the kitchen. She brushed past him and whispered "this evening." Before he could reply, she moved away. He watched as she joined a group of kitchen maids bent over in laughter and pointing to two kitchen lads pummeling each other.

"I'll not be rude," Adam said to himself. "I'll meet her. But I will not touch her." Perhaps she was right. He had been "doing so" and enjoying it almost every night since he lay with her last.

Adam was later than usual that afternoon when he went to the storeroom. A light rain had fallen, and Adam brushed off his wet hair before he opened the door. It took a minute before he saw them. Betty was bent backward over a table. A large man was vigorously heaving-and-hauling over her. Only Betty heard the storeroom latch open, and she looked up. She smirked at the shocked Adam.

Betty pushed the man off her. They both turned to face Adam. Adam recognized the man as Tom, one of the gardeners, a young man several years older than Adam. His wet, red sex pointed at Adam. Tom was embarrassed and said nothing.

Betty grabbed Tom's sex and laughed. "He's not as well hung as you, Adam. But, damn, he knows how to use what he has. Go back to bed, Adam, and jerk yourself. Maybe someday you will be a man."

Betty laughed again. Tom caught the joke and joined her laughter. "Get out, boy," he shouted, "or I will take you, too."

Adam wanted to hit both of them. Instead though he shouted, "Damn you both" and slammed the storeroom door on their laughter. Adam ran from the kitchen yard past the great terrace to the formal garden and into a maze. Since boyhood he had found his way deep inside to a bench where the maze turned back upon itself. He sat down on the bench, his head in his hands.

Adam was hurt and angry. Betty had invited him to the storeroom only to laugh at him. After that first evening he had not performed well enough for her. Now she had taken her revenge. What should it matter to her what he did to himself in bed. His hand grabbed closer than her nest. It felt better there in his bed than with her.

But something more than Betty's joke pressed on Adam's mind. The sound he kept hearing was not Betty's laughter but Tom's cry, "Get out, boy, or I'll take you, too." The image repeatedly thrusting itself before his eyes was not Betty but Tom's bare butt as he plowed Betty and his swollen sex when he shouted "I'll take you, too." That was exactly what Adam found he wanted. He did not want to replace Tom on top of Betty. He ached to be under Tom's body. It was the first time consciously that Adam admitted to himself that he was attracted sexually to other men.

As he sat there on the bench, what amazed Adam was how readily he accepted his desire for other men. He knew that for a man to lie with another man was called an unnatural act. It was a crime punishable by death. He had heard the jokes made in the stable yard about sodomites, and he had heard the curse "up yours." Still Adam felt no shame in his desire for another man's body. That desire seemed a natural part of himself. He accepted it. But, he sighed, how could he act upon that desire? "I want to lie with a man, but I don't know how to go about finding the man. I don't even know what I'd do in bed if I were with another man."

During the Christmas season of 1747-1748 Adam quickly learned what to do with a male bedfellow. He was now seventeen. His only sex since the incidents in the storeroom had been in "doing so." That self-pleasure relieved the ache in his groin, but still Adam yearned for something more. His bedfellow arrived as a holiday gift.

Lord and Lady Cromley were known throughout Kent as the best and most lavish party hosts during the Christmas season. Invitations to the several balls and suppers had been delivered a month earlier. Some guests came for only one day of festivities. Others, more prominent in social rank, were invited to stay for all five days.

Dozens of carriages with richly dressed people arrived at Cromley Hall the first afternoon. With each carriage came a coach with a small retinue of servants and trunks. Adam helped to unload the baggage from each arriving coach. One of the last carriages to arrive was that of a famous elderly earl.

One of the drivers of the earl's carriage immediately caught Adam's eye. The young driver got down to open the door of the carriage. "Thank you, George," an elderly man said, as the driver helped him descend from the carriage.

A bit older than Adam, George was a tall, handsome man of dark complexion. Above his full lips was a small mustache of black hair. A short pigtail of black hair fell behind his tricorne. His livery of green, white, and gold covered a manly body. His tight white breeches boasted a large pouch on the left side of his crotch.

Adam waited until Lord Cromley had greeted the earl, his wife, and daughter and led them into the great hall. Then he and the other servants set to work. George climbed up on top of the coach. As he unstrapped the trunks, he looked down at Adam and smiled. In return, Adam nodded.

When Adam reached up to take a valise, George grabbed Adam's hand. He studied Adam's middle finger intently. "Is your private twice the length of this finger?" George asked in a low voice.

Adam blushed deeply at the surprising question. He did not know how to respond. George merely laughed and handed Adam the valise. "I hope to find out," George told Adam. Before they could talk further, the steward called to the two young men, "Make haste there."

Adam did not see George again until late that evening when the servants gathered in a large room near the two kitchens for a light supper. The housekeeper was busily telling the visiting servants where they would sleep during their stay. She motioned to George and brought him to Adam. "Your room is the smallest in the servants' wing, Adam, but you'll have to find a place for this young man," the housekeeper said. Adam could not believe his good fortune. Behind the back of the housekeeper, George winked at Adam and wiggled his middle finger.

Four hours later, by candlelight, the two men undressed. Afraid to display his hard sex, Adam kept his back to George. Although his body quivered with excitement, Adam was uncertain whether George had only been teasing or whether he truly wanted to see Adam's size. Quickly he pulled a coarse linen nightshirt over his head and down his body. Only then did he turn around to look at George.

George was naked and erect. He burst out laughing. "Do you think you are bloody royalty wearing that thing to bed?" he asked. "Get it off. I want to see you raw." George roughly pulled the nightshirt back over Adam's head. He tossed it on the floor beside the bed. "We can use it to clean up later," he said.

The two men looked at each other's naked body for a short time. Then, George said, "You've a good one there. Now come here, Adam, and kiss me."

Adam had never kissed a man before. Although he longed to be in George's arms, he stood still. *What is about to happen?* he wondered.

"Damn you, come here," George cried.

Adam went to him and quickly found himself folded in George's embrace. George ran his hand down Adam's back and over his smooth butt. Adam felt the pressure of George's lips and tongue against his lips. He opened his mouth to receive George's tongue. Soon his lips and tongue were racing over George's. They kissed for a long time.

Finally George pushed Adam down on the bed and dropped on top of him. Again they embraced and kissed. For a long time Adam relaxed as he delighted in the way George's hands explored his body. His hands, too, moved over George's hairy body. Suddenly George's hand moved up from Adam's thigh to his crotch. He seized Adam in a firm grasp. "Adam, you are hung like a horse," he cried out and laughed. Adam chuckled but said nothing. He simply pressed harder against George's body. The candle cast a dim light over their wild movements. The flame flickered from the breath of their steady moans.

George broke their play by saying, "I'm going to take you, Adam. Have you been buggered before?"

"Never. You'll be the first. I do so want it. But I'm afraid. I don't want to get hurt."

George kissed Adam. "I promise you, more pleasure than pain."

At first Adam thought he could not take the pain. His plea for George to pull out met with a firm "No." Instead George massaged Adam's tense body. Soon Adam was ready for George to have his way with him. By the time George finished, the candle was about to go out.

George pulled Adam into his arms and asked, "Pleasure or pain?"

"Both, but more pleasure than pain."

George kissed Adam again and said, "Good night."

"Good night," Adam replied.

Soon George's steady breathing told Adam that George was asleep. Adam was too excited to sleep, even though he was tired from the long day's work and the night's initiation. He lay for a long time, his finger gently tracing the small of George's back. Tonight had been what Adam had yearned for since his recognition of his feelings about men as he sat on the bench in the maze. Their kisses, their explorations of each other's body, and George's taking of him had far exceeded what Adam had expected. He lightly kissed the nape of George's neck and cuddled closer. Shortly he, too, was asleep.

During the daytime hours of the festivities Adam did not see George. His duties sent him scurrying between the great house and the stables. In the kitchen he began the morning by herding the lads to fetch in the day's supply of firewood. Later, he helped serve and clear the tables where the guests ate and talked at their breakfast meal. Afterward he was at the stable. Horses had to be groomed before and after the ride. Adam hated a few of the guests who rode. Too often they had drunk too much wine. They did not know to handle the horses well, and it took Adam and the other hands longer than usual to calm the excited horses. Then he was back in the kitchen for whatever task he was needed in serving the lavish supper banquet. Chores over, he was weary and hungry. However, after the servants' light supper and a cup of wine, Adam was ready for what lay ahead in his room.

As they undressed, Adam and George recounted the humorous episodes that had occurred to each of them during their long day apart. Soon though they were naked in bed, embracing. Adam enjoyed the lengthy foreplay almost as much as he did the later union of their bodies. When they kissed, the bristles of George's trimmed mustache tickled the smoothness above Adam's upper lip. Adam's hands quickly discovered those special places on George's body to elicit his heavy sighs. Adam's lips and tongue scarcely missed licking a spot on George's hairy body. And Adam quickly learned to imitate George's handling of Adam's sex with his mouth.

When both young men were near orgasm, Adam turned willingly to whatever position George wanted to use in taking him. Every night Adam found the penetration easier for him to take. He soon found ways to move his body to give pleasure to both George and himself. Usually the two men reached orgasm at the same time, George spilling his seed within Adam, and Adam spilling his on their bodies.

Only one thing marred their nightly pleasure. George would soon leave.

One night before turning to sleep, George remarked, "The earl is fond of me. Every season he takes me to London as his second valet. Perhaps Lord Cromley will bring you someday."

"I doubt that," Adam replied. "My aunt goes regularly with her ladyship, but Lord Cromley hardly knows who I am. He rarely speaks to me, and only then with a morning or evening greeting. He seldom sees me except at the stable, where I am but one of a dozen stable lads. I am hardly one to serve him in his private rooms."

"Pity," George said. "We could be companions in London. I would show you places in the city that do not exist here in the country."

"We shall have to wait until next Christmas season to lie together again," Adam sighed.

On the night before George was to leave, he was late in coming to Adam's room. "I had to tend to preparations for our departure tomorrow morning," he explained. Adam lay naked in bed, and he anxiously watched George shed his clothes.

"Come bugger me," Adam told George.

George dropped down beside Adam and propped himself up on his elbow.

"No, Adam, not tonight. It is your turn to bugger me. I have waited for you to take me of your own accord, but you haven't. Now I ask you to plow me with your sex."

"I would be afraid. I would be too clumsy."

George burst out laughing. "Four nights ago you were a virgin with men. You have learned very quickly how to give and get pleasure when lying with a man. You will not be clumsy. I want to feel you inside me very much. I will not wait until next Christmas season."

As George had predicted, Adam was not clumsy. Adam knew from George's moans that he was giving him pleasure. And Adam knew as soon as he had penetrated George that he himself was experiencing a new and wonderful pleasure. The two young men reached orgasm all too quickly.

They stayed locked together until every trickle had found its way out. After several minutes they pulled apart. Adam cuddled into George's arms. They lay quiet for a long time. Then George said, "You were far from clumsy, Adam." They kissed and wrapped themselves in each other's sweaty, naked body. They slept soundly.

George was gone when Adam awakened the next morning. The earl's carriage had been the first to depart, the steward told Adam. Adam was disappointed that George had not roused him for a farewell kiss. Still, he smiled. What George had left with him was the clear knowledge that he wanted to lie only with men.

The next five months were the happiest Adam spent at Cromley Hall. The steward assigned him the important task of recording household expenses in the large ledger. Adam appreciated the trust the steward placed in him, and he went about his new duty with the greatest care. At the stable the stable master turned over to Adam the care of Lord Cromley's favorite mare. "You've a good hand with horses, Adam," the stable master told him. "Handle Nell with your best attention. She is his lordship's favorite mare." Adam delighted in both new tasks.

What surprised and pleased Adam most though was that he met two men servants who were more than receptive to Adam's advances. Both men were in their early twenties. One of them was as new to sex with another man as Adam had been until the past Christmas season. Adam delighted in his role as instructor. The other, however, was even more experienced than George had been. With him, Adam once more became the pupil. Seldom was there the need now to lie in bed "doing so."

On a sunny but crisp February morning the stable master formally introduced Adam to Lord Cromley.

"Your lordship, this is Adam, the young man I have selected to care for Nell. He will do you good service."

Adam bowed to Lord Cromley.

The nobleman studied Adam for several minutes. Then he said, "Nell is my favorite. Treat her well, and I shall treat you well."

"Adam is the nephew to Sarah, her ladyship's maid," the stable master said.

"Ah! Then he comes highly recommended," Lord Cromley replied and nodded. "Lady Cromley swears she cannot do without Sarah, especially when she is to appear in court during the season. Now what other news have you for me, Mr. Henley?"

Adam stood respectfully at a distance while the two men talked. As he looked at them, he suddenly realized that, although Lord Cromley's words were directed to the stable master, the man's eyes were on him. Adam briefly returned the stare. Then, not to be rude, he dropped his eyes.

Although not a tall man, twenty years ago Lord Cromley was considered a handsome man with an athletic build. Now, at forty-two, he had developed a paunch, and his face had grown slightly flabby. At the estate, the nobleman was more inclined to watch his horses being exercised than to ride them himself. During the dark evenings he had become too fond of his port. In London he was often at the gaming table, where luck and skill made him a frequent winner. He had always enjoyed young women, straying frequently from the marriage vows of his wife's bedchamber. Recently he had also discovered that he enjoyed the bodies of young men.

Until Adam took sole charge of the grooming and exercising of Nell, Lord Cromley had barely taken notice of Adam in the stable yard. Now, however, the two met almost daily. At first the nobleman stopped only to study the handsome young man. When Adam became aware that he was being looked at so intensely, he paused and pretended to be more busy with his work than he actually was. Soon though when they met, Adam found that Lord Cromley's hand was across his shoulders and from there working its way down his back. Just as often the hand was on Adam's butt. Adam was puzzled. He knew the difference between the physical contact most men allowed themselves to display with another man, and that of two men lying in bed together. The nobleman's hand on Adam's body was much more like the caresses of a bed partner than the fatherly pats the stable master gave Adam.

The more Lord Cromley's hand touched Adam's body and the more that touch was like that of a bed partner, the greater was Adam's bewilderment. Surely these caresses were not sexual overtures, he kept telling himself.

Adam badly needed to talk to someone about these encounters with Lord Cromley. He knew he could not broach the subject with his aunt. Neither of the two young men with whom he took sexual pleasure would give sensible advice. The one he met well inside the left rear maze would have been too shocked to believe that Lord Cromley was interested in Adam's body. He would call Adam mad. The man he buggered in the hay of the large feeding trough of the cattle barn would only have farted and said, "Let him have you. Then slit his throat."

What Adam wanted most was the advice of George. The earl's coachman had told him how the many ways of the city and the court differed from those of the country, how the aristocrats of the land had their unique ways of behaving. Perhaps, Adam tried to convince himself, he was completely wrong in finding Lord Cromley's hand on his body anything more than the nobleman's way of saying what the stable master said in his. However, when he was most clear headed, Adam admitted he did not know what to make of the caresses. He forced the worrisome questions to retreat to the back of his mind. In time, he came to accept the caresses, even to enjoy them.

In the late spring, Nell came into heat, and Lord Cromley decided to breed her with the roan stallion. "They will produce a fine colt," the nobleman said. On the afternoon of the insemination, a large crowd of onlookers from the stable and great house gathered around the enclosed area, anxious for entertainment. "Get out of here and back to your business," Lord Cromley shouted. "Let them do it in private." Reluctantly the crowd went its way.

"Stay here with me, Adam," the nobleman commanded. "You'll need to take care of the mare later. Until then, we can watch in the stable." Adam followed Lord Cromley into the stable. Adam went to an open window.

The two horses were engaged in a courting dance. The stallion nipped at the rump of the mare. She, in turn, snapped at his neck. The stallion's thick penis emerged out of its covering of skin. After a long foreplay, Nell let the stallion mount her. Adam excitedly watched the roan sink his long tool into the mare. Adam felt his own sex begin to stiffen.

Suddenly Adam smelled the body heat of Lord Cromley behind him. Then he felt the firm pressure of the nobleman's body. Adam was certain that much of that pressure came from an erect cock. Lord Cromley rubbed Adam's neck and behind his ears. As the nobleman pulled Adam's body back closer against his, Adam's sex arose to erection.

Adam stood still, not knowing what to do. Lord Cromley pulled Adam's shirt out of his breeches and ran his hand around Adam's chest. He gently pulled at the hairs at the top of Adam's chest and grasped the smooth muscled mounds with their hard nipples.

"They are enjoying themselves, aren't they, Adam, the roan and Nell?"

"Yes," Adam murmured.

"And are you enjoying what I am doing, Adam?"

Adam hesitated before he said, "Yes." Wasn't it risky to have sex with a nobleman? Where did the greater trouble lie, in pushing Lord Cromley's hand away or in letting the nobleman have his way with him? Adam was sexually excited, but he was also very frightened. To play with either of the two young men in the maze or in the trough was one thing. To play with a nobleman, even one who was making the advances, was quite another.

Outside in the enclosure the two horses were going at it. Lord Cromley roughly turned Adam around and pulled him into a tight embrace. He kissed Adam fully upon the lips. Adam opened his mouth to thrust his tongue against the nobleman's. Adam knew there was no turning back now.

Lord Cromley moved his hands to Adam's waist. He untied the drawstring of Adam's leather breeches. In one quick stroke, he yanked the drawers to Adam's feet. "Get out of them, and go kneel down over that bench," Lord Cromley said excitedly.

"My lord, do you think . . . ," Adam started to ask.

"Be quiet, Adam. I know what I am doing, and I know what I want. And I think you want it, too."

Adam knelt over the bench. His bare butt was high in the air.

Lord Cromley quickly shed his coat and waistcoat. Adam watched as the nobleman undid just enough of his other clothing to reveal his erect cock. Lord Cromley knelt behind Adam. He spread Adam's legs. Then, in one swift plunge, he buried himself deep inside Adam.

Adam raised his head and shouted, "Pull out. You're hurting me." Lord Cromley's only response was to press Adam's head down to the ground. He fell on top of the young man and kissed his neck and ears. Soon Adam surrendered himself. Lord Cromley pumped furiously, unconcerned about any pain he might be inflicting. Outside in the stable yard, the horses broke into a wild frenzy. Their fun was being completed. In the barn, Lord Cromley shook violently and unloaded. In the stable yard both horses whinnied. Inside the stable both men took in deep breaths and sighed.

Finally the nobleman put his hands on the ground and pulled out. Adam stood up. He turned to look at his buggerer. Lord Cromley was grinning. "My stallion and I give good service, don't we, Adam," he said.

"You do," Adam replied. "Now it's my turn."

"You impudent young cur," the startled nobleman shouted, hardly believing what he had heard. "No," he snarled. He began to adjust his clothes.

"Yes, my lord. It's my turn now," Adam said firmly.

Adam's sudden remembrance was that of George their last night together. "It's your turn to bugger me," George had said, wanting to return the favors of the several nights before.

"Yes, my lord. It's my turn now," Adam repeated. "I'll not be a nobleman's boy whore."

Lord Cromley glared at Adam for a few seconds. Sneering, he turned to leave.

Angry, Adam quickly tripped the nobleman and wrestled him to the ground and up over the bench. Lord Cromley was strong but no match for Adam. With one hand on Lord Cromley's neck, Adam held the nobleman to the ground. With the other hand he lowered the nobleman's breeches.

As Lord Cromley had done to him, Adam entered in one swift plunge. He ignored the nobleman's muffled cry, waited a few seconds, and then started to pump. But Adam was too excited. He quickly lost his large supply of jism inside the nobleman. Still holding Lord Cromley's head down with his hand, Adam rested over the squirming body. Finally he pulled out and got up.

Adam looked at his erect sex. It was dirty. He went to a water bucket near the stable door and cleaned himself. He put back on his leather drawers. Dressed, he turned around. Breathing heavily, Lord Cromley was staring hard at him. There was a malicious smile on his face.

"You'll pay for what you did, Adam," Lord Cromley said in a low angry voice.

"I only gave what I got, my lord," Adam replied quietly. "What's more, we both enjoyed ourselves."

"That may be, but no one buggers Lord Cromley."

Common sense told Adam not to reply. Too late, he realized that earlier his common sense had been overcome by a too strong sexual passion. Suddenly he was afraid of the consequences.

The two men stared at each other. Lord Cromley finally broke the silence and barked, "Tare care of the mare, Adam. I'll tend to you later."

For two weeks Adam fretted, wondering what Lord Cromley was thinking. He doubted that the nobleman would simply forget about the incident. That was too much to hope for. Adam was still caring for Nell; he had not been dismissed from that daily duty. Several times Lord Cromley had passed Adam in the stable yard, but the nobleman had not spoken to him, had barely even looked at him. Adam berated himself. If only he had let Lord Cromley have his way with him and then said nothing. But Adam hadn't, and he knew he could not turn back time.

At the end of the uneasy two weeks, the steward told him one afternoon that Lord Cromley was waiting to see him in the library. The steward had a puzzled look on his face.

"Have you offended Lord Cromley in any way, Adam?" the steward asked.

"I played the fool," Adam admitted. He offered no further explanation.

"Then mind your tongue when you speak to his lordship," the steward warned as he gave Adam a friendly pat on the shoulder. Adam followed the steward to the library. His fists clenched and his mind in a whirl, Adam imagined a dozen different punishments awaiting him. The steward opened the door to the library and announced Adam.

"You may go," the nobleman told his steward.

A bust of Shakespeare looked down on Adam as he walked slowly across the room to face Lord Cromley. The inscription at the base of the bust read, "The quality of mercy is not strained." Lord Cromley turned away from Adam and went to a large oak sideboard. He poured himself a glass of port, savored the aroma, and drank a bit. Adam could not determine the nobleman's mood. He stood quietly and waited for the nobleman to speak.

When Lord Cromley returned to where Adam was standing, he stood and studied Adam's body. He smiled slightly and shook his head in a strange, ambiguous way. Suddenly Adam wondered if the nobleman wanted to bugger him again. If that were his punishment, he would accept it and say nothing.

Finally Lord Cromley spoke. "Adam, what we did in the stable was no sin, no matter what the archbishop of Canterbury claims."

"I believe so, too, my lord," Adam replied.

Lord Cromley nodded. He paused, then he frowned. "When you took my body, however, you transgressed a far more important law. You broke social boundaries. For that you must be punished."

"Why so, my lord?" Adam asked, fighting to keep anger from his voice.

"We will not argue that question," Lord Cromley replied. "You are here to listen to what I have decided."

The two men stared at each other.

"You have only two choices, Adam," Lord Cromley said.

Adam said nothing.

"Unless you choose otherwise, I shall see to it that you are sent to Justice Howard. He will find you guilty of the charge of attempt at sodomy, and he will sentence you to be hanged."

Adam exploded, "What attempt! That's a lie. We buggered each other."

"Justice Howard will believe whatever story I tell him. He is my friend and neighbor. We understand each other. He, too, recognizes the unwritten law of social boundaries. He will be horrified at the thought that one of my servants made an attempt to use my body unlawfully. He will not believe any story you tell, if you even have a chance to talk with him," the nobleman said.

Adam bit his tongue to keep from saying what he really felt, and he clenched his fists to control them. Then in a restrained voice, he asked, "And my other choice?"

"Lady Cromley's youngest brother lives in the colony of Virginia. He is a prosperous planter. He writes me that he needs an intelligent young man to help manage the business of his warehouse on the river."

"How does that concern me?" Adam asked.

"You can go over as an indentured servant, bound to Mr. Ashley for a term of seven years. After that you'd be free to go your own way, or you could continue to work for him in a new indenture. Before you leave England, you will sign a statement swearing never to return here," Lord Cromley explained.

"What if I don't want to go?"

The malicious smile Adam had seen in the stable on Lord Cromley's face reappeared. "Lady Cromley and I will hate to lose the service of your aunt. She is her ladyship's favorite maid. But she can be replaced."

The irony of his "choices" infuriated Adam. He knew he had no choice. Enraged, he glared at the man whom he had willingly let take him but whom he had to take by force.

Then, with great self-control Adam said calmly, "I'll sign the indenture papers."

"A wise decision. Despite what you did to me, I would not like to see you hanged. You're too handsome for that, Adam. Besides, before you were hanged, your privates would be cut off while you were still alive. Your horse's cock deserves better treatment than that," Lord Cromley said and laughed.

Adam had nothing more to say.

"I'll have the steward see to the details. The ship captain who is Mr. Ashley's agent sails in two weeks. You'll be aboard his ship," the nobleman explained. He finished his glass of port. His hand waved Adam's dismissal.

Adam turned his back to Lord Cromley. He left the room without bowing. That breach of courtesy was the only revenge Adam ever got.

# 1747-1750: Williamsburg

On the morning after the third auction Lance stood at the window of the captain's quarters. He watched the last of the prisoners being rowed to land. Even at a distance Lance could tell they were a despondent lot of men, headed to cut and clear the wilderness. He was thankful he was not among them. "This afternoon we will go to Williamsburg," Captain Henry had told him in the early hours of the morning.

For the five nights since Captain Henry first took him, Lance had shared the captain's bed. Their lovemaking had been the most intense each of them had ever experienced. Lance was astonished at the strength of the captain's body, but it was welcome weight upon him. Never had the captain been touched with such passion. Lance's hands found spots that had never been touched by another man. And those places on his body were touched with a firm gentleness excitingly new to the captain. Captain Henry awakened each morning with something akin to the intimacy that he yearned for. He had even thought briefly that he should try to keep Lance aboard as a crew member. But he knew he could not. He kissed Lance all the harder and went about the ship's business.

Except for the early morning hours, Lance spent the day in the captain's closet. However, he was neither chained nor naked, and the captain saw to it that he ate more than bread and water. Lance listened as Captain Henry issued orders for the day and made the plans for the auctions. Only after the evening mess with the officers were the captain's quarters private. Then Lance stretched his legs and inhaled the fresh air off the ocean. He waited for the captain to return from the deck.

In a strange way which neither of them could have explained and which neither of them truly acknowledged, a bond grew between

doi:10.1300/5623_03

them in that short time. However, since neither the older nor the younger man was especially gifted at conversation with a new acquaintance, especially that of an intimate kind, what little talk they had was superficial. They knew better how to communicate with hands than with words. It surprised Lance, then, when shortly before they were to leave by flatboat up the James River to Williamsburg, the captain said, "I shall miss you, Lance."

"And I, you. But I understand why I cannot stay aboard ship."

Captain Henry nodded his thanks.

Any regrets that Lance had about leaving the ship quickly faded as the two men traveled to Williamsburg. Lance had never been so close to running water as he was on the flatboat. He was like a little boy as he leaned over the side of the boat and let the water splash over his hands. The native boatmen shook their heads and whispered that a lunatic was with them. The walk from the river to the outskirts of the town, even though Lance carried his heavy bundle of new clothes and bedding, provided endless surprises. He had known only the dirty streets of London. Here, for the first time in his life, were trees, shrubs, strange grasses, and even wildflowers. Lance stopped frequently to look and to sniff. London streets stank, even in the most fashionable districts. Here the woods had a clean smell that worked through his nose to his head. *Here is a new life indeed,* Lance thought.

"Don't tarry," the captain often called back to Lance. "I can taste the chess pie." Since Captain Henry, too, had once experienced for the first time the freshness of this wooded wagon trail, he was hesitant to break into Lance's discovery of the new country. However, he knew the woods were not the life ahead for Lance. "You won't be in these woods, Lance, for seven years," he warned. "Hurry now, we are losing the sun."

Although Lance knew Williamsburg would not be London, he did not know what to expect. Hampton had been largely warehouses around the busy wharves. When the flatboat had passed a collection of dilapidated buildings, Captain Henry had told him, "That is Jamestown, the old capital before it was moved from those swamps to higher ground."

Lance was taken by surprise, then, when the wagon trail ended at a large clearing. Not far away was a large H-shaped brick building with a tall cupola. Lance stopped to admire the handsome structure. "That is the capitol, as they call it here in the colony," the captain informed Lance. "It's a place where topics are debated and laws made."

"And what is that building over there?" Lance asked and pointed.

"A place you do not want to be. The public gaol," the captain replied. "Come along."

As the two men turned west down the broad Duke of Gloucester Street, Lance was even more amazed. Before him lay a busy little town. Houses and shops fronted the street. They were surrounded by large plots of fenced ground with a number of outbuildings. Smoke rose from the chimneys of the kitchens behind the main buildings. A few of the larger houses were brick, but most were constructed of wood, painted white. Exterior shutters were on each side of the windows. The entire scene breathed vitality. "I belong here," Lance murmured to himself.

"Watch your feet," Captain Henry called to the gawking Lance. "Horses don't mind where they shit."

It was dusk. Shops were being closed. But men still gathered in groups to enjoy a pipe and to exchange news of the day. Several of the men called a greeting of welcome to the captain, who, in turn, inquired about their health. Children were taking advantage of a last bit of freedom to finish their noisy games before being called to supper. Shortly after the two men crossed Botetourt Street, Captain Henry pointed to a house on the north side of the broad avenue where they were walking and said, "That is your new home, Lance, and that is your new master at the door."

The next ten minutes were a hubbub of greetings. The captain and John Thomas embraced as old friends. Summoned from inside, Mistress Thomas gave the captain a welcome hug and thrust her six-month-old babe at him to admire. Lance could not hear what was being said, but he sensed that Captain Henry was being given a warm welcome. Finally Thomas pointed and asked, "Who is the lad with you?"

"If I get the price I will ask, he is your new indentured servant. His name is Lance Morley," the captain replied.

Thomas glanced from Lance to the captain and then back to Lance. "We will talk business later. Let us go inside for a cup of cider now."

Inside the shop, two apprentices were still at work. One was a boy, a bit older than Lance had been when he entered his apprenticeship. He smiled at Lance. The other was a young man about Lance's age. He looked up at Lance with a somewhat surly expression.

"Timothy," Thomas said to the young boy, "give Morley here the shoe you are working on. Then go give the new harnesses a final oiling. I must deliver them tomorrow, and I want them in the best of condition." Turning to Lance, Thomas said, "Dudley will show you any tools you will need. I'll see how good you are at work before I talk your price." Then, holding the captain's arm, Thomas said, "Come, Captain Henry, let us sit over there and talk. I want to hear your news of the home country, and I want you to tell me about this lad you want me to buy, paying, no doubt, far more than he is worth."

No sooner had Timothy handed Lance the shoe to be finished than Lance saw that the stitching on part of the left side was badly wrong. He did not want to cause the boy trouble, but neither did he want to be unfairly blamed for a poor shoe the first hour after his arrival. So with hesitation, he approached Thomas. Thomas and the captain looked up at Lance. "What is it?" Thomas snapped.

"Sir, the cut and the stitching don't match here," Lance said, pointing to the spot on the shoe. "I will need to redo some of the work."

Thomas grabbed the shoe, looked at it briefly, and then flung it at Timothy. "Damn, you are as worthless as a man's tits," he shouted. "You're fourteen and still too dumb to do even the simplest stitching."

Timothy burst into tears. Dudley stopped his work and glared hard at Lance. *Damn,* Lance said to himself. *I have got off on the wrong foot with the two people I must work with. Why didn't I keep my mouth shut!*

For a minute the only sound in the shop was Timothy's sobbing. Then Captain Henry broke into a loud laugh and exclaimed, "You are right that a man's nipples are useless, but our chests would look strange without them." The captain glanced at Lance and smiled, recalling the pleasure of Lance's lips on his large dark nipples.

Thomas looked at the captain and said, "Funny thing to say." Then he barked at Timothy, "Stop whimpering, and go about the harnesses." He paused, shook his head in disgust, and then told Lance, "Fix the shoe."

While Dudley and Lance worked at the bench without talking or looking at each other, the cordwainer and the captain talked and drank the cider Mistress Thomas brought them in large tin cups. Only once in their conversation did either of them raise a voice so that it could be heard by the young men at the workbench. "A felon," Thomas had cried out in a shocked voice. Lance's heart sank. Dudley looked up questioningly. Lance busied himself with the shoe as if nothing had happened.

Shortly before supper, Thomas called to Lance. "Show me the shoe."

When Lance handed it to the cordwainer, Thomas examined it carefully and then said, "You do good work, Morley. Your London master taught you well."

"Thank you."

"Have you ever made a harness?"

"No, that would be new to me."

"I will teach you. We make as many of them as we do boots here in the colony."

"I am sure I can learn."

Thomas nodded. Then, he said, "Captain Henry tells that you were sent to Newgate for hitting a constable, but that you had good reason."

"That is so," Lance replied. He was thankful that Captain Henry must not have mentioned the charge of attempted murder for which he had been convicted.

"I will tolerate no such behavior here, even if you have good cause," Thomas said sternly.

"I have learned," Lance hastily assured him.

"Let us hope so," Thomas said, as the shop door opened and Mistress Thomas called, "Come to the table."

After the light supper of cold pork, dried apples, hot bread, and finished off with what Captain Henry hoped for, chess pie, the cordwainer and the captain left for the Raleigh Tavern for a game of cards.

"We will settle on your price tonight," Thomas said to Lance. "Dudley, acquaint the new servant with the quarters."

No sooner had Dudley shut the door to their small room at the rear of the shop than Timothy jumped at Lance. He repeatedly hit him in the belly before he gave him a hard blow in the groin. Surprised by the strength of the young boy, Lance doubled in pain with the blow to his scrotum. Dudley whooped loudly as he watched Lance grab his crotch in an attempt to relieve the pain. "Serves you right," he shouted at Lance.

"Why did you tell on me?" Timothy asked, although now he was ashamed of his blow at Lance's sex.

"I had to, or else take the blame on myself and find misfortune with Master Thomas my first hour here."

"But you could have redone my stitching and not told," Timothy insisted.

"Did you know it was badly done?"

"No," Timothy admitted with reluctance.

"Then I will show you how to do it properly tomorrow."

"He'll be your new master," Dudley interrupted. "He'll treat you just as badly as does that bastard Thomas."

Looking only at Timothy, Lance said, "No, Timothy, I will not become your master. But I would like to be your friend. I promise I will help you at the bench when you need it."

For the first time since he arrived as an apprentice, Timothy heard words of kindness and encouragement. "I will be your friend," he said.

"And shall we be friends?" Lance asked Dudley.

Not answering that question, Dudley asked, "Are you a felon?"

"Yes," Lance answered in a strong voice, "but let me explain."

The three of them sat close together while Lance told his story. He did not know it, but his version of his being sent to Newgate duplicated exactly what the captain had told the cordwainer. Timothy was fighting sleep by the time Lance stopped talking. But he turned to Lance and said, "Yes, you did right. I am sorry I hit you where I did." He pulled his blanket over his small body and was quickly asleep.

"And shall we be friends?" Lance asked Dudley a second time.

Dudley's only answer was, "Stay on your side of the bed, and keep your hands to yourself."

"Do not bother yourself on either account," Lance answered sharply. He knew that he would keep his distance from Dudley in more ways than simply sharing a bed with him.

Lance was too full of the day's events to fall asleep immediately. The trip up the river, the walk through the woods, the excitement of the busy little town, all this clashed against the trouble he had caused Timothy. He was happy though that Timothy seemed genuinely sincere in saying that he wanted Lance to be his friend. Slowly the exhaustion from the long day overcame him, and Lance slept.

For two days Lance worked without talking to Captain Henry and with little talk to anyone in the shop. He did, however, explain Timothy's mistakes to him, and he answered questions from the young boy several times a day. Each time Timothy smiled at Lance before he returned to the workbench. Four or five times during the day Thomas took Lance's work from his hands and examined it. But finding nothing wrong, he said nothing. After having been so long away from leather and tools, Lance was delighted at having his fingers back at their accustomed movements. He was pleased he had lost none of his skill during the months in Newgate or aboard ship.

On the morning Captain Henry was to go back to the *St. George,* he asked permission from Thomas to say a few private words with Lance.

"Not trying to steal him after you have robbed me of twenty-five pounds, are you?" Thomas asked. He was never in the best of moods after paying a bill or settling a gambling debt.

"No, John," the captain replied patiently. "You have more than your money's worth in Lance Morley. I only wish a few last words with him before I leave him in your hands."

Thomas shrugged and motioned for Lance to follow the captain.

Captain Henry took Lance to the woodshed at the far end of Thomas's half-acre property. Once out of sight, the captain took Lance in his arms and kissed him.

"Do you want to have me?" Lance asked a few minutes later.

"No, Lance, I do not want us to part in that way. That can wait until I see you again next year. Something more important is on my mind."

"What?"

"I want to talk with you about two things."

Lance waited for the captain to continue.

Finally, the captain spoke. "First, be alert around your new master. Down deep, John Thomas is a sour man. He is not to be crossed, especially when he has drunk too much at the tavern. Sooner or later, he will be jealous of your good work. Hold your tongue when he insults you. Seven years is a long time. You need not add extra years to your indenture just to satisfy your quick temper for the moment." He paused, then said, "Please, Lance, be careful."

"I know I lose my temper too quickly. I promise you, I will try to control it."

"I hope so."

"And the other thing?" Lance asked.

"It is harder to talk about, because Englishmen cannot talk openly about it. Of course, when they condemn it, their voices are loud enough even though most of them know nothing actually about it."

Lance instinctively knew what was on the captain's mind. "Did we do wrong?" Lance asked.

"No," the captain replied firmly and grasped Lance's shoulders. "No, we have done no wrong, but we have gone against the accepted way of the world." He paused and looked hard at Lance. "Lance, there are men here in Williamsburg who feel as we do, even do as we did. I hope you meet one of them. But you must be careful. If you mistake a smile for an overture and are caught in a false move, you will be punished. Believe me, Lance, a conviction for an attempt at sodomy will bring you far worse punishment than for the attempt to murder."

"I hear your caution, sir. I don't think I can be without lying with another man for seven years. But I will careful."

Captain Henry only shook his head. "I have said all I can say. Good-bye, Lance, until next year." He kissed Lance and then left the woodshed.

Lance returned to his workbench without speaking to anyone. He did though smile at Timothy.

When Captain Henry entered the shop, Thomas called to him, "I see you are ready to leave for the trip down the river. I will walk with you to the trailhead." The two men left the shop for the street.

For the next two years the daily routine in Thomas's shop remained much the same. One day repeated the one before and the one to follow. Every workday morning the apprentices arose before dawn for a breakfast of hot mush, cold cornbread, and sometimes a piece of pork. They worked in the shop until the large meal of the day shortly after noon. After a rest period of half an hour, it was back to the workshop until early evening. Before the light supper at the end of the day, Thomas allowed the apprentices to enjoy a brief relaxation in the streets or at the Exchange, the large open area outside the brick walls surrounding the capitol. After supper and a trip to the necessary house at the far end of the property, the three apprentices were dismissed to their small quarters.

Although the workday hours remained the same, Lance had two new experiences in those years that excited him and relieved the dull repetition of the routine. Several days after Captain Henry left, Thomas showed Lance how to make a harness. "There is a great demand for them, both for oxen and for horses. I can sell as many as we make, and at a handsome profit." Thomas said. He was pleased that Lance so quickly mastered the new technique. Lance himself was glad to have another kind of work to do in the shop.

The other new experience was a complete surprise. It came in a large box on the wagon delivering goods from the ship at the harbor at Hampton. Lance and Dudley carried the box from the wagon into the shop.

"What's in it?" Mistress Thomas demanded.

"Something that will make our shop even more popular," her husband replied.

When the box was opened, Thomas took out an assortment of shoes. He held up two pair and said, "This one is what the fashionable ladies in London wear for dancing at balls, and this one is what the gentlemen wear on such occasions." He arranged all the shoes in a line before his wife and the apprentices. "These are the shoes of people who play more than they work, if they work at all."

"And what are we to do with them?" his wife asked sarcastically.

"We will use them as patterns for shoes we will make. There are people here in this town and in the great houses up the river who wear shoes like these at their parties and balls. They have sent to England for them." He paused, then shouted, "Now they will buy them at my shop."

The apprentices tapped their feet as the Thomas couple danced a jig.

But bad news also came with the delivery wagon. Lance did not hear it until the next evening. The word was that the captain of the *St. George* had been buried at sea on the return voyage. Some reports said the captain had died of a strange fever, crying out in a crazy way about "ants." Others claimed that the captain had been murdered by his second mate, although no charges were filed against him. Shocked, Lance fled to the woodshed and wept. What had happened? Was he to blame in any way? Lance asked himself. Slowly he retrieved from all his short time with the captain only the smile on Captain Henry's face as he kissed Lance good-bye in the woodshed. When Lance recovered himself, he silently thanked the captain for what he had done for him and for what they had done together.

Thomas set Lance to the task of determining the patterns and the techniques for making the new shoes. Lance basked in the responsibility. Within a week, he told Thomas that his shop could begin making the shoes. Always niggardly in his compliments to his apprentices, all Thomas mustered to acknowledge Lance's quick accomplishment was a curt, "I am pleased to hear you say so."

Frequently during the two years Lance recalled the warning about Thomas that Captain Henry had given him in the woodshed. As the now-dead captain had predicted, Lance often had to shut his ears to insults and threats. And when Thomas was too harsh and unfair in his treatment of Timothy, Lance had to sit on his hands to keep from using them in defense of the boy. Lance worked at his best when Thomas was still half-asleep in the morning, or when he was out of the shop, as he often was in the late afternoon.

With each of the two apprentices Lance had a different relationship. He quickly became Timothy's teacher, and two grew into a strong liking for each other. Thomas was all too happy to have Timothy's instruction off his hands. Lance and Dudley, however, seldom spoke to each other except when they needed to in their work. Lance sensed that Dudley recognized the quality of his craftsmanship and resented it.

The only free time Lance had was on Sunday. Even then, half of it was spent with Thomas, his family, and the other two apprentices at Bruton Parish Church at the end of the Palace Green. Although Lance had been frequently outside of St. Paul's in London, he had never attended a church service there. His affairs outside the cathedral had been of a different nature. Here, though, in the small brick church, Lance repeated the prayers and the liturgies without thinking about the meaning of the words. The sermon meant little to him, and, because of its length, he usually fought back sleep before it had ended. He was always glad to be outside the church and away from the torrent of words.

The brief hours of Sunday afternoon were the only times Lance felt truly free. Usually, with Timothy, he walked the length of the Duke of Gloucester Street from east to west, from the capitol to the Wren Building on the grounds of the college named in honor of their majesties William and Mary. Then they walked the numerous side north-south streets. Always Timothy plied Lance with questions about London. Through these questions, Lance recalled the many good times of his youth there.

"I wish we were in London together," Timothy said one afternoon.

"Yes, I too. But it is foolish to wish for things which cannot be," Lance replied, as he sent Timothy off to play with companions his own age.

Whenever Lance joined the other young men at the Exchange, he often felt unwelcome, although he was never excluded from any group. He had once seen Dudley point to him, and the group with whom he was talking turned toward Lance and laughed. On occasion, too, he had overheard the word *felon.* During the two years the only man who approached Lance and sought him out for conversation was a bearded man who always stood alone at the edge of the Exchange. Shortly before it was time for the indentured servants to return home, this large man frequently hailed Lance.

"We have something in common," the bearded man said the first time the two met.

"It's not beards," Lance replied, rubbing his own smooth face.

"No," the man replied and laughed.

"We are both indentured?"

"Yes. But we are also both king's men."

After a long silence, Lance said, "I try to forget that."

"You may try to. But this place won't let you," the bearded man said, pointing down the Duke of Gloucester Street. "Even when you get your pardon, if you ever do, the men who make the laws here will still remember that you are a man who came from Newgate."

Lance had no words to respond. He was happy to have their brief introduction interrupted by Timothy who came up running and shouting, "It's time to go home, Lance." The bearded man and Lance looked at each other and exchanged names. "Good night, Ben," Lance called as he and Timothy started to race each other back to the shop.

Lance and Ben continued to meet and talk briefly late Sunday afternoons, even though Lance found he had little in common with the older man. Still, his chats with Ben were better than standing in a group of other young men and finding himself all but excluded from their gossip and jokes. It annoyed Lance that occasionally their jokes were about "filthy sodomites." Lance never joined in the loud laughter that these jokes aroused.

Late on a Sunday afternoon in December 1749, Ben told Lance that he intended to run away that evening just as it turned dark. Lance was shocked. "But where will you go?" he asked in a troubled voice.

"I will follow the river, and then I will take to the woods in the hills."

"But you'll get lost. You don't know the way."

"No, I won't. But I am willing to take that risk. I hate it here; there's no life ahead for me here. Come with me, Lance."

"No. I escaped life in the wilderness two years ago. I will not go on my own into it now. I think you foolish, Ben."

Lance saw Timothy in the distance waving to him. He shook Ben's hand and said, "Fool that you are, I wish you safety, Ben." As he and Timothy walked back to Thomas's house, Lance twice looked back at

Ben, still standing near the wall surrounding the capitol. Lance shook his head each time.

"Is something wrong?" Timothy inquired.

"No. It is getting chilly. Let's run."

Less than an hour later, supper was interrupted by loud knocking at the shop door. "Who can that be?" Thomas said as he left the table.

"I hope it is not trouble," Mistress Thomas remarked. She and the apprentices had stopped eating. When Thomas returned, he was accompanied by three men, one of whom looked especially angry.

"Stand up, Lance," Thomas snapped. "You were seen at the Exchange this evening with an indentured servant named Ben. His master here says he has run away. What do you know of the matter?"

"Nothing," Lance answered quickly.

"He said nothing to you about running away?" the angry man asked.

"No," Lance replied, looking straight into the eyes of Ben's master and owner.

"Do you believe that?" the angry man asked Thomas.

"Yes, I do. Lance does not lie," Thomas said quickly, not really caring whether Lance was lying or not. He simply did not want Lance associated with aiding the runaway. That well might cause Lance trouble with the magistrates, and that, in turn, might jeopardize Lance's work in the shop. Thomas cared far more about Lance's hours in the shop than he did about the truth of Lance's statements.

Ben's master looked hard at both Thomas and Lance, and then said, "Let's go. A posse is forming. We will find that bastard and beat him to death."

"I hope you do," Thomas said, as he followed the two men back to the shop door.

There was silence around the supper table until Thomas returned.

"I trust you were telling the truth," he said to Lance.

"Yes," Lance replied, avoiding the questioning look on Timothy's face.

Lance slept uneasily that night, and for good reason. As he had expected, Ben was caught. He quickly discovered that finding his way up the land along the river was not as easy as he thought it would be.

Before noon the next day the posse came upon him struggling through the underbrush.

That evening in the grounds around the gaol Ben was stripped of what remained of his shirt and made to stand for forty lashes. He fell to the ground before the lashes were half completed. Yanked to his feet, he was locked in the pillory for the rest of his lashing. His screams stopped after the thirty-first lashing. His head dropped. He was unconscious.

Thomas, like many another master with indentured servants, took Timothy, Dudley, and Lance to the gaol grounds. "You need to see what will happen to you should you ever run away," he told the apprentices.

Outside the Williamsburg gaol, Lance cringed as he saw Thomas and Dudley gleefully watching Ben's lashings. As the gaol master shouted out the strokes, Dudley shouted them back and raised his arms in the air. Thomas nodded his approval at Dudley's wild actions. When Lance looked at Timothy, he saw that the boy's eyes were tightly closed. Soon he felt Timothy's hand grabbing his. Lance returned the firm grasp. Their bodies moved closer together. Lance wanted to put his arms around Timothy to console him, but he knew that gesture would bring a reprimand to them both. He only held Timothy's hand the harder.

When the lashings were done and the crowd began to disperse, Lance wanted to go to Ben. *What's the use though?* he said to himself. *Ben is unconscious and cannot hear me. Besides if I go to him, I shall be caught in my lie.* A hard squeeze from Timothy's hand brought Lance to his common sense, no matter how cowardly he also felt in not going to the collapsed figure in the pillory. "We ought to go home," Timothy said in a more mature, deeper voice than Lance had heard from the boy until now.

The next several weeks were only a blur for Lance, even though his hands worked the leather accurately and steadily. Ben died in a small cell in the gaol just at a time when holiday wreaths began to decorate doors and windows. Through Twelfth Night Williamsburg relaxed its work hours to accommodate a welcome season of merry making. A light snow fell on the first day of the new year, 1750. Had Lance been in London that year, when he turned twenty in May, he would have become a journeyman, free to go work where he pleased. In Virginia he still had five more years of his indenture to serve.

Before the buds turned to leaves that year, John Thomas's shop lost an apprentice and gained a competitor. The servant to go was Dudley. A prosperous baker offered to buy the remaining years of Dudley's indenture, and Dudley was willing, even anxious, to leave the cordwainer. Thomas was at first reluctant to sell Dudley's indenture, never liking to give up anything. However, when he took into account that Dudley had never really produced quality shoes, that now he had Lance, and that Timothy, under Lance's tutelage, was making shoes of dependable quality, Thomas settled on a good price with the baker.

Neither Lance nor Timothy was sorry to see Dudley leave the shop. His vacant workbench did mean extra work for them. But they went about it willingly, since now they felt free to chat in low voices as they worked. Thomas tolerated their talk, but only because he recognized that it helped the two to work more quickly.

Where Dudley's leaving was most welcome though was in their small sleeping room.

"I shall share your bed now," Timothy announced the first night they were alone in the room. "It will be easier for us to talk. Besides, I am too big now for that bundle of blankets in the corner over there."

Lance smiled at the boldness of the lad and said, "You are welcome to your half of the bed. But do you recall what Dudley told me the first night I slept here?"

"No. But I still am ashamed of how I hit you that night."

"You felt I deserved it, and I have since forgotten that incident. But what Dudley said was 'Stay on your side of the bed, and keep your hands off me.'"

Timothy laughed. "Well, don't say that to me. For I don't know if I would keep my promise."

Lance laughed again at Timothy's boldness. And, for the first time. he felt a sexual yearning for the youth. Timothy's voice had deepened, and he now had a cluster of light brown pubic hair. His sex was no longer that of a boy but of a growing sixteen-year-old. *He has probably begun to touch himself,* Lance thought. *But I must resist any temptation. He is too young still to know what it truly means to lie with another man. I am too fond of him to hurt him in any way.*

"What are you thinking?" Timothy asked.

Lance hesitated, then said, "About Captain Henry, the man who brought me here."

"What about him?"

"I wish he were alive and had visited us again."

"Even though he sold you, did you like him?"

"Yes. But it is late, and we need to rise extra early in the morning to finish those harnesses. Come to bed. But remember what Dudley told me."

"I'm damn glad Dudley is gone," was Timothy's only response.

The competition to John Thomas's shop came from a cordwainer who arrived from England and set up an establishment several blocks away. The cordwainer brought with him his three sons and an indentured servant, all of whom worked in the new shop. Even though Williamsburg, a growing town of nearly 2,000 residents, needed a second cordwainer, Thomas resented the new arrival. His shop still prospered, but not as it had before. With the loss of that revenue from his shop, Thomas's gambling debts became a bit harder to pay. By late summer Lance and Timothy found that their talk was less tolerated and that Thomas's temper often flared without cause.

The two young servants simply took deep breaths and accepted Thomas's outbursts and curses. They even joked about the cordwainer's ill nature as they lay in bed at night. However, they found it far less easy to accept when they began to hear Thomas, before his customers, claim that what they had worked on was his. About the harnesses they did not care, and Thomas seldom claimed a harness as his work. Boots and the fashionable shoes were a different matter. Lance prided himself on the boots he made, and he was especially pleased that the royal governor had praised the boots he had purchased. For Thomas, then, to claim that those boots were his work angered Lance. But he did not know what he could do to stop the lying.

One afternoon Timothy finished a pair of lady's dancing shoes. It was the first he had made, and he could hardly contain his joy.

"Look, Lance, they are finished. I have just put on the silver buckles with their pink tassels."

Lance rose from his workbench and stretched out his hand. He took the shoe and ran his hand over the smooth leather. "It is beautiful," he exclaimed, tousling Timothy's wavy hair. "Master Thomas," he called, "look at Timothy's shoe. Isn't it beautiful!"

Thomas looked up from his workbench and asked, "What is the fuss about?"

"Come see. Timothy has made a shoe fit for the governor's wife to dance in."

Thomas took the shoe from Lance and looked at it for a minute before he said, "Yes, it is nicely done."

"It is more than nicely done," Lance retorted. "It is delicate perfection. Someday Timothy will be the best cordwainer in Williamsburg."

Just at that moment Mistress Thomas came into the shop. She paused, looked at her husband still smarting under Lance's remark, and asked, "And what is that pretty thing in your hand, Mister John?"

Lance and Timothy waited for the reply.

"It is a beautiful dancing shoe. I made it especially for you, Madam, when you next attend a ball at the Royal Palace." Both Thomas and his wife knew they would not be invited guests at the colonial palace. "No one's hands have touched this shoe but mine." Thomas bowed before his wife.

Looking only briefly at the farce, Timothy shouted at Thomas, "No, I made it. You didn't."

Quickly Mistress Thomas turned on Timothy and asked angrily, "Do you call my husband, your master, a liar?"

"But I made it. He didn't. Didn't I make it, Lance?"

"Liar," Thomas shouted and hit Timothy hard across the mouth, bringing blood.

Lance lunged toward Thomas.

"No, Lance, no," Timothy screamed.

Lance struggled with his quick temper. Blood rushed to his face, but he stopped himself.

"Go to your bench," Thomas shouted.

Lance knew that to intervene would only bring on more trouble than that which was going to happen. He went to his workbench and picked up the leather he had been cutting. He turned his back to the others.

"Drop your breeches, Timothy," Thomas ordered as he chose a leather strap from the wall. "Now bend over. I will teach you not to lie."

Lance counted the dozen slaps, but he heard no sound from Timothy. He felt the silence of the room unbearable.

Then Tomas asked in a loud voice, "Now who made these shoes?"

"You did, sir, if you say so," Timothy replied in a weak voice.

"Now pull up your breeches. Don't show your bare arse to your mistress," Thomas said, giving Timothy's butt another beating.

Grabbing Timothy by the ear, Mistress Thomas cried, "Get to your room. Liars get no supper tonight."

An hour later, all was quiet in the house. Thomas had gone to the tavern. Mistress Thomas was upstairs with her children. In the shop, Lance repaired a broken harness. When his anger had finally subsided and he was sure he could walk about without being heard, Lance went to the shop's medicine cabinet and took out the oil used when sharp instruments slipped and cut the hand. Then he went outside to the kitchen. Bread and dried apples were in the cupboard, and Lance took a generous amount of both. When he saw a jug of cider left on the table by accident, he poured half of it into a pitcher. "That bitch that wanted dancing shoes which didn't belong to her may miss this cider in the morning, but she will think her drunken husband drank it when he returned home from the tavern," Lance said bitterly.

With Timothy's supper in his hands, Lance hurried to their sleeping room. Timothy was awake, lying on his side. He wore only his shirt. When Lance came in, he leaned up and propped himself with his elbow.

"I've stolen your supper," Lance said.

"I'm not hungry. What are we going to do, Lance? He keeps on lying, and I finally couldn't take it any longer. I made those shoes, and he knows it."

"We'll think of something. It won't do to complain to the magistrates. They wouldn't believe us, and we would only get into more trouble here in the shop."

"But, we ought . . . ," Timothy cried out.

"Hush, Tim, for now let's forget about it. You've got to eat, hungry or not. Also I've brought some ointment for your butt. Does it hurt?"

"Of course not. It feels good," Timothy laughed. His spirits raised just talking to Lance. He grabbed a handful of dried apples.

As Timothy was eating his stolen supper, he chuckled and said, "This is better than eating in the kitchen." When he had eaten it all, he wiped his mouth. "Share the cider with me, Lance."

Lance drank from the pitcher, and then handed it to Timothy. "Now I want to put the ointment on your butt. Take off your shirt and lie down on your belly."

Timothy pulled the shirt over his head and lay down. Looking back at Lance, he smiled and said, "Remember what Dudley said."

Lance laughed. "You've got ugly black stripes back here, but you aren't bleeding. Does this hurt?" he asked as he ran his hand over the small firm mounds of Timothy's butt.

"No, not if you don't press too hard."

Lance poured a small amount of the ointment on Timothy's left butt cheek. In slow, firm circular motions he rubbed the ointment over the marks the strap had made. After several minutes he moved to the right butt cheek.

"That helps," Timothy told him. "It takes away some of the sting."

Suddenly Lance realized that, although he had thoroughly worked in the ointment, he still wanted to rub his hands over Timothy's butt. Several times the tips of his fingers slipped down into the crevice. He heard Timothy sigh as his body quivered. Lance felt his own sex grow hard.

Timothy turned to lie on his side. The two looked at each other intently, their mouths slightly open. Each knew what he wanted. Quickly they were in each other's arms. Lance kissed Timothy's neck and face. Then he pressed his lips against Timothy's. Slowly Timothy opened his mouth, and their tongues met in a long passionate kiss.

Lance knew he ought to stop at this point. He could easily joke about their boyish play, and that would be the end of the matter. However, it had been too long, and Lance desperately wanted the feel of another man's body against his.

Lance pulled Timothy over on top of him, hard sex against hard sex. Lance clasped his arms around Timothy's body and pulled him into a tight embrace. Again they kissed. Soon Timothy started to move his hips rapidly. Lance's body moved upward to meet the thrusts. Quickly they both reached orgasm. Their bellies were wet with their jism.

When they pulled apart and lay down facing each other, Timothy said, "I have never done anything like that before. Have you, Lance?"

"Yes, ever since I was your age, even younger."

"I liked it. I've so wanted to lie against your body. I didn't know how to tell you. Tonight it all came so suddenly without having to think about it."

"I know," Lance said. "That's the best way for it to happen."

"But did we do wrong, spilling ourselves against each other?"

"No," Lance answered firmly. "But most people would say that we did wrong; and, if we were caught, we would be punished."

"Then I guess we had better not get caught," Timothy said. He pulled up close to Lance. Soon they were both asleep.

The next day was an uneasy one in the shop. Both Lance and Timothy wanted to talk. Lance wanted to assure Timothy once again that what they had done was not wrong, but that if Timothy did not want now to share the bed, then Lance would move to the blankets in the corner. Timothy wanted to tell Lance how he longed for night to come so that he could lie again on top of him. Timothy sensed that he had more to discover, and that Lance could teach him, just as he had with the shoe making.

Thomas was puzzled by the strange looks on the faces of his two servants. *Damn those two*, he said to himself. *That young bastard insulted me before my wife. He's due for another whipping.* Thomas waited until Timothy got up from his workbench and went to the leather cabinet. Then pretending he did not see Timothy, Thomas got up and walked in front of him. "Damn you," Thomas snarled, "don't walk into me, you clumsy little bastard."

Quickly Lance was on his feet and between them. All the bitterness he had felt for three years surfaced in his eyes. And his eyes glared hard at Thomas. Thomas stepped back, astonished. Then, without saying anything, he turned back to his workbench.

"Get back to work, Tim," Lance said, almost as if he were the master of the shop.

The tension of that day hung over the shop for the next three weeks. More frequently and for longer periods of time, Thomas was gone from the shop. On many occasions Lance even had to conduct some of the business with customers. He had always measured for shoes, but only Thomas entered into the ledger. Now he did.

Then one night, as Lance and Timothy lay in bed, Lance decided that it was time for more than just lying on top of each other. Since their first night of sex, Timothy had shown no regrets about what they were doing. His hands were always ready to explore Lance's body. His lips had found their way to the large head of Lance's sex.

"Tim, tonight I want you to enter me," Lance said.

"No! That would hurt you too much."

"There you are mistaken, Tim. It will feel very good for both of us."

Despite that assurance, Timothy was frightened about what Lance told him he wanted him to do. Still, he was excited and eager for the new experience.

Lance wadded a blanket and lay down with his belly over it. "Come at me," he called.

Timothy used his hand to guide his hard sex. The penetration was easier than Timothy had imagined it would be. Once fully inside, Timothy embraced Lance tightly and kissed the back of his neck. "It feels so good inside you," Timothy whispered.

"Work your cock," Lance replied. "That will feel much better for both of us."

As Timothy moved back and forth inside Lance, he kept whispering, "I love you, Lance, I love you." He felt their two bodies had joined as one. Shortly he reached orgasm. Lance wet the blanket under him.

After he pulled out, Timothy turned Lance over and lay on top of him.

"We are brothers now, Lance," he whispered.

"We are more than brothers, Tim," Lance replied. They kissed.

Before they fell asleep, Timothy said, "No matter how bad it is, or gets, in the shop, we have each other here."

Things did get worse in the shop. The more Thomas's debts increased, the more he drank. And the more he drank, the nastier he was in the shop. Although he was still afraid to lift a hand against either of the two servants, especially to Lance, he frequently shouted his curses and reprimands. Also, because he knew it angered Lance, Thomas continued to claim Lance's work as his before almost every customer who came into the shop. "The shoes these two servants of mine turn out are fit only for slaves," Thomas constantly complained. "Now this fine boot comes from my workbench." Lance did not know how much longer he could control his anger at the lies and at the arrogance with which they were told.

On a Wednesday morning in late October 1750, the inevitable occurred.

It began when Madam Howard, the wife of a wealthy lawyer, came to the shop with her young daughter, Elizabeth. They had come for the young girl's dancing slippers. Elizabeth was one of four young girls to be presented before the governor and his wife at a special ball to open the winter season. The ball was a special one not only for Elizabeth but also for all of Tidewater society. Elizabeth tried to match her mother's calm composure, but her eyes betrayed her anxiety.

The slippers were the second pair Timothy had made. He had carefully scraped the deerskin and dyed it a rose color. The white tassels had been made by the milliner. The stitches were invisible. Timothy was delighted with his work Even though Timothy had not the least interest in attending the governor's ball, he knew that his slippers would lend Elizabeth the grace she wanted.

When the cordwainer handed the slippers to the young girl, she gasped and cried out, "Look, mother, aren't they beautiful."

"Yes, they truly are," her mother replied. "They will go perfectly with your new pink gown from London. You will have every young man at the ball looking at you."

"I don't care about all the young men. But I shall die if William does not tell me how pretty I look," her daughter replied.

Madam Howard only smiled at her daughter.

"I am honored that you like them so much," Thomas said. "I tried my best to make them beautiful."

Timothy and Lance exchanged glances of disgust. Lance bit his lips to keep his mouth shut. Their reaction to his lie angered Thomas. After a quick bow to Madam Howard, he went to Timothy's workbench, grabbed him by the ear, and pulled him to his feet. "Now if this dumb cur could only learn to do half as well what I do, I might think him worth his keep." He pushed Timothy backward. Lance caught the stumbling youth, but Timothy quickly regained his feet. He put his hand on Lance's shoulder and said in a whisper, "Control yourself, Lance. Sit down. I still have my ear on the side of my head." Knowing that Timothy was right, however, did not stop the flow of blood to Lance's face. But he sat down. Shutting his eyes, he tried to erase this insult along with all those since Captain Henry had left him here under an unwilling seven-year indenture.

Madam Howard settled her account, barely taking notice of Thomas's treatment of Timothy. After she thanked him for his good service, Thomas escorted the two women to the shop door. Just as they were about to leave, a well-dressed gentleman appeared. Surprised at their meeting, he greeted Madam Howard and her daughter warmly. They stood in a group at the door, talking and laughing. Thomas stood at a respectful distance. Finally the new customer bowed, and the two women went out into the street.

The gentleman-customer came into the shop. He nodded graciously to both Timothy and Lance, who returned the warm greeting with a "Good morning, sir." Then he turned to Thomas and said, "John, I hope that my boots are ready. I have little time away from the Landing, and I have come here this morning especially for my boots and to settle a few other more important matters."

"They are ready, sir," Thomas said, going to the cabinet to fetch them. "Here are your riding boots. You won't find a better pair even if you send to England for them. I've made them myself, every cut and stitch."

Lance sensed that the customer knew and appreciated quality, that he was accustomed to quality. The gentleman rubbed the smooth leather. He gave the cordwainer a smile that both puzzled and amused Lance. Then he said, "The boots are fine indeed. You do excellent work, Master Thomas."

Suddenly Lance exploded. Before he could control himself, he cried out, "He lies. I made those boots."

Both the customer and the cordwainer turned to Lance in surprise. Timothy looked up from his workbench in shock.

"He lies. I made those boots," Lance repeated in a bold, loud voice.

"Don't call me a liar, you bastard convict," Thomas shouted.

The furious cordwainer picked up a sharp-pointed hammer and lunged at Lance. Lance knocked away the cordwainer's arm. He hit Thomas solidly on the nose. Blood flowed. The customer rushed to restrain Lance from any new attack on Thomas. Lance was surprised by the strength of the man who held him back. Looking anxiously at Lance, Timothy helped the cordwainer up off the floor. For a minute, the room was a frozen tableau.

Then Thomas came up to Lance, pinioned in the arms of the customer, and screamed in his face, "I'll see that you are whipped until the blood from your back runs down to your ankles. Then I'll sell you to South Carolina, you son of a whore. You'll work with slaves in the rice fields. You'll die soon enough from that labor. And good riddance of liars like you."

Lance knew that once again his quick temper had thrust him into trouble from which there was no retreating. He could not bring himself to look at Timothy.

The shouts from within the shop roused Mistress Thomas. When she burst into the shop and saw the blood on her husband's face and shirt, she ran into street shouting, "Murder, murder." Soon the shop became a bedlam of loud voices and frantic movements. Lance shut his eyes to the turmoil. He felt his body being released from the steady hold of the customer to the rough grasp of several other men. His shoulders drooped, reminding him again that his temper had too quickly robbed him of his common sense. He doubted that there would be a Captain Henry to help him this time. He shuddered more at the fear of laboring in the rice fields though than at the cordwainer's loud threat of whipping him until his back ran with blood.

Suddenly the shop settled into a stillness. Lance looked and saw Thomas and the customer talking in low voices. Finally the gentleman, his boots in hand, shook his head, looked back briefly at Lance, and left the shop. For an inexplicable reason, Lance sensed that his only protection was gone. At his workbench, Timothy sat with his head buried in his hands. His body shook with his crying.

The next two hours before a magistrate in a crowded room were a nightmare that Lance thought would never end. Thomas's loud shrill voice shouted statements blatantly untrue. Lance's denials were lost in the laughter of the hostile crowd. Even those to whom Thomas owed money called for the punishment of a servant who struck his master. Lance's mind moved to the dirty, cramped quarters of the *St. George*, and then further back to the filth of Newgate. He barely heard the magistrate's order that Lance be whipped forty lashes.

Another two hours later Lance, stripped to the waist, stood locked neck and hands in the pillory. Black welts stung his back. The blood from the forty lashes now ran only in trickles. Lance was alone. The laughter from the crowd at the whipping had ceased. The taunts from jeering children were cut off by mothers herding their offspring home. Occasionally young men, his Sunday afternoon companions, on their way to supper had passed by with a sneering laugh. Now only curious dogs sniffed at his feet. Lance shivered under the crisp air of the fall wind. A light rain began to fall. He wondered if he were to stay here all night. He tried in vain to fight back tears.

Suddenly Lance heard footsteps from behind the pillory. Timothy appeared before him. He took Lance's face in his hands and kissed him on the lips.

"Don't," Lance said. "You'll get yourself in trouble, too."

"I'm not afraid. I've brought you cider."

"I can't drink it. I'll choke."

Timothy poured some cider in his cupped hand and rubbed Lance's lips with it. Lance greedily sucked several handfuls.

"Did Thomas beat you after I was taken from the shop?"

"No, and I doubt that he will. With only me to work for him now, he cannot afford to have me in ill health."

"I shall pray for your safety, Tim."

"I don't want you to be sold to the rice fields. Lance, I . . . ," Timothy started to say. But he stopped. He saw lanterns at the far end of gaol yard. "Someone is coming. I must go. I love you, Lance." He quickly kissed Lance again and dashed off in the opposite direction from the approaching lanterns.

Lance cringed as he listened to the several male voices coming towards him. A cloaked figure came up to the pillory. When Lance looked up, he faced the gentleman customer who had held him back from striking the cordwainer a second time. Lance didn't understand why he was here.

The gentleman took Lance by the chin and raised his head. He looked hard into Lance's eyes.

"Who made my boots?" the gentleman asked.

"I did. I am no liar," Lance replied in a firm but low voice.

"I believe you," the gentleman responded.

The gentleman turned to one of the other men with him and said, "You have read the papers signed by the royal governor releasing this man to my immediate custody. He is now my property."

Then he turned back to Lance and said, "I am William Ashley of Ashley Landing. I won you in a card game from Master Thomas."

Lance was weak with relief.

While the constable unlocked Lance's neck and hands, Mr. Ashley continued talking to Lance. "I need you to make shoes for my slaves and for sale in my warehouse to neighbor planters for their slaves. I trust you will do as good work on them as you did on my riding boots. Give me good service, Lance, and I'll see that you are well treated. I am not the kind of master the cordwainer is," Mr. Ashley said.

"I promise," Lance said before he fainted.

# 1748-1750: Ashley Landing

Late one morning in September 1748, Adam stood on the deck of the *Queen Anne*. Before him was the busy harbor of Hampton in the Colony of Virginia. Adam was among a small group of indentured servants waiting to climb down the rope ladders and be rowed to the wharf. Their bundles of clothing were gathered in a large net ready to be dropped to a boat below.

"We are finally here in the new country," one of the men said, speaking as if he alone knew where they were.

"For better or for worse to us all," another man replied sharply.

"And what do you think, Adam?" a young man of Adam's age asked.

"I shall be happy to have my feet on ground again, no matter where it is," Adam said and laughed.

"Well you can afford to laugh," still another man said. "You are a lucky one, young man. At least you know where you are going, even if you know nothing about the place. That's much more than the rest of us know."

Adam did not reply. What if Mr. Ashley were only another Lord Cromley? Would he be better off here than back at Cromley Hall? Adam shrugged away such thoughts and went to the ship's railing. He stared down at the still water of the bay. There on one of the few occasions of the eight-week voyage, Adam's mind moved backward in time.

The bitterness of the last few days at Cromley Hall had evaporated much more quickly than Adam thought possible. The newness of the subsequent events to that afternoon in the library took care of that. A tearful farewell with his aunt who did not understand at all why Adam was leaving was the start of a journey that ended in London with Adam in the custody of a portly ship captain.

doi:10.1300/5623_04

"Until Mr. Ashley pays me, you are my property, Bradley," the captain said. "I trust you will cause me no trouble on the voyage."

Adam's bristled slightly at the captain's statement about "property." But he quickly replied, "I intend to be of no trouble."

Despite the unaccustomed confinement of the ship, Adam delighted in the voyage. He was continually amazed at the long stretch of the water and the endless amount of sky. Since the cargo of the *Queen Anne* was mostly merchandise and supplies and carried only eighty indentured servants, the freedom given them to stay on deck was much greater than usual.

Adam watched the crew go about the ship's business. Occasionally a young crew member spoke to him, and Adam plied him with questions about life aboard ship. Most often though he talked with the other indentured servants. Most of them did not know much more about what lay ahead in Virginia than Adam did. And, since many of them had only grudgingly signed indenture papers, they were disgruntled about their new lives. Like these men, Adam, too, had signed the indenture paper, giving himself first to the ship captain who would then receive payment from Mr. Ashley. But he had not signed of his own free will. Here on ship, however, he began to feel a freedom he had not experienced at Cromley Hall. He found himself, if not exactly looking forward to life in the colony, at least not afraid or dreading it. He was even able now to laugh at the two quick sexual encounters in the stable that had led to his being here aboard ship. *I wish only that I had been able to stick it to him longer and harder.* He wondered when in the new country he would have the pleasure of another man's body. He laughed aloud and said to himself, *That will have to take care of itself. There's too much ahead to learn to worry about my cock.*

"Be alert there," Adam heard a loud voice cry out. "Get your thumbs out of your arse holes. It's time to disembark. Who's first down the ladder?"

"I'll go," Adam quickly volunteered.

"Then get about it," the large crewmember shouted. "Now the next man doesn't start down the ladder until this lad is halfway down. Only two men on the ladder at a time."

Adam went to the side of the ship. He put his left leg over the railing and found the first rung of the ladder. Steadying himself with his hands on the sides of the ladder, he hoisted his body over the railing and slowly started down the rungs of the rope ladder. Above he heard a crewmember shout and laugh, "Be careful going down, lad. There's big fish over here. They will eat you alive if you fall."

When he reached the large rowboat, a short burly sailor greeted Adam with, "You did that like an old salt. Now get back there, and be ready to man an oar. My partner and I here don't intend to row the thirty of you to the wharf."

Half an hour later Adam was among the first group of indentured servants from the ship to step ashore in Virginia. Before he had time to look around, he heard a voice bark, "Collect your bundle from the pile over there. Then stand in a line here before me." Adam searched through the large pile until he uncovered his bundle of clothing. He hoped he could put on a clean shirt soon. As he joined the formation of men with their bundles, Adam glanced at the well-dressed men who were talking in small groups nearby.

When all thirty of the indentured servants were in a line, the man in front of them announced, "I am Mr. Thomkins, the agent for the captain of the *Queen Anne.* Some of you men are already spoken for; the rest of you will be sold at auction later this morning. Now I need to separate five men. Step out when I call your names." He paused, then shouted, "Bradley, Garrison, McAfee, Smyth, and Stoner." Adam and the four other men stepped forward. The captain's agent then turned and called to a group of gentlemen. "Sirs, will those of you claiming one of these men, please come and make your claim." The man who was waiting for the name "Bradley" to be called was William Ashley II.

At thirty-seven, William Ashley was one of the wealthiest men in the colony. Twenty years ago he had come to Virginia with his father. When his father died, Ashley inherited 360,000 acres of productive land and woods. And when Ashley was twenty-five, he returned to England only long enough to marry a young woman to whom he had been engaged since his boyhood. Lord and Lady Cromley attended the wedding, and Lady Cromley wished her new sister-in-law happiness in the new country. Shortly after their return to Virginia, the young couple saw work begin on their Georgian great house facing the James River.

Adam hoped the tall man approaching him with a warm smile on his face was his new master. "You are Adam Bradley?" the tall man asked.

"I am, sir."

"Welcome to Virginia, Adam. I am William Ashley. I also welcome you to your new home at Ashley Landing."

"Thank you, sir."

The two men shook hands. Adam felt that Mr. Ashley's firm handshake was a genuine welcome to the new country.

"How old are you, Adam?"

"Seventeen, almost eighteen."

"I was your age when I arrived here. I have come to love this country. It is now my home. I hope that will happen to you."

Adam was so overcome by the warm welcome that he could not find words to respond before Mr. Ashley called out, "Joseph, come meet our new servant." A tall redheaded bearded man approached and grasped Adam's hand. "Welcome," he said. "You have come to a good place." Again Adam felt a firm handshake.

Mr. Ashley smiled at the two men. "Joseph is my stable master; and when he is not tending to the horses, he is the master of my riverboats. He has been here in Virginia almost as long as I have. When you need help, Adam, turn to him."

"That I will," Adam said.

Before the three of them could speak further, the wharf master called to Mr. Ashley. "We are ready to load your wagons, sir. Your crates are in the second shed."

Adam looked around the wharf. The first group of indentured servants had been led away. A second group was being rowed from the ship. Now the wharf was beginning to fill with horse-drawn wagons. They were headed to four large flat-topped sheds, open on all sides. In them was the ship's cargo, which had been unloaded and sorted during the three days before.

"Come along," Mr. Ashley said to Joseph and Adam. "We have much to do before evening." The three of them walked quickly to the second shed. Beside an empty wagon, four black men and two white men stood awaiting instructions. Adam had never seen a black person before, and he looked at the four men with curiosity. Joseph saw the look on Adam's face, and he pulled Adam aside, while Mr. Ashley read papers he had pulled from his coat pocket. "The black men are slaves, belonging to the wharf master. They are good workers and, in my opinion, much better fellows than the two white men, who are indentured prisoners from London. You will get accustomed to seeing and working with slaves at the plantation, Adam."

"I am sure they are good fellows, just different from us in color," Adam replied.

Mr. Ashley interrupted them, saying, "I read here that I have fifty-three crates belonging to me. Those two over there are special ones." He pointed to two rectangular crates that stood out among the rest, which were all square. "The larger of the two contains a mahogany secretary for my office. The other is a rosewood dressing table. It is a surprise gift for my wife. Those crates will be loaded last. Adam, make sure they are handled with care."

Adam nodded. "I will, sir."

"Joseph, tell the wharf hands to start loading the first wagon. Then accompany it to the riverboats and stay there to see that all goes well at that end. Adam, you stay here and keep count of the crates being loaded."

The work took much longer than Adam had expected. Some of the crates were heavy, and there was a contest between the slaves and indentured convicts to see who would handle the lighter crates. Often it took all four of the slaves to lift a crate onto a waiting wagon. It was late afternoon when the last of the square crates in the shed were loaded and on their way to the riverboats. Only the two special crates remained. When an empty wagon returned, the four slaves lifted the larger crate onto it. One of indentured convicts started to push the smaller crate along the shed floor with his foot.

"Mind what you are doing there!" Adam shouted.

The activity of the shed came to a halt. Mr. Ashley and the wharf master, who stood some distance away, looked at Adam intently. The four slaves stared, frightened and wondering what they had done wrong. The indentured convict who had been pushing the crate with the rosewood dressing table in it stopped and turned toward Adam with a ugly scowl on his face. The other indentured convict yelled at Adam, "And who are you to tell my mate what to do?"

"I am in the service of Mr. Ashley," Adam replied in an authoritative manner, but without any trace of arrogance. "The two of you load that crate carefully. It contains a special gift for my mistress, Madam Ashley."

The two men looked past Adam to the wharf master, who signaled them to obey Adam's order. Mr. Ashley watched the scene with amused delight. "That young man handles himself with dignity and assurance. I think he will be worth much more than the ship passage and clothes he has cost me," he said to himself. Then he and the wharf master joined Adam.

"Thank you for making sure that crate was handled properly, Adam," Mr. Ashley said.

Before Adam could reply, the wharf master said, "That is all your crates, Mr. Ashley. I wish you good evening."

"Mr. Ashley," Adam said quickly, "I have counted only fifty loaded square crates. Yet there are no more here."

"You must be mistaken then in your counting," the wharf master said.

Mr. Ashley look at Adam but said nothing.

"I am sure I have not miscounted," Adam said to the wharf master.

Just then an empty wagon returned from the riverboats. Sitting in it was Joseph. He jumped down and joined the three men.

"I have just passed the wagon with the two special crates. There was no square crate on the wagon, and I have only fifty loaded. One is missing," Joseph said.

"Another man who cannot count," the wharf master snapped.

"Perhaps," Mr. Ashley replied calmly. "But perhaps also my last crate has been misplaced. As you know, such has happened before during busy days like these. Getting the cargo off the ship and to shore is difficult, but I think your task of sorting the crates is a much more demanding one."

"Yes, it is. And my hands are not always the most reliable. Most of them cannot read the lettering on the crates, so I and my two assistants are always having to point where a particular crate is to go. But, look, three of the sheds are now empty. Those boxes and crates in the far shed are all marked for Williamsburg."

"However, you have no objection, I am certain, to our looking among those crates," Mr. Ashley replied.

"None. But I doubt you find it there. I am sure it is already loaded on your riverboat."

Leaving the obviously annoyed wharf master standing by the empty wagon, Mr. Ashley, Joseph, and Adam walked to the fourth shed. "Joseph, you go to the far end and look. Adam and I will look here." Shortly the three men met in the middle of the shed where there was a large amount of cargo covered over by a thin leather tarpaulin. Joseph on one end and Adam at the other, they threw back the tarpaulin to reveal seven large crates. One of them was marked ASHLEY LANDING. Some of the lettering on the crate was in a language foreign to Adam, but beneath that lettering were the words WINE MERCHANT. Mr. Ashley burst out laughing. "So my year's supply of port and Madeira was destined for someone in the capital. I wonder who."

Both Adam and Joseph were surprised at how light-hearted Mr. Ashley was about the matter, believing as he probably did also that the wharf master knew exactly where the fifty-first crate was. "I am pleased that you two can count so accurately. Go find a wagon, Joseph, and tell the wharf master that we need two of his hands to complete the loading of my crates. I think just by telling him that he will understand."

That night Adam shared a bed with Joseph in a back room of a tavern near the river.

"I wish you had seen the look on the wharf master's face when I repeated what Mr. Ashley said. He tried without luck to hide his anger under a pretense of innocence and surprise."

"What did he say?" Adam asked.

"He mumbled something about giving a good lashing to one of the hands who made the mistake."

"Is Mr. Ashley always so good-natured and composed?"

"Yes. You will like working for him."

"Are you, too, indentured?"

"I was for five years under Mr. Ashley's father. When I was free, I signed another five years under Mr. Ashley. Now I am a free man with papers, working for wages. Some people think that I should move west out of the Tidewater. But I am married now with two children, and life for the four of us is more comfortable at Ashley Landing than it would be in the frontier. I hope you like living there, Adam, as much as I do."

"I am anxious to be there."

The next week was one of the busiest Adam had ever experienced. He began that week though cheered by a brief exchange between Mr. Ashley and himself as the slaves had steered the riverboat toward the landing wharf at Ashley Landing.

"Adam, Lord Cromley did not explain in his letter your reasons for signing the indenture papers. My intuition tells me that it was not of your free will. I do not ask now that you tell me your reasons. I do ask, however, that whatever bitterness you felt at Cromley Hall be left behind. You can make a good life for yourself here. It is your choice."

Adam knew that here, on a river whose banks had more wild growth than he had ever seen before, he had a real choice, not like that one in the library at Cromley Hall. "It is not a hard decision to make, sir. Already I am at home. Look, what is that strange bird?"

Mr. Ashley placed his hand on Adam's shoulder. The great blue heron squawked at the intrusion of the boat.

Every night that week Adam went to bed exhausted in his small room at the far end of the servants' brick quarters. But he went to bed far happier than he had been in even his best days at Cromley Hall. He slept without dreaming of his various activities since arriving at Ashley Landing. He had directed the unloading of the riverboats, pleased at how easily he and black slaves worked together. He had been introduced in a formal way to Madam Ashley, and he became acquainted with the two other young indentured servants. He had exchanged greetings with the two overseers of Mr. Ashley's properties when they came down river for their monthly reports. He had eaten a large supper with Joseph and his family and had held their young baby without dropping her.

What most excited him were the hours he spent in the warehouse. He climbed ladders and opened barrels as if he were discovering a new land. He began an inventory of the many items he thought in something of a disorder. The instructions of his old friend, the steward at Cromley Hall, served him well now. "I think, Mr. Ashley, that if we put these stacks of skins over here, it would be easier to keep account of them." Mr. Ashley nodded his assent.

The person he liked meeting most was the large black woman who ruled the kitchen and the servants' table where they ate. Though much of what Hannah set before him were dishes Adam had never tasted, he liked all of them.

"And what is this long thing with all these small juicy bits?" Adam asked one noon.

"Corn," Hannah replied to what she found a strange question. "You'd best get used to it, 'cause you'll get fed a lot of them ears."

"Fine. So long as I don't get fat or drunk on eating it."

Hannah roared. "You'll never get fat, Adam, and you've too much sense to get too drunk."

"Then give me another ear of corn, please," Adam said.

After that week, the routine and the pastimes of the next two years quickly established themselves.

Most of his time during those two years Adam spent in the warehouse. He was especially busy when shipments of tobacco and meal were loaded on the flatboats destined for Hampton where they were put on ships to England. However, since the Ashley Landing warehouse served the Tidewater community, Adam busied himself more often with almost everything from horseshoes to barrels of salt pork, from rum-laced cider to freshly made bricks. Adam loved his work, and Mr. Ashley soon realized how fortunate he was to have Adam.

"Adam is a quiet one," Mr. Ashley remarked to his wife. "There is something deeper within him which we do not know. But his heart is his own. His quick wit, his sharp eye, and his ability to work easily during the most trying of times serves me well in the warehouse. Still, I hope he finds pleasure in something more than his work."

Not all of Adam's working hours, however, were in the warehouse. Joseph soon discovered that Adam had a way with horses that was just short of his own. "If you need a bit of fresh air," he often called into the warehouse, "come exercise one of the horses." Adam loved the long rides, and he sometimes wondered if he were not taking the horses onto trails and through woods where they had never been before. For his own relaxation as much as theirs, Adam also helped to rub down the horses. He did it with such attention that Joseph asked him jokingly one day, "Are you soothing that horse or yourself?" Adam laughed, but blushed and hoped that Joseph did not notice the bulge his sex made in his breeches.

Also relaxing in a very different way were those hours when Adam and two black slaves worked under Madam Ashley's direction in trimming the formal garden. Unlike that at Cromley Hall, Ashley Landing's had no tall mazes or topiaries. The herbs and flowers of the formal garden here were practical as well as decorative. The garden was outlined by a low-growing boxwood hedge. *No one will ever get lost in the turns of this garden,* Adam remarked to himself, *or have sex,* he added, remembering the trysting spot where he met the young man at Cromley Hall. What pleased Adam even more was his work in the several acres of informal gardens being laid out in the hilly area south of the great house. Madam Ashley was planting azaleas and rhododendrons of every color and variety, both native plants and those she had imported from England. "It will take ten years," Madam Ashley sighed, "before these plants are at their best. But then it will be the most beautiful spot in the Tidewater."

Even though Adam thoroughly enjoyed his work and threw himself into it with his full energy, he always looked ahead to his free times. After supper on weekdays he often sat with the other two indentured servants in the kitchen to drink a tall cup of pumpkin beer and to exchange any news of the day. Adam got along well with Matt and Gregory, both five years older than he, but with neither was he a close friend. Adam sensed that both men resented him because his work at the warehouse put him in a higher position in the rank of servants than either of them. Also there was a surliness about Matt that Adam mistrusted. Still, Adam's brief contact with the two men in the kitchen at meals usually passed agreeably enough. However, there were exceptions.

"Did the brick making go well today?" Adam asked Matt one evening.

"I paid Mr. Ashley my indenture cost," Matt replied in a tone that revealed the resentment of his indenture.

"Well, when you have your freedom papers, you can go to Williamsburg and set up your trade. Then you'll be your own master," Gregory chuckled.

"And you'll have to find someone else to do your cooking," Hannah chimed.

"Oh, I once saw what's hung between his legs," Gregory hooted. "Matt will have no trouble finding a woman to fix his food."

"Hush that talk in my kitchen," Hannah said sternly.

"Your kitchen!" Matt retorted in a loud voice.

"Yes. My kitchen," Hannah replied in a calm but firm tone.

Everything stopped for a moment. The black kitchen help, pots in hands, turned their backs to the table. The black servants at the table looked at each other with expressions that showed they wished themselves back in the safety of the great house. Matt and Gregory exchanged glances and nodded as if they knew better than a black slave did.

Adam turned to look out the window into the dark. He did not like for Hannah to be made fun of. But ashamed, he had to admit that, despite his distrust of Matt, he would very much like to see what hung between Matt's legs. On occasion the tightness of Matt's breeches revealed a long member. More than once during the two years, Adam had longed to touch it. Since he had arrived at Ashley Landing, he had touched only himself. He wanted another man. Still, Adam agreed with Hannah. He didn't like that kind of talk in the kitchen. It was part of the coarseness and inconsiderateness that prevented Adam from being more than kitchen acquaintances with Matt and Gregory.

However, Adam developed a much deeper friendship with Joseph and his family. The older man took a liking to Adam, and Adam often ate his light supper in the kitchen of that family. The two men could talk with greater ease and on many more topics than Adam did with Matt and Gregory. Adam sometimes reminisced about his life at Cromley Hall, but he never told Joseph about his reason for signing the indenture papers.

"Would you like to return there some day, Adam?" Joseph once asked.

"No," Adam said firmly. "I shall always remember with pleasure the best of my days there, but I am now a Virginian."

"I hope that when you earn your freedom papers in another five years, you will consider doing as I did. I have not regretted staying on here at Ashley Landing."

"Five years seems like an eternity away," Adam laughed.

"It always does to twenty-year-old young men," Joseph said as he gave Adam a swat on his shoulders.

On Sunday mornings Adam and the other two indentured servants either walked or rode horseback behind the Ashley carriage for the four miles to the small Anglican church that served that portion of the Tidewater. The words of the service ritual had not much more meaning now for Adam than had those of the clergyman when Adam was a young boy at Cromley Hall. But here Adam felt he was a member of a warm community, and he came to look forward to that part of service when he took a sip of wine and ate a wafer. Perhaps, Adam thought, just being part of a community is all religion is about.

The best free times of all though were his Saturday and Sunday afternoons. Then Adam wanted to be alone. He explored the woods and nearby waterways. He hunted and fished, finding game and fish all too easy prey. Sometimes he walked for miles in the virgin forests, using animal trails as his footpath. But just as often he simply lay in the cool woods and watched the wildlife. He knew that there were several dozen varieties of birds, but he could not name a single one of them. He began to give each species a name of his choosing. *That bird,* he said, *with the cheerful note can only be called a redbird because of its flaming color.*

Almost always when he lay on the ground in a secluded spot, Adam unbuttoned the flap of his breeches and played with himself. Usually he lowered his breeches and let the ferns provide a cushion. Adam knew just how to handle himself. He watched his limp cock slowly extend to its full inches. He stretched the tip of his foreskin out as far as it could go. Then he started to move the foreskin back and forth over the mushroom head with its pink lips. The further the foreskin slid down the shaft, the harder his sex got. Finally when the foreskin was pulled back tight, thin lines of bulging blue veins graced his tool. His cock was now bone hard.

Adam then started to pump himself, his hand just below the crown. He glided the foreskin back and forth over the cockhead, rubbing hard against the ridge. He pumped hard, slowing down only when he sensed that he could stop himself. "What's the use of being hung like horse if this is all I can do?" he said aloud and laughed. Then he spit on his finger and went for his hole. Just the nudge of his fingertip there brought back the excitement of the three nights George had entered much further and had left Adam exhausted but complete. Quickly his hand was covered with thick sticky cream.

As he cleaned his cock with green grass or dry leaves, depending on the season, Adam shut his eyes and often asked himself, "Can I go on like this? I am not touching myself sinfully. Of that I am certain. But my hands need to be around another man's body, not my cock. Matt and Gregory are of no help. They would only call me ugly names if I approached either of them. I am sure Joseph would be kind if I were to tell him of my frustration, but his counsel would be of no use outside the room where we talked. I need someone like myself." Fortunately his work at the warehouse and on the grounds kept such thoughts from his mind most of the time.

The late Indian summer of 1750 finally gave way to October. There were occasional rainy days. Most often though days were sunny but with a crispness in the air. Adam reveled in the cooler weather. The one thing he had not completely adjusted to were the hot days of the Virginia midsummer. Fortunately the warehouse was cool, and Adam frequently ended those summer workdays by going to a secluded bend in the river and swimming naked. Now the cool evenings had put an end to those swims. The last time he swam, he came out on the bank with goose bumps almost as large as the nipples on the two fuzzy mounds of his chest.

On a Thursday evening Adam stood outside the warehouse and watched the October wind ripple the river. He was about to leave the warehouse for supper in the kitchen wing of the great house. His stomach was ready to take on the cold ham, squash pudding, hot corn bread, and cider. As he went back inside for a last bit of work and then to hang up his work apron on its peg, he heard a loud shout from the dock at the landing. Adam went to the warehouse door to see what was happening.

"Boat comin'. Masta' comin' home," an excited black boy called.

Shortly, from the stately front door of the great house burst the three young Ashley children, all in their nightclothes. A black woman tried unsuccessfully to corral them as they ran down the broad expanse of sloping lawn that stretched to the river. Adam smiled at their exuberance and their shrill shouts of "Papa, Papa." No doubt they knew that their father brought treats from Williamsburg.

As Adam started toward the dock, one of the slaves ran to meet him. When the black man reached Adam, he said, with a puzzled look on his face, "Funny person on dat boat." From a distance Adam studied the figures on the flat-bottom boat. He easily recognized the tall Mr. Ashley and the several slaves who handled the boat. Yes, there was a stranger, dressed in a very odd way. Knee breeches and stockings suggested a man. A long gray shawl covered the person's head and hung back waist length. Mr. Ashley brings home a strange guest, Adam murmured to himself and shrugged his shoulders. *Who is he?* Adam asked himself.

Adam ran to the end of the dock to help secure the boat. He saw that the stranger was indeed a man. *About my age,* Adam noted. The young man held the shawl away from his body, exposing his muscular chest with its rich mass of reddish-brown curls. A thin line of hair ran down his belly and disappeared into his breeches.

Lance was no longer in severe pain. The ointment that a slave accompanying Mr. Ashley had gently applied last night had taken effect. Still the wounds on his back stung. Lance was grateful to Mr. Ashley for telling him not to wear his shirt and coat today, and for buying the shawl to keep him warm. Lance's arms were tired from trying to keep the shawl from touching his back too much.

On the trip up the river from Williamsburg, Mr. Ashley had talked briefly with Lance about the kind of shoes he wanted made. They were mainly work shoes for his slaves. They would also be sold to neighboring planters for their slaves.

"I shall make them with the same care as I made your boots," Lance told Mr. Ashley.

"I cannot ask for anything more," his new master replied.

After that brief exchange, Mr. Ashley moved away and left Lance sitting alone. He sensed that something more than shoes was on Lance's mind. His intuition was correct, too, for Lance was not so much rejoicing in his own good fortune as he was worrying about Timothy. He hoped that with Timothy as his only help in the shop, Thomas would treat him decently. Lance knew that he would miss Timothy both as a friend and as bedfellow. He hoped he would see him again someday. But he knew that time would have to be years away. He wondered if Timothy would want to see him after such a long separation.

As the boat neared the dock, Lance looked intently at the people on the dock. He smiled at the nanny's near futile attempts to keep the three children from leaping from the dock, across the water, and into the boat. Only Mr. Ashley's call of "Stay there" kept them from attempting the leap. What most attracted Lance's attention though was the man about his age who was helping to secure the boat. The young man was of good proportions from his neck to the calves on his legs. His ash-blond wavy hair hung shoulder length. Strong features gave him a handsome face.

When the boat was fastened, Mr. Ashley jumped to the dock and, in turn, embraced each of the children. Slaves greeted one another in a medley of happy voices. Only Adam and Lance stood and said nothing. They looked at each other without blinking their eyes. Each wanted to move toward the other. Each was shy about doing so. Each wondered to himself why he was so reluctant to greet the other. After a few minutes, Mr. Ashley disengaged himself from the children and turned to Adam and Lance, still standing awkwardly silent.

"Adam," Mr. Ashley said, "this is Lance Morley. He joins us here at Ashley Landing as an indentured shoemaker. For a few days I turn him over to your care. Show him about. I think that you have room for him to house in your quarters, don't you?"

"Of course, sir," Adam replied.

Mr. Ashley caught sight of his wife at the door of the mansion. He waved. When he turned back to Adam, he said, "Lance's back will need attention. Get more ointment for it." Then he turned to Lance and said, "Rest for a few days before we attend to setting up your shop. Keep the tools I bought from Master Thomas with you." He paused and looked at Adam and Lance. "Lance," he continued, "I hope you find life here as good as I think Adam does. Welcome to Ashley Landing." Mr. Ashley nodded good night to them and raced his children up to the mansion and into the arms of his wife.

Lance and Adam were now alone on the dock. Adam took a deep breath. Something told him that here was another major change in his life. "Yes, welcome to Ashley Landing. I'm Adam Bradley," Adam said and extended his hand. Lance took it in a firm handshake. Their hands lingered together for a long moment.

Finally Adam asked, "What's this about your back and ointment? And why are you wearing that shawl over your head? Do you always dress like that?"

Lance shook his head. He pulled the shawl off his body. He glanced briefly at Adam and then turned around.

Adam gasped. Actually he gasped twice. Naked to the waist, Lance's body at first shot tremors through Adam's cock. However, when Lance turned around to show his scarred back, Adam's cock shrank. His balls ached in pain at the black and blue streaks. Red clots peppered the streaks.

"Damn, what happened?" Adam cried.

"I was whipped. Unfairly, but still whipped. I hit my master. He claimed that he had made Mr. Ashley's boots. I was the one who made them as well as the several dozen other shoes the bastard had claimed as his."

"Then I'd say you did right in hitting him," Adam said.

"Yes, but I still got whipped and put in the pillory for everyone in the town to jeer at. Thank God Mr. Ashley was in Williamsburg or I would be dead from another beating by now," Lance said.

"Yes, I am glad he was there." Adam responded so quietly that Lance could not hear the words. But Lance did detect the welcome of Adam's reply.

The two young men stood quietly looking at each other. Then Adam asked, "Are you indentured?"

"Yes."

"What brought you to Virginia?"

Lance hesitated, then said, "I was forced to come. I was taken from Newgate prison."

Adam looked shocked and involuntarily stepped back from Lance. He recalled the two surly convict-workers on the wharf the day he arrived three years ago.

Lance laughed and grabbed Adam's shoulders. "I'm no murderer," he said.

"What then?" Adam asked.

"I hit a drunken constable who insulted my master's little daughter. He deserved what he got. I didn't. But, like yesterday, my quick temper got me into trouble, that time into prison."

"You didn't look like a murderer," Adam laughed.

"And you, Adam. Why are you here?" Lance asked.

Adam wanted to match Lance's honesty. But he didn't want to risk telling the truth.

"I got on the wrong side of a lord at Cromley Hall," Adam replied in an ambiguous version of the truth.

Lance waited, expecting more details.

Adam smiled and said, "I won't bother you with the story now. Another time maybe."

Neither seemed to know what to say next. When Adam saw Lance shiver from the cold, he said, "Let's get up to the quarters. You must be as hungry as I am."

During the next two hours Adam and Lance settled into the beginning of a friendship. While they ate the supper of cold ham and bread, which Adam brought back from the kitchen, each flooded the other with questions. They told details of their lives both in England and in Virginia. They became acquainted with each other's likes and dislikes.

They laughed over funny and strange incidents in their years of growing up.

Adam was surprised that Lance had never hunted or fished.

"People may hunt in London's back streets but not for animals," Lance said.

"Then for what?"

Lance only responded to Adam's question with a brief laugh.

And Lance was amused that Adam did not know the pleasure of a pipe at the end of the day.

"I do not like the smell," Adam said, "but perhaps I will try a pipe with you someday."

"No. I can do without my pipe if the smell annoys you."

Adam admitted that the only thing he missed about England was the Yorkshire pudding the cook at Cromley Hall made. Lance said his ears sometimes heard the busy London streets but that the call was never strong enough to make him want to return.

"At first I thought Williamsburg a pretty but crude place. I missed seeing places like St. Paul's. But I soon got over that. Except for that bastard cordwainer, I came to like Williamsburg. I made one good friend there."

"Who?"

"An apprentice lad in the shop, Timothy."

"Will you miss him?"

"Yes, very much." Lance paused, took a deep breath and then asked, "But what about you? What did you think of Ashley Hall when you got here? And have you made a good friend here?"

"The great house here is a doll house compared to Cromley Hall. But it is a much better place to live, even though I have not, like you, made a special friend."

What they really wanted to know about each other, they did not ask. To Lance's question, "Have you been with a woman?" Adam nodded a yes and said, "But not over here."

Lance responded, "It is the same with me." That brief exchange was all that was said about their sexual experiences. Adam wanted to say but didn't, "But I do love to lie with other men." Lance, too, wanted to say but didn't, "Be Captain Henry with me, Adam."

Suddenly Lance winced and gritted his teeth.

"Are you hurting?" Adam asked quickly.

"Yes. But what is worse than my back is that I just heard again all those jeers while I stood in the pillory. Men shouted that I should be whipped even more. One man even kicked me in my privates. It hurt so much I threw up."

"May he rot in hell," Adam exclaimed. "But did no one try to console you?"

"Yes, the lad from the shop. Timothy brought me cider after everyone had gone. As he left he ki— he said he hoped we would meet again. Then Mr. Ashley arrived."

Adam wondered what Lance had started to say about Timothy, but he did not ask. Instead he said, "We have yet to eat our pie."

After they had eaten the two generous wedges of Hannah's nut pie, Adam helped Lance arrange his few belongings and clothes in the room. Once, by accident, Adam's hand caught and held Lance's arm as Adam helped Lance with his box of shoe-making tools. He felt Lance quiver. Adam quickly withdrew his hand. They stared at each other for a long moment without saying anything.

"Clumsy me," Adam said at last.

"No harm," Lance replied. "Your hand will be all over my back soon if you remembered to get the ointment when you went for our supper. My back is beginning to hurt again."

"I have it," Adam said. "First though I need the privy. It's over back of the hedgerow just north of here. Or there's a chamber pot under that bench if you'd rather."

Adam lit the candle in a lantern and left for the privy. He was glad to be away from Lance for a while. The brief physical contact with Lance's arm had aroused Adam. His cock was half-erect. He had not felt such a strong sexual urge since he left England. However, even if Lance liked men too, which Adam doubted, Adam knew that Lance was in no condition tonight for any sexual play. Best to take care of his business in the privy and then go beyond the vegetable garden to the orchard and self-pleasure himself. At least he could fantasize about Lance as he pumped himself. He needed the safety measure of shooting his seed if he were not to slip and make a fool of himself in bed with Lance during the night.

From within the grove of apple and peach trees Adam heard the singing of the slaves from their quarters. It was beautiful, even though Adam could not understand the words and despite the undertone of sadness. Adam unbuttoned his flap and lowered his breeches. He peeled the foreskin off the cockhead. He spit on his hand and wet his crown. Then he sheathed himself and rubbed more spit on the foreskin. With quick, rapid thrusts he moved his foreskin back and forth over his cockhead. In almost no time he shot. He continued to pump himself though, thoroughly wetting his long shaft.

When Adam returned to his quarters the room was dark. He held up the lantern to find Lance. Adam sucked in his breath. In the bed Lance lay on his belly. He was naked. The sight of Lance's round butt cheeks and his hairy muscular legs hardened Adam's cock again. Adam was thankful that the lantern cast only his dim shadow on the wall.

"Lance," Adam called softly. Lance uttered a low groan but did not speak.

"Lance," Adam repeated. This time there was no response.

Adam set the lantern on the table and got the ointment. He smeared his fingers with the oily lotion and very gently started to rub Lance's back. Lance stirred a bit but made no sound. It took Adam a long time to cover Lance's back. When Adam came to the long wide strip where the whip had cut the deepest, he saw Lance clench his left hand. Lance groaned loudly but did not awaken. The thin scab broke, and blood trickled over Lance's back.

Adam could not stop himself. He took Lance's hand in his. Lance's hand covered Adam's tightly. Holding Lance's hand in a firm grasp, Adam worked the ointment gently into the deepest cuts on Lance's back. Their hands were in an embrace much tighter that their handshake when they met at the landing.

When he was finished, Adam slowly extracted his hand from Lance's. He pulled the blanket up over Lance's bare ass. He let his hand run over the firm butt cheeks as he raised the blanket. Lance sighed deeply. Adam blew out the candle in the lantern, undressed, and got into his side of the bed. He listened to Lance's deep breathing. Adam, too, was soon asleep.

When the light of dawn shone through the one window of the room, Adam awakened. And suddenly he was very much awake. Adam lay on his side. Lance was snuggled up against Adam's back, his leg over Adam's. Lance's hand rested in Adam's crotch. Adam's cock was erect. Adam wasn't sure, but he thought that he could feel Lance's hard cock at his butt.

Adam didn't know his next move. Without awakening Lance and possibly creating an embarrassing situation, Adam had no way of knowing for certain if Lance knew what he was doing. After all, perhaps Lance was having an erotic dream and grasping for whatever was handy. Or perhaps Lance only had a morning piss-hard. Even if Lance did want sex with him, Adam knew this was not the time. He needed to get to the kitchen for breakfast and then to the warehouse. Mr. Ashley would be there early to learn what had happened here during his visit to Williamsburg.

Still, before he left the bed, Adam wanted to be sure. Slowly he moved back against Lance. Yes, Lance had an erection. Adam felt Lance push up against him. Adam moved back even further. He was sure that Lance's cock nudged forward as if seeking Adam's hole.

The breakfast bell rang.

Lance's body rolled away from Adam's. Adam lay still for a minute. Then he got out of bed. Lance did not seem to awaken. Adam dressed hurriedly, forcing himself not to look at the sleeping body in the bed. Quickly he left the room. Walking briskly up the path to the kitchen, Adam said to himself, "I must find a way to learn if Lance likes to lie with men, or if this morning is only the crazed ending to all the cruelty he has suffered since he hit his master."

As he watched Adam dress, Lance pretended to be asleep. Until the morning bell had jarred him awake, Lance had slept well. Too soundly, in fact. He had fallen asleep even before Adam returned from the privy the night before. He barely was aware of Adam's rubbing his back with the ointment. During the early hours of the morning he had dreamed of Timothy and the cider he had brought to the pillory. Lance tasted Timothy's fingers as he sucked the cider from them. He dreamed of lying next to Timothy and feeling his strong body. He held Timothy's hard sex. But when the morning bell aroused him, Lance found that it was Adam's hard cock he held in his hand. He quickly rolled away from Adam's body.

After Adam left, Lance lay there in the bed on his belly. "Damn me," he said aloud. "If my quick temper does not get me into one kind of trouble, my cock does now. What must Adam think of me!" Lance worried about Adam's haste in leaving. Perhaps he only needed to get to the warehouse early today. But Lance knew there was also the strong possibility that Adam had been angered by Lance's advances. Although Lance did want to know Adam sexually, he also very much wanted his friendship.

The kitchen bell sounded again.

Lance left the bed. He dressed quickly, taking care as he put on his shirt. His back still stung, but he couldn't go to the kitchen half-naked. As he tied his long hair back with a ribbon, he mused, *Today begins my life at Ashley Landing. I am certain that I shall like it here. If Adam says anything about this morning, I will find a way to explain myself.*

When he left the room for the privy, he looked back at the bed. Sleeping there naked with Adam would be either a hell or a paradise.

# 1750: After a Hunting Trip in the Woods

It took more than five weeks for Lance's back to heal. Even then there were thick dark crusts over the deepest cuts. Lance's back would be scarred for the rest of his life.

During that time neither Adam nor Lance mentioned the episode in bed that first morning. Both thought about it, and both wanted to talk about it. But neither did. Lance convinced himself that Adam had never felt the groping in his crotch. Adam repeatedly told himself, *Lance did not know what he was doing.* Thus both found ways of avoiding what they most wanted to know about the other.

As the weeks passed, the friendship between them deepened. They were now free to joke with each other. "I might grow a beard," Lance announced one morning.

Adam guffawed. "It will take you a year to grow what Joseph trims off every week."

"I doubt that. But, at least, at twenty I have more than the baby fuzz on your face."

Adam blushed slightly. He needed to shave only once a week. "I make up for it other places," he bragged.

"Well, don't go around lowering your breeches to show how much of a man you are."

A few times they even argued, although never seriously. Once after supper when they had returned to their quarters, Lance said angrily, "I wish to hell I knew why Matt hates me so much."

"Hate you? He doesn't hate you," Adam replied sharply.

"Yes, he does."

"You're wrong."

"No. I'm not wrong. I see it in his eyes."

"Just because he doesn't joke with you as I do doesn't mean he hates you."

doi:10.1300/5623_05

"I know hatred when I see it in someone's eyes."

"I think you slipped in a pile of shit and are trying to blame someone else for it."

"You're so blind that you'll be the one to slip in the horse shit."

"Now look, Lance. I don't especially like Matt. I don't trust him. But you are simply imagining things that aren't so."

"You'll see someday that I know what I am talking about," Lance snapped, having to get in the last word.

The two young men looked hard at each other, then broke into broad grins. They gave each other friendly punches and put their disagreement behind them.

As if they had carefully planned it, Adam and Lance never saw each other fully naked during those five weeks. When they met occasionally in the washhouse, each was only without his shirt. At night they undressed in the dark. During the night as they slept, their bodies never touched. They did lie close enough so that they took in each other's body heat and inhaled the strong musky smell of each other's body. Each often had to fight from handling his hard cock. In the mornings Adam rose first and was gone to the privy by the time Lance got up and dressed.

Their avoiding the topic of sex and their odd routine of undressing and dressing did not, however, translate into a lack of sexual interest in the other. Adam often recalled Lance's bare ass the night he applied the ointment. He wanted badly to run his hands over Lance's ass again, this time letting his finger slip down the crevice and gently work its way in. All that in preparation for what he wanted to do the most. Just as frequently Lance remembered awakening with his hand in Adam's crotch that first and only morning their bodies had touched. He longed to feel Adam's cock again. He wanted to taste Adam's seed. Each fantasized of the other when he self-pleasured himself, Adam usually in the orchard at night, and Lance in his small workshop when he was alone.

The five weeks after Lance's arrival were one of the two busiest, almost frantic, times of the year at Ashley Landing. During the months of tilling the ground, planting, and cultivating, life at the plantation moved at a steady but easy pace. Once crops were ready for harvesting, everyone, including Mr. Ashley, moved faster. In September the barrels of wheat and barley flour moved through the warehouse to the riverboats for loading on ships bound mainly to the West Indies. Now in early December it was tobacco. The dry leaves had been stripped of their stalks and pressed into hogsheads. These containers waited in the warehouse for loading on the tobacco boats which would take them to ships bound for England. Despite the hard work, Adam enjoyed this busy time. Often his voice grew hoarse from shouting orders to the slaves loading the hogsheads on the tobacco boats. At the end of these December days Adam wanted only supper and sleep.

During these weeks Lance, too, had his work. He soon had his small shop in order and was busy making shoes. Occasionally he wished to have Timothy at the nearby workbench, but he knew that could not be. Mr. Ashley praised Lance's work. He wanted his slaves well shod for work early next spring. But he also knew the shoes were a highly marketable item in his warehouse. He often told himself that he was as fortunate in having Lance as he was in having Adam as workers. He was pleased that the two young men had become good friends.

On the night before the last shipment of hogsheads were to be loaded the next day, Adam trudged back to their quarters from supper a weary man.

"Lance, I'm glad all this is about over."

"You've worked too hard."

"Had to, if it got done. But I do ache."

"Where?"

"My neck and shoulders, for some reason."

"Want me to rub you?"

"Do you mind?"

"Wouldn't offer if I did. Take off your shirt."

Adam pulled off his shirt and sat down cross-legged on the bed. Lance squatted behind him. Lance could not believe his luck. He was about to touch Adam's body. Slowly but firmly his hands moved over Adam's neck and shoulders. He rubbed for a long time.

Only once did Adam speak. "Next Saturday afternoon we will have time to go hunting."

As Lance continued to rub Adam, he thought back on the first Saturday they had gone hunting. Adam had been amused that Lance had never handled a rifle before, and he barely suppressed his laughter at Lance's clumsiness. "Don't fire so quickly," Adam kept admonishing. "Take better aim. No sense in wasting shots." Lance had gradually improved, but he knew it would be some time before he could match Adam's sure aim.

"Ache gone now, Adam?" Lance asked.

"Yes. Thank you, Lance. I'm going to bed."

Without bothering to blow out the lantern, Adam got out of his breeches and into the bed. Lance could not believe how quickly Adam was asleep. After a trip to the privy, Lance, too, undressed and got into bed.

Sharing a bed with Adam all these weeks since his arrival was certainly not the paradise Lance yearned for. But neither was it a hell. Simply lying there talking, as they often did, was itself a kind of paradise. Still, Lance continued to want more. He wanted to find out if Adam was bent as he was. His rubbing of Adam's neck and shoulders tonight had only increased his need to find out. *There has to be a way for me to find out. If it does not come my way by chance, I shall have to make the opportunity.* With that resolution, Lance drifted into sleep.

The morning of the final loading brought the first hard frost. Plants were flattened. Winter announced its coming. The brisk cold weather hurried the loading at the landing. By early afternoon the last tobacco boat was on its way down river. Everyone on the landing waved a friendly farewell to the men on the tobacco boat.

"I appreciate all your good labor, Adam." Mr. Ashley said.

"Thank you. It's good, isn't it, to have the crop year at an end."

"You have become a Virginian, Adam," Mr. Ashley said with a smile on his face. "Good shooting Saturday." Mr. Ashley allowed Adam to keep one out of every six pelts from the animals he shot. Adam had enough skins now to fill a box for shipment to England. He had told Lance that they would split the money on the next box, the one they would fill together.

That Saturday Lance and Adam were in the woods for the first time that month. They were both relieved to have the activity at the landing at an end for the year. Lance could tell that Adam had recovered his energy.

"My back rub did you good, didn't it?" he asked

"Yes. It got me through the last loading." Adam wanted to say more, about how he wanted more of Lance's hands on his body. Instead he said, "Let's head east up that animal trail."

By late afternoon, Adam and Lance were pleased with their bag— four raccoons and two foxes. The fox pelts were a special prize. Lance was proud that one of the foxes had been his kill. When they began to lose the sun, they turned back toward home. Adam took the lead on the trail.

Suddenly he stopped. "I need to piss," he said. He unbuttoned his flap. Soon he let loose a steady yellow stream. Steam rose as the warm liquid wet the cold ground.

*Now is the time,* Lance told himself. *I must find out if Adam is like me.* Before Adam finished, Lance walked around to face him. "By God, Adam," he said and laughed, "you've got a good-sized sex. Hung like a horse, I'd say."

Adam blushed deeply. *It's about to happen,* he said to himself. No sooner had the last drops fallen than his cock began to harden.

"Look at that grow," Lance teased. His eyes brightened, his mouth broke into a wide grin. Adam shook with excitement. His cock reached its full inches.

"I want you, Lance," Adam said in a husky voice.

"And I, you," Lance quickly replied.

Adam hurled himself against Lance's body. Their arms pulled their two bodies together in a tight embrace. Lance moved his hand over Adam's shoulders and back and then down over his butt. Adam ran his hand up under the back of Lance's thick chestnut hair and massaged his neck. Their open lips met in a kiss. It was the kiss both of them had been lusting for. Their tongues explored every curve of the other's mouth. Their lips took turns sucking the other's extended tongue. Their tongues wrestled with each other as the lips pushed firmly together. They kissed for a long time.

Finally Lance broke apart, held Adam away from him by the shoulders, and said, "I've waited for that kiss for all of the time I've been here."

"I was beginning to fear that I would never be able to tell you how much I want you," Adam replied.

In celebration of their new relationship they flung themselves into each other's arms again and kissed wildly. When their lips parted from this second kiss, Lance exclaimed, "I want a closer look at your roger and balls, Adam." He dropped to his knees before Adam.

Lance ran his hand along the shaft, thick at the base and tapered slightly at the cockhead. Lance pulled the foreskin back tight. He ran his finger around the crown. He looked up at Adam and said, "Your cockhead is as big as some of the wild mushrooms we've seen in the woods. I wonder if it is as good to eat?" As if to find his answer, Lance took Adam's cock in his mouth. He sucked the head for several minutes. Then he worked the long, hard shaft, racing the foreskin up and back with each movement of his lips.

Adam was ecstatic. But he realized he was near to letting loose. He pushed Lance's head away. "I want to get at you," he told Lance.

Lance stood up. Adam searched frantically for the flap in Lance's leather drawers. "Where the hell is the opening?" he cried out.

Lance laughed. "There isn't one. My work drawers do double duty. When the backside gets thin, I'll turn it around to the front. Just untie the drawstring, Adam."

Quickly Adam had Lance's drawers down, and he was on his knees before Lance's hard sex. Adam kissed it, and then pulled back to look. "I think I beat you in length," he said, "but you're much thicker, and I want it." Adam took Lance's cock. He sucked hard on the head. Then he swallowed the stubby shaft. All the time he sucked, he played with Lance's balls. Lance's balls were huge, and the ball sack hung down low. Adam could tell from Lance's groans that Lance was having as much enjoyment as he was.

Lance suddenly realized how close he was to coming. He pulled away from Adam's lips. "I want to do you at the same time you suck me," he said.

"How can we do that?"

Lance took off his jacket and told Adam to take off his. "Give it to me," Lance said. He took their jackets and spread them on the ground. "Now lie down on your side," he told Adam. When Adam was down on the jacket on his side, Lance lay down, too, his head toward Adam's feet. He had his mouth at Adam's cock, and Adam's mouth was at his. "How's this for our getting at each other?" he asked.

"It seems natural," Adam replied, fondling Lance's sex.

Lance ran his tongue down the underside of Adam's cock. He sucked his balls. Then in a swift dive, his lips traveled down from Adam's cockhead to the base of his shaft. His lips and tongue kept a steady move up and down Adam's quivering cock.

For a few minutes Adam kept fondling Lance's sex. He shut his eyes and enjoyed the double pleasure of playing with Lance's cock and of having his own sucked. "Damn, Lance," he moaned, "that feels good." Then he went down on Lance. His lips and tongue raced all over Lance's cockhead and around his shaft.

Both of them were hot, too hot to last. Each knew the other was near orgasm. They sucked all the harder. They exploded at the same time. They drained each other's jism, using their lips to force the last drops up the shaft. They drank the sweet juice.

When they pulled apart and sat up, Lance said, "I've never tasted better stuff."

"As good as wild mushrooms?" Adam asked mischievously.

"Oh, it's a tad better, I guess," Lance answered, returning the puckish look in Adam's eyes with a mock serious look.

Adam and Lance embraced and kissed. Neither seemed anxious to leave. Finally Adam said reluctantly, "We need to get back before it's too dark. Are you cold?"

Lance laughed. "After all that! What a crazy question. Let's go."

During the three-mile trek back neither Adam nor Lance said much. They walked briskly on the narrow trail. Occasionally they stopped, and, without setting down their rifles or the bags with the pelts of the skinned animals, they kissed lightly on the lips. Just as the lights of the dependencies came into view, Lance stopped abruptly.

"Adam," he called.

Adam turned and came back to Lance.

"I love you, Adam," Lance said quietly.

"And I, you, Lance," Adam softly replied.

"It's another kind of indenture, isn't it?" Lance said.

"But there are no years attached to this one," Adam replied.

With that quiet declaration of their feelings, Adam and Lance sealed their bonding.

By the time Adam and Lance got to the kitchen wing of the great house, Hannah was banking the fire in the huge fireplace for the night. Hannah supervised the five black slaves who prepared the meals both for the dining room of the mansion and for the table seating the indentured servants and the house slaves. Her cooking had made the Ashleys' table the envy of aristocratic Tidewater plantations.

"Where you two been so late? Keepin' out of mischief, I hope," she scolded. The grin on her face partly belied the cross tone of her question.

"Hunting," Adam replied.

"What mischief is there to get into?" Lance asked.

"Menfolks always knows where mischief is, and how to get into it," Hannah told Lance.

Adam and Lance said nothing, but they glanced at each other with amused smiles.

"Ham or turkey for your bread, or a bit of both?" Hannah asked. Lance took turkey, Adam the ham. Hannah piled two plates with dried apples. She took bread from the warmer oven and covered the slices with the meat. Adam took two cups and went to the wine cellar for cider.

"Eat your suppers. Then get out of my kitchen," Hannah said. She was a bit grumpy, but she liked these two young men and couldn't get too cross over their tardy appearance. Adam and Lance ate in silence, listening to Hannah hum as she went about finishing her chores. Both ate slowly, but since supper was the light meal of the day, they soon cleaned their plates. Hannah cut each a generous piece of pound cake to take back to their quarters. "Good night, Hannah," they both called as the two young men left the kitchen. "Night," Hannah responded. "Don't be late for breakfast." The last thing Adam and Lance heard Hannah mutter was "Menfolks, uh."

Crisp clean air replaced the warmth of the kitchen with its good smells. "Turning to winter," Adam said. "I'd better make a detour to the woodshed and get enough wood for a small fire tonight and in the morning. Go on ahead, Lance." Adam got the wood and went to their quarters to build and light the fire in the small fireplace. The fire soon lit the room with dancing shadows.

Then Adam headed to the privy and the washhouse. He did not find Lance at either place. In the washhouse Adam stripped off his shirt. He cleaned his face and neck and ran a soapy rag under his armpits and over his chest. He lowered his breeches just enough to clean his privates. As he washed behind, Adam said to himself, *I want Lance's cock here tonight.* His member stiffened slightly at that thought.

Lance was squatting before the fire when Adam returned to the room. He was naked. The two men smiled at each other. Lance stood up. "Get out of your clothes, Adam," Lance said. Lance watched intently as Adam undressed. When at last Adam stepped out of his breeches, he, too, was naked. Silently they stood in the light of the fire and took in each other's body.

Lance was the taller of the two, his build a bit on the stocky side. The muscles of his chest were covered with a mass of reddish-brown hair. His large nipples peeked through. Down his flat belly and past his navel ran a thick line of dark curls to join the rich mass of hair surrounding his sex. The foreskin lay in a generous fold behind the crown of his pointed cockhead. Like Adam, Lance's arms and legs were well muscled.

The blond fuzz on Adam's firm chest matched his shoulder-length blond hair. His stomach was smooth and hairless. A thin line of fuzz ran from his navel to his light brown cockhairs. The underside of his foreskin extended in a long tip. Like Lance, he had good-sized balls.

Lance broke out in laughter. "Damn," he said to Adam, "at last I get to see you completely naked."

"Yes," Adam responded, "no more hiding and undressing in the dark."

Adam went up to Lance and kissed him. He untied the ribbon that held Lance's hair. The pigtail hung just below Lance's shoulders. Adam ran his fingers through Lance's hair, now free from its confine.

Quickly the two young men embraced. Their hands and lips worked in a wild ecstasy all over each other's body. Then they kissed passionately for a long time. The fire in the fireplace was at its height.

"Let's get to bed," Adam said, still tight in Lance's embrace. In no time they lay in bed. Adam was on his back, with Lance's leg over his sex and Lance's arm across his chest.

"Tell me, Adam. Were you aware that first morning that I was playing with your hard cock?" Lance asked.

"Yes," Adam said.

"Why didn't you respond then?"

"I was afraid. I didn't know whether you were conscious of what you were doing, or whether you were still asleep and having a dream of some kind."

"You could have found out."

"No, it was time for breakfast. Anyway, even if I had found out, your back was in no condition for any wrestling around, Lance."

"It's better we waited. This way we have got to know each other. I love being naked with you, Adam, but sex is only a part of the strong affection I have for you."

The two men looked at each other and smiled. Adam nodded his agreement. Then he asked, "Does your back ever hurt you now?"

"At times. And I know it is not a pretty sight for you to have to look at. I wish it was as smooth as yours," Lance said.

"Don't talk like that," Adam said and pulled Lance down on top of him.

Their arms folded them in an embrace. Their lips and tongues met in a kiss. Lance moved his hips so that his cock rammed against Adam's with each forward thrust. He kept at it until their panting announced approaching orgasms. Lance stopped. Still keeping his cock against Adam's, Lance raised up on his hands. He smiled down at Adam. Then he buried his mouth in Adam's hairy right armpit.

"You taste good," he told Adam, as he went for Adam's nipples.

"I want you inside me," Adam said.

"Not yet. I just want to lie here for a while and let my hand run over your body." Lance rolled off Adam and snuggled up close. "It is going to be paradise sleeping like this with you." His hand played over Adam's face. "You've not been with many men, have you, Adam?"

"How many is many?"

"Can you count them on your hands?"

"All of them on just one hand. You're the fifth."

"Who were the others?"

"I lost my virginity to George, the coachman to an English earl one Christmas season. He was a good teacher, and I learned through him that I liked to lie with other men. Then I played around with two young servants at Cromley Hall. We had a good time, but I have all but forgotten them."

"That's only three," Lance said.

"Do you recall that I told you I got on the wrong side of a nobleman?"

"Yes, you said that when we first met on the landing."

"Well, I let Lord Cromley bugger me one afternoon in the stable. Then I made the mistake of buggering him by force. He blackmailed me into signing indenture papers by threatening to let my good aunt go from his wife's service. I couldn't hurt my aunt."

"So that's what you meant by 'wrong side.'"

"Yes. I wish I could have been honest with you then, as you were with me."

"Do you ever regret taking Lord Cromley by force?"

"No. He angered me with his arrogance. Also, I would not be here with you now if I had not got angry and buggered the old fart."

"I'm glad you did," Lance said, giving Adam a kiss.

"And how about you?" Adam asked.

"It will take your hands as well as mine to count them," Lance replied.

"I don't believe that."

"Adam, I got a much earlier start on you. And London is full of men of our persuasion."

"But how did you find them?"

"There are several places where men like us gather. I went mainly to St. Paul's but occasionally to Covent Garden. Adam, I am ashamed to tell you, but I often sold my body at those places."

Adam raised up, shocked. "How could you do that!"

Lance bit his lip. "I'm sorry I told you."

"No. Better for us to be honest with each other. I don't like your having done that. But all that is past." He lay back down and kissed Lance.

"I didn't always get money. The young men and I simply found a dark place in the street and pleasured each other, either by mouth or by hand. It was the older men, many of them married and with children, who paid me."

"And did you go with them to the dark places?"

"No. They took me to a room in a tavern where men like us gather. There they had the pleasure of my body."

Adam was silent for a time. Then he asked, "Did you ever feel any affection for these men?"

"No. I have forgotten their faces and names, if I ever knew their names."

"Am I the first then for whom you feel as you do?"

"Yes, and no," Lance replied slowly. "No, because I felt strongly for Captain Henry, although he, too, in a way paid for my body. But when he left me in the woodshed one afternoon at the cordwainer's, he went out of my life."

Lance paused. Adam said nothing.

"And, no, because I loved Tim. But he was like a little brother to me. I still love him in that way. I am sure though that he will forget his boyish affection for me. I hope that he will not hate me for the few nights we had in bed together."

"I would like to meet him someday," Adam said.

Lance sighed. "Time plays tricks on us all. Perhaps the three of us will meet someday. But to answer your question, yes, you are the first man I truly love."

The two young men pulled even closer together. They kissed briefly and lay still. Each of them had an erect cock. As he handled Lance's cock, Adam said, "I want that inside me."

Lance smiled at Adam and nodded. He moved between Adam's legs and went down on Adam's cock. As he sucked, his finger searched for Adam's hole. He rubbed his finger over the wrinkles. Slowly he worked his finger past the muscles. The more he probed, the more Adam's hole expanded. Lance added another finger and pushed deep inside the cavity.

"I want your cock up my ass," Adam repeated. He shoved Lance away and turned over on his stomach.

"Are you deaf? I want you up my ass," Adam said a third time.

"I heard you," Lance laughed. "But not that way. Turn on your side, Adam."

Adam turned and lay on his right side. Lance lay down on his side, his cock against Adam's butt.

"Raise your leg a bit," Lance told Adam.

Lance reached over Adam to play with his nipples. As he pinched them, Lance guided his cock to Adam's hole. Slowly he pushed the cockhead in. Adam winced at the pain.

"Relax, Adam. I'll take it easy. Next time I'll bring some oil I use on leather in the shop."

Adam took several deep breaths. "I can take it now, Lance. Push in."

As Lance kissed Adam's neck and ears, he plunged his cock deep into Adam's hole. Lance pulled Adam closer to him. He continued to kiss Adam's neck and to rub his chest. "Go at it," Adam said.

Lance started at it, sliding easily now. At times Lance almost pulled out, leaving only a bit of head in. Then he would tunnel back in and pump furiously. As he buggered Adam, Lance reached for Adam's cock. He pulled the foreskin over the head and jacked him. The rhythm of his hand kept pace with the thrust of his cock. Adam moaned in delight at the double pleasure.

"I'm coming," Lance cried suddenly. He held Adam tight and let loose. Adam welcomed Lance's juice. His own cock quivered and then shot.

Feeling Adam's shaking body, Lance cried out, "No, Adam, don't come. I want you to take me."

For a few seconds, each of them groaned with climatic release.

"Too late, Lance."

Lance felt Adam's cock. It was drenched in jism. Lance wiped it with his hand. He licked his hand clean.

Lance pulled out of Adam. Adam turned and lay on his back. Lance put his leg over Adam's sex and his arm around Adam's chest. They snuggled together.

"Tomorrow you bugger me," Lance told Adam. Adam promised with a kiss.

For a while they lay without talking. They watched the last of the fire turn to glowing embers. Adam pulled a blanket over their naked bodies. Turning to Lance, he asked, "Do you think what we did is sinful?"

"No. Hell no. Why is that question on your mind?"

"Didn't those young men in the dark places or in the tavern room ask it?"

"No. There it was only a matter of doing, not talking. Had I asked that question, I would have been thought a madman."

"But the Bible . . ."

"Bugger the Bible." Lance pulled apart from Adam. "Do you believe what happened was sinful? Are you sorry you let me have your body?"

"No, not at all." Adam paused, then added, "It is only another way of having sex." Again he paused. "It won't make babies. But it is our way of showing love."

"If you feel that way, then why did you ask that question?"

"I guess I wanted to make sure you didn't feel guilt about what we were doing."

"Guilt! Adam, I loved what we were doing. My only regret is that you didn't get to take me, too."

"We have plenty of time."

"Yes. But we do have to be careful, Adam. Men are hanged here in Virginia for what we just had fun doing. What's even worse is that sometimes those men have their privates cut off while they are still alive. We don't want to end up on the gallows."

"We won't. We'll stay well hung, but not hanged." Adam turned to Lance and kissed him lightly on the lips.

"I love you, Lance," Adam said.

"And I, you, Adam," Lance replied.

# 1751-1752: New Good Names and an Ugly Old One

Adam stirred. He missed the warmth of Lance's body. Suddenly he was awake and sat up. In the light of a candle, he saw Lance propped up in bed against the wall of the room. "What are you doing?" he asked.

"Drawing."

Adam rubbed his eyes. "Becoming an artist at this early hour of the morning?"

"No."

"Then what are you doing?"

Lance handed Adam the piece of paper he was drawing on and asked, "What do you think of it?"

Adam studied the drawing on the paper for several minutes, turning it upside down and sideways. Then he threw it back to Lance and lay down and covered his head.

"So you don't like my invention?"

Adam raised up. "Invention? Are you out of your head this morning?"

Lance gathered Adam into his arms and kissed him. His hand covered Adam's sex. "Now look again, damn you."

Adam looked but he obviously could not see what Lance wanted him to see.

"What do you see there?" Lance finally asked.

Adam was now fully awake and in the mood to joke. In a loud voice he answered, "A big turd. Big on one end and little on the other."

Lance pushed Adam back down.

"No, blind man, it's a clog."

"A what?"

"A clog."

doi:10.1300/5623_06

Adam stared at Lance. "It's too early to play word games. Come lie down."

"Not now. I want you to see the new kind of shoe I want to make."

"Is that what you call a 'clog'?"

"Yes. Now sit up and look."

Adam realized that Lance was in earnest. It was not part of an early morning game where they lay head to foot and pleasured each other by mouth. He lay back against Lance's bare chest. Lance reached around for Adam's sex. "I want you to have me later," Lance said.

Adam nodded. "First though tell me about this new shoe."

"It will have a thick sole, cut to fit most men's feet. I will make it by sewing several layers of deerskin together. See that's the long part of the drawing. Then across the shoe just above the toes, I will nail a three inch wide strap. See it on the drawing? That's all there is to the clog. The toes and back of the foot and heel will be exposed."

"Your explanation is much clearer than your drawing. I still hold you drew a large turd."

"I'll turd you."

The two young men playfully wrestled for a minute and then kissed.

"So how do you think it is going to stay on anyone's foot?" Adam asked.

"The tight leather strap will see to that. It may take a bit of getting used to walking in the clog. But the foot will keep pushing forward as the men walk. It won't come off."

"Make me a pair to wear in the warehouse. Then I'll tell you what I think of your clogs."

"I will have to experiment for a while. So don't expect your clogs for a couple of weeks."

"I'll wait. Oh, why do you call them clogs?"

"Can you think of better name?"

"No, but I can think of something better that I'd like to do, Lance."

After their first night of lying together, not just sharing a bed without touching, there was never any more talk about guilt and sin. What they did in bed they considered natural, simply a part of their love. They boldly explored each other's body; there wasn't a crack they left untouched by hand or by lips. A little over two months ago they had discovered what they decided to call "ringing."

One night they had been lying on their sides sucking each other's cock. Lance was also fingering Adam's hole. Suddenly Lance pulled his mouth off Adam's cock. He rolled Adam over on his back. Lance got on his hands and knees, his head at Adam's crotch. He spread Adam's legs.

"Let me get a better look at your hole," he said. "I've had it, but I really have never looked at it." Lance spread Adam's butt cheeks. Adam's hole was long and oval, surrounded by dark wrinkles. A ring of light fuzz surrounded the wrinkles. "I want that," Lance said in a low voice.

Adam gasped when he felt Lance's mouth where it had never been before. It was tremendous. Adam spread his legs so that Lance could get it better. "Damnation," Adam shouted, "that feels good." Lance pulled Adam's butt cheeks even farther apart. His tongue dug deeper into Adam's hole.

"Let me get at you, too," Adam said. Adam raised his head. His hand spread Lance's butt cheeks. Thick brown lips surrounded Lance's round opening. Like the rest of him, Lance's rear end was hairy. Adam pushed the butt cheeks farther apart. He saw the soft pink flesh just inside the hole. His tongue headed for it.

The lips of their mouths kissed the lips of their assholes. Tongues worked their way inside the soft flesh of the hole. Both of them got deeper and deeper. This new sexual experience excited each of them so much that their cocks, already hard from the sucking, oozed large creamy drips. The longer they kept at it, the more excited they became. Finally, without even touching their cocks, both men shot just as their tongues reached the deepest penetration of their holes.

Adam and Lance fell back exhausted. Adam flipped so that he could hold Lance in his arms. "What made you think of that?" Adam asked.

"I don't know. Suddenly I just asked myself, if your hole likes my cock, how would it like my tongue. I decided to try it."

"Tasted like wild mushrooms, didn't it?" Adam said and grinned.

"A hell of a lot better," Lance replied. "Yes, I definitely like ringing."

"Ringing? Is that what it's called?"

"I don't know what other men call it, but I want to call it 'ringing.'"

"Why is that?"

"Adam, you can't see it, but you've got a ring of fuzz circling the puckers of your hole. When I got past that ring of fuzz and the puckers, I was inside you. So why not 'ringing'?"

"Well, you ought to see yours. You've got a big patch of hair I need to penetrate. So 'ringing' it is."

They loved ringing and continued to ring each other after that night. But it never replaced pleasuring each other by mouth. "There's just more to work with down at your prick than at your asshole," Lance told Adam.

Their best pleasure came, however, when one of them buried himself deep inside the other. They could go at it that way for a long time, and they usually reached climax at the same time. "Doing this," Adam once said, "makes me feel at one with you, Lance. Like our two bodies had become one."

Lance shook Adam. "Are you so excited about getting clogs that you forgot that I said I wanted you to take me?"

Adam laughed. "That's something I never forget. Lie down on your back and put your legs over my shoulders." Adam squatted before Lance. His erect sex nudged Lance's hole. He pushed in and paused.

"Bugger me, Adam."

The two young men were unusually excited this morning, and both let loose much sooner than they ordinarily did. As Adam pulled out, he said, "That happened all too fast."

They lay back down against each other. As he played with the hair on Lance's chest, Adam said, "I wish we had our own name for what we did just now. 'Bugger' has always sounded ugly to me. It doesn't really describe the pleasure we both feel."

"Maybe you'll come up with another name for it. Tell me when you do," Lance replied.

They found the new name late one August afternoon that year when they had finished exercising two geldings from the Ashley Landing stable. Joseph was always glad to have the two young men help at the stable. As with hunting, Adam had to teach Lance how to ride. But Lance learned to control his horse more quickly than he learned to shoot with complete accuracy

As they led the geldings to the stable after the run, Adam and Lance passed a barn where a young black boy was feeding a large flock of chickens with handfuls of corn kernels.

They smiled at the boy, talking to the chickens as he fed them from a large bucket full of kernels.

"Where did you get so much corn?" Adam called.

"Shelled it," Abe answered with a shrug. He thought the question a rather dumb one.

"That must have taken a long time. What did you use? An oyster shell?" Lance asked.

"No, I cornholed it," Abe responded.

"You what?" Lance asked, a quizzical look on his face.

"I cornholed it," the boy repeated.

"What's that?" Adam asked.

"Want me to show you?" Abe responded. The smile on his face said that he was obviously pleased to know something these two grown-ups didn't. Both Adam and Lance nodded. They tied the horses to a fence post and followed Abe to the side of the barn. "See that hole in that board," Abe said and pointed.

"Yes," Adam said.

There was a long nail just above the round hole. Abe hung his bucket on the nail. He picked up a long ear of corn. He stuck the end of the ear in the hole. "Now watch," the boy instructed Adam and Lance. Abe shoved the ear of corn through the hole. The kernels dropped into the bucket. The shelled ear fell inside the barn. "That's how I do it. That's cornholing," Abe announced, a big grin of accomplishment on his face.

"Let me have a try at that," Adam said. Adam picked up another ear of corn. He rubbed his hand over it. He looked at Lance. Lance snickered in return. The phallic-shaped ear of corn was about nine inches long. Adam put the end of the ear at the hole in the board. Again he looked at Lance. This time Lance burst out in laughter. Abe looked at Lance in astonishment. Abe thought that the young man had gone crazy over nothing. Adam shoved the ear of corn through the hole. "That's cornholing," Adam said, looking only at Lance. Lance continued to laugh.

"What's funny?" Abe shouted.

Adam and Lance stood silently as they looked deep into each other's eyes. Finally Lance nodded his head at Adam. Then he turned to Abe. "Nothing, Abe. Just that watching Adam do that reminded me of something. It's a private thing between Adam and me."

"Oh," Abe said, thinking it must be as crazy as he suspected before.

"Thanks for showing us something new, Abe," Adam said. "You'd better get back to feeding the chickens. Lance and I have to rub down the horses."

That night in bed, Adam said, "I promised I'd find a new name. So bugger off, 'bugger.'" Adam leaned over and fingered Lance's asshole and said, "Big cornhole you have."

Lance grabbed Adam's hard cock and replied, "Large ear of corn you have. Cornhole me, Adam."

Whether it was the new name for it or not Adam and Lance didn't know, but sex that night seemed better than ever. They each cornholed the other before they settled in for the night.

Adam and Lance had been lovers for almost a year. For giving and getting it up the ass during that time, Adam and Lance had enjoyed a variety of positions. Not often did they use the same one twice in a week. They loved taking each other in any position—on hands and knees, standing against a tree in the woods, on the back with legs over the shoulders, or squatting coming down on a waiting cock. Or whatever the moment suggested.

However, tremendous as sex was, their greatest pleasure was a much less strenuous one. And for it they needed no name. That pleasure was simply snuggling naked, hands roaming gently, and kissing when they settled into bed for the night, and then sleeping, their bodies entwined. Their only prayer was "May we live together for as long as we live."

It took Lance much longer to make the first clogs than he had told Adam. Demands for Lance to repair harnesses and to make new ones came from the overseer of the north plantation. For a month there was no time for clogs. In late spring, however, Lance finished the first two pairs. One of them he gave to Adam. The other he showed to Mr. Ashley.

Adam tried hard to be enthusiastic, and he was sincere in his praise of Lance's craftsmanship. But, after a day of wearing his clogs in the warehouse, he had to admit to Lance that he had his reservations.

"It's just that I can't move as quickly as I need," he told Lance

"Are they too loose?"

"No. But I feel like I am shuffling along, not walking. And I wouldn't attempt to run in them. I'm sorry, Lance. I guess I'm just a clumsy ass."

"Don't apologize. And you are not an ass."

"Where I think I'll try wearing them is in our quarters. They might just be right for there."

When he was presented the second pair of clogs, Mr. Ashley, too, had his reservations. "It's an interesting idea, Lance," he said. "And I am pleased to have you think of something that will help our blacks in the field. But I wonder if most of them wouldn't prefer to go barefoot."

"Can we test them though?" Lance asked.

"Certainly. Let's walk to the vegetable garden and see if a field hand is there or close by."

As they approached the garden, they heard several voices singing. The slave who was leading the singing was hoeing the ground alongside the young plants. He was barefoot.

"Moses," Mr. Ashley called, "leave off, and come here."

"Yah, sir," the big black man replied. When Moses came up to the two men, he stared at the clog in Lance's hand. "What dat?" he asked.

"A new shoe Lance has made. He would like for you to try it on and to walk around in it," Mr. Ashley said.

Moses took the clog, and Lance showed him how to slip his foot in it.

"Now walk to the far end of the garden and back," Mr. Ashley said.

When Moses returned about ten minutes later, he had a broad grin on his face.

"I'd say we have an answer, Mr. Ashley," Lance said. He was delighted by the grin on Moses' face.

"Do you like them, Moses?" Mr. Ashley asked.

"They keeps the bottom of my feet from the rocks and the twigs. And they air my toes right well. But I wants shoes when it's cold and snowy."

Mr. Ashley clasped Lance around his shoulders and congratulated him. "Make a dozen pair, and we'll see how the hands at the north plantation like them. My guess is that they will like them better than Moses here. It's rougher work there than here in the vegetable garden."

The most enthusiastic response to the clogs came unexpectedly. Lance had finished the first of the clogs for the north plantation and was showing it to Mr. Ashley and Adam. With Mr. Ashley was his ten-year-old son, William. No sooner had Lance handed the clog to Mr. Ashley than the little boy cried out, "I want that."

The men laughed, and his father said, "Isn't your foot a bit small?" He put the large clog next to young William's foot. "See."

"Then make one smaller, Lance," the boy declared.

"Please," his father reminded him.

"Yes, please, make me one," the boy said.

"Do, Lance, and soon. He will pester me until he has them on his feet," Mr. Ashley said, and tousled his son's hair.

"I'll be pleased to make you a pair, William. But you must promise not to pester your father."

The boy nodded assent.

That night in bed Adam leaned over and kissed Lance hard. Then he said, "I'm proud of you, Lance."

"I'm a bit proud of myself." After a long pause he murmured, "I can hardly believe that I was ever in Newgate."

Adam thought for a moment and then said, "There are new gates here, but not like that old one. Both of us have opened new gates ever since we came here. I'm sure more are to be opened. London's Newgate is the past. Virginia's new gates are our future."

Lance's body relaxed. He sighed and said, "Does that mean I have to make even more clogs?"

"Probably."

Both of them laughed.

"Are you getting used to your clogs when you wear them here?" Lance asked.

"Gets easier every day."

"That's all I can ask. Except right now I want your cock."

"Which way?"

"Any way you want."

That night Lance had a strange but pleasant dream which mixed up the clogs with Adam's cock.

On May 23, 1752, Lance turned twenty-two. Adam was not to be that age for another five months. That night there was a celebration for Lance in the kitchen. For the occasion Hannah had made a berry cake which she handed out in generous portions, each topped with a dollop of thick spiced cream.

"Happy birthday, Masta' Lance," Hannah sang out.

"Happy birthday," the rest of the room responded.

"Thank you," Lance said.

Besides Matt and Gregory, the house servants were seated at the long table. They were full of the special light supper Hannah had prepared. Adam had been given permission to go to the wine cellar for a large pitcher of cider.

"I propose a toast," Adam said solemnly He poured cider into everyone's cup. "All stand up and raise your cup." The entire kitchen rose, black and white, and raised their cups. They looked at Adam.

"To the inventor of clogs at Ashley Landing. Happy Birthday."

"Thank you, again," Lance said. He smiled at the guests at his celebration.

Shortly after that, the house servants left to finish their chores of the evening. Although Adam and Lance were anxious to get back to their quarters, they stayed to drink another cup of cider with Matt and Gregory.

Matt had a special reason to celebrate that night, too. At the end of the week, Matt would complete his indenture and receive his freedom papers. He was more thinking about that than he was about Lance's birthday.

"What are you going to do after you have your freedom papers? Adam asked.

"Call it my walking papers. For as soon as I have them in hand, along with the freedom money Mr. Ashley has to give me, I'm walking the back trail down to Williamsburg."

"That's a far piece," Gregory remarked.

"I can make it if I start early and walk late. Hannah will send along some food for the trip, won't you, Hannah?"

Hannah nodded. She was not sorry to have Matt leaving her kitchen. He seldom spoke to her, and when he did, it was usually to ask for something more to eat.

"At Williamsburg what will you do?" Adam asked.

"I may stay there if I can find carpentry work. But I think I'd rather head out of the Tidewater and into the hills and frontier beyond. The Tidewater is big land. Beyond here, there's more room, more opportunity, for us little men. I hear carpenters are in demand there. I'll be my own master there."

"I wish you luck," Lance said.

"I, too, Matt," Adam added.

"What will the two of you do when you get your freedom papers?" Matt asked.

"That won't be for several more years. But right now I think I'll stay here. Joseph did, and he's happy. I would be, too."

"Joseph is a damn fool," Matt grumbled.

No one replied to the remark. Neither Adam nor Lance wanted to spoil the birthday celebration with an argument.

"I think I'll stay here, too," Adam said. "But, at the moment, I am more thinking about tomorrow than three years from now."

"Goin' to be hot tomorrow, Masta' Adam. I can tell from how still everything is," Hannah called from her table where she was scrubbing supper dishes.

"If it is as hot as Hannah claims it will be, then perhaps we ought to have our first swim at the bend before we come to supper, Adam," Lance said.

"The air may be hot, but the water is still going to be chilly. But if you want, I'm game," Adam replied.

Adam and Lance said goodnight to the other two men. As he was leaving the kitchen, Lance hugged Hannah warmly and said, "Thanks for the cake and cream."

"It was nothin'," she told him. "Happy birthday, Masta' Lance." She smiled at Adam and Lance as they left the kitchen. Then she turned to Matt and Gregory, still seated at the table. "I needs to go to the great house and get orders from the mistress about dinner tomorrow. I hopes you all is gone out of my kitchen when I returns." With that, she left for the great house.

"Her kitchen," Matt snarled. "Someday these rich planters here will pay for having brought these nigger people over here."

"Oh, they are all right in their place," Gregory replied.

Matt drained his cup and looked in the pitcher to see if there were more cider.

"Damn," he said. "Adam should have brought more."

They sat silent for a minute. Then Matt said, "That's a strange pair."

"Who, Hannah and Lance hugging?"

"No. Him hugging a nigger was bad enough, but I'm talking about those two men, Adam and Lance."

"What about them?"

"There's something unnatural about them."

"How do you mean unnatural?"

"Except when they are working, they are always together."

"Well, some folks might say the same about us."

"But they look at each other in ways we do not."

"Are you saying that they are unnatural like in the Bible it says two men shouldn't be?"

"Maybe."

"Maybe you're saying that, or maybe they are."

"I'd bet half my freedom money that they are damn filthy sodomites."

Gregory took in a deep breath. He looked at Matt. Finally he said, "You must be only half sure if you are betting only half your money."

"Half is good enough."

"Maybe. They seem like nice young men to me. I'd say they were more like brothers."

"Brothers, hell. I'm going to the bend in the river tomorrow afternoon. I wager you I can prove you wrong."

"I won't bet with you. Whatever they are is not my business. They have never harmed me. And if you are smart, Matt, you'll let them be. Just get on to Williamsburg and worry about your life, not theirs."

"I guess I'm not that smart, for I'm going to the river."

Gregory shrugged his shoulders and said, "Let's get out of here."

As Hannah predicted, it was hot the next afternoon, much hotter than it usually was so early in the season. Everyone moved at a slow pace.

"A freak day," Joseph told Mr. Ashley. "By late tomorrow night though we will be back to May weather, not this. Not even the horses like this kind of sudden burst of August heat in May."

"I hope you are right. But tonight will be another matter. Just walk the horses."

At times at his workbench Lance couldn't see because of the sweat running down his forehead into his eyes. Repeatedly he wiped it away and tried to get back to work. Adam all but stopped work in the warehouse. Rather than move around, he sat on his stool to add the numbers in the ledger. Both of them were ready for their swim in the river.

On the mile and a half walk to the river, Adam and Lance were so anxious to get undressed and into the water that they barely spoke. When they arrived at the large area of thickets which hid the shore of the river, Adam called back, "Watch out for snakes."

"They'll get out of our way," Lance replied as he followed Adam on the animal trail through the thick brush.

Shortly they emerged, with a few scratches, from the thickets out onto the wide stretch of sandy shore. Here on the east side of the river, the water was shallow for several yards out as the bank gradually sloped into the river. After that it was over their heads. The current at the bend was not so strong that the young men couldn't easily swim across to the west side where tree limbs and vines hung into the water. Adam and Lance had not tried to venture into the woods on the west side.

Quickly Adam and Lance were naked and into the water. They shouted loudly as they splashed themselves and each other before they started to swim.

"Feels good, doesn't it?" Adam yelled.

"It's a bit chilly. But, yes, it does feel good," Lance yelled back.

"I'll race over and back," Adam challenged.

"You're on," Lance replied.

Like he had taught Lance to hunt and to ride, Adam also had to teach Lance how to swim. But Lance took easily to water, and quickly he swam with more energy and grace than Adam. When they raced, Lance usually won. This afternoon, however, Adam stroked with greater speed, and he arrived back on the east shore a bit ahead of Lance.

Adam stood up in the shallow water and cried out, "I won this time."

"Yes, but by getting a head start on me," Lance teased.

Adam scooped large handfuls of water and splashed Lance. Lance returned the volleys. Soon the target was each other's sex. Quickly both had erections.

"Now that I've cooled off, I'm hot," Adam laughed.

"So I see. But I can do something about that," Lance replied.

Lance waded over to Adam and took him into his arms for tight embrace. They kissed. Then Lance knelt before Adam and took his sex in his mouth. Lance's lips worked the head so expertly that Adam let loose in less than a minute. Lance stood up and scolded, "No fair. I didn't get long enough on you."

"Don't worry. Let me have another swim, and I'll be ready to go again. But now I want you." Adam knelt before Lance's stubby swollen cock. He licked the slit and then covered the cockhead with his lips.

No sooner had Adam taken Lance than there was a loud crash in the thickets. Adam pulled away quickly. Both men stood up and froze. They looked at the thickets. There was no other sound. They saw nothing but the brush.

Finally Adam asked, "What was that?"

"I don't know. Sounded like a branch hitting something."

"I hope it wasn't somebody."

"Who would it be?"

"A field hand wanting a swim. Or maybe it was just a deer needing a drink."

"Let's hope it was just a deer. I wouldn't want a field hand, or anyone for that matter, seeing me down on your sex," Adam said.

"Nor I."

By now their cocks hung limp.

"Let's just take another swim and head back. Hannah will be angry if we are too late for supper," Adam said.

By the time they reached the kitchen they were sweating again. The air was still and muggy. Hannah's greeting to them was "It's goin' to be some storm soon. Then things will cool off. It's not good for it to be so hot so early in the year." The house servants had eaten and gone back to their evening chores. Only Gregory was at the table.

"Where's Matt?" Adam asked.

"Don't know," Gregory answered him.

"Maybe he decided to take off early for Williamsburg," Lance suggested.

"I doubt that. He still wants his freedom money. All of it, not just half," Gregory responded and chuckled.

Adam and Lance did not know what to make of Gregory's reply. But Gregory was not in a talkative mood, so the three of them ate their supper without saying much. Several times though Adam and Lance were aware that Gregory was looking at them in a strange way. However, neither said anything about it. When they had finished eating, they all said good night to each other and to Hannah.

Once outside the kitchen, Adam turned to Lance and asked, "What was wrong with Gregory? Did you see how he was looking at us?"

"I guess he was just in one of his moods. It's not worth our time trying to figure that man out."

"You're right there," Adam agreed.

"Adam, I'm going back to the shop for a spell. I didn't get much done this afternoon before we left for the swim. I have a couple of little chores to tidy up. I'll only be a few minutes."

"I'm going to the privy and back to quarters," Adam said

Each went his way. After Adam had relieved himself, he stepped out into the muggy air again. *I sure hope Hannah is right about things cooling off. It is going to storm, too. The damn air seems like it is just waiting to explode,* he thought to himself. As he started back to their quarters, he was startled when Matt stepped from behind the privy and stood blocking his path. Matt had a strange smirk on his face.

"Evening, Matt. You surprised me. We missed you at supper."

"Did you now."

Adam didn't think Matt was asking a question. He said nothing.

"I'd like a word with you, Adam. I'm leaving in two days; now seems the best time."

"What is it, Matt?"

"A private matter."

Adam hesitated, then said, "We can go to my quarters."

"No. It's better just you and me."

Rain started to fall.

"The storm is coming," Adam said.

"That's not all. We needn't get drenched out here while we talk. Run for the stable barn."

Adam sensed that something was wrong, but he replied, "Yes, let's run."

Adam and Matt ran quickly to the stable barn in the heavy rain. Their shirts and breeches were wet. Several of the horses whinnied at the sudden intrusion.

At his workshop Lance had gone to the door to look at the rain. Then he saw Adam and Matt running to the stable barn. *What's all that about?* he wondered. *I'll finish up and go see.* He went back to his workbench.

Inside the barn Adam and Matt shook the water from their shirts and rubbed their breeches.

"Perhaps now it will get cooler," Adam said. "What did you want to say to me, Matt?" Then he realized that Matt had the same strange expression on his face that Gregory had at supper. Only Matt's was also ugly.

"Speak up, Matt, or I'm leaving."

"Not before you pleasure me, you're not."

Adam was stunned. But after a few seconds he blurted out, "I don't know what you mean."

"Like hell, you don't, you filthy sodomite."

Adam looked toward the barn door. Matt stepped in front of him.

"You're not going anywhere, Adam, except down on your knees pleasuring my cock."

"Matt, I don't know what makes you think I'd do that. I'm not bent that way. So if that's what you wanted to say to me, I'm leaving now."

"You did it to Lance down at the river. That's how I know you do that."

The heavy rain beat on the roof of the stable barn, accompanied by loud claps of thunder. Adam winced and shut his eyes. *So that's what that noise was,* Adam realized. He opened his eyes and looked at Matt. Matt still had the same ugly smirk on his face.

"Do you also bugger each other? Hell, of course, you do."

Adam said nothing. A dozen different thoughts raced through his mind. Thoughts from denying it all to those of fighting. Finally Adam clenched his fists and said in a low firm voice, "Yes, I am that way. But Lance isn't. He just lets me do it whenever he needs relief."

Matt looked at Adam as if he didn't know quite what to say. Suddenly Adam felt he was in command.

"What if I don't pleasure you?"

The angry look returned to Matt's face. In a voice to match the look on his face, Matt snarled, "I'll go to Mr. Ashley. It's his evening to work in his library. I'll tell him that he has two sodomites working for him. He will have you both punished. Since your bedfellow is a king's prisoner, a bloody convict, he'll be hanged for sure. And good riddance of that bastard."

Adam suddenly recalled what Lance once said about Matt's hatred of him. He was right.

"And what if I do pleasure you?"

Matt grinned. "That will be it," he said. "We'll each just go our own ways."

Both men stood, waiting for the other to speak.

"No," Matt said, "that's not all. I want a pair of new boots. You can get them for me from Lance's shop."

"I'm no thief."

"Just call my new boots and my getting pleasured a part of my freedom papers."

"I pleasure you, and you don't say anything? Right?"

"That's what I said. And I get my boots."

"You'll get your damn boots." Adam took a long deep breath and said, "Lower your breeches, Matt."

As Matt fumbled with his breeches, Adam shut his eyes as his mind whirled. He wasn't sure he trusted Matt to keep his word. He wanted to talk with Lance. Together they might find a way to avoid Mr. Ashley's learning about them. *I'd best humor Matt now though. Make him enjoy my pleasuring him. Even promise him another before he leaves if he wants it.*

"Are you going to do it, or are you just going to stand there praying I'll disappear?" Matt asked and laughed.

Adam opened his eyes. Matt's cock was erect. It was the largest Adam had ever seen. It was thicker than Lance's and longer than his own. The foreskin was pulled back tight on the long pole.

*Now or never,* Adam told himself. He took Matt's large bulb of a cockhead in his mouth. His lips and tongue caressed the smooth skin. Matt's sighs were a hum of delight. Soon Matt was moving his hips to thrust his cock further down Adam's throat.

Neither of them heard Lance enter the stable barn.

"What the hell! What are you doing, Adam?" Lance shouted and hurled Adam away from Matt's body.

"You bastard," Lance yelled at Matt and lunged at him, pushing him to the sawdust ground of the barn. "Pull up your breeches, and I'll give you a thrashing."

"No, Lance, go away," Adam cried out.

Quickly Matt adjusted his breeches and rushed toward Lance, fists clenched to strike. Adam got between the two men and pushed against their chests.

"Get out of my way, Adam," Lance shouted and gave him a shove. Matt gave Adam a much harder blow and sent him on his back. His head hit the corner of a stall. Things turned black. The disturbance sent the horses into a fit of whinnying.

Joseph and his wife Agnes were still sitting at the kitchen table. Agnes was nursing her latest baby. The noise from the stable barn reached the kitchen. Joseph stood up quickly. "What's going on?" he exclaimed. He grabbed his rifle from the rack on the wall and ran out of the room.

What Joseph saw in the stable barn shocked him. Adam was rubbing his eyes and stumbling to his feet. He seemed to be crying. On the ground Matt straddled Lance, pinning him with a tight hold. Both had bloody faces. Matt's hand was firmly around Lance's throat. Lance's feet were flaying the air in desperation. Joseph quickly pulled Matt over Lance and hurled him backward.

The rain on the roof stopped. A breath of cool air came in through the door Joseph had left open. For a long minute the four men formed a silent tableau.

Then Joseph broke the silence and said, "Go calm the horses, Adam. And you two stay where you are." Joseph went to help Adam rub the necks of the excited horses. Lance and Matt glared at each other for a few minutes, before they turned and walked in opposite directions. Lance found a water bucket and cleaned his bruised face. He took off his shirt to wipe himself dry.

Once the horses had been calmed, Joseph called to the three young men. "Now come here and give me an explanation for all this nonsense."

The three young men gathered around Joseph, but none of them spoke. Lance didn't want to say what Adam had been doing that caused the fight between Matt and him. Matt didn't want to admit that he had asked to be pleasured. And Adam was ashamed to tell Joseph that he taken Matt's cock in his mouth.

Finally though Adam started to say, "Joseph, I was . . ."

"Shut up," Matt interrupted. "I don't want to hear your lies, you filthy—liar."

"Then you explain, Matt," Joseph demanded. "And I hope you have done nothing to jeopardize your freedom papers."

Matt hesitated. Avoiding looking at Adam and Lance, Matt spoke directly to Joseph. "I had gone to the privy after I left from supper. When I came out these two accosted me and said they would like a word with me. Since it was starting to rain, we came here. I shouldn't have come, for I have known for a long time that Adam and Lance do not like me. Adam said something to me which I found indecent, and I told him to shut his mouth. Then Lance started a fight with me. I was about to get the best of the fight when you came in."

"And that's all?" Joseph asked.

"That's all. They started the fight."

Joseph turned to Adam. "Did you say something indecent to Matt?"

"No, I didn't."

Joseph looked first at Adam and then at Matt. Turning to Lance, he asked, "Anything to say?"

"No."

Joseph chuckled. "I don't think I am getting the true version of what happened. Shall we all just go and get ready for bed and leave the horses in peace?"

"No, I'm going to Mr. Ashley," Matt said.

"Why?" Joseph asked.

"I have something to tell him about these two."

Joseph looked at Adam and Lance. He was sure that Adam's lips were quivering. Turning squarely to Matt, he said in a firm voice, "I doubt you will tell Mr. Ashley anything about Adam and Lance that he does not already know."

Both Adam and Lance were surprised. They glanced quickly at each other, with the same question on their minds: *Does Mr. Ashley know that we lie together and make love?*

"Maybe, and maybe not," Matt retorted.

"I think I shall go with you, Matt. I, too, have something to tell Mr. Ashley."

"About Adam and Lance?" Matt asked.

"No. Something about you. Something that will keep you from getting your freedom papers day after tomorrow."

"And just what is that?" Matt snarled.

"Surely you haven't forgotten. Think back a little over a year ago when I found you here in this barn. You were plowing that black girl so hard that neither of you heard me come in. I sent her packing. I told you I would forget the incident, despite the fact that you had broken a colony law about white men having intercourse with black women. I have kept my word. But if you go spreading ugly talk or lies about Adam and Lance, I'll tell Mr. Ashley my story."

"Damn you," Matt shouted at Joseph. He picked at the dried blood on his nose. "I hope I never see any of you again. I'll be glad to leave this damn place." He paused and grinned, "If I do see you again, Adam, remember that we have a bit of unfinished business."

No one spoke, and Matt turned and walked away. The air within the stable barn was much cooler now. The freak storm had blown past the Tidewater over the hills and into the colony's frontier.

"Thank you, Joseph," Adam said.

"I don't know what caused the commotion tonight, and I don't want to know. But don't repeat what I said about Matt to anyone. He will be gone soon, and he won't be missed."

Both Adam and Lance nodded.

"My throat hurts. I need to get some sleep," Lance said.

"Let's get to quarters, Lance," Adam said. He turned to Joseph, who was watching the two of them, and said with a smile on his face, "Thank you again, Joseph."

Joseph returned the smile and nodded.

The three of them said good night. As they left for their quarters, Lance clasped Adam around the waist and whispered, "You've got a lot of explaining to do."

"If Matt hasn't deafened you with blows on your ears, you have a lot of listening to do," Adam replied. He grabbed Lance's hand and squeezed it hard.

# 1753: Williamsburg

No one could believe it; everyone was puzzled. It was late July, and the weather was still like that of late spring. Ordinarily in two weeks the tobacco stalks would need cutting for hanging in the drying sheds. But Mr. Ashley and the overseer for the tobacco fields wondered if the cutting shouldn't be delayed for several weeks.

Fortunately tobacco was not the major cash crop for Ashley Landing now. Grain and corn brought in more money. Since Mr. Ashley had been practicing crop rotation for several years, his extensive land holdings were still arable. Mr. Ashley had tried hard to convince his Tidewater neighbors that the constant planting of tobacco was exhausting the soil. Until recently though his comments had been met only with patronizing smiles. The prosperity of Ashley Landing had brought about second thoughts.

"Let's wait another ten days," Mr. Ashley told his overseer. "Then we'll cut and set it to dry just before we go off to the fair." The overseer nodded agreement. He, too, thought that waiting was better.

During the unusual late July summer days, both Adam and Lance abandoned their full day's work in the warehouse and the shop. Instead they shed their shirts, rolled up their breeches, and worked in the large azalea and rhododendron garden that Madame Ashley was nurturing. Working together, they cultivated the ground, carried buckets of water from the well to drench the areas around the main stalks, and hauled wheelbarrow loads of wood chips from the carpentry shop to mulch the ground around the young plants. Tiny beads of sweat dotted their foreheads, and from their armpits trickles of sweat ran down their muscled bodies, now tanned by the afternoon sun. At the end of the workday and before supper, Adam and Lance went to the bend in the river to refresh themselves with a swim. The water was cool, even a bit chilly in the deep part out in the middle of the river.

doi:10.1300/5623_07

The swim always left them hungry for the light supper Hannah had waiting at their return.

Over a year had passed since the incident in the stable barn with Matt. Matt left Ashley Landing without telling Mr. Ashley about the scene between Adam and Lance he had witnessed at the river. And if Joseph suspected that more had happened among the three young men than he knew about, he let the matter drop as none of his business. He was glad to have Matt gone, and very glad to have Adam and Lance still at the plantation. In a strange way the incident in the stable barn brought Adam and Lance even closer together. Lance's anger at first seeing Adam's mouth around Matt's cock quickly disappeared after he knew how Adam was trying to protect them against exposure and probably the end of their lives together.

"If only I had been there," Lance exclaimed.

"But you weren't. I'm just glad you were outside the shop and saw Matt and me going for the barn door in all that rain. I'm not sure just what the two of us could have done even if you had been there."

"I would have killed the bastard."

Adam kissed Lance and said softly, "Then where would your quick temper have landed us?"

Lance sighed, returned the kiss, and said, "So right you are. It's better this way."

"But we do have to be more careful from now on, Lance."

"Yes. And I must guard against my quick temper."

Adam and Lance kept on swimming at the bend in the river, and they kept on having sex after their swims. But they soon found a much safer place to suck each other and to cornhole than on the open beach. One afternoon a young deer showed them where the dense thicket gave way to a small sheltered spot of ferns. Here only a few birds disturbed their lovemaking.

Perhaps it was the unusual July weather, but when they lay down naked this afternoon among the ferns, Lance suddenly recalled the barn stable. He raised up and stared down at Adam. "Did you like sucking Matt's cock?" he asked.

Surprised, Adam returned the stare. Then he exclaimed, "What kind of question is that?"

"Adam, I'm just curious. Did you like sucking Matt, even when you really didn't want to be doing it?"

Adam pulled Lance into a tight embrace. "Well," he said, "Matt did have the biggest cock I have ever seen, not that I've seen all that many. He was much thicker than you are, and he was much longer than I am. I guess, looking back, I was a bit excited even though most of me was angry with rebellion. Does it bother you that I say that?"

"No. I suspect I would have felt the same way." Lance paused and then said, "I wonder if someday it will be possible for us to have sex together with another man. Someone we both like, but someone who will not come between our love for each other. Someone whose body we can both explore and enjoy, and someone who can enjoy each of us without falling in love with either of us. Do you think that is possible?"

Adam lay on his back for a long time. Then he said, "Yes, I think both of us would enjoy such play with a third man. It would not change my love for you. But hadn't you better turn me over and ram your thick cock up my butt and forget about someone else being here with us?"

Lance laughed loudly. He turned Adam over and pressed his swollen cock against Adam. They made love for a long time before they walked back to Hannah's kitchen.

The next day the weather changed. Overnight it went from late spring to midsummer. When Mr. Ashley and the tobacco overseer met, Mr. Ashley said, "Our timing is just right. Get the hands ready for the cutting a week from today." After cleaning up from the large midday meal, Hannah went outside the kitchen and called out, "Thank ya, Lord. You is doin' it right now." The late afternoon swim felt better to Adam and Lance than it had anytime earlier in the summer. Every day for the next week the weather got warmer and warmer. As Hannah had said, the weather was "doin it right."

The first week in August the tobacco cutting began. Both Adam and Lance left their usual activities and helped. Lance went with the tobacco overseer to the fields up river and inland. He helped supervise the cutting and stacking for loading the bound sheaves on the flatboats. At night Lance slept on a pallet on the porch of the overseer's three-room house. He went to his bed tired every night for ten days. He missed having Adam's body next to his, but he quickly fell asleep, knowing the cutting would start again after sunrise the next morning. At Ashley Landing Adam supervised the unloading of the riverboats, keeping count of the number of sheaves for his warehouse records. He, too, missed his usual bed partner. When word came that the loading up river was all but completed, Adam went with Mr. Ashley to the tobacco fields. Mr. Ashley wanted not only to inspect the fields but also to thank his slaves for their hard work. Adam accompanied Mr. Ashley more or less as a holiday to celebrate the bringing of the last riverboat of tobacco to the drying sheds at Ashley Landing. He shared Lance's pallet that night. But, as they lay down for the night, Lance whispered, "We take no chances, Adam. We must wait until we are back at quarters. Try to go to sleep now." It was hard to keep their hands from straying after such a long time apart, but both turned over, so that their butts touched only slightly, and went to sleep.

Two days after their return to Ashley Landing, when he was nearly ready to go to Lance's shop and pry him away from work for their walk to the bend in the river, Adam heard young William Ashley shouting in a shrill voice as he ran toward the warehouse. Adam knelt down. He opened his arms and caught his young visitor.

"Now what is all this about?" Adam asked.

"We are going to Williamsburg," Will announced in a voice that suggested he was making the most important statement of his life.

"And what are you going to do there?"

"We are going to the fair," Will said, breaking away from Adam's arms and looking at him with a grin that said he had even more to tell.

"That should be fun for you," Adam said and smiled.

"Oh, you are going, too. You and Lance."

Adam did not know whether to believe young Will or not. Mr. Ashley had said nothing about Lance and him going to the fair. He guessed that Will had simply misunderstood something that had been said at the dinner table of the great house.

"I doubt that, Will," Adam finally said.

Will stamped his foot and replied, "Yes, you are. Just ask Papa."

Adam looked and saw Mr. Ashley approaching. He was shaking his head and wagging his finger at his young son.

"I see Little Mister Big Ears has beat me here with my news," Mr. Ashley said.

"I told you so, Adam. He wouldn't believe me, Papa," Will said.

"As well Adam shouldn't believe everything he hears from little mouths. And, Will, you must be more careful about repeating what you hear—or think you hear—at the dinner table between your mama and me."

"I'm sorry, Papa," Will said, biting his lip.

"It's all forgotten now," Mr. Ashley said and hugged his son. "Yes, Adam, I have arranged for you and Lance to go to the fair for two days and two nights. You'll accompany Madam Ashley, the children, and me on the boat down to Williamsburg. But I'm afraid you will have to walk the long back trail home. When you return here, Joseph and his family will come to Williamsburg for their short holiday. While you and Lance are gone, Joseph will look after things here. You will do the same when he leaves."

"Thank you, Mr. Ashley," Adam said. "I've never been to Williamsburg. I'm truly surprised, and I am delighted. I hope I know how to act there so that I will not be a disgrace to Ashley Landing."

"You will be the kind of young man there that you are here," Mr. Ashley assured Adam.

"There will be horse races, and all sorts of contests and games to see who wins," Will chimed in.

"And plays. A troupe from London is touring the colonies. I will see that you and Lance have seats, Adam," Mr. Ashley said.

"May I go, too?" Will asked.

"There will be puppet shows for you but not plays," his father said. "You need to be a bit older for *The Merchant of Venice*. You will find the puppet shows much more fun. Perhaps if you ask properly, Adam and Lance will take you to one of the morning puppet shows."

"Will you please, Adam?"

"Of course, Will, if your mother and father say it is proper."

Mr. Ashley nodded a yes, and Will danced around the warehouse. "I'm going to a puppet show" he kept singing in his boyish voice.

Suddenly Adam furrowed his brow. "Mr. Ashley," he said, "will it be safe for me and Lance, as indentured servants, to be free to walk the streets in Williamsburg?"

"Don't worry about that, Adam. I will give each of you a slip of permission, dated for the days you are there and signed by me. If you should need me, we will be staying with the George Wythe family. Their large brick house faces the Palace Green. You would have no trouble finding it. I'll make arrangements for you to bed at the Widow Larson's rooming house on Henry Street on the edge of town. She will also provide you breakfast and supper. I'll see that you have pocket money to buy sweets and cider at the booths set up around the capitol."

"And slices of roast pig?" Will added.

"I'm sure there will be, and enough other delicacies to trouble young stomachs," his father said. "Now run back to the house, Will. I have something I must speak to Adam about," Mr. Ashley said and patted the lad's head.

"Not for little ears, I guess," Will said and grinned.

Mr. Ashley and Adam waited and watched until young Will opened the front door of the great house and waved back at them. Then Mr. Ashley turned to Adam and said, "Adam, I heard your concern about your walking the streets of Williamsburg. Let me speak to you frankly."

"Do, sir."

"Let me begin by saying that I wish you and Lance a happy two-day holiday. And thank you for taking Will to a puppet show."

"I probably will be more eyes than Will at the puppet show," Adam replied.

"If so, you will be even more attentive when Portia confronts the Jew."

Adam did not understand and so said nothing.

Mr. Ashley looked steadily at Adam and said, "I have no qualms about you and Lance going to Williamsburg. Neither of you will invite trouble. Still, I have three prohibitions you must accept."

"They are?" Adam asked.

"First, you and Lance must stay out of the taverns. My permission slip will be worthless there. Drink the cider at the booths. But nowhere touch spirits."

"You have my word, and Lance's, on that, sir," Adam said.

Mr. Ashley nodded. Then he said, "Adam, you are in no danger in Williamsburg. Lance could be. He is still a king's prisoner even though I own him now. My permission slip will be worth nothing if he violates the laws of the city. Make sure he controls his quick temper."

"I will, believe me," Adam replied. "And your second prohibition?"

"It concerns Lance. Keep him away from John Thomas, his former owner."

"That should be easy. We simply will not go near the cordwainer's shop."

"It will not be that easy. I know that Thomas has lost his shop. It's now owned by the cordwainer who came to Williamsburg several years ago. I don't know, however, what happened to Thomas. He may be working for the new owner of the shop. He may not. But whatever, I do not want Lance to meet Thomas. Lance may believe he has put the mistreatment at the cordwainer's shop behind him. But I would not want to have that belief tested should the two of them meet."

"Nor do I want them to meet," Adam answered. "But I know that Lance felt strongly about a young apprentice in Thomas's shop. He often befriended him against Thomas's curses and blows. Lance will want to see Timothy again."

"Then you, Adam, and only you, must go into the shop and inquire after the lad. If Lance and he are to meet, it must be through your arrangement."

Adam wondered how he could make such an arrangement, for he knew Lance would want to see Timothy again. And Adam shared Mr. Ashley's fear about what would happen should Lance and Thomas meet. Somehow though he knew he could find a way for Lance to see Timothy without meeting Thomas.

"And the third request you have of us?" Adam asked finally.

Mr. Ashley blushed slightly and rubbed his lips and chin. Then he said, "After the bonfires are lit in the evening, there will be women about."

Adam waited for Mr. Ashley to say more; when he didn't, Adam said, "So?"

"Loose women, Adam. Women all too ready with an invitation for young men to lift their petticoats. You and Lance must restrain yourselves. As you know, sexual intercourse outside of marriage is prohibited to indentured servants."

Adam almost burst out laughing but didn't. Still, an amused smile erupted across his handsome face. "Again, Mr. Ashley, I promise you that you have no need to worry."

Mr. Ashley seemed at a loss as to what to say next.

Adam helped him out. "Neither I nor Lance is a virgin, Mr. Ashley. However, we have not been with a woman since we came to the colony. Sometimes it has been hard, but we have managed. And, to be honest, I have on occasion handled myself. I suspect Lance has done the same."

Mr. Ashley smiled and said, "I did the same before I was married, so I do not fault you there. Sometimes I even wonder if the biblical injunction against men lying with other men isn't very foolish."

The statement took Adam by complete surprise. He did not want to pursue the topic, and he certainly did not want to make a confession of his love for Lance to Mr. Ashley. He quickly returned to Mr. Ashley's third prohibition.

"Mr. Ashley," Adam said, "let me repeat myself. You have no need to worry about Lance's and my behavior after the bonfires are lit."

"I trust your word, Adam."

Adam sensed that Mr. Ashley would welcome a change in the conversation away from men's sexual activities. "Will there be balls for you and Madam Ashley to attend?" he asked.

Mr. Ashley appreciated Adam's question and quickly replied, "Yes. Probably more than I shall want to attend. I fear, Adam, I am more at ease on a horse than on the ballroom floor."

"You sound like you are glad the fair comes only once a year," Adam said with a grin.

"True, Adam. But I am glad for the holiday for Madam Ashley and the children. All of life must not become tobacco cutting." He paused and then said, "Oh, please tell Lance that Madam Ashley will wear the dancing shoes he made for her at the Palace Ball. And our eldest daughter will wear hers at a special cotillion for young women coming of age. Thank him, and I shall thank him again when I next see him."

Two hours later Adam and Lance lay naked in the den of ferns near the bend in the river. Adam had not told Lance the news either on the walk to the river or during their swim. Still Lance knew Adam well enough to know that he was excited about something.

"What's causing that crazy bounce in your butt?" Lance had called to Adam as he followed him down the trail to the river.

"You'll find out," Adam teased and walked out of Lance's hearing distance.

Once in the water, they raced to the other bank and back. Lance won.

"I'm a bad loser," Adam cried out, pretending to pout. "Maybe I just won't tell you about my bouncy butt," Adam said. He had splashed the winner of the race with handfuls of water.

In their den after several long kisses, Adam told Lance about the conversation that afternoon with Mr. Ashley. Then Lance flooded Adam with answers to questions.

"Of course, I want to see Timothy."—"No, I don't want to run into Thomas, that bastard."—"Yes, I will control my temper. But you must find a way for me to see Timothy again."—"Umm, perhaps he is the one we should have as a third man in bed."—"No, I hope he now has a life of his own, just as we have."—"I can hardly believe that Mr. Ashley told you that he once pleasured himself. I guess all men do."— "Like you, Adam, I have no idea what he meant by saying that the biblical injunction was foolish."—"I agree, we must still keep our love for each other secret."—"Yes, I am happy about our two days in Williamsburg. I shall be your guide to the city."—"No, I won't give in to the women at the bonfire. Will you?"—"I didn't think so."— "Why should I want spirits? Not when your lips feel so good down there. That's better than any spirits."

Lance lay back and announced, "I am ready for Williamsburg."

Adam replied, "And so am I."

On the morning of the first day of the fair the landing at the river that served Williamsburg was a busy place. People arrived in all sorts of boats, some from down river at Hampton, but most from the Tidewater up river. Among the several waiting carriages was one for the Ashley family from their hosts, the Wythes. Like most people though, Adam and Lance walked the trail from the landing to the city. At Mr. Ashley's request, the two young men had gone first to the Widow Larson's to introduce themselves, leave their bundles, and give her a letter of payment. "It's always a pleasure to accommodate the fine young men who are Mr. Ashley's servants," the widow had said. Adam suspected that it was the contents of the letter which more pleased the widow. Adam did notice, however, that the widow's eyes lingered over both his and Lance's crotch. *Best look to other guests,* Adam thought.

Once accommodations arrangements were completed, Adam turned to Lance and said, "Walk me the city." For their walk west through the city, Lance decided to go down Francis Street instead of the main thoroughfare. Their return would be down Duke of Gloucester with its multitude of shops, offices, taverns as well as houses.

For Adam—never having experienced anything other than his parents' hovel, the grandeur of Cromley Hall, only the briefest glimpse of London on the way to the ship, the busy wharf at Hampton, and then Ashley Landing—Williamsburg was a new world. It was more cluttered, much more noisy than Ashley Landing. At first it was more exciting, but only because it was new to him. It had its own kind of vitality, different from, but certainly not better than, that at Ashley Landing. What Adam most noticed was how crowded Francis Street seemed. Even though each house had a parcel of ground around it large enough for a big garden and several out-buildings, the houses seemed to Adam too close together. "No room for privacy," he said to himself. "There's land and wildlife at Ashley Landing; here it's too many people and animals in too small a space." Still Adam was enjoying himself, and Lance delighted in playing guide.

More than a dozen times during their first hours in the city, Lance tugged at Adam's shirt sleeve and whispered, "Don't stare so hard, Adam. People probably already know we are strangers. But we don't have to put on purple dunce caps to flag it. Besides I don't want people looking at me and suddenly recognizing who I am."

"You're right. Sorry. I know though why little Will was so excited."

"When do we take him to the puppet show?"

"Late tomorrow morning," Adam replied. "And we see that play in the afternoon. Mr. Ashley said there would be benches at the back for us. He gave me money for us to get in. I've never seen a play before. I don't know what it will be like."

"Like the first time you got cornholed," Lance teased.

"Maybe. But it will be different. In its way I know it will be just as good."

"Nor have I seen a play. But I have watched men go to the playhouses in London." He paused and chuckled. "Many a time, Adam, there was a quick one with some of those gentleman before they went inside."

"There's more to your life in London than you have told me, Lance."

"Nothing worth the telling, Adam." He leaned over and in the shade of a big elm in the yard of William and Mary College, Lance kissed Adam lightly on the lips.

"Now who's being careless and wearing the dunce's cap? But I did like what you did." Adam looked around. They were alone in the college yard. He returned the kiss. Then he said, "Let's head in the other direction now."

As they passed the gates of the college and looked east down the broad, busy street, Lance asked, "How soon are you going to inquire after Timothy?"

"I think this afternoon."

"I will point out the shop as we pass it. But don't go in then. I want us to go on to the capitol and then to the gaol and that damn pillory where Mr. Ashley found me."

"I'm not sure I want to see the pillory."

"Well, Adam, you've had to look at the scars on my back all this time, you might as well see the place where I got the blows."

"Do you want to see it, Lance?"

"Yes, I think I do. Just so I can be even more thankful for how bloody lucky I've been since that time."

As they walked down Duke of Gloucester Street they became part of the crowd of people. Booths displaying every sort of ware or edible had been set up both in the Market Square and on the other side of the street in the large area around the Magazine. Adam had never been in such a crowd. Everyone was in the best of spirits. Shouts blended with laughter. Adam jostled elbows. He bumped shoulders and excused himself. He smiled at people he had never seen before and would never see again. He laughed as wives steered their husbands away from pretty young women. He was amused at the young children tugging at their parents to buy a sweet or a toy. Certainly it was not the warehouse at Ashley Landing. Much though he was enjoying himself, Adam was thankful that he would return to another kind of life after his holiday at the fair.

Occasionally Adam saw Lance's body tighten as a young man passed them, who stopped and turned back to look as if he somehow recognized an acquaintance, before he finally went on his way. Suddenly Adam wondered if being in Williamsburg was as much fun for Lance as it was for him. Was being here bringing back the memory of too many bad experiences? Or was Lance apprehensive about the possibility of meeting a young man to whom he had been attracted, perhaps even had sex with? Whichever it was, Adam did not want Lance to be unhappy or worried. Surely his new life at Ashley Landing had blotted out all but the deepest dark moments of his life in Williamsburg. And if there were a lingering affection for Timothy, Adam could accept that. Much though he loved Lance, he did not own him. Nor did his intense love for Lance give him the freedom to pry into Lance's most private self.

With thoughts like these, Adam saw and admired the capitol and bumped about in the crowd at the booths set up on the Exchange. He even ate with relish the slice of roast pig on corn bread which Lance handed him. Then, as he was wiping the grease from his hands on the seat of his breeches, Lance motioned to him and said, "Time to go."

It was only a short walk to the gaol and pillory. Adam was shocked at the complete contrast to the scene they had just left at the Exchange. No booths, no crowds here. As far as Adam could tell, he and Lance were the only people around. It was as if the city authorities had set aside this ground to remind merrymakers that they should not get out of hand. Adam followed Lance as he walked slowly around the pillory. Then, suddenly, Lance raised his hands in the air, his fists clenched, and shouted, "To hell with you."

Quickly Adam gathered Lance into his arms, not caring if anyone was close by and saw them. "Let's get away from here, Lance. All that is past."

"Adam, please go on to the shop now. If possible, I want to find what was good in my life here."

When the sign of the cordwainer's shop came into view, Lance pulled at Adam's shirt sleeve, and they stopped. "You go on the shop. I'll turn down here," he said, motioning to the side street. "I'll be somewhere down there waiting for you."

The two young men looked hard into each other's eyes. Finally Adam said, "I'll do my best. I only hope I do not run into Thomas." Lance puckered his lips into a kiss and walked away, down the side street.

The top half of the door to the shop was open. Adam lifted the latch and entered the large room. From their benches, two men looked up at him. One of the men was about Adam's age. The other was a sturdy, handsome younger man. Adam wondered if he were Timothy. The older man rose from his bench and walked toward Adam. "Good afternoon," he said in a pleasant voice, "What may I do for you?"

"Good afternoon," Adam replied. "Is Master John Thomas about?"

"No," the man before him snapped.

"Does he no longer own this shop?" Adam asked. Adam, of course, knew from Mr. Ashley that Thomas no longer owned the shop, but he did not know whether Thomas had stayed in the shop as a worker.

"You must be a visitor in Williamsburg, if you ask that question. No, he does not own this shop now, nor does he work here."

Adam was relieved to hear that Thomas was not in the shop. Just as he was about to speak again, the older man interrupted him, asking, "Why do you wish to see Thomas?"

"I don't really want to see him. I'm Adam Bradley, an indentured servant at Ashley Landing." He extended his hand.

The younger man put down the shoe he was working on, and looked up inquiring at Adam.

"I'm Alan Tisdale," the older man replied and shook Adam's hand. "What is it you want here, if you are not asking for Thomas?"

"I'm looking for a young man named Timothy. I am a friend of Lance Morley, who also is at Ashley Landing. Lance knew Timothy when they both were in the shop several years ago."

"I'm Timothy. Where's Lance now?" the younger man cried out, jumping up from his bench.

"He's down the street," Adam told him.

Timothy bolted out the door, but quickly returned. "Down which street? he asked breathlessly, his face all smiles.

Alan looked at Adam and Timothy and laughed. "Tell him quickly, Adam, or he'll burst a seam."

"He's somewhere on the first side street to the right going towards the Exchange," Adam said.

"I'll find him," Timothy yelled back at the doorway.

"And bring him back here, Tim," Alan called.

Alan then turned to Adam and smiled. "You might just as well sit down, Adam. It will be a while before Tim brings your friend back here, even if they have now already met. You and I can get acquainted, while those two are catching up with news about each other and plying each other with questions."

"I suspect you are right there," Adam said. Adam wondered how much Alan knew about what had happened between Lance and Timothy.

"Let me put my work away for the day, and we can go in the yard in the back and enjoy the fresh air. It's time to start my holiday. A cup of cider for you?"

Alan was right. It was a long time before Timothy and Lance came to the shop. For the two hours while Alan and Adam waited, they sat on benches behind the shop and talked. Alan placed a large bowl of unshelled peanuts between them to go along with the cider. A mixed-breed dog rested her head on Alan's foot. One of the first questions Adam asked was, "Do you own the shop?"

"No, my father does. He bought it about a year after we arrived here from England. Thomas was heavily in debt, and drinking too much. He was glad to get the money my father offered him. Tim was still in his apprenticeship; and, since we liked both him and his work, we kept him on."

"So your father owns the two cordwainer shops in Williamsburg?"

"Yes, he and my two brothers are in the shop down the street close to the capitol. Tim and I are here. But the two shops are not in competition. Actually we do more of the making here."

"What has happened to Thomas?"

"When he is sober, he works as a handyman, mainly carpentry. But it's his wife who keeps the larder stocked. She is an excellent seamstress."

"As you can guess, Lance's stories about Thomas have not made me like the man very much."

"You are not alone there. In fact, not too many people now think Lance was to blame in striking Thomas. I doubt now that anyone thinks Lance wanted to murder Thomas, as Thomas claimed in court. Quite a change from that afternoon when people were clamoring for Lance to be whipped to death. My family didn't know what to think back then. We barely knew Thomas, and we had never met Lance. Tim must have been the only friend Lance had at that time."

"Yes, he was an especially good friend. But let's forget about Thomas. Tell me, Alan, would you and Timothy like to own this shop someday?"

Alan did not reply. He took a couple of peanuts from the bowl, cracked the shells, and popped the meats into his mouth. He washed them down with a long sip of cider.

"Sorry if my question was impertinent," Adam said.

"No, you weren't impertinent. You only asked the question that Tim and I wrestled with a few months ago."

"What did you decide?"

"We are leaving Williamsburg this fall."

It was not the answer Adam expected. His head jerked, and then he said, "Where will you go?"

"To the hills. Then over the hills to the land beyond."

"What will you do there?"

"Make shoes for the folks who are building new communities far away from the Tidewater. We will have no trouble keeping food in our mouths and shirts on our backs."

Adam thought for a moment, then said, "But aren't you giving up the known for the unknown?"

"In some ways, yes. In other ways, no."

"How so?"

"We do not know the land beyond the hills. We do know that it will not have the fancy carriages of the Williamsburg rich folks. That difference does not frighten us. It excites us. We will not know people there, but Tim and I do know each other. We both feel we will be happier there in the unknown territory than here where we do know the pressures."

"Pressures?" Adam did not understand.

Alan raised his foot. The dog looked up. "No, sweetheart," Alan said, "I'm only changing positions. My foot is going to sleep." Alan shifted his body, and the dog lay back down, her head against Alan's other foot.

"See, Adam, she adjusted to change. So will Tim and I."

"But what pressures are there against you here in Williamsburg?"

"I am twenty-four."

"I am a year less. So?" Adam demanded.

"Isn't it time that you were married? Even an indentured servant can get permission to marry. Shouldn't you be carrying babies to the altar to be baptized? Isn't there something unnatural about your still sharing quarters with another man your age?"

Overwhelmed by Alan's outburst, Adam sat dumb.

"Yes, that is the pressure I feel here in this known territory. Perhaps it will creep over the hills and into the land beyond. But it will not be—I am sure of it—before I am too old for it to matter."

Adam said nothing. He knew nothing of such pressures at Ashley Landing.

"Tim is still not old enough to feel such pressures. No one asks him yet when he intends to marry. Of course, mothers with eligible daughters eye him and make plans for his future. But whatever stirs in his breeches, he keeps from them. For me, it is different. My brothers are both married. Much though my parents love me, they still are bothered that I am a bachelor. What they do not understand is that it is against my nature to marry. What they do not understand is that Tim and I . . ." Suddenly Alan broke off his explanation, realizing he was revealing much more than he intended. He took another handful of peanuts and said, "Another cup of cider, Adam?" As Alan stood up, the dog stood up also.

"Please," Adam said.

When he reached for his second cup of cider, Adam's finger lightly grazed Alan's hand. Still Adam felt a warmth there, perhaps an invitation for both of them to say more. They sat still for several minutes, each of them looking at the dog who had so easily adjusted to her changed position on Alan's foot.

"Do you and Tim lie together?" Adam asked, about like he was asking for the time of day or the price of a pair of boots.

Alan leaned back and answered in a low voice, "Yes."

There was a brief pause, and then Adam said, "I thought so. I hoped so."

"And you and Lance?" Alan asked.

"Yes. Almost ever since he came to Ashley Landing."

Then both young men broke out in laughter, joining the holiday laughter outside on the street. They stood up and embraced briefly, but without any sexual contact.

When they sat down again, Alan said, "You are the first man to ask me that question."

"And I have never asked any man so directly."

Before they could go beyond their admissions, they heard the latch on the front door click and then the voices of Timothy and Lance.

"Where are you?" Timothy called.

"Back here," Alan answered.

"Come on, Lance," Timothy said. "Let's go tell them."

As soon as Timothy and Lance were in the yard in back, Timothy announced proudly, "We were all made in the same way. Bent in a different direction."

"We already know," Alan said calmly.

"You already know! How did you find out?" Timothy asked, surprised that the news he wanted to tell was not news at all.

"I asked him," Adam said.

"And I told him," Alan added.

"Well, I'll be damned. What a pair you two are," Lance exclaimed.

Then suddenly each young man gave a friendly hug to each of the other three men. When all was done, no one seemed to know what to say until Adam laughed and said, "Now that we all know, let's not sit around and talk about it. That would be like looking at each other's navels for the rest of the afternoon. Let's go out and join the crowd at the fair."

"Yes, let's," Timothy agreed. "The three-legged contest is going to begin soon. A couple of us should compete."

"A three-legged contest. If that's what it sounds like to me, then Adam has already won," Lance said and rubbed Adam's crotch.

Everyone laughed, except Adam, who blushed bright red. "Don't anyone go for a ruler. I'm not entering that contest."

"No, it's not that kind of third leg," Timothy said. "Although I suspect from what Lance has told me, you would have won handily."

"What a conversation you two had. No wonder it took you so long out there," Alan teased.

"Well, if it's not that, then what is a three-legged contest?" Lance asked.

"It's a race, four couples at a time. Then the winners of each race run against each other."

"That still doesn't tell me why it's a three-legged race," Adam said.

Alan explained. "The left leg of one man is tied fast to the right leg of his partner to make a third leg. Each man puts his arm around the other's waist. Then the four couples start out running for thirty yards."

Lance put his right leg forward and imagined it tied to his partner's left leg. He started to run. "That's easy enough," he proclaimed.

"You'll find out," Timothy said, slapping Lance on the back.

"Let me lock up the shop, and let's be off," Alan said.

On the walk to the Palace Green, Timothy walked with Adam, Alan with Lance. The young men asked questions about what they wanted to know from each other. Alan told Lance about the plans to go to the frontier soon. Lance responded by telling Alan about life at Ashley Landing. Timothy told Adam how hard it had been for him after Lance left the shop and how happy he was to discover that Alan, too, liked to lie with other men. Timothy said he would always have a strong affection for Lance, who had introduced him to sex with men, but that now his love was for Alan. Adam, in turn, told Timothy about how it had taken several months for him and Lance to learn about each other. Adam said he was happy that Timothy had found a lover. He hoped they would enjoy their life out of the Tidewater and that it would be a prosperous one. When they reached the Palace Green, they found the three-legged races already underway.

"Who's going to be partners?" Adam asked.

"Alan and Lance should be," Timothy said. "They are both the same height. It will be easier for them to hold on to each other. That's important."

"Fine with me," Lance said.

"Me, too," Alan added. "Let's go find one of the judges to strap us together."

Once they were tied together, Lance quickly discovered that even walking with his partner was much more difficult than he imagined earlier. "Hell, when we start to run, I'll fall flat on my face."

"Or your butt," Timothy told him.

"That's all to be expected. Most couples take at least one tumble. We'll just have to help each other up as best we can and then start running again," Alan said.

"Next couple," a judge called, pointing to Alan and Lance. They joined the three other three-legged couples at the starting line. "On your mark. Get set. Ready. Go!" shouted the judge.

Alan and Lance had gone only a few feet before they were on the ground. But, then, so were two other couples. Alan and Lance struggled to their feet and started off again. It was easier now. Still halfway up the course, they stumbled again.

"Damn," Lance cursed. "My fault."

"Hush about fault," Alan shouted at him. "Let's just get our butts off the ground."

Again they struggled, but finally got up. As they started off again, Lance heard a shrill voice calling, "Run, Lance, run. Win the race." Lance looked across the green and saw Will and his father among the crowd watching the race.

"Who is your young admirer?" Alan asked.

"Mr. Ashley's little son. I don't want to disappoint him. I think we are in stride now, Alan. Let's pick up some speed."

"Go, Lance," Alan said in a low voice. "Just pretend our tied-together third leg is really our third leg hanging down between the other two. Let's use it like we would the real one—pumping ass like hell."

Adam and Timothy, joined by Will and Mr. Ashley, were at the finish line to greet Alan and Lance as they came in several feet ahead of the couple behind them.

"You won, you won, I knew you would!" Will yelled excitedly.

"I don't know if I am happy or not," Lance said. "Now we will have to compete in the elimination races against the other winners. Can we get untied, or do we have to stay like this until we race again?"

"I'm afraid we are bound together until we drop out of the races," Alan said.

"But, at least, not until death do you part," Timothy whispered to Lance.

It wasn't long though before the elimination races got started. To their surprise, Lance and Alan won the next two races. They were sweating heavily by the time for the final race.

"If age has anything going for it, you two will be final winners," Mr. Ashley remarked.

Alan and Lance looked at the other winning couples. All of them were still in their late teens. "This one will be our hardest," Alan said. "It will take all we've got to race these young bloods."

Race they did. And they tried hard, not falling even once. But they came in third.

"I so wanted you to win, Lance," Will said sadly.

"Don't fret, Will. It's all been fun, and that's what matters. Just think of the fun we will have tomorrow at the puppet show," Lance consoled the young boy.

Shortly Mr. Ashley and Will said "good evening" to the four young men, after having made arrangements for Adam and Lance to come to the Wythe house to get Will the next morning.

"What now?" Timothy asked.

"I'm going to collapse," Lance announced.

"No, now it's your turn to watch others compete. There's horse-shoes down there, and wrestling over that way," Timothy told him.

For the next two hours the four young men watched other men try to outdo each other. None of them found horseshoes all that exciting, and whether it was the energy of the wrestling contests or the half-naked bodies of the sweaty young men which more attracted their attention, none of them would say.

"How would you like to wrestle with that one?" Lance whispered to Adam. He pointed to a tall, dark-haired, well-muscled young man with a chest covered with dark curls.

Before Adam could respond, Alan walked up to them. "If I can take your eyes off that young beauty for a minute, may I invite you to my father and mother's house for supper?"

"Thank you," Lance replied. "Are you sure though that we would not be barging in too unexpectedly to suit your mother?"

"Not at all. She will be delighted for your company. Tim and I will go on soon to alert her about her guests."

After the four of them watched the last of the wrestling matches, Alan said, "Come when you can. You'll recognize the house by the sign on the shop on Duke of Gloucester Street near the capitol."

It was dark by the time supper was almost over. Six people sat at the table in the large kitchen. Their spoons were scraping the last bits of the creamy custard pudding out of the small bowls. A light breeze carried the jovial sounds of the street through the windows as the merrymakers headed to the Exchange for the lighting of the bonfires. As Alan had promised, Martha Tisdale was delighted to have company for supper, and Adam and Lance were more than pleased to be her guests. Both young men suspected that Martha's dishes at supper had been much superior to anything the Widow Larson would have placed before them.

Supper had probably taken longer than usual because of the constant talking. Henry Tisdale had inquired endlessly into every detail of Lance's shoe making at Ashley Landing. He was especially interested in Lance's description of the clogs, interested but a bit skeptical. Martha Tisdale wanted to hear about the great house. She had heard that it was the largest and finest great house in the Tidewater.

Only one thing during the table conversation slightly annoyed Adam. He learned what Alan meant about the pressures young unmarried men Alan's age felt in Williamsburg. Adam realized, of course, that Alan's mother did not intend to be annoying or offensive in any of her remarks. Still, he knew that he shared Alan's discomfort occasionally during the meal. Martha Tisdale had exclaimed several times her joy in seeing four such handsome young men at her table. "It's a shame we don't have some pretty young girls here for you four to look at," she said. She hoped that Alan and Timothy would meet pretty young women in the new land beyond the hills. "I just pray though they will be the right kind of young women." To Adam and Lance she had remarked that, when the time came, she would be more than happy to introduce them to suitable young women in Williamsburg. Adam saw Lance squirm in his seat at that offer.

"Martha," her husband said, "leave our guests be. I think they are quite capable of finding and choosing young women for themselves."

"Sorry," Martha said. "I do not mean to be impolite. It's just that when I see such handsome young men, especially when one of them is my own son, I want them to be happy and married. I think all of you sitting here must be shy. You need a bit of prodding. I'm not talking about Henry there, of course. He was always the forward one."

"As I recall, Martha, you had as much, if not more, to do with my courtship as I did," her husband said.

"Henry," his wife cried out, "you know that's not true."

Alan let out a loud happy laugh and rose from the table. "I think my father and mother need some time to themselves," he said. "Shall we go join the crowd at the bonfire?"

Adam and Lance thanked the Tisdales for their hospitality. They promised to visit again at the next fair. Timothy kissed Martha on the cheek and whispered something no one else heard. Henry shook hands all around and told the young men to enjoy themselves for the rest of the evening.

At the Exchange noise and light greeted them. Four bonfires were ablaze. From somewhere behind the capitol men kept bringing armloads of firewood. The higher the sparks rose, the louder the laughter of the crowd. Small groups of people were singing around the several fiddlers. Couples were beginning to dance.

Alan looked at the revelers and then turned to the other three young men and said, "I don't know about you, but I'd prefer to sit somewhere on the edge of things and talk." All of the others quickly agreed, since there was not going to be much time the next day for them to get together again.

"I said this afternoon that I did not want to sit around and talk about the way we are bent. But I guess now I do want a little navel examination," Adam said. They all laughed.

"Well, it is plenty warm. Let's take off our shirts." Timothy said. Before the others could respond, Timothy pulled his shirt over his head. He pushed his breeches down a bit, just low enough to expose his navel. "Don't be bashful. Join me. I promise I won't ask that we take off anything more." Within a matter of minutes, the four shirtless young men were sitting apart from the crowd and talking.

"I apologize for my mother and her talk about suitable young women and marriage," Alan said.

"No need for apologies," Lance quickly replied. "I admit I did squirm a bit, but I know your mother meant all for the best."

"Yes, she loves me and wants only the best for me," Alan said. "It doesn't help to have my two older brothers married and bringing grandchildren to my parents' house."

"Do you think your mother knows?" Adam asked.

"That Alan and I are already a married couple?" Timothy quickly interrupted.

"Yes."

"I don't know," Alan admitted.

"Would she accept it if you told her?" Adam kept at it.

"An even harder question. I don't know."

Timothy and Lance were listening intently.

"Could you tell your father and mother?" Adam asked Alan.

"No."

Adam paused before he spoke. "So going over the hills to the frontier is a way of avoiding facing pressures in Williamsburg, especially from two people whom you love very much. Two people who might, but might not of course, accept you and Tim into a new kind of house-hold." It was a statement, not a question.

Alan bristled slightly and stuck his finger in his navel. "Yes, per-haps you are right, Adam. But I hope it is not merely an escape. We are not leaving Williamsburg just to avoid the pressures to marry. We are both ready for a change, for new adventures and new opportuni-ties. Meeting those challenges will be exciting. That's what Tim and I want most."

"Very much," Timothy added quickly.

After a long silence, Lance asked, "Will Adam and I be escaping the pressures by staying at Ashley Landing then?"

"No," Alan and Timothy shouted simultaneously.

"In some ways, you and Adam will have to confront more difficult situations than we will," Alan said. "With the two of you sharing quarters year after year, you could become suspect. What would you do then?"

"I don't know. Face it when that time comes, if it does," Adam an-swered. "But I know what I will not do."

"What's that?" Timothy asked.

"I won't marry and pretend to be someone I am not. I know what would happen. I would still meet Lance at the bend in the river where we swim. I would still take his cock in my mouth, and I would want to feel him deep inside me."

"Yes, that is what would happen," Lance said.

"A lot of people think that two men lying together is wrong," Adam continued. "But I think that leaving the marriage bed and finding the real pleasure in secret with another man is what is wrong. It is dishonest and cowardly behavior."

Again there was a long silence. The four young men listened to the revelry beyond them.

Finally Timothy broke the silence. "Would anyone like to see my navel?"

Before anyone else could answer, Lance laughed and said, "Tim, I've seen your navel, and Alan here has seen it much more. Adam now has seen it only once, only tonight, but I will answer for him that once is enough. It's time for us to leave. Let's get our shirts back on."

Shortly the four fully dressed young men stood awkwardly not knowing quite how to end the evening. Finally Adam said, "It has been a long and strange day. I would never have guessed when I walked from the landing this morning that I would end the evening with two friends who share the feelings that Lance and I do."

Without speaking any further Alan embraced Adam, and Timothy caught Lance in his arms and gave him a brotherly kiss. Then Timothy pulled Adam into a deep hug and whispered, "Thank you for loving him so much."

At the same time Lance and Alan embraced, and Lance said, "I am happy for you. Take care of him."

Alan replied, "I promise."

Lance turned to Adam and said, "It is time we got to the Widow Larson's. She will be angry if we are too late and disturb her."

"That is, if she is there. I suspect she is out there among those dancers, one of those who will be there until the bonfires are only embers."

"Do you want us to walk you there, or can you find the way by yourselves?" Alan asked.

"I can find the way for us," Lance answered, "but walk us there anyway, just for company."

The four young men locked arms and walked four abreast the short distance to the widow's house. It was dark, and there was no answer to the knock on the door. However, the door was not locked.

Adam laughed. "I told you she would not be here. She is rather foolish, I think, to leave her house unlocked."

Alan snickered and replied, "The Widow Larson has a reputation for often leaving her door unlocked. She likes the company of young men visitors, I understand."

"She may just want to see your navel, Lance, so be careful," Timothy teased.

They all laughed. Then the four young men said goodnight again, and Alan and Timothy turned toward their quarters at the shop.

Adam and Lance entered the house. They found candles on the table, lit one of them, and went to their small bedroom. About an hour later they were awakened by low voices. One of them was that of the widow, the other a male voice. Shortly the door to the widow's bedroom clicked shut, followed by a loud giggle.

"They will be going at it soon," Lance said. He ran his hand down Adam's body. He poked into Adam's navel and then reached for his cock. "Shall we follow suit?"

"Yes," Adam replied and turned to kiss Lance.

There was no sign of the widow's visitor the next morning at breakfast.

"I trust you slept well last night, m'am," Adam said.

"Very well indeed. I heard you two come in late, but you did not disturb me," she lied. "I hope you, too, slept well."

Adam and Lance smiled at each other across the table but said nothing. As they were leaving to fetch Will at the Wythe house, they told Widow Larson that they would not be there for supper since the Tisdales had asked them to eat with them.

"Tomorrow morning we will have to leave before daylight. We have an eighteen-mile walk home. Tonight could you leave our breakfast on the table so that we will not have to disturb you so early?" Adam said.

"Gladly," she responded, "and I will pack some meat and bread for you to have midday on your walk home."

"Thank you," Adam said. "Perhaps we had best say good-bye now, for again we may not come back here until much after you have gone to bed." Lance turned away so that the widow could not see the amused look on his face.

Several hours later that morning young Will was seated on Lance's broad shoulders, looking over the heads of people in front of him at the puppet show. They had been watching long enough for Adam to understand why Mr. Ashley was glad not to have to attend the performances every day of the fair with his son. He knew though that Will could stay here all day. He clapped at the antics of the clowns; he booed at the villain pirates; and, along with the other young spectators, he sang when the fiddler asked the crowd to join with him in a song. When his hands weren't busy clapping and his mouth was not shouting or singing, Will reached into his vest pocket for peanuts.

"Will," Lance pleaded, "I know you are enjoying the peanuts. But, please, be a bit more careful not to drop the shells down the front of my shirt." Then he realized that the puppet acts were repeating earlier ones. "Shall we go now?" he asked.

"No, I want to see more," Will replied.

Many in the crowd, however, were moving on to something new. Will saw space open up close to the makeshift stage. "Let me down," he cried. Lance squatted, and Will jumped off and ran to a choice spot for viewing. "We'll wait back here," Lance called to him. "But remember our promise to have you back by noon."

Adam and Lance moved back away from the crowd.

"Enjoying your holiday in Williamsburg?" Lance asked.

"Yes. I am especially glad you found Tim, and without seeing Thomas."

"Tim has changed. When we were here in the shop together, Tim was a bit shy, too uncertain of himself, and certainly often afraid of Thomas. Now he is confident and bubbling over with happiness. Being with Alan has been good for him, and they obviously love each other."

"I wish them well after they leave Williamsburg. But I would not want to be going where they are."

"Nor I, Adam. I like Ashley Landing too much." Lance paused, then asked, "Do you think that Alan was right when he said that the longer we share quarters, the more we will become suspect?"

"I think it is possible."

"What will we do?"

"I only know what I will not do."

"What is that?"

"Should either Joseph or Mr. Ashley ever ask me if I am bent in the direction I am, I will not lie to them."

"You would tell them?"

"Yes."

"Even if it meant our separation and our punishment?"

"That will not happen. Joseph would not approve of our behavior, but he is too much our friend. My admission to him would not go beyond him."

"And Mr. Ashley?"

"He, too, would not approve. But I firmly believe that he would not turn us over to the magistrate."

"If and when that time comes, I hope you are right."

"But it hasn't come yet, Lance, and it may not. Right now I am on holiday. Let's think about seeing the play this afternoon. Hadn't we best pull Will away from the puppet show? I don't want him, or us, scolded for being late."

It was easier than they thought to convince Will to leave. No doubt, despite the peanuts, he was looking forward to the full table in the dining room of the Wythe mansion.

Lance and Adam were finishing their roast pig on corn bread when they joined the throng of playgoers outside the theater at the end of the Palace Green.

Williamsburg was proud of its theater, the first to be built in all of the colonies. In the spring of that year the students from William and Mary College had presented *The Tragedy of Cato* to an appreciative full house. More recently an amateur acting group in the city had offered both *The Recruiting Officer* and *The Beaux Stratagem*. The plays had been called a success. This afternoon the touring company presenting *The Merchant of Venice* was that from the famous William Hallam of London. In the colonies the principal actors were Hallam's brother Lewis, his wife, acclaimed the best Shakespearean actress of the day, and their twelve-year-old son Lewis Jr. Along with two other actors, they were going to present a much abbreviated version of Shakespeare's play.

When Lewis Hallam, acting as manager, took their money, Adam and Lance were instructed to choose a place on any of the benches in the last four rows of the theater. The fashionable folk had already filled the front rows close to the stage when Adam and Lance squeezed in beside a young bearded man. After they exchanged greetings, the young man leaned over and said, "It's my first time in a theater. I'm excited."

Lance replied, "My friend and I are, too."

The two hours of playing time passed quickly. Adam and Lance listened intently to every word, caught up by a kind of language they had never heard. Occasionally Lance was distracted when the bearded man's leg seemed to be rubbing intentionally against his. But when Lance turned to his neighbor, the young man's face was looking straight at the stage. Lance quickly returned his attention to the actors. At the end of the performance Adam and Lance joined in clapping the actors back to the stage again and again.

When they stood up to leave, the bearded man turned to Lance, rubbed his crotch, and said, "Yes, the play was as exciting as the time I lost my virginity."

Lance hesitated, then rubbed his crotch and said, "I know what you mean."

The bearded man smiled and said, "I wish you and your friend a good evening."

The three of them separated quickly after leaving the theater.

"Adam," Lance said, "if we were in London, I would say that man wanted to be the third man in bed with us."

"Perhaps," Adam replied, "but I am glad we are not in London."

It was too early to go to the Tisdales. Adam and Lance bought cider and sat on the grounds of the Palace Green to talk about the play.

"Did you like it?" Lance asked.

"Yes. But I didn't respond quite like so many people there."

"How so?"

"Despite his nasty nature at times, I had a lot for sympathy for Shylock," Adam said.

"Even when he was willing to let Antonio bleed to death?"

"Of course I didn't like that. But I understood why he so much wanted revenge. He had been spit upon in the streets, called dirty names, and ridiculed for his religion. Besides, in the courtroom Portia tricked him."

"No, she didn't. She gave him every chance to let Antonio go and still get his money back."

"Well, even if she didn't trick him, his punishment at the end was too severe."

"What makes you say that?"

"He was forced to give up his religion. Forced, Lance, forced! That's not right. No one should be forced to be someone they are not." Then after a moment of silence, Adam asked, "How did you like the play, Lance? Who was your favorite character?"

"The more I think about it, Adam, the more I believe that no one in the play was perfect. Everyone had a weakness, a fault, or a nasty streak somewhere."

"But among all those people, who was your favorite?"

"Antonio, the friend of the young man who wins Portia in that riddle contest."

"Why?"

"I guess for something of the same reason you have sympathy for Shylock. The way I see it, Antonio too was mistreated, not as badly as you say Shylock was, but still Portia makes damn sure at the end of the play that her marriage to that young man means more than the friendship between the two men. Didn't you notice at the end how, when all those couples are dancing around, Antonio is left standing there alone. I may be very wrong, Adam, but I think Antonio was one of us."

"You mean you think Antonio and his young friend had been lying together?"

"No. I wouldn't go that far. I think the young man was something of a bastard. I guess he loved Portia, but he also loved her money. He professed an affection for Antonio, but I don't think he ever realized how much Antonio loved him."

"That doesn't mean he was one of us."

"Maybe not. But maybe the man who wrote that play couldn't be more open about Antonio's feelings for the young man."

"I see your point."

For several minutes the two young men sat, absorbed in their own thoughts. Then, suddenly, Adam jumped up and said, "We had better watch it. It's time we were at the Tisdales'."

When they reached Alan's parents' house, they found only Alan and Timothy there. Alan explained that his parents had accepted an unexpected invitation to have supper with close friends and then go to the Market Square Tavern for an evening of dancing in the Great Room. His mother had been reluctant to accept the invitation since she had invited Adam and Lance to supper, Alan said, but his father had convinced her that the four of them would get along just fine without their company, especially since it was our last night together. "My mother has left us supper here as well as a large parcel of food for your midday meal tomorrow," Alan said. When she had heard that the Widow Larson was going to provide that meal, she remarked, "I know her. I must see to it that those two young men have enough to eat on that long walk."

After they had eaten, the four of them started out for the Exchange, again to watch the bonfires. Just as they arrived to join the crowd, Alan stopped them. "On our last night together, do we really want to sit in that mob? Let's go to our shop and sit outside in the back. It will be easier to talk there." The other three readily agreed.

The conversation in the yard back of shop went in a dozen different directions. Occasionally it concerned Ashley Landing, at other times the land beyond the hills. Some of the talk centered around the making of shoes. They all hoped they could keep in touch through letters, although they knew it would probably be easier to get a letter to Ashley Landing than it would be for Adam and Lance to locate Alan and Timothy.

When Timothy saw Adam yawn as if he were ready to excuse himself for bed, Timothy arose and said to Adam, "It's our last night together for a long time, if ever. May I have a few private words with Lance before you leave?"

"Of course. He probably wants the same with you. Alan and I will sit here and talk and wait for you, just as we did yesterday afternoon."

Lance got up, and he and Timothy went outside the shop and stood in the street,

"The last time I said good-bye to you when just the two of us were together was when you were in the pillory," Timothy said. "Will it be too painful if we go there tonight?"

"No. Adam and I were there yesterday. I think I exorcised all the ugly memories of that place then. Tonight I will recall only the best moments, those when you came bringing me something to drink just before Mr. Ashley arrived."

They turned up a side street to the north and got to Nicholson Street which ran straight to the gaol. The street was deserted of revelers. Lance and Timothy locked arms and walked, almost without speaking, to the gaol. Like yesterday, the area around the gaol was deserted. The two young men walked up to the pillory and stopped.

"When I left you here that night, I was certain I would never see you again. After I heard the men approaching and I ran off, I hid behind the gaol. I watched you leaving with Mr. Ashley. Somehow I knew you were in good hands."

"All that's past, Tim, but I am still grateful for your coming to comfort me here in the pillory and for bringing me the drink."

"But I am the one who owes thanks. That's why I wanted to have a few private words with you."

"Thanks for what?"

"Lance, you taught me to be myself. Even before you came to the shop, I knew I was different. I was scared of that. It wasn't until the first night we truly lay together and felt each other's body and kissed, that I accepted who I was. Those few weeks we had together enjoying each other's body gave me a confidence I never had before. I didn't have to feel guilty anymore about who I was. I was suddenly glad to be the way I was. I owe all that to you."

"I'm glad I did that for you."

"Then, Lance, I did it for Alan."

"For Alan?"

"Yes. After his father bought the shop and left Alan in charge with me as the only helper, Alan and I shared the bed in the backroom. For weeks we were careful not to touch in any way. I was burning up. And I felt that Alan was too, except that he was afraid to make a move. He was a bit timid about seducing a younger man. Then, one night, when I was handling my cock fantasizing about the first time you and I were together, I simply reached over into Alan's crotch, found his hard cock, and pulled him over on top of me I think I shocked him out of a year's growth of beard. We went at it almost all night long. Alan told me later it was that night that he accepted who he was. So, Lance, both Alan and I owe you thanks."

Neither said anything for a minute, then Tim said, "I am going to kiss you."

Timothy pulled Lance into his arms. They embraced tightly, then they kissed. It was not the brotherly peck of the night before. It was a long, passionate kiss. Both quickly had erections. Timothy's hand reached down and covered the hard bundle in Lance's breeches. Lance pulled back from Timothy.

"No, Tim. I loved having you kiss me again. But we cannot go any further."

Timothy sighed. "Not even to look at our navels?"

"No. Stop being a tease. I am going to kiss you now and kiss you very hard, but that is it. After that we are heading back to the shop."

When their lips finally parted, the two young men stood looking at each other in the darkness. Both still had erections, but both were satisfied.

"Good-bye, Tim. In my way I will always love you. I hope I meet you and Alan again someday."

Timothy waited a minute and then said, "Good-bye, Lance. In my way I will always love you. I hope I meet you and Adam again someday."

They hugged.

"Let's race back to the shop like we used to do," Lance challenged.

As usual, Timothy won the race. In the yard at the back, they found Alan resting with the dog at his feet. Adam was asleep on the ground. Lance gently nudged him. Soon the four of them were standing awkwardly on the street outside the shop. No one knew what to say since all that mattered had been said.

Finally Adam said to Alan, "Again, thank your mother. Lance and I will think of you when we stop for our midday meal tomorrow. Let's go, Lance, before I drop asleep here in the street."

The widow was not at her house when Adam and Lance got there. Nor was she around the next morning. Well before daybreak the two young men ate the breakfast the widow had left for them. They packed their few belongings in their bundles. They latched the front door quietly, hoping not to rouse the widow and any guests she might have.

At the well in the William and Mary College yard they filled their canteens with fresh water. As they left the yard, they saw five sturdy walking sticks on the ground, as if dropped in a hurry.

"Shall we?" Adam asked.

"Yes," Lance answered without hesitation. "They are of more use to us than to whoever dropped them so carelessly." Lance chose the best of the lot. He handed one to Adam and kept the other for himself. He waved it into the air and shouted, "This may come in handy." Then, walking sticks in hand, Adam and Lance set out on the long walk to Ashley Landing just as the red of the approaching sun appeared in the east. It was over a two-mile trek from the college yard before they reached the back trail.

The back trail stretched for thirty-eight miles from the port at Hampton to deep into the Tidewater on the east side of the river. The back trail, cut through private land, was used mainly by people, either on horseback or on foot, who did not have convenient access to the river. The portion that Adam and Lance needed to cover before dark was the eighteen miles from Williamsburg to the trail where they cut off west to reach Ashley Landing. Several trails branched off the back trail to the east, but the major junction was twelve miles up from the capital. The trail at that important junction then led to the main road to the hills and beyond.

When they started out from the college yard the two young men chatted back and forth about their holiday in Williamsburg. Both agreed it had been a full and enjoyable two days. They were happy to have been with Timothy and Alan, but neither of them wished they were going with the two adventurers into the frontier of the colony. "Our quarters at home will look good to me," Lance said. Adam quickly agreed.

As soon as they reached the back trail, however, conversation became difficult. Since Lance was the taller of the two, he had the longer stride, and he was soon ahead of Adam by several yards. Adam did not try to keep up with him; he knew he would only tire himself doing that. So the two young men walked in silence, listening to the birds and watching wildlife scamper across the trail from time to time. Occasionally each stopped for a drink of water from his canteen or to take a piss. Mainly though they kept up a steady stride, each at his own pace. They met only one party, an overseer from another plantation and his family. There was a brief exchange of greetings and news, but everyone was too anxious to be on their way for anything more than that.

Shortly before they reached the important junction twelve miles from Williamsburg, Lance stopped and waited for Adam. "I need some food," Lance said. Each chose a tree for a back rest, and they opened the two parcels of food. As Alan's mother had predicted, there was hardly enough in the widow's parcel to feed one of them. The one from Mistress Tisdale, however, more than made up for the widow's stinginess. After they washed down with water the generous slabs of pound cake from Alan's mother, they stood up. Lance looked quickly up and down the back trail to make sure no one was approaching and then pulled Adam into his arms. They kissed. "That will give us sustenance for the rest of the walk," Lance said. They picked up their bundles and started walking. Once again Lance was soon well ahead of Adam.

As Lance arrived at the important junction, he stopped and yelled back to Adam, "We are more than halfway home." Adam was certain that he heard a horse's whinny answer Lance. Adam watched Lance quickly go into the woods. Just as Adam starting trotting toward where he saw Lance disappear into the woods, Lance reemerged.

"What's the . . . ," Adam started to call, but he stopped when Lance hastened toward him, his finger over his lips and his head shaking.

When the two young men met, Lance said, "There's a horse tied back there. There are full travel bags behind the saddle. But there is no one around."

"That's right. There is no one over there. That's because I'm behind you," a loud male voice announced.

Both Adam and Lance froze. Both shuddered. Even without turning around, they recognized the voice. It was Matt's. "Damn," Adam said softly. He felt certain that this meeting was no more chance than had been the one over a year ago when Matt accosted him as he stepped out of the privy on Lance's birthday night.

"Aren't you glad to see me again?" Matt asked. "Turn around so that I can see the smiles on your faces."

As they stood there, their backs to Matt, Adam said in a low voice, "Control your temper. Let me do the talking."

They turned around to face a Matt much fatter than the one who had left Ashley Landing. He had a grin on his face as broad as his belly.

"Afternoon, Matt," Adam said as calmly as he could.

"Surprised to see me?" Matt shot back.

"Yes, must say I am. I supposed by now that you had made your fortune over there," Adam said and pointed to the northwest.

Matt chuckled. "No. I stayed in Williamsburg. I'm good at wood and nails, and there's plenty of that kind of work there. But I'm going to the frontier very soon."

"Then why are you here?" Adam asked.

"I came to meet the two of you."

Adam knew that Lance's body shook at that answer. But trying to remain calm, Adam said, "Meet us here. How did you know we would be here?"

Matt waited a minute and then answered, "I saw your sodomite friend there two days ago in Williamsburg. I made inquiries and learned that you would be walking back today."

Lance moved forward, fists clenched. Adam pushed him back.

"And just who told you we would be walking back? And why should it matter to you if we were walking back?" Adam asked calmly.

Matt laughed. "One question at a time. A widow friend told me."

"Widow Larson?"

"I never ask the name of the widows I plow," Matt replied.

Adam was disgusted by Matt's crudity. But without showing it, he asked, "And just what do you want from us so much that you have come out of your way to meet us?"

"We have two matters of business to settle, as you may recall," Matt snarled.

Lance stepped forward a bit and shouted, "If you think you are going to get Adam's mouth around your cock again, then you are bloody well mistaken."

Matt grinned and rubbed his crotch. "If it's been around yours all this time, why shouldn't it be around mine for a couple of minutes?"

"Because I won't let you."

"I think this will persuade you otherwise," Matt said. He pulled a dueling pistol from his vest. "Now drop those walking sticks."

After hesitating for a second, Lance threw his walking stick to the ground. Adam pitched his to Matt's feet.

Surprised by the pistol but still in control of himself, Adam asked, "You said two matters of business. One is my pleasuring you. What is the other?"

"Lance."

"Lance?"

"Yes. I once was about to kill that bastard for hitting me. Now I will."

Again Adam pushed Lance's tense body backward.

"Then where will the two of us be? What then?" Adam asked, still trying to keep his voice as calm as possible.

Matt laughed loudly. "I've learned about men like you since I've been at Williamsburg. I prefer widows, but I'm not against men like you. I might persuade you to go with me over the hills. Until I find a woman, I'd let you do all the pleasuring."

After a long silence, Adam said, "I'll pleasure you, Matt. It would be fun to do that."

"Like hell you will," Lance shouted.

"Shut up, Lance," Adam shouted back. He gave Lance a hard blow on his back and sent him to the ground close to Matt's feet. Adam's blow surprised both Lance and Matt.

"Now listen to me, Lance," Adam said. "I'm going to suck Matt's cock. I'm damn tired of handling only that dwarf thing of yours. I want a real man's cock. Matt has the biggest cock I've seen, and I want it."

Matt howled. "It will do me good to see Lance's face as he watches you take my cock, Adam. And don't try anything, Lance, or I'll blow Adam's head off and then yours." He pointed the pistol at Lance.

"Bloody right, Lance," Adam said loudly. "Stay out of this. I want Matt's cock, and this time you and that stupid Joseph won't interfere."

"What the hell are you saying?" Lance cried out.

"A lovers' quarrel," Matt snickered.

"Now get up, Lance, and lower your breeches and whack off while I take on Matt," Adam said.

The image of Lance pumping himself while he watched Adam sucking away sent Matt into another fit of loud laughter.

Adam leaned down and grabbed Lance by the shirt and yanked him up. As he did, he whispered quickly, "When I say 'go,' let's rush him. A quick look of understanding shot across Lance's face. Adam shouted, "Go." What happened in the next two minutes seemed to pass like two seconds.

Adam and Lance rushed at Matt, taking him by surprise in his laughter. Matt fired wildly at Lance. Lance cried out in pain, grabbed his arm, and stumbled backward. Adam grabbed Matt's arm.

"Let go of that gun," Adam shouted.

The two men wrestled about, Adam keeping a firm grip on Matt's wrist. Adam felt Matt's hand waving frantically. Matt fired. For a second the two wrestlers froze. Then Matt fell to the ground. Little geysers of blood spurted from his neck. Adam looked down at the dying man. Matt was trying to scream, but all that came from his throat was a heavy flow of blood. His wild eyes seemed to be pleading. Without hesitation, Adam picked up the pistol, aimed at Matt's left temple, and fired. Soon Matt's bloody body lay still.

Adam hurried to Lance and helped him to his feet. No sooner was he up though than Lance leaned over and emptied his stomach. When Lance finished wiping his mouth, Adam said, "Let me see your arm."

Lance held it out. From the torn flesh just above his left elbow ran a trickle of blood. "It's only a bad scratch. I was lucky," Lance said.

Adam got his canteen and told Lance to wash out his mouth. Then, exhausted, he sat down on the ground and put his head between his hands and started to cry. Lance was quickly beside him. He put his good arm around Adam and pulled him close.

"I killed a man," Adam murmured.

"No, Matt shot himself. He was dying. You only put him out of his pain. It was an act of mercy on your part," Lance assured him. "He would have killed both of us except for your clever little game."

Adam waited a long time before he said slowly, "I suppose so."

They sat for a few minutes without saying anything. Finally Lance said, "We've got to get away from here." They both stood up. They knew certain things had to be taken care of before they started out.

Adam took off his shirt. With water from his canteen, he wet a portion of the shirt. As best he could, he washed Lance's wound. It was not a deep cut, but Adam could tell that it was throbbing and that Lance was in pain. Adam tore his shirt into several pieces and wrapped a large dry portion around Lance's arm. He started to use the other dry portion to tie around the bandage. Instead he dropped the torn shirt and unloosened the string around Lance's pigtail. With it, he tied the bandage.

"We look like two madmen, Adam. You shirtless. Me with a bloody bandage and my hair hanging down my neck," Lance said. "I hope no one meets us on the trail."

They both laughed. Instantly they knew that somehow they would make it safely back to Ashley Landing.

"Matt goes over there," Adam said pointing to an opening in the brush. Together they pulled Matt's body by his feet toward a final resting place. As they did, something fell from his vest pocket. Adam picked it up. It was a tiny bundle but heavy with coins. "Let's get him into the woods, and I'll drop this on his face out of revenge," Adam said. They left Matt's body far enough off the back trail for only the hawks to reveal it to any travelers.

Again on the back trail, Adam picked up the dueling pistol. He looked at it with a combination of anger and relief. Then he hurled it into the brush as far as he could. Now only the matter of what to do with the horse remained. They untied the mare and brought her out of the woods.

"Do you want to ride her, Lance?" Adam asked.

"No. It's only about six miles more."

"But there's two more miles off the trail to home."

"I can make it."

"No," Adam said firmly. "You ride most of the way. When we get close to the trail to get us back home, we'll decide what to do with the mare. But not here. Now get up into that saddle and let's get the hell away from this damn spot."

Adam watched Lance and the mare go down the trail. He turned slowly to survey the scene around him. There was no sign of the violence that had taken place such a short time ago. He started after

Lance, then suddenly he stopped. He bent over and relieved himself of all he had eaten that day. His retching over, he straightened up and took a drink of water. In the distance he saw Lance waving him forward. Without looking back, Adam waved to Lance and started out to catch up with him.

Whether it was the heaviness of their thoughts or the heat of the late afternoon or a combination of both, the rest of the journey took longer than either Adam or Lance expected. At last though Adam saw the large white marker with the initials AL. It was the beginning of the 3,000 acres around the great house and its various dependencies. Adam breathed a sigh of relief. Ahead he saw Lance standing, the mare at his side. In a few minutes he joined them.

"What do we do with the mare?" Lance asked.

"We can't take her with us. Give her a good pat on the rump and head her back down the trail. She'll make out on her own," Adam replied.

Lance removed the reins and the bit from the mare and threw them into the woods. He gave the mare a swat on her rump, and she was off. Lance laughed and said, "She'll be in Williamsburg before we are in quarters."

Adam could tell that, despite the lightheartedness, Lance was tired. "Walk on slowly, Lance. I'm running to get Joseph," he said. He drew Lance close to him, making sure that he did not touch the bandaged arm. He kissed Lance lightly on the mouth. Then, without saying anything more, he started his race to Ashley Landing.

Adam's body was drenched with sweat when he unlatched the gate into Joseph's yard. From the kitchen window Joseph saw him and immediately knew something was wrong. He spoke quickly to his wife at the table and then bolted outside to Adam.

"I want water," Adam called to him. Joseph returned inside the house and poured water into a large cup. Again he spoke to his wife before returning to Adam.

Adam sat on the front step of the porch and slowly sipped the water. Between sips he told Joseph what had happened, giving him an abbreviated version which left out all the details about the sexual offer and the game he had played to confuse Matt.

"That son of a bitch," Joseph exclaimed. "I'm glad he shot himself."

Adam was relieved that Joseph made no comment on his putting the pistol against Matt's temple and firing.

"Are you rested enough to go back up the trail, Adam, or shall I go by myself?" Joseph asked.

"I'll go with you."

The two men started out together, but soon Joseph was well ahead on the trail. Adam's spirit was still energetic, anxious to get to Lance. However, his leg muscles ached from the more than twenty-five mile walk since they left the college yard that morning. Also, after they let the mare go, Adam had carried both his and Lance's travel bundles. Light as two feathers when they started out, the bundles had felt as if they contained bricks when Adam dumped them at Joseph's front porch step.

Adam was over halfway up the trail when he saw Joseph and Lance coming toward him. Lance had his bandaged arm around Joseph's shoulder. He was using his walking stick with his good arm. Adam stopped and waited for them to join him.

"How are you feeling?" Adam asked.

"Hungry. And I'm not ready at the moment to walk back to Williamsburg." Joseph and Adam were glad to hear that, despite the pain, Lance still had his sense of humor.

When they reached home, Adam said, "I want to wash up." The three men went to the washhouse. Quickly Adam and Lance stripped completely and washed their sweaty, tired bodies. Joseph did not bother to turn his head from the two naked young men, but he looked without interest at their nakedness. As soon as they had finished washing, Joseph said, "Let me see the wound, Lance." He was glad that Lance was right that it was little more than a deep cut. "Get to your quarters," he told them. "I'll bring you meat and bread as well as an ointment for the wound and new bandages."

While Joseph spread ointment over Lance's wound, Adam asked, "What do we tell Mr. Ashley?"

Joseph thought a moment while he tore cloth for a fresh bandage. He looked at Adam and said, "I can't think of a good reason why you should tell him anything. There, Lance, that should take care of you. Keep a shirt on, and no one will know you have a bandage on your arm."

"Sooner or later, Matt's body will be found," Adam persisted.

"Probably true. But that doesn't mean you and Lance know anything about the matter," Joseph replied.

"Joseph's right, Adam," Lance said. "The best thing for us to do is to get back to day-to-day business."

Adam waited a minute, then said, "I suppose so."

"I'd best leave now, and let you two get some sleep," Joseph said, considering the discussion of telling Mr. Ashley over.

Adam and Lance looked at each other, both thinking the same thing. Then Adam said, "Joseph, once again we owe you thanks. You helped us out once before where Matt was concerned. And now you've done it again."

"Yes, thank you, Joseph," Lance said.

"I didn't do much either time. I have forgotten the episode in the stable barn. Now I'll forget this one. Now I'll say good night to you."

As Joseph was about to leave, Adam called to him, "Joseph, you and your family have a good holiday in Williamsburg. We may not see you tomorrow before you take the boat down river."

"Yes, Joseph, have a good holiday. Be sure that little Joe gets to the puppet show," Lance added.

It did not take long for Adam and Lance to get to bed and asleep.

Three weeks later news arrived at Ashley Landing that the decomposing body of a naked man had been found in the woods near the main junction on the back trail. A traveler had noticed hawks circling above the spot and had investigated. There was no way to identify the dead man. Every stitch of his clothing was gone as were any possessions he might have had with him. All that remained for the hawks was the rotting flesh of a once rather fat man. It was whispered about, out of hearing of the womenfolk, that the only part of the man's body which the hawks had not pecked away at was the extraordinarily big sexual member.

# 1753-1754: Ashley Landing—Letters

During the months between the Williamsburg fair of 1753 and that of 1754, life for Adam and Lance followed its usual patterns of work in the warehouse and in the shop. They stopped going to the bend in the river in mid-October and started again in early April. The water was chilly both when they stopped and when they started their swims again. However, both preferred the goose bumps on their naked bodies to their half baths in the washhouse.

In the late fall of 1753 Gregory's term of indenture ended, and Mr. Ashley gave him his freedom papers. Like Matt, Gregory decided to leave Ashley Landing and seek his fortune in the land beyond the hills. Adam and Lance wished him well. Two new indentured servants arrived from England. George and William were the same age as Adam and Lance, now twenty-four. However, since the two new young men were most often with overseers on lands up the river, no close friendship grew out of the occasional meals the four shared in the kitchen at the great house.

Both Adam and Lance had pushed the episode with Matt on the back trail into the furthest recesses of their minds. Only occasionally did the memory of the bloody face reemerge to confront them, and then only in the worst of nightmares. True to his word, Joseph never mentioned the story that Adam had told him on the steps of his front porch. Everyone soon forgot the news of the dead man whose body was found in the woods off the back trail.

In the time between the two fairs, unexpected news came to Ashley Landing through several packets of letters. Two packets crossed the Atlantic Ocean, one from Cromley Hall and the other from London a short time later. The other packet came up from Williamsburg. The news in all of the letters was surprising.

doi:10.1300/5623_08

The first packet from England arrived in late October. It was addressed to Mr. Ashley from Lord Cromley. The letter began,

*It is with great sorrow that I inform you of the death of Lady Cromley, my beloved wife and your sister. Although Lady Cromley had not seen you since your departure for the Colony of Virginia, she often spoke of you with great affection. I extend my sympathy to you at your loss.*

Mr. Ashley had no special memories of his sister. She was older than he, and her marriage to Lord Cromley and then the Atlantic Ocean had put even greater distance between them.

Lord Cromley's letter went on to say that he now planned to spend more time at his London residence than at Cromley Hall. There would be distractions there from the sorrow at the loss of his wife. Then, for the first time in any of his annual letters to the Ashleys, he mentioned Adam. He said that Sarah, her ladyship's favorite personal maid and Adam's aunt, would be retained in service at Cromley Hall. She would attend the Cromley's eldest daughter, Jane Elizabeth. He trusted that Sarah's nephew had been in no trouble since he arrived in the colony.

"Adam in trouble!" Mr. Ashley exclaimed. "If anything, what that young man needs is a bit of getting into trouble."

The second packet of letters from England arrived shortly before the Christmas season. It came from a prestigious London solicitor. There were three letters in the packet. The first was addressed to Mr. and Madam Ashley. It was the solicitor's brief official announcement to the Ashley family of the death of Lord Cromley on September 12, 1753. The new Lord Cromley was the eighteen-year-old eldest son. Any further communication between the two families, the solicitor advised, should be addressed to the new lord. The solicitor also said that he assumed the new Lord Cromley would write regarding the personal details of his father's death.

Then, in a separate envelope marked POST-SCRIPT the solicitor wrote that the will of Lord Cromley left to one Adam Bradley the sum of ten pounds, *"in recompense."* The solicitor said that he understood that Adam Bradley was an indentured servant at Ashley Landing.

Upon verification of that fact and as soon as details of the will were settled, that bequest would be honored.

When informed of the bequest, Adam was surprised. He did not know what he had done for Lord Cromley for which he now deserved any payment. Had Lord Cromley regretted his forcing him to leave England? That hardly seemed in character with the arrogant lord Adam had known.

When he told Lance about the ten pounds, Lance burst out laughing and exclaimed, "Well, that's a damn lot more than any of my gentlemen friends ever paid me. What are you going to do with that much money?"

"I won't think about that until I have the money in hand. Then, we will decide together," Adam replied.

The third letter in the packet was for Adam. It was from his aunt. Only once since Adam arrived in Virginia had Sarah Mann and her nephew exchanged letters. Several months after he was settled at Ashley Landing, Adam had written his aunt telling her how happy and excited he was with his new life in the colony. His aunt had replied that although she was still baffled by Adam's sudden decision to leave England, she wished Adam "great happiness and prosperity" in Virginia.

Now his aunt's letter to Adam began with news about herself. She was well and busy in London attending her new mistress. She got along well enough with Jane Elizabeth, his aunt said, but she missed Lady Cromley. She sensed that the young girl would prefer a younger woman as her private maid.

His aunt also sent greetings from three of Adam's favorite people at Cromley Hall. The stable master hoped that Adam was where he could still ride horses. The steward wondered if all those hours of keeping records for him were of any use to Adam now. His aunt said that the message from the tutor was an enigma to her; she assumed it was a private joke between the two of them. The tutor told Sarah to ask Adam if "he had learned to handle himself well." Adam smiled as he read their greetings, especially the question from the tutor. "If only they knew how much I am indebted to all three of them," Adam mused. After this personal news, his aunt wrote, "Now, Adam, I must turn to news of far more importance than I have related so far." Adam quickly read through the rest of the long letter. Then he raced to Lance's shop.

"What are you so excited about?" Lance asked as Adam burst into the shop.

"Lord Cromley was murdered, and my aunt is coming to Williamsburg."

"What?"

"Lord Cromley didn't die of natural causes as that solicitor's letter to Mr. Ashley suggested. He was murdered. And my aunt is coming to Virginia."

"Why? Did she murder him?"

"Don't be funny, Lance."

"Well then, Adam, you calm down and tell me what your aunt says in her letter. And keep your two stories separated. Don't scramble the murder with your aunt's coming here."

Adam laughed. "I guess I did make it sound like she killed him."

Adam paused and then said, "Aunt Sarah's letter confuses me a bit, but from what I can make of it, here's what happened. After the burial of Lady Cromley last August, Lord Cromley took his two oldest sons and his oldest daughter to London. My aunt went with them as private maid to Jane Elizabeth. About a month later Lord Cromley was found murdered. His throat had been cut. His body was found in a very disreputable neighborhood. One of those where there are lots of fights between drunken men. Lots of taverns and even more houses of 'ill repute,' as my aunt puts it."

"How did she know all that?"

"The penny newspaper."

"Damn, old Lord Cromley must be turning in his grave to hear that his death was reported in those scandal rags."

"But Aunt Sarah says there were even stranger things than the bad area where his body was found. He still had money in his purse. So robbery was not a motive. What really puzzled my aunt though was how he was dressed. He wasn't wearing his usual finery. He was wearing the clothes of a laborer, one who might work at one of the wharves alongside the Thames."

"All of that in the penny newspaper? Where was he found? Does your aunt say?" Lance asked.

"On the South Bank, somewhere off . . ." Adam looked again at the letter and after a minute said, "Off Blackfriars Road."

Lance sucked in his breath and let out a loud whistle.

"What's the matter?" Adam asked.

"That's the worst area in all of London. Do the city authorities know what happened?"

"No. The new Lord Cromley—or Jason as I used to call him—got the whole mess hushed up. But you're making me get ahead of myself in the story."

"Adam, I know what happened, even if the authorities don't."

"Oh."

"Adam, no man in his right mind goes into that area during the day. And men like Lord Cromley don't go there at night unless they are hunting for one thing—sex. And when they do go there, they certainly do not go in their best clothes. My guess is that Lord Cromley propositioned the wrong young man. Lord Cromley wanted to do the buggering, and the young man didn't go for that. No doubt, the young man was willing to do the buggering, but Lord Cromley didn't go for that. Probably Lord Cromley lost his temper just as he did with you that afternoon in the stable. Only this time his lordship got more than you gave him."

For several minutes Adam said nothing. In his ears though he heard the heavy panting of Lord Cromley behind him in the stable. He felt the heavy hand in his crotch.

Finally he said, "I know you are right. No wonder then, if Jason had even the slightest hint of what his father was doing in that part of London, that he went to one of the king's ministers to help get the murder hushed up."

"Are the Cromleys that powerful?"

"Yes. The king listens to them but not to you or me."

Lance laughed. "Yes, his majesty wasn't much concerned about me when he stamped me as one of his prisoners to be sent over here."

"And I am sure the penny newspapers gladly accepted a bag of coins in exchange for switching to other stories of more interest."

Adam paused and then asked a bit too playfully, "How do you know so much about that area, Lance? Is that where you went?"

"No, damn you!" Lance exclaimed. "I played around, you know that. Even whored, since I accepted money. But you should bloody well know that I wouldn't go to a stinking place like that."

Lance got up from his workbench. Looking as if he could hit Adam but didn't, he ran from the workshop. He was gone for a long time before he returned. He found Adam sitting there, his chin in his left hand. His eyes were wet.

"I'm sorry, Lance. I really didn't mean that like it must have sounded."

"I'm sorry, too. I didn't mean to snap."

Quickly they hugged in a hard embrace. They stayed clinched until each felt the other's body relax. Then they kissed. When they broke apart and looked at each other sheepishly, Lance said, "Go on now. I'm anxious to find out why your aunt is coming to Williamsburg." Adam began again as if he were a young boy reciting his history lesson.

"Lord Cromley was buried beside his wife in the family burial grounds at Cromley Hall. But Jason and his sister, Jane Elizabeth, did not stay long in the country. Jane Elizabeth was soon to be presented at Court. Jason, too, was anxious to return and see the young woman to whom he had become officially engaged at the age of sixteen."

"And your aunt with them to London?"

"Yes. But here's where something is missing in her story. The first part of her letter, telling about Lord Cromley's murder, was written after they returned to London from the funeral at Cromley Hall. The second part where she tells me that she is coming here was written after they had been in London for several weeks."

"How do you know that?"

"She says so. 'It is hard for me now to pick up my pen. So much has happened since I started this letter to you. However, I hope that you will rejoice with me. Next summer I shall join you in Virginia.' Also there are dates three weeks apart within the letter."

"What do you think happened?"

"I can only guess. But, like your telling of Lord Cromley's murder, I think I know what happened."

"And, like me, you are probably right. So tell me."

"First, she says that Lord Cromley left her one hundred pounds in his will, as he did to the steward and the stable master."

"A one hundred pounds!" Lance exclaimed.

"Yes. She was worth that and more for all her good service to that family. However, Aunt Sarah and Jane Elizabeth did not have the same good relationship that my aunt had with Lady Cromley. Jane Elizabeth did not have the patience to listen to the 'good advice' my aunt says she gave. So either my aunt or Jane Elizabeth went to Jason and told him of the situation."

"I hope it was your aunt."

"I think it must have been, for she writes, 'Lord Cromley has honored my request to leave my service with the family and come to Virginia, and he has offered to pay my passage to the colony. I have accepted his generous offer.'"

Both young men thought for a moment about Sarah's decision.

"How old is your aunt?" Lance asked.

"Let's see. I was five when she brought me to Cromley Hall. Aunt Sarah must have been about my age now. That would make her a little over forty now."

"She's a brave one to freely choose a new life in strange place!" Lance exclaimed. "What will she do?"

"She says she can earn her livelihood as a housekeeper."

"But why Williamsburg?"

"She considered the larger cities of the northern colonies—Philadelphia, New York, Boston—but she wants to be in a more rural area but one with a busy social life. However, she says her main reason is to be near me."

For several minutes neither young man spoke. Adam went to the door of the shop and looked out. Lance picked up the shoe he had been working on. When Adam came back to Lance's workbench, Lance looked up and said, "I wish we could do something to help her."

"I think we can."

"What?"

I've thought of two things. I'm going to ask Madam Ashley to write her friends in Williamsburg. They are prominent people, the kind who would be in need of an experienced maid. Also I am going to write to Alan's mother. She might know of some family in need of a housekeeper."

"You are right about both Madam Ashley and Martha Tisdale. They will help. Will you write your aunt soon?"

"Yes, and I want to ask Mr. Ashley permission to go to Hampton to meet Aunt Sarah when she arrives this summer."

"Don't get too far ahead of yourself, Adam. Unless you have more surprising news, I'd best get back to work."

After he left Lance, Adam walked to the landing and sat down at the end of the large loading dock. He needed time to sort out his feelings about the several pieces of news. About Lord Cromley's death he felt no sorrow. Nor did he gloat. Although he disliked Lord Cromley for his arrogant treatment of him, Adam was grateful for how much the forced indenture had changed his life.

Adam could dismiss Lord Cromley from his thoughts but not his aunt. He was delighted that his aunt was coming to Williamsburg. And he was certain that she could find a responsible position as a housekeeper. Still he was apprehensive. How well would she like Williamsburg? Would she find it too new—much too raw—after her life at Cromley Hall and in London? Would she soon miss the aura of the established and the traditional and become disturbed by the ever-changing energy of colonial life?

Then, suddenly, Adam recalled what his aunt had said to him that first afternoon at Cromley Hall as he stared trembling at the magnificent grand staircase. "Don't be frightened by your new life here, Adam. Don't be afraid of change. Change—that's what life is about." He hadn't understood what she had meant that afternoon. He had not even recalled her words until this afternoon. But there on the landing dock Adam knew for certain that his aunt would do well in Williamsburg.

The festive Christmas season of 1753 kept everyone busy. Both before and after Christmas the Ashleys hosted suppers and dances and, in turn, attended parties at other Tidewater plantations. Hannah worked more than her usual long hours to keep the dining room table in the great house overflowing with everything from roast pig to the daintiest of pastries. Adam and Lance occasionally abandoned their usual tasks to help keep the wood supply ready for numerous fireplaces.

On one morning before Christmas Day Mr. Ashley asked Adam to accompany him on the ride to take gifts to the three overseers and their families on lands to the northeast of the river. On the ride back when they stopped to let the horses drink from a stream, Adam told Mr. Ashley of his aunt's intention to come to Virginia and of his hope that Madam Ashley would write to her friends about Sarah. Adam said that he also planned to write Martha Tisdale.

"I am pleased for you that your aunt is coming, Adam. I am certain that Madam Ashley, as well as Mistress Tisdale, will be glad to help her find suitable employment. I'll speak to Madam Ashley tonight."

"Thank you. It is still hard for me to realize that by the time of the Williamsburg fair next summer, I will see Aunt Sarah again after these six years apart."

On Christmas Eve day Adam and Lance each said they had important details to finish up at work before they went to Hannah's special supper that night. Each wondered what the other had left to be done. When they joined George and William and the black house servants that night in the kitchen to taste Hannah's large fruit cake, both Adam and Lance looked rather pleased with themselves. That night they made love with a special intensity.

"Christmas cheer," Lance said as he cuddled close to Adam.

"Yes, the same to you," Adam replied. Soon they were both asleep.

On Christmas morning Adam stirred, annoyed by something heavy on the cover at the foot of the bed. He opened his eyes and looked down. A pair of shiny riding boots lay across his feet. He raised up and looked down at Lance, who seemed to still be asleep. Adam reached down and picked up one of the boots. It was handsomely made.

"Merry Christmas," Lance shouted. He pulled Adam back down on the bed and kissed him for a long time. When they broke apart, Adam responded, "Merry Christmas to you. Thank you for the boots. They are far too good for likes of me. But, Lance, I need to piss before I wet the bed. I'm going to the privy."

In a few minutes Adam returned. He stuck his head in the door and said in a firm voice, "Close your eyes, Lance, and don't move."

Lance looked puzzled.

"Do as I say, damn it," Adam said.

Lance closed his eyes. He had no sooner closed them than he felt a heavy covering over his head.

"You can open them now," Adam told him.

Lance lifted the covering off his head. It was a round cap with a flat top, all made of beaver skin. He held the cap out in front of him, turning it around several times. Then he put it back on his head and pulled Adam into his arms. "Thank you, Adam. It is the most handsome hat I have ever seen."

"Now you can get rid of that silly rag you wear every winter to keep your ears warm," Adam said.

The both burst out laughing. "Merry Christmas," they said simultaneously.

They looked at each other and grinned. Then Adam pulled Lance back down on the bed.

"Let's celebrate Christmas by skipping breakfast and being naughty," Adam said.

"Naughty?"

Adam got out of his breeches and exposed his erect sex. "Yes, naughty," he said.

Adam and Lance did not leave their quarters until time for the Christmas feast.

And feast it was—slices of turkey and ham, roasted quail, baked yams, squash pudding, dried apples spiced with cinnamon, hot biscuits, and, from the storehouse, fresh apples in a special combination with nuts and raisins. All of this was washed down with generous pitchers of cider. Reluctantly both Adam and Lance declined a slice of fruit cake, but they asked Hannah to save them a piece for later. They glanced across the table and knew each other's mind. They wished the company Merry Christmas and went out into the brisk December air.

"I'm too full," Lance complained.

"Me, too. Let's walk to the river bend. That will help."

"Do you want to go swimming!" Lance exclaimed.

"No." Adam paused and smiled. "My ballocks are small enough without getting them shriveled in that cold water."

Lance laughed. "No, your ballocks are not small. They are just tightly wrapped, not loosely hung low like mine. But, again, do you want to swim?"

"I will, if you dare."

They had almost reached the bend when Adam stopped and turned to Lance. He had one of the most serious looks on his face that Lance had ever seen. "What's wrong?" Lance asked.

"I'm thinking about Hannah."

"Her good meal?"

"No. How hard she has worked. Will she get a Christmas present?"

"Yes, like all of us, she will get something tomorrow on Boxing Day."

"But what about today?"

Lance looked at Adam and said, "You have something on your mind. Say it."

"Let's go back. I want us to make something to give Hannah after all the others are gone tonight after supper."

"What?"

"A muff, I think."

"Adam, slaves don't carry muffs."

"Well, she will. Not where folks can see her perhaps, but where it will keep her hands warm on cold nights."

Lance waited for a moment, then said, "You're mad but good. Let's go back. I'll help make the muff."

They walked quickly back to the warehouse. They opened the box of furs they were saving for shipment to England. An especially fine raccoon skin attracted them. It was the right width and length for a woman's muff.

"You oil the inside skin lightly," Adam told Lance. When Lance had finished his part of the work, Adam said, "I'll get the needle and thread." Adam was not the most accomplished seamster, but after an hour he had the two edges of the skin sewn together neatly. Then he handed the muff to Lance.

"Hannah will love it," Lance said. "And will she be surprised!"

Adam and Lance waited to go to the kitchen that evening until they knew that the house servants would have finished eating and left to do their chores in the great house, and that George and William would be almost done. With Lance holding the muff behind him, they entered the warm kitchen and quickly sat down. Lance put the muff on the floor at his feet. They greeted the other two indentured servants and Hannah.

"You'se late. Where you been?" Hannah asked.

"Working," Lance replied.

"Working!" George exclaimed in a loud voice.

"Yes, finishing up something we had not thought of until this afternoon," Adam said.

"You two are a queer pair," George continued, shaking his head. "Here it is the one day of the year when we have a full free day, not even a church service to interrupt it, and you say you've been working. It's just not natural."

Adam and Lance glanced briefly at each other. They both thought the same thing. *Please, not another Matt.*

William got up from the table and turned to George. "You ready to head out?"

"Yes," George replied. "Good night and again Merry Christmas. And you two don't do any more work tonight."

"No, we're through for the day. Only fun tonight. Good night and Merry Christmas," Lance replied.

When George and William were gone, Adam said to Hannah, "I'm not really too hungry after that feast at noon. I'd like just that piece of fruit cake I didn't have at noon and a cup of hot tea."

"The same for me," Lance said.

Hannah cut two large slices of fruit cake and set about making the hot tea. "Workin,'" she grunted loudly.

The two young men ate the fruit cake and drank the tea without saying anything. When they had finished eating, Adam rose from the bench and said, "Hannah, that was the best cake I've ever eaten. You've done yourself proud with all the good dishes you cooked today."

"Thank you," Hannah said and smiled broadly.

"Will you do us a favor now?" Adam asked.

"What's that?"

"Close your eyes and hold out your right hand."

"Why's that?"

"I can't tell you."

"Then I won'ts do it."

"Please, Hannah," Lance said.

"You two up to some mischief, I s'pects."

"It's Christmas and time for some fun. Please do us the favor."

"Don't you get me into no trouble now," Hannah said, as she closed her eyes and held out her right hand.

Lance quickly slipped the muff over her hand. Wondering what was going on, Hannah opened her eyes. She gasped and cried out, "What's this!"

"It's your Christmas present," the young men exclaimed together.

Hannah's face beamed her delight, but she said, "This is not for me. It belong to the mistress of a great house."

"It's for you," Adam insisted. "You are the mistress of this kitchen."

As tears gathered in her eyes, Hannah stuck the other hand into the muff and held it close against her large bosom. Then she put the muff on the table. She gathered first Adam, then Lance into her arms for a long hug. "Thank you, thank you," she repeated joyfully.

The three of them stood awkwardly, not knowing quite what to say next. Finally Adam said, "Well, Lance, we'd best get back to work. Merry Christmas, Hannah."

"Merry Christmas, Adam. Merry Christmas, Lance," Hannah replied.

As Adam and Lance left, they saw Hannah, her hands in her new muff, humming and dancing around the kitchen.

Boxing Day was a full day for the Ashley family. Shortly after breakfast Madam Ashley assembled the house servants in the large drawing room. With the help of her two youngest children, she handed out gifts to each of the black servants. Madam Ashley had several words of personal gratitude for each of the servants. Each of the children added their thanks as well. Then, in the early afternoon, Madam Ashley and the two children went to the kitchen behind the great house to greet Hannah and her helpers. After the gifts were distributed, Madam Ashley and her daughters left the kitchen to a chorus of "thanks you."

After the midday meal Mr. Ashley began his round of distributing gifts. Trying to act older than his eleven years, William accompanied his father. Outside the stable Joseph had assembled the numerous black men and the few black women who worked the various dependency buildings and the gardens surrounding the great house. It was a large gathering. It took Mr. Ashley almost all afternoon to hand out his gifts and to offer a word of thanks to each worker. When he finished, he and his son accompanied Joseph to his house where he had gifts for all of Joseph's family.

"It has been a good year, Joseph," Mr. Ashley said. "Much of the thanks goes to you."

"And to the good weather," Joseph replied.

The two men smiled and shook hands.

Adam and Lance were waiting for Mr. Ashley outside the door of his office in the east wing of the great house. "Come inside," Mr. Ashley said, welcoming the last two persons on his Boxing Day list. Once inside, Mr. Ashley looked steadily at the two young men and said, "I shall be brief in my thanks. Each of you knows all too well how much I depend on you for the well-being of Ashley Landing. And Madam Ashley extends her thanks as well for all of your help in her new garden."

Neither Adam nor Lance knew what to say.

"I hope these watches will in some small way repay my year's debt to you," Mr. Ashley said as he handed each of them a small pocket watch.

Both Adam and Lance were like Hannah with her fur muff. The gift was one they never would have expected. They stuttered their thanks, looking with surprise and delight at the watches. Finally Adam said, "It's more than my service is worth. But I accept my watch with many thanks."

"As do I," Lance added at loss for any other words.

Mr. Ashley put an arm across the shoulders of both young men and said, "Let's hope for another good year at Ashley Landing."

Adam and Lance nodded agreement and started to leave.

"Oh, Adam," Mr. Ashley called, "Madam Ashley says to tell you that she will write her friends in Williamsburg about your aunt. But

she will wait until the middle of next month. Williamsburg folk celebrate the holidays longer than we do here."

"Thank her for me," Adam said. The three men bade each other a
good evening.

Parties at the Tidewater great houses continued through Twelfth
Night but then stopped. The rest of January 1754 was a quiet time. It
was too early to till the fields. Tobacco seeds would not be planted in
flats until next month. There was only ledger work for Adam in the
warehouse; and, since Lance was ahead of himself in his shop, the two
young men spent several afternoons each week in the woods hunting.
The skins in the box for shipment to England doubled.

Shortly after a late January snowfall, the packet of letters from
Williamsburg arrived. One letter was from Henry Tisdale. The letter
contained bad news. Martha Tisdale had died from pneumonia in late
November.

"I am sorry for Master Tisdale," Adam said. He hesitated before he
went on. "I don't mean to sound selfish, but I am also sorry that Mistress Tisdale will not be there to help Aunt Sarah."

"No, you are not selfish. Best that you go ahead and say what is
only natural for you to feel. I had thought the same thing," Lance replied. "But what else does he say?"

Adam picked up the letter again and read,

*Since Martha's death I have had many people looking after me, and
many people offering advice on what I should do with my life now. Several of my older close friends tell me that I should remarry. I'll not accept
that counsel, at least until I feel much differently than I do now. One of
my sons wants me to live with him and his family. I doubt I'll move from
my house though. Although the rooms seem vacant without Martha, they
are still the most familiar rooms I know. They are the rooms I want to
live in. My oldest son's wife gives the advice I shall probably take. She
says that I need a housekeeper, someone to see that the kitchen help pre-
pares meals and to tend to all the household duties while I keep busy in the
shop. That is what happened between my late wife and me, except, of
course, I had the added pleasure of sharing my bed with her. My oldest*

*son says a good housekeeper with an honest reputation will be hard to find, but his wife says not. As of this writing, I fare well enough alone.*

"Damn," shouted Lance, "that's the place your aunt needs to be."

"It is almost too good to be true," Adam replied. He was already thinking of letters he had to write. But since nothing would happen that day, he turned his attention back to the letter at hand.

"He's enclosed a letter from Timothy and Alan," Adam exclaimed.

"Before we read the rest of his father's letter, let's open the one from our friends," Lance said.

"You open it, and read it to me," Adam replied.

Lance tore open the letter. "There's no date on it. Here's what they say."

*Dear Lance and Adam,*

*This is only a short message to let you know that we are well and happy. I hope Alan's father is able to send it to you. After we left Williamsburg in September, everything took twice as long as we had expected and was twice as hard. We are now settled in Charlottesville. We stopped at three places before we arrived here, but none seemed right for us. For now, we are content in Charlottesville. We have rented a shop, and, although good leather is hard to find, we do enough shoe-making to keep us in food. The town is small but growing. It is in a valley overlooking the Rivanna River. To the west on a clear day we see tall mountains with a blue haze above them. We hear that the valley beyond those mountains is the richest in the colony. I am willing to push on and to farm there, but Alan isn't. I send my greetings and my love to you both. Now I'll turn the pen over to Alan.*

*Tim*

"I'm glad they are settled," Lance said.

"Yes, but for how long? It sounds to me like Tim may get a bit restless and want to cross the mountains. What does Alan say?"

Lance started reading again.

*Dear Adam and Lance,*

*I do not have much more to add to what Tim has already told you. I must admit that I miss Williamsburg more than I thought I would. But Tim's energy and love keep me here, and happy to be here. We will miss seeing you at the fair this summer. Come fair time, on the second night, take off your shirts and look at your navels. Tim and I will do the same here. Over all the rough country between us, we will be together.*

*Alan*

"It's good to hear from them. We must try to get a letter to them. What do you think of Alan's suggestion?" Lance asked.

"I like it. But, Lance, right now I need to sit at the privy for a minute or two. I'll look at my navel out there as I take care of business."

While Adam was gone, Lance read the rest of Alan's father's letter. When Adam returned, he found Lance sitting on his bench, staring intently across the shop with his left hand propped under his nose.

"What are you thinking about so hard?" Adam asked.

"Master Tisdale wants me to come to Williamsburg when my indenture ends."

"To work in his shop?"

"Yes. He says that since Alan and Tim left, he and his two sons have hardly been able to supply all the requests for shoes."

"Would you like to go to Williamsburg?"

"Not unless you also went, and I don't think you want to leave here."

"No, I don't. But we won't get our freedom papers until late next year. So you—or we—don't have to make a decision now."

"No, we don't, and when the time does come, it will be our decision, not just mine. But, Adam, his letter also says that if I didn't want to go to Williamsburg, he would be happy for me to supply shoes from here to his shop."

"That would require Mr. Ashley's consent even when you become free and were working for wages here."

"Yes, that's true. But, as I said, we don't have to decide today. Master Tisdale says we can talk about the matter when we come to the fair. Oh, by the way, he extends an invitation for us to stay there with him."

"Of course, we'll accept," Adam said. "If all goes as I hope it will, Aunt Sarah will be there as the housekeeper."

"Are you going to write him about your aunt?"

"Yes, and soon. But I want to speak to Madam Ashley about it before I write."

The next day after the midday meal Adam went to the great house and asked permission to speak alone with Madam Ashley. When a house servant announced that Adam wanted to speak with her, Madam Ashley was surprised. She sensed that Adam had something bothering him, for this was the first time since Adam arrived at Ashley Landing that he had asked to speak with her privately.

As soon as he entered the room, Adam said, "I am sorry to bother you, Madam Ashley."

"Don't apologize, Adam. What may I do for you?"

Adam started to speak several times but couldn't. Finally he managed, "I—I—I want—"

"Adam," Madam Ashley said kindly, "simply tell me quickly and plainly what is on your mind."

In a quick flow of words Adam told her that Martha Tisdale was dead, that her husband now needed a housekeeper, and that he hoped his aunt could obtain that position.

Calmly Madam Ashley replied, "Then you must write to Master Tisdale at once and tell him that your aunt is coming to Williamsburg and is in need of a position as housekeeper. Mr. Ashley is going to Williamsburg soon on business. He will take your letter, and he will speak to Master Tisdale on behalf of your aunt. I will delay writing my friends there until I hear what Master Tisdale has to say."

Adam breathed a sigh of relief. The worried look on his face disappeared. He said, "Then what I want to do is proper? I will not seem to pander my aunt?"

"Goodness no!" Madam Ashley exclaimed firmly. "Adam, we woman are not as free as you men. Often we need the offices of men to get along in life. You are doing your aunt a kind favor in offering to help her. You are simply doing what many a man—father, brother, nephew—has done for a woman he respected and loved."

"Then I will write Master Tisdale at once and bring you the letter to give to Mr. Ashley."

"And I will tell my husband exactly what to say to Master Tisdale to ensure that your aunt gets the position."

"Thank you, m'am," Adam said as he left the room.

After he had gone, Madam Ashley shook her head and smiled. How good Adam was, she thought, to think so carefully about his aunt's reputation. But she also thought how brave Sarah was in her decision to come to Williamsburg on her own, without knowing how Adam had plans to see that she had an appropriate position.

More surprising news came to Ashley Landing during the next two weeks than Adam thought possible. The good news which Mr. Ashley brought back from Williamsburg was that Henry Tisdale very much wanted Adam's aunt as his housekeeper.

While at the capital Mr. Ashley had arranged for a packet of three letters to be sent to his London agent who would then see that the packet was forwarded to Adam's aunt. One of the letters was from Henry Tisdale saying how happy he would be to have Sarah as his housekeeper. If she accepted his offer, he wrote that he would make arrangements for her travel from Hampton to Williamsburg after she arrived here. Another of the letters was from Tisdale's daughter-in-law, who welcomed Sarah to Williamsburg, described the widower's needs, and detailed at length what Sarah would find life to be like in the colony. The third letter to Sarah Mr. Ashley took upon himself to write on behalf of Adam.

"Adam," Mr. Ashley said, "I trust I have done the right thing. I wanted your aunt to get Master Tisdale's offer as soon as possible. I have told her what you have done for her, and how happy you are with her coming to Williamsburg. You will, I'm sure, write your own letter, but it probably will not reach her until after she has made her plans for leaving England."

"Thank you for all you have done. I guess now it is only a matter of waiting," Adam replied.

The surprising news which Mr. Ashley brought back from Williamsburg concerned a business venture he was strongly considering. At the capital he had talked at length with an Annapolis shipbuilder, Captain McGaw. The captain's proposal was that Ashley Landing join with him in building a small cargo ship. Then goods from Annapolis and the warehouse at Ashley Landing would be shipped to the West Indies. On the return sailing the ship would bring back sugar and spices for sale in the southern colonies. The captain and Mr. Ashley had all but signed the final papers for the business venture.

"There is little risk and much to gain," Mr. Ashley explained to Adam and Lance one afternoon. "You both will be busier than ever. Your shoes, Lance, will be a major export."

Lance looked at Adam, who nodded. It seemed the appropriate time for Lance to tell Mr. Ashley about Master Tisdale's invitation to join his shop.

After listening to Lance, Mr. Ashley said, "I had always hoped that you would stay here after your indenture ended."

"I intend to, especially now," Lance said. "I appreciate Master Tisdale's offer for me to join his shop. But I really do not want to live in Williamsburg. There are too many bad memories. But, more than that, life here is too good for me to leave it. Master Tisdale can find young apprentices to help him and his sons in their two shops there. I want the new challenge here."

"We will be busy," Adam quickly added, "but I like that."

"I am pleased to hear what both of you say," Mr. Ashley said. "But, out of courtesy, Lance, you should write Master Tisdale of your decision to stay here and also to thank him for his offer of employment. I'll take your letter to Williamsburg next month, and I'll explain to him about the new Ashley Landing venture which needs your help."

"I'll do that," Lance promised.

"Captain McGaw comes to Ashley Landing late this year. He will want to talk with you both," Mr. Ashley said. "Until then we have work to do. It's near planting time."

Not until late June did Adam hear from his aunt. By that time of the year, the tobacco plants had been moved from the flats to the fields where they were now growing. Field hands were carefully freeing the

plants from worms, pruning the young leaves, and hoeing the ground
to keep it rid of weeds. The tobacco crop looked in prime condition.

His aunt's letter arrived at the landing by boat along with boxes
from England and letters to Mr. Ashley from his London agent. As
soon as a house servant brought the letter to Adam and he saw his
aunt's handwriting on the envelope, Adam left the warehouse for
Lance's shop.

"I've heard from Aunt Sarah," he shouted as he entered the shop.
"What does she say?"

Adam tore open the letter and started reading.

> *Dear Adam,*
>
> *I am in London waiting for conditions to be favorable for our ship to go
> down the Thames. I am staying at the Cromleys' house in the city. The
> young Lord Cromley insisted that I be comfortable until my departure.
> He has been most generous in paying for my passage to Virginia. My bag
> is ready, so when word comes that the tide is right, I can leave quickly for
> the ship.*
>
> *I don't know which will get to Virginia first—my letter or me. I am
> told that we should be at Hampton by early July.*

"She might be already here," Lance exclaimed.

"She may be," Adam agreed, hoping that she had arrived safely. He
was sorry not to be able to be there to greet her. He returned to the
letter.

> *Adam, I cannot tell you how grateful I am for all you have done in help-
> ing me to secure employment. While I was willing to go to Williamsburg
> and there search for a position as housekeeper, you have made my life
> much easier. Master Tisdale's letter makes me certain that he is a pleas-
> ant and generous person, and I shall do all I can to run his house effi-
> ciently. His daughter-in-law was most thoughtful in writing to me about
> details of the widower's house and about the everyday concerns in living
> in Williamsburg. I think I shall be comfortable both in Master Tisdale's
> house and in the city itself.*

Adam quickly skimmed the rest of the letter and then said, "She writes that Master Tisdale has made arrangements for her to stay at a Hampton inn until he has word that she has arrived. Then he will go to bring her to Williamsburg. She says that Master Tisdale has told her of his invitation to us to stay at his house during the fair."

"That will be a great reunion for the two of you," Lance said.

"Yes. She says she wonders if she will recognize me." Adam read from the letter, "I certainly remember you as a young boy, Adam. And I can still picture you as a lad of seventeen. But you must be quite a young man by now. Have you grown a beard?"

"Grown a beard!" Lance exclaimed. He howled as he ran his hand over the light blond stubble of Adam's face. "Where you have hair is down here, not on your face," Lance said as he grabbed Adam's crotch.

Adam tried to pull away from Lance's grasp. But Lance held him tightly in his arms. He rubbed his crotch hard against Adam's. Soon each had an erection. They kissed.

Finally Adam pushed Lance away. "That's dangerous," he said. "We shouldn't do that here. Someone might come in unexpectedly, and we'd be hard pressed to explain ourselves."

"You're right. But hard pressed is just what I want to do one more time." Again Lance pulled Adam into his arms and pressed hard against him.

Adam gave in for several minutes, returning the hard contact of Lance's body. Then he wiggled out of the embrace and said firmly, "Now stop it, Lance, and listen to the last of Aunt Sarah's letter."

"Spoil sport," Lance said, feigning anger. "Go on, read me the rest of the letter."

*Adam, I am anxious to be in Williamsburg, even more anxious to see you. You may not hear from me again before I see you at the time of the fair. I am delighted that you and your friend from Ashley Landing will be guests at Master Tisdale's house. I look forward to seeing you very much.*

*Love, Aunt Sarah*

"Yes, seeing you, even without a beard," Lance teased, grabbing Adam's crotch once again.

"Not now, damn it," Adam said. "I've got to get back to the warehouse."

"You are really going to get it tonight," Lance said and laughed. He grabbed his own crotch and squeezed hard.

"Fine. I can take all you've got to give," Adam responded.

"And that's plenty," Lance boasted.

"Don't I know!"

The two young men grinned at each other as Adam left the shop. They both were anxious for the day to pass into night.

The summer heat matured the tobacco crop. During the first week of August, Mr. Ashley announced that it was time to cut the tobacco and take it to the drying sheds. From then until almost time for the fair, almost everyone worked longer hours than usual. As he did last year, Lance went to plantation fields up river to help supervise the cutting. He missed being with Adam, but he went to bed in the overseer's house too tired to care about anything but sleep.

When Lance returned to Ashley Landing after the cutting was done, Adam greeted him with "You look a bit tired."

"I am. Thank goodness there's nothing more to be done with tobacco until October. Then we'll bust our ballocks getting it into hogsheads. But for now, it's up to the hot wind to do its job in the drying sheds."

"Are you ready to go to the fair at the end of this week?"

"I'll be ready by then."

"Are you too tired to go to the bend for a swim?"

"No. That water will soak new life into me."

Over an hour later the two naked young men lay in their hiding place near the river. Their skins were still wet from their swim. As usual, Lance had won the race across the river.

"Feel better?" Adam asked.

"Much. And ready to do a little feeling." Lance reached for Adam's cock and peeled back the foreskin. Almost immediately Adam's cock responded. Lance squatted before Adam and took the long sex in his mouth. He kept on it for a long time.

Finally Adam pushed him away. He sighed deeply and then chuckled and asked, "Did you handle yourself while you were away?"

"No. I was too tired when I went to bed to even think about it. Did you?"

"Yes, thinking of you as I did it."

"Well, think of me now." Lance lay back down, his cock at Adam's mouth.

They were in their favorite position with each of them at the other's sex. The two young men took each other. They were so excited, however, that in less than two minutes each unloaded in the other's mouth. When they finally pulled off each other, Adam shifted himself so that he could take Lance in his arms. They kissed and then rested.

Lance fell asleep. Adam let him doze for a short time, then shook him awake. "If you sleep too long, we'll miss the fair."

Lance raised up and exclaimed, "Wouldn't want to do that."

Shortly after noon on Saturday the flatboat took the Ashley family and the two indentured servants to the landing outside Williamsburg. Everyone was in high spirits. The two Ashley girls were full of talk of parties. Young William announced that he and a friend would win the three-legged race this year. Their parents listened and smiled. They were thinking of their own festivities.

"Please, will you take me to the puppet show again?" William asked Adam and Lance.

"Yes," Lance replied, "but only if you promise not to get peanut shells down the front of my shirt again."

William nodded and laughed.

"Take me, too," little Caroline demanded.

"Only if your mother says it is proper," Adam told her.

"If you want Adam to take you to the puppet show, then ask him properly," Madam Ashley reprimanded her daughter. "Don't shout at him."

Caroline bowed her head and then turned to Adam and said softly, "Please, take me to the puppet show, Adam."

"Of course, I will," Adam told her. "But no peanut shells down my shirt."

"Thank you. Don't worry about peanut shells though. Young ladies do not eat peanuts in public," Caroline said in a manner far beyond her years.

No one laughed out loud. But even the black hands in charge of the boat had a hard time suppressing their amusement at the young girl's pronouncement.

"Who told you that?" her brother demanded.

"Nobody. I just know such things," his little sister answered in a tone of voice that declared the matter settled.

Before the argument could go further, the landing came into sight.

Friends had sent their carriage to take the Ashleys into Williamsburg. After saying good evening to the family and setting a time to take Caroline and William to the puppet show, Adam and Lance picked up their small travel bags and headed down the wide trail. Other people were walking, too, but Adam tugged at Lance's sleeve and said in a low voice, "Let's not join the others."

"Oh, fine. Is something the matter?" Lance asked.

"I guess I'm a little frightened."

"Of meeting your aunt?"

"Not that really. But what if she doesn't like it here, or if she does not like Master Tisdale? Or what if he doesn't like her as a housekeeper?"

"I think you are worrying without any cause."

"I hope so. And I suspect you are right. It's just that I want this to work out well for Aunt Sarah."

"Come on, Adam, let's join the other people and talk about something else."

Thirty minutes later the two young men stood beneath the cordwainer's sign on his Duke of Gloucester Street shop. Henry Tisdale looked up from his bench and saw them standing at the open door. He quickly went to greet them. He gave each of them a fatherly hung.

"How are you, Master Tisdale?" Lance asked.

Henry Tisdale snorted. "What's with this 'Master' nonsense!" he exclaimed. "My name is Henry. That's what I want you to call me."

"Greetings, Henry," Adam said. "How are you?"

"Fine, fine, and happy to see you two," he said. Then he went to the back of the shop and called, "Sarah, our guests are here."

Soon Henry Tisdale and Lance stood smiling as they watched Adam and his aunt embrace each other warmly. When Sarah finally pulled away and held Adam at an arm's length to look at him, she said, "It's so good to see you, Adam. I would have recognized you. I am glad you have not grown a beard."

Adam heard Lance chuckle. The four were so excited that no one quite knew what to say next.

Finally Henry Tisdale said in a loud voice, "Welcome to our home."

The "our" startled the other three people. They looked at him with surprise.

"Yes, our home," he said again.

All of the fears Adam had expressed on the walk to Williamsburg quickly disappeared.

# 1754: Ashley Landing: A Winter Visitor

"How much longer?" Adam asked

"Two, three days at the most," Lance answered.

The late summer and early fall hot breezes had dried the tobacco hung in the sheds. Now it was time to strip the leaves from the stalks and to press them into hogsheads. The tobacco from the north plantations up river had arrived by boat at Ashley Landing. One of the overseers had come to supervise the arduous task. Mr. Ashley had asked Lance to help the overseer.

"Been hard work?" Adam asked, already knowing the answer.

"I'm glad it's almost over. I'm ready to get back to my shop."

October had been the busy month for Lance; November was now the busy one for Adam. The hogsheads now had to be labeled and counted, then these figures entered in the warehouse ledger. Once the bookkeeping was completed, Adam had to supervise the loading of the hogsheads onto the flatboats for the trip down the river to Hampton for shipment to England. It was late in November before the business of the year's tobacco crop was over.

"Glad to see the last of the flatboats leave the dock?" Lance asked Adam. They were lying close together in bed.

"Yes, very much."

"Even happier, I suspect, to have that letter from your aunt," Lance said.

The letter from Williamsburg had arrived that morning. It was the first news Adam had from his aunt since he had seen her at Henry Tisdale's house almost four months ago. Adam was delighted with what his aunt had to say. She thoroughly enjoyed her new life. She felt more contented than she ever had in England. Henry's family had made her feel a part of them. Once a week the two sons and their families sat at Henry's table for a meal. Martha Tisdale's friends also wel-

doi:10.1300/5623_09

comed Sarah. They frequently quilted together. On several occasions one of the women had whispered to her that she hoped Sarah would someday marry the widower. Sarah wrote, "I did not come to Williamsburg to find a husband. But, Adam, should Henry ever propose to me, I think I would accept him."

"Are you pleased?"

"Of course, Lance. I must admit though I am a bit surprised at how quickly she has taken to life here in the colony."

Lance did not respond to that. He waited a minute or two and then said, "Well, I have another surprise for you now."

"What's that?"

"It's no surprise if I tell you."

"True. But give me a hint."

"This morning Mr. Ashley asked me to ride to the southeast fields to take a message to the overseer there."

"So?"

"I enjoyed the ride. Whisper is a good horse. So I gave her an extra ear of corn when we got back."

Adam laughed, "You cornholed the ear?"

"Yes, and I did another ear and brought it back here."

"What for?"

"Don't ask so damn many questions," Lance said. He reached over and rubbed Adam's bare chest.

"You're a strange one tonight," Adam said, as he felt Lance's hand slowly caress his face and neck, and then move to play with the hair of his armpit. Once again his hand rubbed Adam's chest before it moved slowly down his firm belly. Lance stopped rubbing just as his hand reached Adam's thick cluster of cock hair.

"You're warming me up," Adam said.

"Just what I intended to do."

Lance raised up and kissed Adam. Then, for a long time, his lips played with Adam's body—over his nipples, down his belly, and into the two sides of his crotch. He pulled Adam's legs apart and let his tongue lick Adam's hole.

"I'll shoot if you keep that up," Adam warned. His foreskin was stretched down his hard cock as far as it could go.

"Let me have your juice then," Lance said as he swallowed Adam's long sex.

Suddenly Adam felt something hard at his hole. It was different from the head of Lance's cock, but it felt good.

"What's that?" Adam raised up and cried out.

Lance pulled his mouth off Adam's cock and pushed him back down. "Just let me do what I want," he said.

Adam relaxed and let the long object penetrate him. He could hardly believe the double pleasure he was getting. The faster Lance's lips moved over his cockhead, the faster and deeper the thing inside him moved. Finally Adam shouted, "I'm there." He let loose his juice in Lance's mouth at the same time the thing kept hitting the hard spot up inside him. A few minutes later Adam rested in Lance's arms. A corn cob lay on the floor beside their bed.

"When did you get that idea?" Adam asked.

"This morning when I came back to the stable. The ear of corn I shelled for Whisper looked so much like my cock."

"As thick, yes. But longer and quite a bit bumpier."

"Did you like it?"

"Yes, it was good. And it was certainly different. Still my preference is this," Adam said as he reached for Lance's stiff sex. Before long, Adam's hand was wet with Lance's cream.

After they had cleaned up and were in bed again, Adam laughed and said, "Well, I guess I really got cornholed tonight."

The two young men settled down for the night. Shortly though Adam raised up and said, "Lance, that Annapolis shipbuilder comes late next week. I had almost forgotten that."

"Adam, that's almost two weeks away. Why are you so concerned about it now, just when I was almost asleep?"

Adam laughed. "From an ear of corn to cornholing to cornmeal. That's what raced through my mind. Besides your shoes, cornmeal is one of the things we'll be sending to the West Indies."

"Well, stop grinding the cornmeal now and go to sleep, damn it." Lance gave Adam a nudge in the ribs and a quick kiss before he turned over.

Two weeks later on the morning the ship builder was to arrive, snow fell. Midafternoon a slave on the dock at the landing shouted that a boat was in sight. The young black man walked through the snow up the long sloping lawn to the great house and around to Mr. Ashley's office. Then he went to the warehouse to get Adam to join Mr. Ashley. "Stay here, Josh, by the fire," Adam told the young black man. "When you are warm, come down to the dock." Adam put on his heavy coat and went to the landing.

Adam watched as the large open boat was secured against the dock. Aboard the boat, with a tent pitched midway across it, were six people, four of them the black men who had handled the boat. The short bearded older man was obviously the shipbuilder.

What surprised Adam was the sixth person, a young man. He wore a short heavy coat and gloves above his dark pants and polished leather boots. Only the features of his finely chiseled face and his uncovered hair gave him a physical identity. His handsome face was the dark color of the shell of a pecan. His hair was deep black; it hung below his neck and was tied in a loose pigtail with a dark blue ribbon. What struck Adam most though was the regal way the young man stood, but without a trace of haughtiness.

While Mr. Ashley and captain exchanged greetings and talked, Adam instructed one of the house slaves to take care of the captain's slaves. However, Adam was puzzled. What to do about the young Indian, who stood silently taking in the scene? Adam had never heard of an Indian slave or indentured servant. He decided to let Mr. Ashley handle the matter. After several minutes, Mr. Ashley turned to Adam and introduced him to the shipbuilder.

"Here's the man who will help us bring new merchandise to our warehouse from the West Indies, Adam," Mr. Ashley said. Captain McGaw and Adam shook hands and spoke briefly. Then the shipbuilder turned to the young Indian and said, "Let me introduce a young man who is like a son to me. This is Martin. Martin, this is Mr. Ashley and Adam Bradley." The three men shook hands.

"I am pleased to meet you," Martin said in a soft but manly voice.

Adam looked at Martin in surprise. *Who is this stranger of color with such good manners and who speaks so well?* Adam asked himself. As if he had read Adam's mind, Captain McGaw answered his question.

"Fourteen years ago I went to Philadelphia to claim the bride my family had arranged for me. There at her parents' house was six-year-old Martin, the orphan son of a former servant. How his mother and he, then a year-old baby, got from their Nanticoke tribe to Philadelphia was—and still is—a mystery. I recognized him immediately as a bright lad, and my bride-to-be and I agreed that he should go back with us to Annapolis. It was a wise decision. Martin is invaluable. I depend on him for a host of things at the shipyard. Also he is like an older brother to our young sons. I hope he is welcome at Ashley Landing," the shipbuilder said.

"Indeed he is," Mr. Ashley replied. "Adam, make Martin your guest while he is here." The winter sky was clear now. The snow had stopped. There was a sharp bite to the air. "Let us get to warm rooms," Mr. Ashley said. Mr. Ashley, the captain and the slaves left the landing. Adam and Martin were alone at the dock.

"Do you have gear?" Adam asked.

"A sleeping pallet and a small kit," Martin answered. "I'll get them."

Adam waited while Martin went to the boat to fetch his things. When he returned to the landing, Martin let his eyes roam over Adam's face and body. Martin broke into a warm smile. When the two young men were face to face, they studied each other briefly. Adam, too, smiled.

"Here I can carry one of those," Adam finally said. As Martin handed Adam the bedroll, their fingers touched. "Thank you," Martin said as he look at Adam and smiled again. "Let me show you the warehouse," Adam said. "I have to tidy up a few things there before we go to supper."

They walked quickly through the snow to the warehouse. Adam and Martin said little as Adam finished his work. In response to Adam's questions, Martin talked mainly about his work with Captain McGaw. When Adam asked him about Philadelphia, Martin replied that he did not remember much. Martin asked nothing about Adam's life. Yet Adam felt no discomfort in the presence of the reserved Martin. Somehow Adam sensed that Martin already knew more about him than Adam had revealed in spoken words.

"I'm done," Adam said, hanging up a broom. "Let's take your things to our quarters and then get to supper."

Martin nodded. The two of them walked toward the quarters without speaking. Suddenly Martin came up to Adam and asked in a low voice, "Do you have a bedfellow?"

The question surprised Adam. He did not know how to respond. When he decided that there was no second meaning to the question, he replied, "Yes, I share my bed with another indentured servant. Lance is our shoemaker. He is several months older than I am. We are close friends."

"Do you want me to sleep on the boat and not intrude on your privacy? There's good cover on the boat from the cold there. Give me an honest answer, Adam," Martin said.

"No, certainly not," Adam responded quickly. Adam sensed that Martin was pleased. He continued, "We have plenty of room for your pallet. There is even room in our bed for the three of us. We might all keep warmer that way. It's cold for this time of the year."

Martin suddenly became very quiet. He lowered his head and seemed to be biting his lips. Then, almost in a whisper, he said, "I'm not sure I could trust myself."

The statement startled Adam. He thought he had heard correctly, but he wasn't sure. "What?" Adam asked anxiously.

Before Martin could reply, a shout from Lance halted the two young men. They stood, facing each other without speaking, while Lance ran toward them. Then Lance stopped. He scooped up snow to form a snowball. He hurled it at Adam. But Adam ducked, and the snowball hit Martin squarely in the face.

"A fine way to treat our guest," Adam shouted to Lance.

His face red with embarrassment and from the cold air, Lance ran up to Adam and Martin. When he saw the handsome young Indian grinning at him, Lance blushed even more. "I'm sorry. I meant that snowball for Adam," Lance explained.

"Yes, I know you did. It was a token of your affection for him," Martin told him.

Both Adam and Lance were stunned. They looked at the clear evening sky as if they were trying to make it snow again.

"I'm Martin," the Indian said to Lance, breaking the awkward silence. "I've come with Captain McGaw about the ship he and your Mr. Ashley are going to have built."

By then, Adam had recovered himself. He introduced the two men, who then shook hands. They laughed about the snowball. "Your snowball did no harm," Martin said to Lance. "Its coldness felt good, and fortunately the whiteness of the snow did nothing to damage my natural color."

Neither Adam nor Lance knew quite how to respond to Martin's remark, but a stiff wind prompted Adam to say, "Let's get out of this cold and to the quarters. Lance, if you'll get wood for a fire, I'll show Martin where to store his gear." When Lance headed toward the woodshed, Martin's eyes followed him. "He is a good fellow," Martin said to Adam.

"Yes, he is," Adam repeated. Adam was still curious as to what Martin had meant about not trusting himself with the three of them in bed. He doubted, however, that this was the time to ask. He was even more curious about Martin's calling the snowball a token of affection. *Surely,* Adam told himself, *after being here less than two hours, Martin cannot know how strong the affection is between Lance and me.* Adam was at a complete loss as to how to ask Martin what he had meant by that remark.

Adam took Martin to the quarters. Inside, Martin looked around the room and asked, "Where shall I put my pallet?"

"You'll be warmest there in front of the fireplace. But, as I said, Martin, if it gets too chilly during the night, you must share the bed with us."

Martin hesitated, then asked, "Are you certain, Adam, that you would not rather I slept on the boat and did not disturb you and Lance?"

"No, Martin," Adam said quickly. "It is not just that Mr. Ashley asked me to welcome you here. I want you to share our quarters.

Lance and I have never had a guest before. It will be fun talking and getting acquainted."

"If you are sure."

"Very sure, Martin." Suddenly Adam felt bold. "Why would you not trust yourself to share the bed with us?"

"Perhaps I'll tell you later when . . . ," Martin began but was interrupted when Lance hurried in and dumped a load of wood in the woodbox by the fireplace.

"There's wood for a start," Lance said. "We can each carry in a load after supper."

Adam was annoyed that Lance had cut off Martin's explanation, but he did not ask Martin to continue. Instead he said, "Yes, it is time to get to the kitchen. Do you need to make use of the privy, Martin?"

"No."

"Then let's be off."

Later, in the kitchen, the three young men found bowls of hot, rich corn chowder on the table along with bread and cold ham. Although Hannah had welcomed Martin to the kitchen and to Ashley Landing, there was an uneasiness around the table. Clearly the two other indentured servants, William and George, resented Martin's presence. They had barely grunted a greeting upon being introduced and had seemed not to see Martin's extended hand. Nor did they speak to Martin as they ate. Martin intuited the reasons for their feelings toward him. Without flinching, his eyes met the bitter looks of the two other men at the table. His dignity reminded Adam of the regal way Martin had stood on the long boat.

Just as the five men finished eating, a house servant entered. He announced that the master and his guest wished Martin to come to the great house. The captain needed Martin to help explain certain details. Martin thanked Hannah for his supper, and he told Adam and Lance not to wait for him. "I can find my way to the quarters," Martin said as he left with the servant.

As soon as Martin was gone, George jumped up from his chair and raised his clinched fist in the air. "Damn redskin!" he exclaimed. "He gets invited to the great house. I don't. We ought to have scalped every one of those bastards instead of pushing them west into the hills." For a minute a hush fell over the kitchen.

Then Adam stood up. "Shut up," he said calmly but firmly. "Martin's a good fellow. True, he's different from us in the color of his skin. But, in a lot of more important ways, he is no different."

George stared at Adam. He shrugged his shoulders at what he considered the stupidity of Adam's statement. "Hell, he's your guest in quarters, not mine. Thank God for that. Will, are you ready?"

William shoved his chair back and stood up. He looked briefly at everyone in the kitchen before he turned to George and said, "I'm with you. I'm ready to leave." Without saying good night to Adam and Lance, the two men stalked out of the kitchen.

Hannah sighed. "Not the best night in this kitchen." She shoved another dirty pan to each of her kitchen helpers for cleaning.

Shortly Adam and Lance headed to the privy before turning in. Back in their quarters, Lance started a fire and lit a lamp. Soon the chill of the room was gone. Then, Adam told Lance about what Martin had said about sleeping three in the bed. "He was starting to explain what he meant when you came in with the wood. He said something about telling us later."

"Well, I don't know what he meant," Lance said and laughed, "but I do know that I wouldn't trust myself to keep my hands off him if he were naked next to me."

Before that conversation went further, Martin returned. He was exuberant. "Your warehouse will get its ship, Adam," Martin said. "That means I'll be visiting here at least once each year, unless, of course, I wear out my welcome this time."

"You won't do that as far as Lance and I are concerned," Adam assured him.

"Maybe when the ship is ready to sail, I'll sign on as a deckhand," Lance said.

Adam laughed and teased, "Tired of staying here on land, Lance?"

Lance turned quickly. "Oh, no, Adam, you know I . . ." Lance stopped himself before he could finish by saying "love you."

Both knowing the unspoken words, Adam and Lance looked at Martin. For some reason, he was grinning with amusement.

"Let's put another log on the fire," Adam said. "I want to hear more about what went on in the library." Lance added a small log and stirred the fire. Adam got a jug of apple juice from the cabinet and filled a large mug. The three of them sat cross-legged before the fire. In turn, they sipped from the mug.

For an hour Martin talked about the cargo ship. Neither Adam nor Lance always understood the terms he used. Martin smiled and explained in other ways. When Martin said that during rough weather he occasionally got sick aboard ship, Lance laughed and said he guessed he would not learn to be a seaman. He reached over and slapped Adam on the back. Adam slapped him in return. Suddenly they all stopped talking. They looked at each other and smiled.

After a minute Martin got up. "I'd better not keep us up any longer." He touched both Adam and Lance on the top of the head. Then without any sign of embarrassment he stripped himself of his clothes. He stood naked before Adam and Lance, still cross-legged before the fire. Adam and Lance did not dare look at each other. They knew they both had erections.

Martin's dark-colored body glistened in the firelight. He was taller than Lance by several inches. His body was slender but well muscled. Large nipples dominated his square chest muscles. His flat abdomen was a perfect U shape. His body was hairless, except for dark patches under his arms and the cluster of dark curls surrounding his sex. Martin's limp cock was almost longer than Lance's hard cock. His ballocks hung low.

Suddenly Lance cried out, "Martin, what's that?"

Lance pointed to Martin's foreskin. Martin looked down. Adam followed Martin's eyes down to his cock. He saw what Lance had seen. On the inside of the tip of Martin's foreskin was embedded a flat, round blue bead. Martin took his limp sex in the palm of his hand. Like his body, his cock was slender. It was triangular in shape. His foreskin was back just far enough to expose the long slit on the dark red head. The blue bead sparkled when the firelight hit it.

"What's that?" Adam asked, repeating Lance's question.

"It is my mark as a special one," Martin calmly replied.

"A special one," Adam and Lance said in unison.

"Yes. At my birth the wise man of our tribe told my mother that she had given birth to a special one. Later he marked me with this bead." Since Adam and Lance still looked puzzled, Martin explained further. "I was only a baby so I do not remember the wise man. I only remember what my mother told me before she died. She told me that the wise man often slept with warriors in his tent. My mother said I was born to be a man who would know both men and women."

Adam and Lance were speechless. They hardly believed what they had heard.

"I was only five when I heard this from my mother. At that time I did not understand what she meant in saying I would know men. I do now."

Adam looked Martin in the eyes. "Do you like to lie with men, Martin?"

"At twenty-two, I am still a virgin," Martin replied in a matter-of-fact voice. "I have known no one—woman or man. But I ache to sleep with another man." As he spoke, Martin's cock hardened.

"So that's what you meant," Adam suddenly realized.

"Yes, Adam. I want my body against your body and against Lance's body. My sex against your sex and against Lance's sex. But do you want me? I know that two men can have a strong affection for each other but still not desire each other's body," Martin said.

Adam grabbed the tense Martin by his shoulders and pulled him into a tight embrace. His lips lightly brushed against Martin's as his hand wrapped itself around Martin's hard sex. Then he pulled away and asked, "Does that tell you anything about how willing I am to have your body against mine?"

"And you, Lance?" Martin asked.

Lance pulled Martin into a hard embrace. "That's my answer."

Again Adam and Lance embraced Martin. Then the three of them put their arms around one another. They pulled their bodies together tightly. Adam's cheek pressed against Martin's on one side, Lance's on the other. Both Adam and Lance felt the pressure of Martin's hard sex. Adam kissed Martin lightly on the cheek. Martin returned the kiss, and then kissed Lance on the cheek.

Martin was aglow. "Let me help each of you undress," he said in a husky voice. "Except for myself, I have never seen a grown man naked. And I have never felt the hard sex of another grown man."

Martin turned to Lance. "Sit down on the bench, Lance. I'll get your shoes and stockings off." Lance sat down, and Martin squatted before him. As Martin pulled at Lance's shoes and stockings, Lance loosened the ribbon around Martin's hair. He ran his hands through the mass of long hair. The palms of his hands massaged Martin's shoulders and back. He felt Martin's body shake with excitement. When Martin raised his head, Lance pulled him up into his arms. Lance put his lips on Martin's. He forced his tongue through the closed lips. Slowly Martin opened his mouth. Lance thrust in his tongue and ran it around Martin's tongue. Soon Martin's tongue was at work. When Lance released Martin, the Indian said, "I've never been kissed like that. Thank you."

"I'm ready for you to help me with my shirt and breeches," Adam called. Martin turned, took Adam in his arms, and gave him the kind of kiss Lance had just taught him. Lance came up behind Martin. He reached around and rubbed Martin's chest and pinched his large nipples. Through his breeches, Lance's stiff cock pressed against Martin's bare butt.

When the three men finally untangled, Lance went to put another small log on the fire.

"Not warm enough for you?" Adam joked.

"It will get hotter soon," Lance replied.

Martin unbuttoned Adam's shirt. He ran his hands over Adam's chest and bent to suck his nipples. As Adam played with Martin's hair, Martin wrapped his arms around Adam's back. Adam thrust back his shoulders and wiggled out of his shirt. They pressed their bare chests against each other and kissed for a long time. When Martin finally pulled his lips off Adam's, he said proudly, "That's what Lance showed me how to do."

"He was a good teacher," Adam replied. "Now get me out these breeches." Martin undid Adam's belt and pushed his breeches down to his ankles. Adam stepped out of them. Now he, too, was naked. Martin stepped back to get his first look at a naked man with an erection. He clapped his hands in delight. He rushed to Adam and pulled his naked body against his. Their cocks met at the same time that their lips did. They stood rubbing against each other and kissing for a long time.

The sight of their kissing excited Lance. "What about me?" he called in a mock plaintive voice. Quickly the two naked men were upon him, Adam at his back, Martin in front. Martin undid Lance's shirt; Adam peeled it off. Martin's fingers traced through Lance's chest hair. Adam untied the ribbon and freed Lance's wavy chestnut hair. As Martin sucked Lance's nipples, he loosened the drawstring holding up Lance's leather work drawers. Martin dropped to his knees, pulling down Lance's drawers as he did. Lance raised one foot and then the other as Martin stripped him of his drawers. Martin stood up. Again he stepped back to look, this time at his second naked man with a swollen sex. Once more he clapped his hands in delight. Then he rushed into Lance's arms for a long kiss.

Adam stood so that he could rub the bare butts of both men. He put his arms around the embracing men and kissed their necks and shoulders. Slowly he tightened his grasp around the two men. Suddenly he pulled backward sharply. The three of them tumbled onto Martin's pallet in front of the fire.

Martin and Lance lay on the their backs with Lance's arm under Martin's neck. Adam moved quickly between their hips and made a space for himself. He kissed the tip of each extended cock. Then while he slowly jacked Lance, he looked at the blue bead embedded in the tip of Martin's foreskin. Playing with the foreskin, Adam rubbed the bead. He watched it go down the shaft as he peeled the foreskin. When Martin's foreskin had disappeared down the shaft, the blue bead was about a third of the way down Martin's long member. Adam kissed the bead and then again kissed Martin's cockhead.

"Time for more serious action," Adam announced. Still playing with Lance's cock, Adam went down on Martin. He took all of the long cock in one dive. He rapidly moved the foreskin up and down the shaft and past the cockhead. Adam heard Martin groaning in delight. Then Adam shifted to Lance's cock. Since his mouth was much more accustomed to that stubby shaft, Adam could move up and down it much faster than he could on Martin's long sex.

Adam took turns sucking his lover and his new friend until he began to taste little gobs of juice at their slits. He pulled off the cock he was sucking and forced himself between the two men. Lance and Martin stopped kissing. Adam lay down between them. Adam turned first to Lance for a kiss, and then to Martin.

As Adam kept moving from one to the other for deep kisses, Lance and Martin reached across Adam's body to get at each other's cock. When they finished playing around there, they landed on Adam. Martin went for Adam's cock, Lance for Adam's balls and the buried cock shaft beneath. Gradually Lance's finger found its way to Adam's crack. Lance rubbed the wrinkles surrounding it. As the muscles relaxed, Lance's finger entered the hole. Once in, his finger shot up as far as it could. Adam groaned in anticipation of getting something better than a finger up him.

Martin listened to Adam's groans, and he watched with fascination the finger in Adam's asshole. Obviously Adam was experiencing a real pleasure. *I want for Lance to do that to me,* Martin said to himself. Martin raised up. He looked down as Lance inserted a second finger into Adam's hole. Adam shut his eyes, opened his mouth, and took in several deep breaths. His moans increased. *Yes,* Martin said again to himself, *I want Lance's finger up me.*

"I want your cock, Lance," Adam cried out.

"Not yet, Adam. Let's introduce Martin to cornholing first," Lance replied. He pulled his fingers out of Adam's butt and give him a good kiss.

Martin sat beside them. He looked puzzled. "That's an odd expression," he said.

"We'll do it first, then tell you how we found a new name for something that's been around a long time. Lie down on your side," Lance told Martin.

Martin lay down on his right side facing Adam. Adam snuggled up close. He rolled Martin's balls as they kissed. Lance got behind Martin and draped Martin's left leg over Adam's body. Lance spread Martin's butt cheeks to expose the hole. Dark folds of flesh surrounded it.

Lance gently separated the folds to reveal the pink flesh. His finger rubbed the exposed flesh.

"That feels good," Martin said.

Lance began to press harder, but Martin's muscles were still very tight.

"Relax, Martin," Lance said. "You aren't welcoming my finger enough."

Adam tried to help Martin relax by kissing him harder and by rubbing his chest and belly. The hole still resisted Lance's finger.

"Virgin territory," Lance laughed. He got out of bed and went to get the oil he always brought from his shop. When he returned, he smeared the crack with oil generously. He covered his finger with the oil and started to work again. This time his finger got past the muscles. Martin shivered a bit but told Lance to press in further. Lance's finger took a deep plunge and buried itself well inside Martin. Martin froze, locking Lance's finger. Adam kissed Martin all the harder. Suddenly Martin's hole expanded.

For a long time Lance used only one finger. Then he inserted a second, and finally a third. By the third finger, Martin was moaning with joy. He was even moving his butt to meet the thrust of Lance's fingers.

"I think you're ready," Lance said as he pulled his fingers out.

Martin felt Lance's cockhead at his asshole.

"This may hurt. Tell me if it does," Lance said. Lance's cockhead pushed in. Martin winced but said nothing. Lance waited a few seconds and then pushed his cock well up inside Martin. Again Martin froze, this time locking Lance's cock. Lance waited. Adam held Martin tighter. After several seconds, both Adam and Lance felt Martin's body surrender.

Lance went to pumping. Adam covered Martin's face with kisses. Martin groaned with pleasure as Lance's cock worked his butt. After some time, Lance pulled out and turned Martin over on his back. Lance looked down at him and said, "That's cornholing."

"Why didn't you let loose inside me?" Martin asked. "I kept expecting you to, and I wanted to feel your wet juice."

"Getting cornholed on your side is good for the first time, but now I want to finish the job another way." Lance spread Martin's legs and squatted at his crotch. "Put your legs over my shoulders and push them back toward your chest," he told Martin. Martin did, and Lance exclaimed, "That's some cornhole you have, my friend. Here comes my ear of corn."

Once again Martin felt Lance's cockhead at his ass crack. This time, however, his well-oiled hole was ready for action. Lance eased his cockhead past the rings, and then in one swift thrust buried himself inside Martin. Martin winced only slightly. Then he moved down on Lance's cock to signal that he was ready. Lance pumped furiously. Lance bent down and gathered Martin in his arms. The two men kissed passionately. Adam massaged Lance's back and turned so that he could watch Lance take Martin.

The harder Lance pumped, the more Martin groaned in delight. Adam knew they were both close to climax. To give Lance an extra charge, Adam wet a finger and drove it well up inside Lance. Lance's lips left Martin's just long enough for Lance to shout, "Finger me good, Adam." Then he went back to kissing. Adam's finger kept time with Lance's sex, thrust for thrust. Just as his finger reached its deepest penetration, Adam felt both men shaking wildly. He smiled as they came.

Adam pulled out his finger and waited while Lance and Martin clung together for a long time. Finally Lance withdrew. Martin's belly was drenched with his thick cream. Lance and Martin lay back exhausted. Adam lay down beside them.

They were quiet for a time until Martin broke the silence by asking, "Why do you call it cornholing?"

Adam explained, much to Martin's amusement.

"We gave you corn," Martin said. "You found a new way to shell it. I am told that my people used sharp rocks or oyster shells. Now you have a new name for what the warriors did in the wise man's tent at night."

"It probably won't be the last name for it," Adam replied. "But it will be the same thing—a cock and a bunghole—no matter the name it's given."

All the time they had been talking, they had played with each other's cocks. All of them had erections. Martin looked at the two lovers. He knew what he wanted to do. He eased himself down to their crotches. A hand on each stiff cock, Martin played with them, moving foreskins up and down. Then, keeping his hand on Adam's cock, he went down on Lance's. He sucked him for a long time. Then he moved to Adam's cock.

"I'm getting too close," Adam said after a time. He pulled away from Martin and said, "Lance, I want your ass."

"And I'm ready to be cornholed. How do you want me? Let's show Martin a new position."

"Get on your hands and knees. I can really ram it to you that way," Adam said.

"Yes, I know you can. You practically come out the other side," Lance laughed. "And it feels terrific." Lance dropped to his hands and knees, his legs wide apart. Adam spread Lance's butt cheeks to expose the thick wrinkles of the hole. To Martin's surprise, Adam leaned forward and sucked Lance's asshole for a long time.

"Your tongue is doing great, but your cock can do better," Lance finally called to Adam.

Adam smeared his cock and Lance's hole with the oil. He knelt behind Lance, his cockhead perched to spring into action. Adam placed his hands on Lance's hips. His cockhead made several quick jabs at the hole. Then in one swift lunge Adam tunneled in full length. Lance's butt closed for a moment over the long shaft. Adam rubbed Lance's hips and reached under to fondle his cock. Lance's hole opened wider. Adam drove his cock back and forth. With every penetration, Lance's hole grew more responsive.

Martin moved around to Lance's face; he kissed him hard. In a flash it occurred to him that, if he lay on his back with head at Lance's crotch, he could suck Lance while Lance was getting cornholed. "Spread you hands a bit," he told Lance. It didn't take Martin long to get under Lance, his head facing Lance's hanging hard cock. Martin reached up and swallowed it. A few second later he felt Lance's lips at his own cock. The two men sucked each other with long, steady strokes. Martin especially liked the way Lance used his tongue to lick the blue bead whenever he could.

With his hands on Lance's hips to steady himself, Adam moved his own hips so that his cock dug deep into Lance. At times he pulled completely out of Lance. Lance then moved back to take on the waiting cock. Once inside, Adam set to work again.

As Lance had said earlier in the evening, it was getting hotter. Finally with a yell of delight, Adam unloaded. His climax was contagious. Both Martin and Lance shot in each other's mouth. They stayed locked together for several long seconds. Then they tumbled apart, wrapping themselves together in a bundle on the pallet.

"I like the taste of your juice," Martin told Lance.

"Better than wild mushrooms," Adam and Lance said in one voice.

Once again they lay quietly together. Shortly Lance's light breathing announced that he was dropping off to sleep. Adam leaned over and kissed him gently on the lips. Lance stirred a bit and snuggled closer to Adam. Adam reached across Martin's chest and rubbed his nipples. Then he moved his hand to explore all over Martin's face. Martin kissed Adam's fingers as they moved over his lips.

"Tired?" Adam asked in a whisper.

"Yes and no," Martin replied. "I've been cornholed for the first time in my life. I can still feel Lance's cock moving inside me. I've sucked a man and been sucked by a man for the first time. I don't know which I enjoyed more, sucking or getting sucked. I do know that I loved the taste of Lance's juice when he unloaded it in my mouth."

"It's been a busy first time for you," Adam laughed.

"Yes. I have lost virginity three different times tonight. I now know what it means to lie with another man. I should be tired, but I am still too excited to sleep," Martin said.

"Let's rest a bit. Then you can cornhole me," Adam said.

For an hour the two young men talked in low voices. Occasionally Adam kissed Martin, but most often they were content to hold hands or to run their hands lightly over each other's body. Unlike their first conversations at the landing and in the warehouse, Martin peppered Adam with questions about his life.

When Adam's hand moved close to the hairs around Martin's sex, he realized that Martin had an erection. The thought of having Martin's long cock inside him caused Adam's sex to reach full growth. The excitement with which they touched each other caused Lance to stir.

He opened his eyes and was soon wide awake. He grabbed the two hard cocks and exclaimed, "I'm in on any new action."

"Wouldn't be right without you," Adam assured him.

"I'll lie down on my back. Get down on your knees before me, Martin," Adam told him. As soon as Adam lay down, Martin squatted before him. Martin pulled Adam's legs into the air and held them there.

"Have a look at this cornhole, Lance," Martin said with a grin. "Hold his legs, Lance. Those lips need my lips." Quickly Martin's lips and tongue were at Adam's hole. Martin was surprised at how easily his tongue found its way up. He loved to lick the soft flesh with his tongue. He didn't know if he wanted to stop. His cock told him he could easily shoot this way. But shortly Martin stopped, and Lance dropped Adam's legs. "Use a little oil," Lance said and handed Martin a small bottle. Martin oiled Adam's hole and his own cock. He shook with excitement.

Adam placed his legs firmly against Martin's hips. Martin moved up into Adam's crotch. His cockhead found Adam's hole. Slowly he pushed in, fascinated by the sight of his long cock disappearing inside Adam. Lance stood behind Martin and rubbed his shoulders and back. His hand ran down to Martin's butt. He fingered Martin's asscrack. Martin shouted with delight and pushed his cock full length into Adam.

"Hold a minute," Adam cried out. "That's the longest ear of corn I've ever had." Martin rubbed Adam's chest and leaned down to kiss him. Quickly Adam's hole expanded, welcoming Martin's inches. "I'm ready for you," Adam shouted.

Martin placed his hands firmly on the sides of Adam's chest near his armpits. He started his hips moving. His cock shot back and forth inside Adam. He didn't keep count, but he imagined that he saw his blue bead slip in and out of Adam at least a hundred times. He was in ecstasy.

Lance moved around and squatted before Adam's face, his hard cock inviting sucking. "Want a taste?" he teased.

Adam rose slightly and accepted the invitation. He sucked Lance as passionately as Martin was cornholing him. Martin was shaking with delight so much that Adam knew he would let loose soon. Adam sucked all the harder on Lance's cock. After a minute or two Adam felt the cock in his mouth and the cock up his ass pulsating violently. Juice filled his mouth at the same time that it filled his ass. Adam drank down Lance's juice after Lance had fired his last shot. Lance moved away. Martin pulled out and collapsed on Adam's chest. The two men kissed for a long time.

"My initiation is complete," Martin announced with joy.

It was now past midnight. The wind outside had died down. The last log on the fire was turning to glowing ashes. Adam pulled a blanket off the bed. The three young men huddled together on Martin's pallet under the cover and fell asleep.

The negotiations between Mr. Ashley and Captain McGaw and the working out of details regarding the small cargo ship lasted for three more days. The shipbuilder kept Martin busy at the drawing board. He was pleased with the extra fine care Martin took in his draftsmanship. With a hand on the young man's shoulder, Captain McGaw said, "You're welcome here, I think." Martin nodded and replied, "Very much."

For the three nights after Martin's night of initiation, the three young men returned hastily from supper to the quarters. William and George were at the kitchen table only one of those three nights. If their stares at Martin were a shred less hostile, the indentured servants were no more friendly than they had been before. What puzzled them was the warm comradery among the three young men.

"What do you think of that friendship?" William asked after they had left the kitchen.

"It's bloody unnatural," George responded.

If the two lovers and their new friend overheard that comment, they ignored it. Too much that was good happened before the small fireplace for them to bother about stupidity.

Frost was on the ground the early morning of Martin's departure. Adam and Lance dressed warmly to escort Martin to the landing. The black slaves were there, ready to steer the boat down the river to their waiting ship. Mr. Ashley and the shipbuilders were walking quickly down the lawn from the great house. The three young men stood a stiff awkward threesome. They had kissed good-bye in the quarters. Here their farewells had to be more formal. They shook hands.

Shortly the boat left the landing and entered the main stream of the river. Mr. Ashley beamed and said, "A new day arrives for us all." He wished good-day to Adam and Lance and walked back up the lawn.

Adam and Lance watched the departing boat. Lance coughed loudly several times. Adam turned to look at him.

"Nothing," Lance said.

# 1755: Williamsburg and Ashley Landing

The summer of 1755 came early. By the time of Lance's twenty-fifth birthday on May 23, the two young men had been swimming at the bend in the river for over a month. The corn was up and ready for hoeing. The field hands were busy ridding the young tobacco plants from the threat of worms. The flourishing azaleas and rhododendrons in Madam Ashley's large informal garden required a good watering once a week. Adam and Lance took turns seeing the watering was done adequately.

In two more months, in July, Adam and Lance would end their indentures and earn their freedom papers. They planned to celebrate their new status as free men at this year's Williamsburg fair.

"What are we going to do differently at this fair to celebrate?" Adam asked.

"I don't know," Lance replied, "except that I think young Will—or William as he tells me he likes to be called now—may not want to go to the puppet show."

"That is fine with me," Adam laughed. "I wish that Tim and Alan could be there to help us celebrate."

"Yes, so do I," Lance answered.

Adam and Lance had assured Mr. Ashley that, as free men, they intended to stay on as paid workers at Ashley Landing. They liked what they were doing there, and they knew how fortunate they were in the freedom they felt in sharing quarters. If anyone, especially Mr. Ashley and Joseph, believed it was time for them to find wives, no one said anything about it. They were as pleased to be staying on as Mr. Ashley was. In another year the small cargo ship would begin its semi-annual sailings between Annapolis and the West Indies.

However, despite all the signs of another year of prosperity in crops, the anticipation of their freedom papers, and the pleasant rou-

doi:10.1300/5623_10

tine of daily activity, Adam felt that something was wrong in quarters after he and Lance settled down for the night. At first, it had been Lance's cough. The cough that Adam had heard at the landing the morning Martin left lingered on for several weeks that winter. It stopped, however, by Christmas. What persisted was a low wheezing as Lance slept at night. But shortly after they started their swims in April, Lance's cough sporadically returned. Lance shrugged it off as a late spring cold. Adam half-heartedly joked about the large cup of cider that Lance drank before he came to bed. By mid-May, however, Adam stopped joking, and he said nothing since any mention of the cough irritated Lance. Finally though one night Adam sat up in bed and, looking down at Lance trying to suppress a cough, said firmly, "You've got to see Berta in the morning about that damn cough."

"And what do you think Berta can do?"

"Lance, you know bloody well how much the slaves depend on her remedies when they get sick. Even Madam Ashley asks her to mix up something when the children are ill."

"Yes, I know, but I'm not sure she can help me."

"Well, let her try. Don't be so damn stubborn."

Lance hesitated, then said, "I will."

Adam leaned down and they kissed. But when Adam reached into Lance's crotch, Lance pushed his hand away and said, "No, Adam, not tonight."

Adam was neither surprised nor offended. Each of them occasionally resisted the other's advances. But since Adam was in good spirits because Lance had agreed to see Berta, he decided to tease. "Well, I've a load I need to get rid of. If you can't help me out, I guess I'll just have to handle myself."

"Go ahead. It won't disturb me if you do. I'm going to sleep."

Lance's reply did surprise Adam. It had been a long time since Adam had self-pleasured himself, and he really did not want to now. He started to become angry but stopped himself. *Something bad is wrong with Lance,* he told himself. He snuggled down and pulled Lance close to him. Lance pushed his body back hard against Adam's and said, "I love you, Adam, you know that don't you, even if I don't want to have sex tonight."

"Yes, I know that," Adam replied and kissed Lance lightly on the back of his neck

The next night at supper Berta came to the kitchen from the great house. "Here y'are," she said and handed Lance a bottle filled with a dark-colored liquid. "Take a big gulp every night 'fore you gets to bed for five nights."

"Does it taste good?" Lance asked anxiously.

"Never you mind how it taste. Drink it," Berta told him.

"I hope it gets rid of his pesky cough," Adam said.

"It will. If'n cough is what's wrong with him," Berta replied.

Back in their quarters Lance took a long whiff of the medicine and exclaimed, "If this tastes as bad as it smells, then I think that you'll have to put up with my cough, Adam."

"Like hell. Do what Berta says, take a big gulp."

"But smell the stuff." Lance handed the bottle to Adam.

Adam put the bottle to his nose but quickly took it away. His face belied what he said, "Smells good to me. Drink it." Lance put the bottle to his lips and drank a large dose. He grimaced as he licked off the brown liquid from around his lips. "I was right. It tastes as bad as it smells."

In five days the potion had done its work. The cough had disappeared, and the nightly wheezing had all but stopped. At his workbench Lance had more energy than usual, and he rested better at night than he had for some time. He seemed back to himself—with one exception. Adam discovered after several nights' attempts that Lance was hard to arouse. In bed they kissed and let their hands run over each other's body, but when Adam played between Lance's legs he most often felt only a limp sex. The one night when Lance did reach an erection, Adam insisted that he wanted to be cornholed.

"It's been too long since you took me. I want your cock," Adam said.

"Don't think that I don't want you. I do very much. But I just don't seem to be able to keep it up."

"Then have at me, damn it."

Adam got down on his knees with his head on the floor. He spread his legs. He felt Lance's body behind him, but Lance was having trouble getting his cockhead where it needed to go. After several attempts at penetration, Adam knew that Lance's sex was limp. A chill swept over Adam. *Something is still wrong with Lance,* he reluctantly admitted to himself. Adam shuddered as he heard Lance tumble down on the floor and start to cry. Adam was quickly beside him and cradling him in his arms.

They lay there, close together, until later the moonlight through the window awakened them. Adam was the first to move about, but he sensed that Lance was also awake. It seemed only moments ago from their unsuccessful lovemaking. Adam hesitated, but he knew he had to ask. "What's wrong, Lance?"

"My cough."

"No, it's not your cough," Adam said softly. "That awful stuff Berta made for you took care of that." When Lance did not reply, Adam took a deep breath and asked, "Are you tired of having sex with me, Lance?"

That question brought Lance on top of Adam. "No, Adam," he shouted. "It's just that I hurt so much sometimes." He buried his face against Adam's. Adam hugged Lance desperately. Finally he asked, "Where do you hurt?"

"My ballocks."

"Your ballocks?"

"Yes, sometimes they are so swollen that I think they will burst out."

Adam knew it was not the time to joke about Lance's large ballocks. "May I feel them?" he asked. Lance lay back and Adam gently touched him. Adam did not think Lance's ballocks were any larger than usual, but he learned from the cry Lance made when he touched him that something was different. Something deep inside was causing the pain.

"I'm going to rub your ballocks," Adam told Lance. "I'll try to be gentle, but tell me if I'm hurting." Slowly and cautiously Adam ran his hand over Lance's sack, barely touching it. He kept at it until he heard Lance starting to snore.

The next morning Lance was awake and about before Adam. "Wake up, Adam," he said and gave him a kiss on the forehead and quick grab in the crotch. "We've got work to do today, and here you are still sleeping." Adam forced himself awake. He stared at Lance, but quickly decided to ask no questions. He pulled Lance down for a long kiss, then pushed him away saying, "Time for me to get up."

For the next month it was as if there were two of Lance, each one on the opposite ends of a seesaw. When one of the two was full of energy, his end of the seesaw was high in the air. But when his twin was hurting and irritable, his end of the seesaw touched the ground. Every morning when Adam got out of bed, he did not know which Lance was awake. Adam did not worry about the energetic Lance. It was the other Lance that frightened Adam.

On the low nights Adam had to rub Lance's body gently until Lance was asleep. On those nights the wheezing occasionally returned. Several times when Adam was certain he would not disturb Lance, he left the quarters. Under the large hickory tree, he handled himself. He did not like what he was doing. It brought relief, but Adam felt too much alone for there to be any real pleasure.

On the high nights, the two young men made love. Lance was able to hold an erection, and he pumped more furiously than he ever had. Since he felt that Lance needed to be in charge, Adam was the one most often lying on his stomach or on his side. He was only too happy that, on those occasions, Lance's cock was firm, not limp.

In mid-June a letter from his aunt in Williamsburg brought another kind of seesaw. The letter arrived via the courier service which had been established along the back trail earlier in the year. The horseman started at Hampton and rode to the end of the Tidewater. The monthly stops at Ashley Landing were an occasion, and Madam Ashley told Hannah to always give the rider a special treat in exchange for the news he carried in his saddlebags.

Adam thanked the house servant for the letter. He was pleased to see his aunt's handwriting on the envelope. However, he was less pleased when he read the opening lines of Sarah's letter.

*Dear Adam,*

*Like my letter to you less than two years ago, this letter also contains both good and ill news. The ill news lies in the enclosed letter from Tim. My*

*own news fills me with happiness. I have accepted Henry Tisdale's pro-*
*posal of marriage. We are to be married in July. My life here in*
*Williamsburg has been like nothing I have experienced before. In the old*
*country I was a servant. Here I am to become the mistress of a house.*
*However, that is not my reason for accepting Henry. We are very fond of*
*each other. At our ages, Adam, it is sometimes difficult to know exactly*
*what is need, what is affection, and what is love. Our marriage, no*
*doubt, is a mixture of all three. But I know that both Henry and I are*
*extremely happy, and I am pleased that his family and his friends are*
*happy for us. I hope that you can somehow arrange it so that you can be at*
*the simple marriage ceremony at Bruton Parish Church. And Lance, too,*
*if that is possible. The date is Saturday, July 26th.*

Although the letter continued, Adam stopped reading. Certainly
his aunt's news was good. He was elated. Sarah deserved the best. By
the time of the wedding Adam and Lance would have their freedom
papers, and Adam felt certain that Mr. Ashley would agree to their
going to Williamsburg for the wedding. Adam wondered though
about Lance. Would he feel like going? Which end of the seesaw
would he be on those days?

The thought of Lance's ill health made Adam remember the ill
news his aunt said was in Tim's letter. He put down his aunt's letter
and picked up Tim's. It was addressed to LANCE AND ADAM. Adam
was torn about what to do. Lance had left that morning in good spirits. They had even made love before going to breakfast, something
that had not happened recently. How would ill news affect him? High
on the seesaw might be the best time for Lance to accept bad news.
But, on the other hand, any bad news might well send the seesaw to
the ground and bring on another Lance. After several minutes of hesitation, Adam decided to read the letter before he went to Lance's
workshop.

Adam tore open the letter. He read the opening sentence, gasped,
and put the letter down. "Damnation!" he exclaimed, shutting his
eyes tightly. Then he looked again at the letter. It read the same, "I
am back in Williamsburg, and Alan is dead." This time though he
quickly read through the entire letter.

The facts were simple enough. In late February Alan had gone hunting. Tim had urged him not to leave the shop since, in the distance, the sky was dark with an approaching storm. But Alan had laughed and said he would be back before the storm clouds broke. Two hours later when the heavy winds swept through Charlottesville, Tim said that a sixth sense told him something was wrong. A day later Tim and a search party found Alan's body. In the wind storm a large limb had broken and fallen. A strong jagged branch had pierced Alan's skull.

Tim said he debated whether to stay on or to return to Williamsburg. Without Alan, the frontier no longer held any attraction for him. "To preserve my sanity, I needed to get back to the familiar, so I am here in Williamsburg." He was once again working in the Tisdale shop. However, he wondered if Ashley Landing might need a second cordwainer.

The longer Adam thought about it, the more he believed that the best thing to do was to go to Lance's shop and there, quickly and simply, tell him of Alan's death and of Tim's return to the capitol.

Less than five minutes later Lance put his head between his hands and moaned, "Poor Tim. He was so in love with Alan." Adam went to Lance's workbench, bent down, and rubbed Lance's back for a long time. Finally, Lance raised up and exclaimed, "It's not fair. They were just starting a life together."

"It will be hard for Tim, alone there," Adam said.

Lance looked steadily at Adam and replied softly, "You may face the same someday soon."

Adam was startled, then a bit angry. "Shut up that kind of talk. No tree limb is going to smash your head open."

"No, perhaps not," Lance laughed. "But my ballocks will get me."

"Shut up, I said. Your ballocks were just fine this morning. Full of good stuff."

They were silent for a time. Finally Lance broke their silence. "What else was in your letter?"

"Oh, I almost forget to tell you. Aunt Sarah and Mister Tisdale are to be married."

A big smile crossed Lance's face. "Good for them," he exclaimed. "When?"

"In late July. They want us to come to the ceremony. We'll be free men by then, and I'm sure Mr. Ashley will let us go. I'll talk with him this evening."

"I should like to go to Williamsburg not only to attend the wedding but also to see Tim," Lance said.

Suddenly Adam recalled what Tim had said in the letter about the possibility of his coming to Ashley Landing. "Lance," he said, "in his letter Tim asks if we need a second cordwainer here. Perhaps you should speak to Mr. Ashley."

"Tim wants to come here?" Lance exclaimed.

"Yes, at least he mentions it. Here, you read both letters."

As Adam started to leave, Lance called to him and asked, "Would you object if Tim did come here?"

"No, I don't think so."

"Would you want him to share our quarters?"

Adam thought for a moment and then said, "No, I would not want him to do that."

Lance said nothing.

"If he shared our quarters, there would be sex among the three of us. You know that, Lance, as well as I do. We couldn't stop ourselves. We talked once about having sex together with another man. Remember? Then we did, with Martin when he was here. And we both enjoyed those several nights. When Martin comes again, after the cargo ship starts making its sailings, I think we will both like lying with him again for a few nights." Adam paused and then said, "But I would not want to have him—or any other man—in our quarters all the time."

He waited for Lance to say something. Lance didn't.

"It might not destroy our love for each other, Lance," Adam continued. "But having a third man in bed every night would change our bonding. One of the three of us would often feel left out. I think someone would finally explode."

Again Lance said nothing.

"You don't agree? Do you want Tim in bed with us? Do you want to make love with him?"

Lance rubbed his hands. He squirmed on his workbench. He did not want to come down from the high seat on the seesaw.

"Yes, I agree with you. It would change us," Lance answered. "But if I want Tim in bed with us, it is for you, not me."

"For me!" Adam shouted.

"Yes, Adam, for you."

Suddenly Adam realized that Lance was again thinking of his swollen ballocks and the pain in his body when he was on the ground end of the seesaw.

"Shut up that kind of talk. Let me tell you exactly how I feel. I do not object to Tim's coming to Ashley Landing, if Mr. Ashley says he is needed. I would welcome him here as a friend. But I do not want him to share our quarters. I do not want Tim as another lover."

Lance nodded. "Let's not talk about it any longer. Give me time to think about what to say to Mr. Ashley."

After supper for the next two nights, Mr. Ashley received two visitors in his office. The first visitor was Adam, the second was Lance.

Mr. Ashley was reading his favorite play, *The Tempest,* when Adam knocked.

"Come in, Adam," Mr. Ashley called. Adam did not like to waste Mr. Ashley's time with small talk so he quickly informed him of his aunt's marriage next month.

"My congratulations to them," Mr. Ashley said. "And, Adam, you must plan to attend the wedding. Lance, too, if he wishes."

"Thank you. I was going to ask if we might go."

"In fact, I will go with you and Lance to the capital so that we can finalize and record your freedom papers."

"Then the visit will truly be a holiday for us," Adam said, not quite knowing how to bring up another topic.

Mr. Ashley studied the silent young man. Then he asked, "Adam, is something else on your mind?" When he saw that Adam looked hesitant to speak, he said, "Out with it, Adam."

In a torrent of words, Adam explained his concern over Lance's health and over his strange oblique statements about his death. It was not just Lance's cough. Berta's strong medicine gave him relief, although it did not cause the cough to go away permanently. The problem seemed to lie in Lance's groin.

"His groin?"

"His testicles. Lance claims that they are often swollen and that his stone sack aches terribly."

"Have you felt him, Adam?" Mr. Ashley asked, a deep concern in his voice.

"Yes, and his stones were swollen. Even when I touched him gently, he cried out in pain. I suspect Berta can do nothing for him."

"No, I think not," Mr. Ashley agreed. "Is the swelling all the time?"

"He says that it comes and goes. I can tell when he is hurting though by his moods."

Mr. Ashley got up from his chair and stood at the office window for a short time. Then he turned to Adam and said, "If he is still hurting when we go to Williamsburg, I will see that Lance visits Dr. Matthews at his apothecary shop. He may be able to help in a way Berta cannot."

"Thank you," Adam responded. "I feel better having talked with you."

"I am glad you did."

Adam started to tell Mr. Ashley about Tim, but he and Lance had agreed that Lance should talk to Mr. Ashley about that possibility. Instead he said, "Lance does not know that I have come here tonight. Should he come to you on his own, please do not tell him of my visit tonight."

"I understand, Adam."

The next evening Mr. Ashley was starting to reread an old favorite, Izaak Walton's *The Compleat Angler,* when he saw Lance standing on the edge of the formal garden behind the great house. He seemed to be hesitant about coming to the office. Mr. Ashley went to the door and called, "Lance, come sit and have a chat with me." He could tell that Lance welcomed the invitation. Once they were seated, they talked briefly about the weather, but Mr. Ashley knew that Lance had not come to discuss the June heat. "How are things at your shop?" he asked.

"Good. But I never seem to get work done as fast as I would like."

"Why is that?" Mr. Ashley felt he already knew the answer.

"I don't always feel too well."

"What's the matter?"

Lance hesitated, then said, "It's my cough. Berta's medicine only helps me for a while."

"Nothing more than the cough?"

"No, just the cough and the aches it brings on."

Mr. Ashley sighed but not so that Lance could hear him. He realized that, unlike Adam, Lance was squeamish and embarrassed. He was not going to talk about his privates with another man, except Adam.

"Well, when we get to Williamsburg next month, I want you to see my friend Dr. Matthews at his apothecary shop. Tell him all that you feel wrong with you."

"I hope he can do more than Berta," Lance replied.

Mr. Ashley waited a moment, then asked, "Is the black boy any help to you in the shop?"

Lance smiled and answered, "Toby tries, and he has learned to cut fairly well. But it takes him half the day. He'll never be a cordwainer, Mr. Ashley. He's best at odd jobs and keeping the shop and my tools in order."

"If you need better help, do you think we could find a lad in Williamsburg who might comes here as an apprentice?"

Lance was delighted. "I know someone. But he's not a lad anymore and he's past his apprenticeship days."

"Who is he?"

For five minutes Lance talked about Tim, from his apprenticeship days at Master Thomas's shop to his present employment at Master Tisdale's shop.

When Lance had finished, Mr. Ashley said, "I should not like to seem to steal someone away from Master Tisdale's shop, especially now that Adam's aunt is to marry the owner."

"Knowing Tim's honest nature, I am sure that he has already mentioned to Master Tisdale that he would like to come to Ashley Landing if there is employment for him here."

"Well, Lance, when we go to Williamsburg, I will talk with both Master Tisdale and the young man. Perhaps some agreement can be reached, if not for now, then for later this year."

"I should like to have Tim here as my helper. Thank you."

"But, Lance, I am concerned about your health. You must agree to see Dr. Matthews about—your cough."

"Yes, I agree. I feel better already."

The two men shook hands, and Lance left the office.

Mr. Ashley shuddered. *No one, neither Berta nor Dr. Matthews, can help that young man. He is very ill, and he knows it.*

For a month Adam was surprised but delighted. From the night when Lance returned to quarters from Mr. Ashley's office to the time for the boat to Williamsburg, Lance seemed his former self. It was as if he had jumped off the seesaw and run away from it completely. Or, Adam hated to admit to himself, was Lance only balancing the seesaw, waiting to see which end would win? They frequently made love, each taking the other with an intensity that shocked both of them. Each of them pushed harder and deeper inside the other than ever before.

"You see," Adam said, "nothing is wrong with you."

"Nothing is wrong when I am with you, Adam. But I may not be . . ."

Adam silenced Lance with a long passionate kiss. As they lay back exhausted, they continued to hold each other tightly.

As soon as Mr. Ashley and the two young men were in Williamsburg on July 25, Mr. Ashley insisted that they first go about business. By late afternoon, the freedom papers were recorded at the court house, and Adam and Lance each had a copy in their coat pockets. While Lance and Adam went to the apothecary shop, Mr. Ashley went to talk with Master Tisdale and Tim. The two visits came to quite different ends.

Tim was to continue working in Williamsburg until the end of his contract. Then, in November, he was to come to Ashley Landing. Although Henry Tisdale said he was sorry to lose Tim, he was glad that Tim was going where he wanted to be. Master Tisdale and his two sons could handle the shop, especially now since more lads wanted to enter an apprenticeship.

At the apothecary shop Adam and Lance waited while the large man in the smock coat talked with an elderly woman. "There, that should do the trick, Mistress Helen," the doctor said. The woman thanked him, smiled at the two young men, and left the shop. "Now what can I do for you two?" Dr. Matthews asked.

"We are from Ashley Landing, and we have a letter for you from Mr. Ashley," Adam said.

"Ah, my good friend, William Ashley," the doctor murmured as he opened the letter. When he had finished reading it, he asked, "Which of you is Lance Morley?"

"I am."

"Mr. Ashley asks that I examine you to see if I can detect what causes your ache."

"It's my cough," Lance told him.

"Oh, Lance, be honest," Adam exclaimed. "It's his testicles."

"Damn you, Adam" Lance cried out.

"Here, here, Morley," the doctor said, "Your testicles are a natural part of your body. If that is where your ache stems from, then I must look at them. I've seen plenty of them in my years of practice. Yours won't be shaped any differently. Come into the back room."

Once they had gone to the room behind the counter, Adam went outside. He wandered up the street looking at the houses and the shops. But he kept an eye on the door to the apothecary shop. It was almost half an hour before he saw Lance step out onto the street. He was carrying a small bottle. Adam walked to greet him. When he got to him, Adam realized that Lance was shaking.

"What did he say?" Adam asked.

"Just what I've been trying to tell you."

Adam winced. It was as if Lance had stuck a knife in his stomach and twisted it. He cried out, "Oh, Lance," and grabbed Lance into his arms. Several passersby turned to stare at them.

Lance pulled away from Adam. "Calm yourself. People are looking at us. I'm not gone yet, and it may take years. Dr. Matthews gave me medicine for when the ache gets too bad. I've got a poisonous infection in my ballocks which he had some fancy name for. He could tell from feeling them that they are badly inflamed. He offered to cut them off."

"Cut them off!"

"Yes, that's what he said. But he couldn't be sure the infection had not spread beyond them."

Adam said nothing.

Lance grinned and said, "I told him I still used them, and I'd prefer to keep them hanging there."

"You joked with him," Adam said in amazement. "You, who couldn't stand to hear me say 'testicles.' I don't believe you."

"Well, I did. And why not. He was doing a good job of feeling my ballocks. I almost got stiff."

The two young men looked at each other. They burst out laughing. Then Lance said, "Come on, Adam, let's go find Tim and hear what his news is."

The next afternoon Tim joined Adam and Lance in one of the back pews at the church to listen to Henry and Sarah exchange marriage vows. Tim sat between the other two young men. As they listened to the words that united Sarah and Henry as a couple, Tim whispered to Adam, "I wish two men could take vows as a couple."

"It would be nice," Adam replied in a whisper.

"That day will come," Lance predicted. Lance reached over Tim and took Adam's hand. Their clasped hands rested in Tim's crotch. Tim placed his hand gently on top of theirs. Soon Adam and Lance felt a hard sex under their hands. They looked at each other, then at Tim and grinned.

Lance leaned over and whispered to Adam, "Maybe he'll let us see his navel later tonight."

Adam smiled and replied, "It's not his navel which will interest me then."

Tim whispered, "Stop talking like that in church."

Suddenly the clergyman's words "'til death do you part" broke their jollity. Those were not the words Adam wanted to hear, given what Dr. Matthews had told Lance. Nor did Tim want to be reminded yet once more of Alan's accidental death. Only Lance accepted the words with equanimity. Surprising both Adam and Tim,

Lance let loose of Adam's hand and placed it in Tim's. Then Lance put his hand on top of theirs. They remained like that until it was time to stand for the benediction.

After the amen, Sarah and Henry walked down the aisle. People in the pews in front of the altar followed. The three young men stood and watched the procession until the church was empty. Adam and Tim still felt the warmth of each other's hand. They looked at Lance. His smile was infectious.

The reception for the newly married couple was at the house of Henry's oldest son, Garth. Although Adam and Lance barely knew anyone, they felt welcome. Tim kept introducing them to people. When one of them heard that Adam was Sarah's nephew and was from Ashley Landing, a good friend of Henry's exclaimed to the room, "Tidewater aristocracy has come to your wedding, Henry."

Adam blushed as everyone laughed. He quickly retorted, "Hardly aristocracy. I just earned my freedom papers yesterday after seven years of indenture, as did the plantation's cordwainer, Lance, here."

The man who had started the matter embraced Adam and turned to the party. "Double cause for celebration. Here's to two free young men and to the new couple. Long life to them all." The party cheered. Adam and Lance acknowledged the toast as did Henry and Sarah.

Adam looked at Lance and could tell he was beginning to tire from too much movement in the room. Adam sought out Tim from the crowd and said, "We should leave. Lance is tired."

The look in Adam's eyes caused Tim to ask, "Is Lance well?"

"No. He is . . ." But Adam stopped.

"Is what?" Tim asked.

"Tired from all the activities here coming so soon after his work back at his shop."

"I'm glad I'm going to help him there."

"So am I. But, please, let's leave."

As the three of them were about to leave, Sarah and Henry joined them and thanked them for coming to the celebration. Then they pulled Adam aside. Sarah spoke first.

"You were only five, Adam, when I brought you to Cromley Hall. Now, twenty years later, I have another home—Henry's and mine—to welcome you to. Please visit as often as you can."

Adam kissed his aunt. Then he felt Henry's arm across his shoulders. "Thank you, Adam, for that letter. It brought Sarah to me." Adam knew the letter, the one he had written after talking with Madam Ashley. He was glad he had written it.

Outside on the street Adam joined Lance and Tim. Tim was dancing a jig and waving a large parcel. "I've swiped food from the party for supper tonight," he shouted. "No," he admitted quickly, "Garth's wife gave it to me. But no matter, we will dine like kings before . . ."

"Before what?" Adam interrupted.

"Before you see my navel, or whatever it was you said might interest you," Tim teased.

Late that night the three young men lay naked on Tim's bed. They had thoroughly examined each other's navel—and much more. Each cock was finally limp, having relieved itself several times during the long session. Again, as in the church pew, Tim lay between the other two young men. Lance was starting to snore.

"Nudge him over on his side and cover him up," Adam told Tim. "That way he'll sleep but not snore." Soon Lance was breathing quietly in a deep sleep.

Tim turned to Adam and pushed him over on his back. Then he placed his hand on Adam's limp member. "Another go at it?" he asked.

"I doubt I can," Adam answered. But, as Tim worked Adam's cock toward erection, Adam pushed his hand away. He needed to talk with Tim, not have sex. "Do you mind if we just talk?" he asked.

"No, although I do like looking at that long thing," Tim replied, admiring Adam's cock. "But it probably is better that we do talk."

"I hope we don't disturb Lance," Adam said.

"Then let's put on our shirts and go out to the yard behind the shop," Tim said.

The two young men got quietly out of the bed and slipped on their shirts, which hung well below their waists but did not cover their cocks. Tim looked at Adam and said with a laugh, "I believe we can both talk and play around a bit, if we want." He twitched Adam's cock and said, "Let's go outside." He picked up a blanket for them to sit on.

Once they were seated, cross-legged, with a cup of cider for them to share, Tim asked, "What's on the tip of your tongue, Adam?"

Adam waited a minute. Then he decided to come directly to the point. "Lance is very ill. He may die soon."

"Yes, I know."

Adam was stunned. "How did you know?" he exclaimed.

"Lance told me."

"When?"

"Yesterday evening while you were talking with your Aunt Sarah. Lance and I came here."

"What did he tell you?"

"All about his cough, his swollen stones, his terrible aches, and now his visit to Dr. Matthews."

"Tim, I'm glad Lance told you. I hated having to do it. I am a coward, I guess."

Tim reached over and kissed Adam lightly on the lips. "No, you're not. You love Lance very much, and I suspect it's harder on you accepting what's going to happen than it is on him. Also you know, don't you, that Lance and I have a strong affection for each other, and you didn't want to add bad news to the ache I still feel over Alan's death."

"How long has it been?"

"Five months. At first I had nightmares, always seeing him lying there crushed by the limb with the jagged branch digging into his head. His face was so bloody I hardly recognized him."

They were silent for a spell.

"I hope Lance holds on until you come in November," Adam said.

"I do, too."

"It's not just that I want you to see him again. You going to have to help me, Tim, when it happens."

"You don't mind my coming to Ashley Landing, do you Adam? Lance told me you didn't."

"No. I'm glad you are coming. Did Lance tell you anything else?"

"Yes, he said I might not be able to share your quarters."

Adam was relieved, for that wasn't quite what he had told Lance. He had been emphatic about Tim's not sharing quarters. But so much had happened since they arrived at the capital, especially in the half-hour at the apothecary shop and in the long session in bed tonight. Now he wanted Tim to share their quarters. Even their bed, for occasional sex, if not for sleeping every night. "Lance must have been thinking that our quarters would be too small for three people. But I think we can manage," Adam said, hoping that Lance had said nothing which made Tim doubt the sincerity of his new attitude.

"I think we should wait and see what works best when I get there," Tim said.

"Wherever you quarter, I do want you to know that I'm very glad you are coming to Ashley Landing."

"Thank you, Adam."

They were silent then. Their thoughts wandered. Neither of them said it, but both realized though that, sooner or later, there would be only the two of them in the quarters.

"We are getting a bit too serious," Tim said. He leaned over again to kiss Adam, this time letting his tongue probe Adam's mouth. Adam returned the kiss. When they pulled away, Tim said, "Adam, you are on holiday and you are my guest tonight. So, as your host, I have a good-night gift for you."

"Oh."

"Yes. Lie down on the blanket."

When Adam was on his back, Tim spread his legs. "Do I get your cock?" Adam asked.

"No. I get yours."

Tim squatted before Adam and leaned down to take Adam's sex in his mouth. Adam's cock hardened as Tim's lips circled the cockhead. Then Tim worked his mouth down the long shaft. Adam couldn't believe how quickly he was ready once again to unload. "I'm going to shoot," he cried. Tim kept at it. Adam groaned wildly as his juice exploded in Tim's mouth. Even after the last shot, Tim continued sucking until Adam pushed his lips away. Adam leaned forward and took Tim in his arms. They kissed for a long time.

"We'd best go in," Adam finally said.

When Tim didn't get up, Adam asked, "Something else on your mind?"

"Yes."

"What?"

"This afternoon just as the clergyman was reading the last of the vows, Lance let go of your hand and put our hands together and then placed his on top of ours. What was he doing?"

"I think it was his way of saying that he wanted us to know one another better. And I do feel closer to you, Tim, than I did last summer at the fair. I would be lying though to say I know you as well as Lance does, or that I have the same strong affection for you as Lance does. But I like you, and I want us to be the best of friends. And, just to make it clear, it's not your cock that makes me like you—although that does add an attraction."

"I guess I see a bit more in what Lance did than you do. But it's getting chilly now, and I don't want to talk any longer. I want some sleep. Let's get back to bed."

"Sooner or later, will you tell me what you think Lance meant?"

"Yes, I think the right time will come. Right now I hope we don't wake Lance."

They didn't, and the next morning Lance asked, "Did you two talk after I fell asleep?"

"A bit," Adam replied. "Only long enough to turn you over and stop that infernal snoring. Hearing that thunder, Tim almost decided not to come to Ashley Landing."

They all laughed.

Four weeks after Adam and Lance returned from Williamsburg it was time to cut the tobacco and hang the stalks in the drying sheds. Once again Lance told Mr. Ashley he was ready to go the plantation lands up river to help supervise the cutting and the hanging for drying. Mr. Ashley replied that this year there was plenty of help.

"I appreciate your willingness to help, Lance, but I think you have plenty to do at your shop. Remember we don't have that many more months before we will need to stock the cargo ship. I'm glad Tim will be here in November to lend a hand."

"I'll miss going to the cutting," Lance said.

"Well, if you wish, you and Adam ride up to the nearest fields one day, just to satisfy any need you two have for a break in the routine down here."

Adam was relieved to hear that Lance was not needed in the tobacco fields. He suspected that Mr. Ashley was as concerned as he was about Lance's health. There wasn't much energy in the young man. Lance attributed it to the late August heat. Adam didn't remind him that it was no hotter an August than those of the past several years.

The two young men still went to the bend in the river in the late afternoon for their swim. But Lance took longer to walk the trail. And he stopped challenging Adam to race across the river. "We can cool off better if we don't exert ourselves so much in racing," he had said.

If he had wanted to tease, Adam would have replied, "That hasn't held you back before." But, since their return from Williamsburg, Adam found it less easy to joke with Lance. Instead he replied, "Suits me fine. I was getting tired of always losing the race. We'll wait until it's cool and near time to stop the swims, then we'll have a final race of the season." Adam wasn't sure, but he thought he heard Lance say something about "a final race." Adam kicked himself mentally and said, *You stupid ass, why did you have to say anything.*

Even though they didn't race, they enjoyed dog-paddling and floating in the water. And, once they were out, they still went to their den of ferns. More often than not, they simply lay there and talked and watched the birds. Usually they just let their hands massage each other's body, stopping frequently for a long kiss.

One afternoon in early October when they in the den, Lance announced, "It's time for me to stop the swims for the year. I think fall is coming early."

Adam didn't agree about an early fall. But he said, "You're probably right. Also it's near time for me to supervise getting the tobacco into hogsheads and ready for shipment next month. I will probably be too busy for swimming."

"Then I think it's time for that final race of the season that we promised ourselves," Lance said.

The suggestion took Adam by surprise. He wasn't at all sure that it was a good thing to do. He turned and grinned at Lance. "I don't think I want to lose one more time, especially on the last race of the season."

Lance stood up and pulled Adam to his feet with more energy than Adam had felt in him for some time. "Then, just to be a good sport, I'll slow down and let you win."

"That's no fun."

"Come on, Adam. Get your lazy butt out there to the river," Lance shouted. He gave Adam's rear a hard swat and ran out of the den and to the river.

Adam did not know what to do. Lance was more like himself than he had been in months. Adam didn't want to refuse the challenge and send Lance back on the low end of the seesaw. But, on the other hand, he didn't want Lance to overexert himself. After a minute, he decided, *I'll race, but I'll keep close to him in case he needs help.*

Lance returned to the den. "I said, come on. What are you doing? Sticking your finger up your ass?"

Adam met that with a mischievous, "Yes. I was pretending it was your cock."

"Don't worry, you'll get that tonight. Maybe sooner."

Adam sensed that something good was happening. He told himself, *Let's get this damn race over and get back to supper.* But when Adam looked and saw that Lance's sex was half there already, he also started to harden. He laughed though and exclaimed, "Not now, Lance. Let's save our energy for the race. I think I might win this one."

They were soon at the river and into the water. Adam was surprised at how much Lance swam like his old self. They reached the other side of the river with Lance ahead but Adam not far behind. "Back," Lance shouted and turned around. Adam touched the tree they had dubbed the halfway mark and started back. He was amazed but pleased. Lance was swimming with long swift strokes. Adam had to push himself to keep up. Lance was on the shore and laughing as Adam reached the shallow water. Adam stood up and said, "I thought you were going to slow down and let me win."

"I did. You couldn't keep up."

"I tried, but I lost." He paused and then said, "But I still want your cock inside me tonight."

"Tonight!" Lance's whoop sent the birds flying to safer boughs. "I don't want to wait. Look at me," Lance said. Adam looked. Lance's thick cock was at its best. "Get down on all fours, Adam."

Adam joyously raised high his clenched fists. He was certain that Lance was on the mend. His fists tried to catch and capture the hot air. "Get down, I said," Lance snapped. Adam dropped to his hands and knees. Lance spread his butt cheeks.

"Back door's open. Come on in," Adam joked.

Quickly Lance buried his thick sex deep inside Adam. With Lance riding Adam vigorously, they stayed locked together for a long time. It was the first time they had made love on the beach instead of their den since Matt had seen Adam going down on Lance. If either of them remembered that, neither said anything about it. The present was too intense to admit the past.

They were at it so long that they were late for supper, but Hannah did not scold. As soon as she saw them come into the kitchen, she could tell from their faces that something special had happened more important than answering the supper bell.

Later, back in their quarters as they undressed for bed, Lance asked, "Do you want to take me, Adam? I had a good go at you this afternoon. It's your turn, if you want it."

Adam pulled Lance into a tight embrace. "No, I only want to lie next to you." The two young men got under their quilt and snuggled closely. They kissed. Then, as he ran his fingers over Lance's face, Adam said, "I love you, Lance."

"I love you, Adam."

"It's been a good day, hasn't it?"

"Yes, it's been a very good day." Lance snuggled even closer and said, "Adam, every day since I arrived here with my back still hurting from the beating at the gaol has been a good day."

"Yes, they have been."

"I think there will also be good days once Tim arrives."

Adam suddenly remembered what Tim had said about Lance's placing their hands together with his on top during the last minutes of the wedding ceremony.

"Lance."

"Yes."

"At the end of the wedding ceremony you put my hand and Tim's together with yours on top. Why?"

"You don't know?"

"No."

"I don't believe you."

Adam rubbed Lance's nipples and said, "Tell me."

"Not tonight. It's been a very good day. I don't want to talk about tomorrow."

Adam waited and then asked, "But you will tell me, won't you?"

"Yes, when the times comes and you haven't already guessed what I meant. Now it's time for me to go to sleep."

Lance pulled Adam into a tight embrace for a long passionate kiss. When Lance pulled away, he exclaimed, "I won the race." Then with a flourish that sent the cover off them, Lance turned over on his side.

Adam laughed and pulled the cover back over them. He kissed the back of Lance's neck. He lay still as Lance drifted into sleep. Although he wondered about what Lance had meant by his action in the church, he really half knew but also half wanted not to acknowledge that he knew. Lance was soon fast asleep. It took Adam much longer.

Lance was right. Fall did come early. Although the days were still quite warm in mid-October, the nights were chilly enough for a small fire in their quarters. In two or three weeks it would be time to strip the tobacco leaves from the stalks and pack them in hogsheads. With the change in season, Hannah declared her own special day to celebrate the end of summer. For the occasion she announced on the night before the special day that she was baking two large pound cakes, one for the dining table of the great house, the other for the servants' table in the kitchen.

Adam listened for the kitchen bell to summon them to the big meal of Hannah's special day. That pound cake was going to taste good. What he suddenly heard though—instead of the bell—was the shrill cry of a young boy. Adam left the warehouse to see the little black boy whom Lance was training as an assistant in the shop running toward him.

"Masta' Adam, Masta' Adam, come quick," the boy screamed.

"What's wrong, Toby?" Adam called.

"Masta' Lance on the floor. He cuts himself with his knife," the boy answered.

Trying to push the worst scene from his mind, Adam raced to Lance's shop. Lance lay unconscious on the shop floor. Blood flowed from the deep cut in his hand. The utility knife beside him was covered with blood. Quickly Adam found a piece of cloth and wrapped it tight around Lance's hand to slow the bleeding.

"Run for help, Toby," Adam told the frightened boy.

Adam picked Lance up and cradled him in his arms. He held Lance's wounded hand close to his chest. Lance's blood stained his shirt. Adam pulled Lance closer to his body, attempting to calm the convulsions wracking Lance's belly. Lance's head dropped upon Adam's shoulder. Lance stirred. "Put me down. I can walk," he stuttered.

"Hush," Adam told him. "Put your arm around me and hold tight." He waited briefly until he felt Lance's good arm on his shoulder. "Hold me tight," Adam cried again. Lance's good arm reached up to grab Adam's neck. Adam pulled Lance's wounded hand all the closer. He felt the blood soaking through his shirt and wetting his chest. "We've got to get out of here," he said.

Struggling with Lance's limp body, Adam started down the path to the quarters. He had not gone far before he was met by two black men running to help. Both of them were much stronger than Adam. One of them took Lance from Adam's arms and ran quickly ahead. "Take him to the quarters," Adam called. Then he told the other man to go to the great house. Madam Ashley was the physician-nurse for the plantation. She would have bandages and medicine.

Suddenly Adam was tired. He sat down on the ground. He knew that whatever was going to happen was out of his hands. When he looked up, he saw Toby waiting patiently for him to move. They were alone.

"What happened, Toby? Adam asked.

"We was workin'. I heard this loud noise. Masta' Lance had fell from his bench. The knife he was workin' with sliced his hand open," the boy answered.

"Has he coughed much this morning? " Adam asked, dreading to hear an answer.

"All the morin'. Got a fall cold," Toby told him.

"Perhaps," Adam said to the boy. But to himself, Adam said, *No, something bad happened. He must have fainted.*

Toby read the concern on Adam's face. "He be fine, Masta' Adam," Toby said and smiled.

Adam gave Toby a hug and said, "Let us pray so. Go on, Toby. I need to stay here for a spell." Toby left, and Adam sat down on the ground. For a long time, he cupped his head in his hands between his legs. His shoulders shook as he cried. He imagined the worst. "No," he shouted, "I'm coming, Lance." He started to run.

When Adam reached the quarters, he found Madam Ashley already there. With her was Berta. Lance lay still. He seemed half-conscious. His hand was bandaged. His breathing was heavy. Madam Ashley looked up at Adam and smiled. She said, "Go eat your dinner, Adam. Lance is sleeping. Berta will watch over him. Your turn will come tonight."

Adam hesitated. "Will he die?" he finally asked.

"I don't know," Madam Ashley replied softly.

"Berta?" Adam asked.

"Masta' Lance may in the sky tomorrow," Berta said calmly. "If we's all as good as he is, we all get there someday."

Adam barely touched his food at the table. He even declined the piece of pound cake. He excused himself long before the others had finished eating. He went to the warehouse. "That man hurtin'," Hannah sighed as she watched Adam leave the kitchen.

Shortly after two that afternoon, Mr. Ashley entered the warehouse. He said he was sorry to hear about Lance and expressed his confidence that he would soon be well again. "We need to inventory the pelts, Adam," Mr. Ashley said. Adam knew it was only Mr. Ashley's way of keeping his mind off Lance. Still Adam welcomed the diversion. However, since Adam had the pelts so well sorted, the inventory took less than an hour. "Lock up the warehouse, Adam," Mr. Ashley said. "Ride with me to the land that is being cleared eleven miles up the river. It will do you good to be out in the air for the rest of the day." Adam appreciated Mr. Ashley's consideration. He enjoyed the long ride which did occasionally take his mind away from Lance. They spent an hour checking the progress of the clearing before they rode back.

After he had rubbed down the mare and fed her, Adam went to the washhouse. He took off his coat and shirt and soaped the upper part of his body. He rinsed in cold water. Refreshed, he went to supper. This time he was hungry. He finished his meal with a large slice of pound cake which Hannah had saved for him.

"He be restin' good," Hannah assured Adam.

"I hope so," Adam replied.

"Tell him I'm savin' his cake."

"He'll appreciate that. Thank you, Hannah."

Rain clouds were gathering when Adam left the kitchen for the quarters. "It's going to pour soon," Adam called back to Hannah.

Adam was anxious but afraid to get to quarters. He walked to the informal gardens and looked at the azaleas and rhododendrons that he and Lance had so carefully attended. The plants were thriving. Next year's spring buds were already forming. *We'll have even more to do next spring,* he told himself. "We," he shouted and headed to quarters.

Adam found Berta holding a cup of hot broth to Lance's lips. Lance took small sips. He smiled at Adam. "He's doin' fine," Berta said. "You can nurse him now. If you needs me, you knows where my cabin is."

"Thanks, Berta. Good night," Adam said.

As soon as Berta was gone, Adam went to the bed. He kissed Lance gently on the lips. "Now you need to drink the rest of this," he said.

It took a long time for Lance to drain the cup. Adam waited patiently. After Lance had finished, Adam asked, "How do you feel?"

"Tired. And so cold."

Adam built a small fire, even though he thought the quarters warm enough.

"I want my shirt on," Lance said.

"Sit up," Adam told Lance. He got behind Lance. With a little effort, he worked Lance's arms into the sleeves and pulled down the shirt. He lay Lance back down. Adam covered Lance with a blanket.

"Warmer?" Adam asked.

Lance nodded.

Adam didn't know what to say next. He listened to the rain starting to fall outside. Soon it was really coming down.

"Adam," Lance said.

"Yes."

"When I die, will you marry?" Lance asked.

"Don't talk like that."

"Sooner or later you'd turn into a good husband, and you'd always make a damn good father."

"I said, don't talk like that. Anyway you know I'm not the marrying kind."

Lance was quiet for several minutes before he said, "No, you're not. Not at least with a woman. But in our way, we are married even if a clergyman hasn't blessed us."

"Yes, we have been married and still are," Adam replied quietly.

Lance raised up. He was—or seemed to be—the energetic, strong Lance of before. He gave Adam a quick kiss and then said in a firm voice, "Now listen to me, Adam, and stop pretending you don't hear me. Do you hear me?"

Adam nodded.

"I'm dying. And if death ends the pain I feel, then I'm glad it will be over. But I want you to continue to enjoy life and the love of another man."

Adam started to respond, but Lance put his bandaged hand over Adam's mouth. Adam tasted the blood that had soaked through. He knew what Lance was going to say next. He took a deep breath and waited. He finally admitted to himself that he knew what Lance had meant when he joined his hand with Tim's and then placed his on top of theirs. He realized also that Tim had more quickly caught the meaning of Lance's gesture that afternoon in the church.

Still looking down at Adam, Lance said, "Tim is coming here. I want him to take my place."

"You are not going to die, so hush that kind of talk," Adam quickly replied.

"Stop pretending, Adam. Stop pretending."

Adam lay back exhausted. Yes, he admitted, Lance was dying. Yes, perhaps, in time Tim could take Lance's place, could even be his lover. But, no, Adam's mind and body shouted to him, he was not ready to let Lance go.

"Do you hear me, Adam?" Lance said.

Adam did not answer immediately. Finally he said, "Yes, part of me hears you. But another part, the larger part of me, doesn't. That part still tells me to rub your back and get you to sleep."

"I'm ready for that, 'cause suddenly I'm tired. Damn tired. But, Adam, you've got to listen to that other part of you as well. I'll say it one more time. Stop pretending, Adam." Lance paused and then finished by saying, "Now rub my back."

Lance turned and kissed Adam before he shifted to lie on his side. "This way I won't snore." Both young men chuckled. Adam rubbed Lance's back for a long time until Lance's breathing indicated that he was asleep.

Lance's remarks had upset Adam. Quietly he got up, slipped on his shirt for warmth, and poured himself a small mug of cider. He put another log on the fire. He sat before the fire to drink the cider. He listened to Lance's steady breathing and the wind blowing the rain against the window.

Adam kept thinking about what Lance had said. Tomorrow was Adam's birthday. He was glad he hadn't mentioned that to Lance, and that Lance seemed to have forgotten it. How unfair, he thought to himself. Here we are both twenty-five, and both free men. Everything was going so well for us until that damn infection spread in his stones. Why did our lives have to turn out this way? How can I live without him, he murmured. Then he thought of Tim. He was glad Tim was coming. He would be of comfort. But he asked himself, *Would I like to live with Tim? I hardly know him. Yes, I know his body, and I loved our sex. But living with him day to day as I have with Lance, I don't know.*

Adam closed his eyes and tried to push away the thoughts of Lance's dying and of his own life after Lance was gone. Slowly the torment subsided. He could settle nothing tonight, he told himself, and Lance was still alive. Soon the sound of the rain made him sleepy. He pulled off his shirt and got quietly into bed. He snuggled his naked body against Lance. Although the shirt covered Lance's back and chest, his body from the navel down was naked. Adam touched Lance's sex. It was shriveled and limp. Adam did not try to make it stiff. Adam took Lance's hand, put it to his lips and kissed it. He kept hold of it as he fell asleep.

Much later Adam awakened to a strange sound. A hard rain pounded on the roof. But that wasn't the sound that had awakened him from his deep sleep. He turned to Lance and felt his forehead. It was covered with beads of sweat. He was talking to himself. Adam bent over to try and make sense of the mumbled words.

"Lance," Adam whispered.

Lance did not respond. His mumbles grew a bit louder.

Adam moved closer and listen intently. He lay there for a long time. What he heard was a jumble.

"Men at St. Paul's. Young men. Handsome. Old men, just like my grandfather. Old men pay.—I made those riding boots, not you, damn you. 'Lash him harder. Teach him not to curse his master.'—Blue bead. I love to suck the blue bead.—I want to stay on the ship. You can bugger me all you want. The bath feels so good after all those weeks of hell below deck.—I want a blue bead at the tip of my cock.—You're hung like a horse, Adam. My hole may not be able to take all that. But I want it.—Old men pay, but young men are more exciting.—Tim, I want you. Lose your cock inside me.—Adam, lie down so we can suck each other. I love your cock in my mouth.—How did you get the blue bead in your tip?—Thanks for the water, Tim. I love you.—I love you, Adam. I don't want to leave you.—I am a good shoemaker.—Kiss me, Adam."

Lance's mumbles became even more incoherent. Adam couldn't make out any more. He leaned over and kissed Lance. "I love you, too, Lance."

Lance was sweating heavily. Adam got up and went for a rag to wet in a bowl of water. He bathed Lance's face. Then he ran the rag over Lance's chest. As he rubbed Lance's belly, he realized that Lance had an erection. Adam took Lance's cock in his mouth. With only a few licks, Lance came. Shortly after that, Adam felt Lance's body relax.

Again Adam snuggled close to Lance. He was soon asleep.

When Adam awakened the next morning, Lance seemed to be resting so peacefully that he did not want to disturb him. Adam washed his face with the rag he has used to bath Lance. He started to dress. Just as he was putting on his work vest, Berta tapped at the door. She had come to take over as nurse. "Go eats your breakfast," she ordered Adam.

Things seemed to be going better this morning. Adam was hungry. He began to hum as he hastened to the kitchen.

He was only halfway there when Berta's loud, shrill lament broke the stillness of the morning. Adam froze. He knew. His legs gave from under him, and he fell to the ground.

# 1755: The Cemetery at Ashley Landing

A month after Lance's death, the tobacco leaves in the drying sheds were ready to be cut from the stalks and packed into hogsheads. Dried tobacco came by flatboat from the plantation's lands up river to add to that close to Ashley Landing.

"Adam," Mr. Ashley said, "this year I think either William or George should supervise the cutting and packing. You will have plenty to do when it comes time to label the hogsheads and enter the numbers in the ledger before shipment."

Adam knew what lay behind Mr. Ashley's suggestion. Although Adam went about his daily business in an apparently normal manner, people could tell that inwardly he was hurting. Ever since Lance's burial, Adam had appeared at the warehouse early and had not left for the noon meal until he knew that the others at the table would be almost finished eating. Often he asked Hannah to wrap some cold meat and bread which he could eat that evening in his quarters.

Just before time for tobacco cutting Hannah told herself, "That young man can't go on like he is." That noon when Adam asked Hannah to wrap his evening meal for him, Hannah braced herself and said, "No, Masta' Adam, I won't pack no supper for you. You needs to come to the table with the rest of folks. I knows you grievin' but that ain't goin' to bring him back."

Hannah's blunt statement surprised Adam, but it also jolted him to accept the hard truth that he did need to come to terms with Lance's death. All month in the warehouse, his hands and a part of his mind performed routine work efficiently, but the greater part of his mind still heard the words read in the prayer book by Mr. Ashley, "Ashes to ashes, dust to dust" and also still saw the mourners throw their handful of dirt down on the wooden coffin. Adam was the last to throw his handful of dirt. Although he tried hard to keep from crying

doi:10.1300/5623_11

before the assembled group, tears ran down his cheeks. Now, outside the kitchen, Adam said to himself, *Yes, Hannah is right. Grieving won't bring Lance back.*

Adam started back to the warehouse. Suddenly though he stopped. *If it is time to start the healing,* Adam told himself, *then there's no better place than the cemetery.* He had not gone to Lance's grave since the afternoon of the burial. It was his way of denying the death. Now he walked quickly to the cemetery.

The Ashley cemetery was in a grove of pine trees a mile from the great house. Lance's simple tombstone lay in the large area outside the enclosed family plot. His tombstone read LANCE MORLEY, 1730-1755, ASHLEY LANDING CORDWAINER.

Adam stayed in the cemetery looking down at Lance's grave for a long time before he started back to the warehouse. His eyes were dry now, and his shoulders had lost the slight slump of the past month. Adam was still not a joyful man, but he was a calm young man willing to face the days ahead.

Adam was glad Tim was coming soon. As he walked, he kept thinking about Lance's wish that Tim take his place in Adam's life. He also remembered he had told himself that, yes, in time, Tim could become his lover. That admission caused Adam's sex to harden slightly for the first time since Lance's death. He recalled the pleasure of Tim's body. As he did, he grinned when he thought about how Tim liked so much to joke about navels.

That evening Adam joined the supper table. Hannah warned the house servants not to say anything about Adam's return to the table. Although George and William had been puzzled by Adam's strong reaction to Lance's death and considered it a bit unnatural, they acted as if nothing unusual had happened. Adam was the last one at the table to leave the kitchen. He thanked Hannah for the supper. As he was about to go out the door, he turned and said, "I appreciate what you said to me, Hannah."

As she watched him leave the kitchen, Hannah remarked aloud, "Believe he's on the mend. I's glad of that."

Had he not gone to the cemetery and recovered a large bit of his old self, Adam might well have assented to Mr. Ashley's suggestion. But now he wanted to supervise the workers and see that the hogsheads were properly packed. "No," he told Mr. Ashley. "I will do it. I want to do it. And I don't think I am boasting too much when I say that I can do it better than either William or George. They're good men, but they don't have my experience—or my patience."

"If you want, Adam, then good," Mr. Ashley replied. He knew Adam's claim was an accurate one. What delighted him was that Adam seemed more like himself than he had seen him since Lance's death.

"Adam," Mr. Ashley continued, "I had news this morning which will interest you."

"News about Tim?" Adam asked.

"Yes, about him and about the cargo ship."

"How soon will Tim come here?"

"Not as early as we had planned. Master Tisdale writes that one of his sons has been ill, and the shop is behind in its work. He hopes that Timothy's leaving Williamsburg can be delayed until mid-December. I shall write that such an arrangement is acceptable to me."

Although he wanted to be with Tim, Adam was also relieved that Tim would not be coming to Ashley Landing before he had more time to fully come to terms with Lance's death. "He'll be sorry to miss his first season of getting the tobacco ready for shipment. But there will be others," Adam said.

"Once he is here, Adam, will it be convenient for him to share your quarters? If you would prefer now to be alone, then Timothy can share quarters with George. William leaves next week to work out the rest of indenture with the overseer at the north plantation land. So there will be room for him in George's quarters."

"No, I would like to have him in our—my—quarters," Adam replied. He blushed slightly at his mistake.

"Are you certain?"

"Yes. I have met Tim on only two occasions, once at the fair two years ago and then at my aunt's wedding. But I know him as a friend. I will enjoy his company in quarters. What news about the cargo ship?" Adam asked.

"Good news. Captain McGaw writes that our ship will be ready for its maiden voyage to the West Indies next July. He comes here next month to settle a few last details and to learn what goods he can expect from our warehouse to add to the cargo he will arrange for in Annapolis."

"That means I need to inventory."

Mr. Ashley laughed. "With the meticulous way you keep your ledgers, Adam, that will not be an arduous task."

"Do you know if Martin comes with Captain McGaw?" Adam asked.

"Yes. So you will again have him as your guest."

When Captain McGaw and Martin arrived at the end of the second week of December, the last of the hogsheads had been placed on the flatboats and were on their way to Hampton for loading on ships bound for England. Adam had worked steadily the last weeks of November and the first of December. Mr. Ashley attributed the smoothness with which the whole process had gone to Adam's patience and to his joking with the slaves at the same time that he demanded that the packing into hogsheads be done properly. He was certain that Adam was now almost his old self.

The appearance that Adam gave to others was a close, but not perfect, match for how felt inside. He still missed Lance. On occasion, he thought "I must tell Lance that . . ." before he caught himself. At those times an intense pain wracked his guts. But he forced himself to an outward composure by reminding himself of Lance's statement: "Stop pretending, Adam." Soon his normal breathing returned.

One morning in early December Adam awakened to find that he was holding his hard cock in his hand. He peeled his foreskin back and rubbed the crown of his cockhead. His cock stiffened even more. Adam massaged his ballocks and slowly moved his finger back to his hole. He took his hard cock in his hand and pleasured himself. Relieved, he licked the heavy load of juice from his hand.

It was a still, cold afternoon when Adam heard a shout from the dock announcing the arrival of a small boat. He knew that it had to be Captain McGaw and Martin. He wanted to see Martin, but he also dreaded the moment when he had to tell him of Lance's death. The pain he had experienced when he threw his handful of dirt on Lance's coffin surged through him once again.

Suddenly and unexpectedly Adam was weak. As he stood up, his knees buckled, and he collapsed onto the wooden floor. He buried his head in his hands and cried. His body heaved with his loud sobs. That was the way Martin found him.

Martin quickly sat down on the floor, cross-legged. He gathered Adam into his arms. Adam's chest lay across Martin's. Adam's head rested against Martin's neck. Martin put his arms around Adam and held him tight. He gently rocked Adam's body until the sobs stopped. Then Adam raised his head and said in a low voice, "Lance is dead."

Martin pressed Adam's head back down against his neck. "Yes," he replied quietly, "I know thy sorrow. Mr. Ashley told me at the landing. I came here as quickly as I could to comfort thee."

"I don't know where to begin," Adam murmured.

"Don't try now. Rest thyself. Cry if it makes thee feel better. There are tears in my eyes, too."

Martin pulled Adam even tighter against his breast. The two young men remained silently in that tight embrace for a long time. Finally Adam raised his head and said, "Thank you, Martin. I feel calm now. And I do want to talk to you about what happened."

"And I want to hear thee. Also, Adam, I have news of my own. I am embarrassed though that my news is good, not thy sad news."

"What is it?" Adam asked, suddenly aware that there was something different in Martin's language.

"Let me hear thee first, Adam. Tell me, where is Lance buried? I should like to visit his grave and pay my respects."

"He is buried in the cemetery close to the Ashley family plot. Would you like to walk there now? We have time before the darkness sets in."

"Yes, we must go there," Martin said. He reached down and pulled Adam up. He folded Adam into his arms in a gentle hug. He kissed him lightly on his cheek.

When they broke apart, Adam stood back and looked at Martin. They smiled at each other. But Adam sensed that in some way this was not the same Martin who had shared the bed with Lance and him last year. When they had hugged, Adam's sex was aroused, but he detected no hard pressure against his. The kiss had only been on his cheek. It seemed more a brotherly gesture than a lover's. But Adam shrugged away such thoughts. Adam put on his heavy coat and pulled on his mittens. "Ready?" he asked.

"Yes," Martin replied.

Outside, Adam pointed and said, "It's down this way." They walked at a brisk pace. The December air did not invite a leisurely stroll. Again he said, "I don't know where to begin."

"Some wise fool once said to start at the beginning," Martin replied and laughed.

"Well, Lance's cough started the day you left here last year," Adam began.

"I hope my being here didn't cause it," Martin said playfully. He didn't want Adam to become dejected as he talked.

"I doubt it," Adam replied and smiled. He grabbed Martin's gloved hand. Martin squeezed Adam's hand hard and then let go.

"What happened next?"

As they walked side by side, Adam told Martin of the yearlong intermittent coughing spells, the frequent wheezing at night, then the pain caused by the swollen ballocks, and finally the visit to the apothecary in Williamsburg.

"Was there nothing the apothecary could do?" Martin asked.

"He offered to castrate Lance, but he declined. Even if he had agreed, the apothecary said the infection could have spread beyond the ballocks."

"Did he suffer badly?"

"He must have. But it was not until he told me of his swollen stones that I realized how much he was hurting. I think the pain got the worst this fall."

"Were there no good times for the two of thee?"

"Yes. We swam all last summer. And, despite his ill health, Lance always won our races across the river." Adam laughed at that memory.

"Nothing more?" Martin asked and grinned.

"Yes. We made love. Not as much as I wanted. Most often we simply lay close together, touching each other and kissing, but occasionally we cornholed." Adam looked at Martin, hoping to catch his reaction to the mention of that joy they had introduced him to last year, but Martin had turned aside to pick up a broken pine branch to smell.

With the pine branch in his hand, Martin turned to face Adam. "I'm glad that the two of thee had such pleasures." Martin paused, then asked, "Did he give up after the trip to Williamsburg?"

Adam had never thought about that. He did not know how to answer. Then he recalled the exchange of hands in the church at the wedding. Adam didn't know why, but he wasn't ready to tell Martin about Tim. Instead he answered, "I don't know. He had some very good days, but also a lot of bad ones."

"I wish I had been here to help thee."

Adam appreciated that, but he wasn't sure it would have been the best thing. "Thank you," he said anyway. "I have come near to accepting his death, and talking with you has helped even more."

"I am glad." Martin stopped and pointed in the distance. "Is that the burial ground?"

"Yes."

"Stay here, Adam. Let me go there and spend a few minutes alone with my good friend."

"I'll wait here. Wave to me when I can join you."

Adam watched Martin find his way to Lance's gravestone. He rubbed his mittens together to warm his hands. He shut his eyes and took a deep breath. He had told the truth when he said that his talk with Martin had helped. He nodded and said to himself that, like Martin, he would soon need to go to the gravestone and acknowledge a final farewell. But not quite yet, he admitted. When he looked up, he saw Martin waving to him.

Adam walked quickly to meet Martin in the burial ground. Martin started to speak, but Adam stopped him. "Let's not talk about Lance's death any longer," he said. "Give me your news. You said it was good news, and I want to hear it. But tell me first, what is all this *thee* and *thy* I keep hearing?"

Martin laughed gently. "I wondered if you had noticed. It is the way I speak now as a Friend."

"A friend?" Adam asked, not understanding.

"It is a long story."

"Then as the wise fool once said, start at the beginning," Adam said and grinned.

"Shortly after I returned to Annapolis from here last year Captain McGaw invited me to attend meeting with him. He and his wife are what many people call Quakers, although we prefer to call ourselves Friends. We are members of the Religious Society of Friends. At first I found meeting strange. Men sit on one side of the room, the women on the other. There are no sermons. In fact, meetings are for silent meditation. No one speaks until the spirit moves someone to pray or to offer almost any kind of comment. Soon I found the meetings very peaceful and satisfying. I felt that I knew myself better than I ever had, both as a young man and a member of the community." Martin paused and smiled. "That's a long way of answering your question about *thee.*"

"It sounds like you are a happy man. I'm glad for you," Adam said. He was not at all sure just how changed a man Martin was. He recalled the brotherly kiss and the lack of response when Adam pressed his semi-erect cock against Martin's crotch. He wondered if the Friends, like other religious groups, regarding men lying with men as sinful.

Martin interrupted Adam's thoughts by saying, "But that's only the beginning of my news. I am leaving Annapolis."

"Where are you going?"

"Philadelphia, where I was when I was a little boy before Captain McGaw brought me to Maryland. There are many Friends in Philadelphia, and I'll be welcomed into a large community of people who will accept me as a young man of color more easily than many people do in Annapolis. But that's not the main reason for going there."

"Then what is?"

"Captain McGaw's sister is married to an architectural draftsman, and he has offered to take me on as an apprentice. Captain McGaw feels that working as a draftsman in the office of his shipbuilding yard limits my abilities. He wants me to do other things than work on the details of his ships."

"You want to do more?"

"Yes. I want to design houses. Not great houses like that here at Ashley Landing, but smaller houses, those built for cordwainers and tailors. For people working hard to put food on the table, and doing it at the same time they are raising a family."

Adam waited a minute before he said, "You are a different person than you were when Lance accidentally hit you with a snowball."

Martin nodded his head. "Yes, different, but still the same. The difference is that I am going to be married."

"Married!" Adam exclaimed.

"Yes. Helen Marie and I will be married before we leave for Philadelphia."

The thunder of Martin's announcement and the thunder in a darkening sky coincided. A slow, cold rain began to fall on them. Martin looked up at the rain, but Adam stared at Martin, not quite believing he had heard correctly. He didn't know what to say. Finally, after taking a long look at Lance's gravestone, Martin said, "We'll be chilled if we don't get back to thy quarters. Stay by my side, and I'll tell thee about the wonderful young woman who is to be my wife." He gave Adam a slap on the shoulder, and they started down the narrow road.

Adam's mind was awhirl, but he kept up with Martin's fast trot. Martin's words came as fast as his footsteps. From them, Adam learned that Martin had seen Helen Marie at meeting. At first, he looked away from her on the opposite of the hall. But, even as he meditated, his eyes kept glancing at her. To his surprise, he admitted, he even felt his sex harden as he looked at her. Captain McGaw's wife had seen the glances, but hopefully not the bulge in his breeches, and eventually she introduced the two young people.

Helen Marie was the illegitimate daughter of a white man and an Indian woman. Abandoned as a baby, she had been reared in the orphanage run by the Friends. Like Martin, she had almond-colored skin and dark hair. Although they were both bashful during the courtship, it did not take long for them to fall in love. Friends at the meeting were delighted to hear of their betrothal. Several of them, on both sides of the hall, broken the silence during meeting to pray for their happiness.

Their coats and breeches were damp by the time Adam and Martin reached quarters. Adam quickly built a fire. The small room soon started to warm. The two young men took off their coats and hung them to dry. Then they stood side by side with their backs to the fire. Martin put his arm around Adam's shoulder and said, "Well, do thee have nothing to say, nothing to ask?"

Adam had questions, but he felt he should wait to ask him. He didn't know whether he should or not, but he put his arm around Martin's waist. Then turning to Martin, Adam said with a smile on his face, "Martin, I must admit you have taken me by surprise. Your news is not that I had expected to hear. But, like your Friends at meeting, I wish you and Helen Marie happiness together."

"Thank you, Adam," Martin replied and kissed Adam lightly on the cheek.

Adam could wait no longer. He had to know. "What about what we did last year?"

Looking at Adam with a smile on his face, Martin said softly, "Many times during this past year I have thought with great pleasure about my visit with Lance and thee."

Although Adam was pleased that Martin had remembered his visit to Ashley Landing, he still thought Martin's answer to his question evasive. "I don't know why you didn't, Martin," he said, "but I don't think you truly answered my question. You must know that I was asking about what you, Lance, and me did lying in bed naked those nights."

"Yes, I knew that was what thee was asking."

"Then why didn't you answer me honestly?"

"I wanted to wait until after we came back from the kitchen to talk about that intimacy."

Adam became impatient. He snapped, "Well, damn it, I want to talk about it now."

With a pained expression on his face, Martin looked at Adam but said nothing.

"So," Adam exploded, "you had a pleasant visit. But you regretted what we did in bed. You were disgusted when you went back to your safe Annapolis—even though while you were here you bloody well enjoyed having your cock sucked and shoving your cock up our butts. Lance and I were just your whores, helping you to get rid of your fears of sex."

"No, Adam!" Martin shouted. "That's not true." Martin reached toward Adam and covered his mouth. "That's not true," he shouted again. He started to pull Adam into an embrace, but Adam pushed him away.

"Then, what is—thy—truth," Adam said sarcastically. "Thy truth," he repeated.

"Adam, do not be angry with me." Martin again moved to pull Adam into an embrace. This time Adam let his body be moved closer to Martin's. "Now listen to me," Martin said, yet once more giving Adam a light kiss on his cheek.

"No," Martin said, "our lying together was not disgusting. Nor did I regret it after I left here. I do not regret it now." Martin paused. He felt Adam's tense body relax a bit.

"Why should I regret what meant so much to me?" Martin continued. "Lance and thee taught me how to love. I was so afraid of my body when I came here last year. It took all the courage I had to undress before thee that first night. Lance and thee helped me rid myself of that fear. The more thee held me in thy arms, the more thee carressed me and made me want to come to thy body, the more I experienced the pleasure of leaving myself and coming to another person, of becoming one with that person."

Martin paused again. "Now that pleasure will be with Helen Marie. But, Adam, if it had not been for Lance and thee, I would never have reached that new pleasure. Thee were not whores. I took thy bodies, yes. And thee gave me thy bodies, too. But Lance and thee gave me much more than thy bodies; thee gave me the inner experience of love. Thee were my teachers."

Adam sighed. Martin's words made him happy. "Then you are not ashamed of what the three of us did in bed last year?" Adam asked.

Martin laughed and gave Adam a hug. "Ashamed! No, I am glad we did what we did."

"Would your Friends be ashamed of you?"

"No. They would accept what we did as only another way of human love."

"And you are not ashamed?" Adam repeated.

"There is nothing to be ashamed of when people make love, no matter what form that lovemaking takes."

Adam hesitated but then asked, "Did you lie with other men in Annapolis?"

"No."

"Did you want to?"

"Yes, very much. But there was no one. Then, after I met Helen Marie, my desires moved in another direction."

"Will you still think of men after you have married?

"I don't know. I probably will. But, after I marry, I will be faithful to my wife. I will not have sex with anyone—woman or man—other than Helen Marie. If I do think of men occasionally, I will not be ashamed of my thoughts."

Adam knew his question impertient, but nonetheless he asked, "Have you been with Helen Marie?"

"No. We will both be virgins the night we consumate our marriage."

"Then you are no longer the special one, marked with the blue bead," Adam commented.

"The blue bead is gone."

"Gone?"

"Yes. My foreskin has been cut away. It is a ritual among some of my people of color. It celebrates manhood."

"When was this done?"

"Three months ago."

"Wasn't it painful?"

"Very much. I was given a stick to chew on while the foreskin was cut away. And my member was in pain for several weeks." Martin paused and gave Adam a hug. "But let's stop talking about me. I want to hear more about thee."

"What do you want to know?'

Before Martin could answer, their conversation was interrupeted by the supper bell. "We'll wait until later," Martin said. The two young men looked at each other. Both wanted to say something more, to ask something more. But neither spoke. "I'm hungry," Martin finally said.

By the time they finished supper the light rain had turned into a heavy downpour. At the kitchen door, Adam looked out, shook his head, and said to Martin, "Make a dash for the privy if you need to. I'll get more firewood, do my business, and meet you in quarters. Give the fire a good stir and put on another log."

Later when he entered quarters, Adam was drenched. The only light in the room was that created by the fire. Adam looked around for Martin. He was surprised to find him in bed. The blanket was pulled up over his nipples. Adam knew from the bare shoulders and arms that Martin wasn't wearing a shirt. He was naked. After the conversation this afternoon Adam expected both of them to wear their shirts to bed.

"Get out of thy wet clothes, Adam, and come to bed. Thee doesn't want to catch cold," Martin called to him.

Adam waited a second or two and then asked, "Martin, shouldn't I sleep on the pallet?"

"Why?"

He must know the answer, Adam thought to himself. He must know that I want his body. He answered, "If I lie naked with you, I won't be able to keep my hands off you."

"Then come to bed, for I want thy hands on me."

Adam was surprised. "But I thought you said . . ."

"Yes, I know what I said," Martin interrupted him. "But, Adam, I am not married yet. And I want thee here by me. We have things to talk about—and things to do. Come to bed."

"Martin, I told you. If I come to bed I will want your body. Are you sure?"

"Yes, Adam, I am sure. Come to bed."

Adam hesitated only for a moment. But he quickly told himself that, if Martin had no qualms about sex with another man when he was betrothed to a woman, then he had no qualms about lying with that man. He shed his wet clothes and placed them to dry before the fire. When he looked down his naked body, he saw exactly what he knew was there—an erect cock.

Quickly he was in bed beside Martin, and they were in each other's arms. As they clung tightly to each other's body, their lips met. Adam kissed Martin with an intensity that made Martin's body quiver. The deeper Adam's tongue probed Martin's mouth, the more Martin's tongue and lips responded. They kissed for a long time.

When their lips parted, Martin whispered, "I've thought about thy kisses ever since I left here. I am pleased to taste thy lips again. But I also have thought about thy large member, and I want to taste it too."

Martin raised up and moved down the bed. He buried himself at Adam's crotch under the covers. His hand worked the foreskin back and forth over the cockhead. When the foreskin was tight down the shaft, Martin took Adam's sex in his mouth. He sucked furiously. It was as it he were either making up for lost time or relishing something for the last time. Every move down his cock brought Adam closer to climax. He pushed Martin off and threw the covers back off them.

Martin's cock was erect. Adam looked at it with studied curiosity. With its sheath missing, Martin's member looked strange, too naked. *It's not natural,* Adam said to himself. *I am glad I am not like that. But if the ritual is important to Martin, then I accept the loss of his foreskin.* Then he flipped so that Martin's sex was touching his lips. He swallowed Martin's very large cock. Martin went back down on Adam.

The rain beat down on the roof of quarters. The flames of the fire flicked long shadows across the room. But the two young men were so lost in a frantic orgy that neither of them of was aware of the steady pelting on the roof and the waving patterns on the walls. Martin's lips made love to Adam's foreskin and cockhead. At first Adam missed having Martin's foreskin to play with, but he soon learned to concentrate on just the cockhead and the firm smooth skin below the crown. It did not take long before each felt the other's cock quiver frantically. Then each tasted the sweet heavy juice of the other. Even when there was nothing more to drain out, their lips continued to circle the cockheads. Finally they let go. Adam turned around to face Martin. They embraced and kissed.

Then without saying anything, they lay back and shut their eyes. They lay like that, close together, for a long time. Finally Martin propped himself up with his elbow and looked down at Adam. "How will thee fare now that Lance is gone?" Martin asked.

"I'll stay here at Ashley Landing. I like my work, and I'll keep busy at it," Adam replied.

"That's not what I was asking," Martin said and poked Adam in the ribs.

"I know that," Adam answered. "I, too, have good news. I have waited for the right moment to tell you."

"I hope that moment is now."

"Yes, it is." Adam paused briefly, then he announced, "I, too, am betrothed. At least I think I am."

"Betrothed! Thee thinks that thee is?" Martin exclaimed, both surprised and puzzled.

"Yes," Adam replied calmly.

"Who is she?"

"His name is Tim," Adam answered with a laugh.

"Another man?"

"That's what I said. His name is Tim."

Martin waited a second or two and then burst out, "Who is Tim? Where is he? How long have thee known him? Have thee lay together in bed? Why does thee only think that thee is betrothed? Don't thee know?"

"I can't answer all those questions at once," Adam said and returned Martin's poke in the ribs.

They both laughed. Martin kissed Adam lightly on the lips and said, "Well, start at the beginning."

"The beginning is when Lance met Tim at the cordwainer's shop when Lance first arrived in Williamsburg."

"Well, that does go back a few years," Martin commented.

"Seven, to be exact," Adam said.

"Were Lance and Tim bedfellows as Lance and thee were bedfellows? Martin asked.

"Yes, they had a strong bond. But they were not together long enough to develop the intense love Lance and I grew to have for each other."

"Go on," Martin said.

It took Adam almost half an hour to tell his story. As he talked, he realized how much he wanted to see Tim again. He forgot that Martin was listening to his words. It was more like he was recounting for himself how Tim had grown from someone he had only heard about from Lance, to an acquaintance he liked at the time of the Williamsburg fair, and then to a good friend on the next visit to Williamsburg for his aunt's wedding. *Soon he might be my bedfellow,* Adam thought with delight. *He will have fun teasing me about his navel.*

Martin brought Adam back to the present though when he heard about Alan's death. He interrupted Adam by saying, "Tim is like thee. A young man who has lost someone very dear to him. Perhaps his sorrow is even greater, for he has lost Lance as well as Alan. Does he know of Lance's death?"

"I think so. Mr. Ashley told Master Tisdale in a recent letter. I am sure Henry has passed the news on to Tim."

"The two of thee will need to comfort one another when he arrives." Martin ran his hand over Adam's face and neck.

"I want Tim here," Adam said. "I'll be glad when he comes. But it will open the wound again. You are right, Martin. Tim and I will need to comfort one another."

Martin nodded and then said, "But I still do not understand what thee means by a betrothal. Thee has been in bed with Tim only once. Adam, that hardly means thee is betrothed."

"Let me finish my story. Then you can tell me whether or not you think I am betrothed," Adam said. This time he kissed Martin lightly on the lips before he returned to his story.

"The three of us were at my aunt's wedding ceremony. Towards the end of the service, Lance reached across Tim and took my hand. Our clasped hands fell into Tim's crotch."

"What did Tim do?"

"He placed his hand on top of ours. His cock hardened and pressed against our hands. We all smiled at each other. Then, as Sarah and

Henry were finishing their vows and pledging to live together until death parted them, Lance let loose my hand and placed it in Tim's. Then Lance put his hand on top of ours and pressed hard. Just at that moment the marriage vows were over, and Henry and Sarah were husband and wife."

Martin thought for a few seconds, then asked, "Did Lance ever explain why he gave thy hand to Tim's and then placed his on top?"

"I asked him why. I told him I didn't understand. He said that he thought I did but didn't want to admit it."

"Then did he explain his reason?"

"No. He said he would later, if I had not guessed by then. We never had a chance to talk about it directly, but the night before he died he told me that he wanted Tim to take his place in my life."

"Doesn't thee think, Adam, that was what he was telling both Tim and thee that afternoon in the church? That he wanted thee two to become bedfellows as he and thee had been bedfellows?"

"I guess it was. I couldn't accept it then, for I still was trying to believe that Lance would not die."

"Did Tim and thee talk about what Lance did with thy hands?"

"Yes. The night after the ceremony the three of us lay in bed together. After we had all spent ourselves, Lance fell asleep. Tim and I put on our shirts and sat in the yard in back of the shop. Tim said he knew what Lance meant by placing our hands together. Like Lance, Tim said he thought I knew, too, but couldn't admit it."

"Before thee three went to thy aunt's wedding, did Tim know that Lance was seriously ill, probably going to die soon?"

"Yes. Lance had told him."

"Adam, I think Tim accepted Lance's approaching death before thee could. Also that Tim knew clearly that Lance wished him to become thy bedfellow, to take his place."

"I know you are right—now. But I could not accept it all when we were in Williamsburg or during the months before Lance died."

"Tim and thee are betrothed—and with Lance's blessing."

"Yes, that was my good news," Adam said.

Martin lay back and pulled Adam into his arms. They kissed. When Martin pulled away, he said, "I'm tired, and we have a busy day tomorrow at thy warehouse. Captain McGaw needs to know what the warehouse here can supply for the ship's first voyage."

"I know. Mr. Ashley asked me to be at the warehouse as soon as I finish breakfast."

"Then it's time for us to sleep. Turn on thy side. Let me keep thee warm for the night."

Adam turned on his side, and Martin moved up close against him. Soon the two young men were asleep.

The next day at the warehouse was a busy one. Adam was surprised at how many questions Captain McGaw had for him. The captain wanted figures from the several ledgers and detailed answers about the contents of the numerous boxes and barrels. Although Adam was a bit tired and happy to hear the supper bell ring, he was pleased that he had been able to answer all the questions to the captain's satisfaction. Both the captain and Mr. Ashley thanked Adam as they left for the great house.

When the two older men were gone, Martin clasped Adam around the shoulders and, exclaimed "Thy abilities impress me. Mr. Ashley is fortunate to have you here."

"And I am fortunate to be here, although no one could have told me that seven years ago. Then I thought I was being indentured to a circle in Hell."

"Virginia is thy home then?"

"I no longer think of myself as an Englishman. I am a Virginian."

"Well, let us go eat some of thy Virginia fare in the kitchen."

Before they had finished the bread pudding, a house servant brought word to Martin that he and Captain McGaw were to leave after breakfast the next day.

"I hoped that you would be staying longer," Adam said to Martin. "I probably will not meet you again. Philadelphia seems as far away as London."

"They aren't," Martin replied. "There's an ocean between here and London. Only waterways and rough roads between here and Philadelphia."

"There's an ocean 'tween here and my country," Hannah remarked as she picked up their empty dishes.

"Do you want to go back there?" Adam asked.

"No. I'se a Virginian," Hannah told him.

Adam raised his cider cup in a salute to Hannah and said, "Yes, Hannah, we are here together."

The black slave and the young Indian Quaker looked at each other in a knowing way and then looked at Adam, who was smiling at them both. Then Hannah said in a mock gruff manner, "Now you two gets out of my kitchen and lets me finish up so I'se can get back to quarters and find some rest."

Outside a cold wind greeted the two young men. Looking up at the clear sky with the emerging new moon, Martin shivered and said, "I think our winter has arrived."

Adam pulled his coat tighter around him and replied, "It will be a heavy frost tonight. The first killing frost of this winter. Go poke the fire, Martin, and I'll get more firewood."

It took Adam longer to get to quarters than he expected. At the woodshed he met George. The two men greeted each other.

"Cold enough to freeze your ballocks off tonight," George commented.

"I hope not," Adam replied and laughed.

"I hear that damn Indian is leaving tomorrow morning."

The unexpected shift from friendly jocularity to ugliness took Adam by surprise. "Yes" was Adam's curt reply.

"Good riddance, I'd say," George continued.

"He's decent company," Adam answered, biting his lip to control his temper.

"If I were you, Adam, I'd let Mr. Ashley have a strong piece of my mind for quartering that bloody redskin with you."

"He's been no bother."

"I hope you're making him sleep in the opposite corner of your quarters."

"No," Adam said quickly and firmly. "Martin shares my bed. He's a guest here at Ashley Landing."

George grunted. "Stupid thing to do. He hasn't tried to prong you, has he?"

Adam gasped. "You mean . . ."

"Yes, that's what I mean. Has he tried to shove his cock up your butt? Damned Indian is probably a filthy sodomite as well."

Angry and surprised at George's comment, Adam thought of and rejected a dozen replies. Finally, in a low, controlled voice, he said, "You've got a nasty tongue, George, and a much nastier mind if you think that."

George came close to Adam and stared at him with an amused grin. "You know, Adam, I think you just might enjoy that sort of thing."

Adam quickly moved so close to George that their noses almost touched. "Shut up with that kind of talk," Adam snapped and glared hard at George.

George backed away. "Calm yourself. You take a little joke too much to heart. Just be careful though, Adam. You don't need to have that son of a bitch in your quarters just because he's a guest here." He paused. "Let's get our wood and out of this cold."

"I need a shit first. I'll come back for my wood. Good night, George," Adam said.

Actually what Adam needed was time to control his anger. In the dark privy he sat with his head between his hands. All of George's ugly remarks infuriated him.

But George's remarks also frightened Adam. Had George somehow guessed about how he liked to lie with other men? Perhaps his expression had revealed more about himself than Adam wanted when the two men were breathing into each other's face. George said he only had been joking about Adam's possibly liking having Martin prong him. But Adam did not trust George. Damn it, he said to himself, when Tim comes, we have got to be very careful around that man. Tim likes to joke and tease so much, sometimes a bit too carelessly. For us to lie together, to take each other's body, to become one through sexual contact would seem only natural for Tim and me, Adam said to himself. But now more than ever before, Adam realized that there were men for whom the only reaction to that kind of lovemaking was hatred.

Adam shivered. He was getting cold sitting there. He pulled himself together and headed back to the woodshed. He had certainly not forgotten his brief encounter with George by the time he got back to quarters, but he thought he had put it enough out of his mind so that he could enjoy his last evening with Martin.

Adam found Martin sitting in front of the fire. He had removed only his coat and his shoes. For comfort, he had pulled his shirt out of his breeches. When he heard Adam enter, Martin turned and said, "Where has thee been? I was almost ready to go out looking for thee."

"Just out doing my business," Adam answered.

Martin could tell from the slightly troubled look on Adam's face that the explanation was only half true. He sensed that something had happened to upset Adam, but he only said, "Do thee intend to spend the evening standing there, Adam? I would like thy company down here by the fire."

"And I yours," Adam replied. He shed his coat and went to hang it on a peg at the far end of the room. As he touched the peg, George's remark about how he and Martin should keep far apart from each other echoed in his ears. "I'm over here hanging up my coat where it belongs," he mumbled, as if in defiance of George's nasty advice.

"What did thee say?" Martin called.

Adam realized that he was not as far away from his confrontation with George as he had thought. "Nothing, just talking to myself," he answered.

"Well, come talk to me. I want to talk with thee about two things," Martin said.

Adam looked at Martin and then asked playfully, "Shall I go to the warehouse and get my ledger so that I can record those two things?"

"No, just listen and record them in thy mind. The first is only a small request which I hope thee will honor. Tonight, on our last night together, I want both of us to sleep with our shirts on. I hope that we can still sleep close to keep each other warm. But we must not have any further bodily contact. I hope that thy sex will remain as limp as mine will be. Will thee still honor my request?"

"Yes, of course, I will."

"Thank you, Adam."

Adam hesitated but then asked, "Do you regret what we did last night?"

"No, Adam. I wanted thee last night, and I am happy that we pleasured each other. I knew when I came here this year, I would want to have sexual pleasure one night with thee. But I also knew that once would be the last."

"Then you're still not ashamed of having been with another man?"

"No, Adam. Like I told thee last night, I still believe that when one man lies with a man friend, they are only engaged in another natural way of expressing their love for each other And, Adam, even when I am married to Helen Marie, I will still love thee as my good friend, even though I will not express that love with my body."

"And I will continue to love you, Martin."

The two young men smiled and kissed each other on the cheek to seal their new relationship. Afterward Adam asked, "And what is this second thing I must record in my mind, Martin?"

"Thee must take Tim as thy bedfellow and loving friend. Lance wanted thee and Tim to be together here. He wanted Tim to take his place in thy life. He betrothed thee two at thy aunt's wedding by joining thy hands together and placing his on top as a blessing."

"Yes, I am betrothed to Tim, and I'm very happy. I want him to come here." Adam paused. "But . . ." He stopped and looked into the fire.

"But what?"

"Martin, last night and tonight—through you—I experienced love, each night in a different way. But tonight, shortly before I came to quarters, I also experienced hatred."

"Hatred! How?"

"Yes. Hatred."

Then in a rush of words Adam told Martin about his meeting with George. When he had finished talking, Adam put his face between his hands. His shoulders shook. He fought back crying. Quickly Martin squatted before Adam and took him into his arms. Martin hummed into Adam's ears for a long time. Finally Adam raised up, dried his eyes, and asked, "Why does he hate so?"

Martin was silent, as if he were in meeting. Then, in a firm voice, he answered, "Not all men, Adam, have thy generous soul. Many do. But some men, a few but too many, believe that only their way of doing things, of seeing things, is right. They cannot accept differences. That blindness causes hatred."

Adam pulled away from Martin. "Tim and I must be careful, or we will feel the wrath of that hatred," he said, more to himself than to Martin.

"Is such hatred new to thee, Adam? Has no one before tonight spewed out his venom at thee as a bent one?" Martin asked.

Adam thought about Matt. Had Matt hated Lance and him because they were that way, or had Matt only been jealous? Twice Matt had wanted to be pleasured. Before he could take Matt in his mouth the first time, Lance had intervened. Then, at the crossroads on the back trail, Matt again had demanded that he pleasure him. Certainly Matt had disliked Lance intensely. No doubt initially it was his jealousy of the favor Mr. Ashley showed to an indentured servant who was a convict. Later he became angry that Lance had struck him in the fight in the barn and was out for revenge when he met them on the back trail. *But,* thought Adam, *Matt must also have been jealous of us. He told us that he had been with other men in Williamsburg. However, he only wanted to be pleasured. He was incapable of giving of himself. He only took from other men. If there was hatred in Matt, perhaps the strongest was a self-hatred. He must have seen the love between Lance and me, hated himself because he could not love in that way, and then perhaps turned that hatred toward us. I did not kill Matt,* Adam said to himself; *Matt killed himself. Long before I pulled the trigger to get him out of his pain, Matt had poisoned his own inner being.*

"Thee has not answered me," Martin said.

"I'm sorry. I was thinking about something that happened two years ago and which has lingered in the back of my mind all this time."

"Do thee wish to talk about it now?"

"No, I don't think so. What you said about blind hatred suddenly helped me to bury the incident. It won't trouble me again."

"Burying that incident won't cause all blind hatred to go away, Adam. As thee said, Tim and thee must be careful."

Adam turned around and looked at Martin. He saw him in a slightly new way. "You have felt a blind hatred from others because of the color of your skin, haven't you?" Adam asked quietly.

"Yes. But like thee and the incident two years ago, I don't wish to spoil my last night with thee by talking about it."

"I hope you experience no more."

"Adam, thee lives in too isolated a world here at Ashley Landing. Even when Helen Marie and I move to Philadelphia, we will encounter prejudice. Not all people in that city practice brotherly love." Martin paused and then said, "But let us talk of more pleasant things."

"Good. Tell me more about the cargo ship."

Well over an hour later Martin was still talking about the ship and the goods it would take to the West Indies and the goods it would bring back to the colonies. When he caught Adam yawning, he grinned and asked, "Have I told thee enough?"

"I think so. Let's get to bed. We need to get up early."

The two young men stepped out of their breeches and pulled off their stockings. Adam banked the fire for the night. He got into bed, his back to Martin. Martin moved close to Adam and reached over and took his hand.

"I love thee, Adam, my friend," he said.

"And thy friend loves thee, too, Martin," Adam replied.

When Adam awakened the next morning, Martin was already up and starting to dress. He had built a small fire, so the chill was gone from the room.

"Did thee sleep well?" Martin asked.

"Yes, and you?"

"Yes. But I dreamed of Helen Marie, and I am afraid, Adam, that I have left a spoiled spot on thy bedcovers."

"Then there are two of them. I dreamed of Tim."

They started their morning with a loud burst of laughter.

"Hurry and dress. We must get to breakfast," Martin said.

They were soon ready to leave quarters. At the door Adam and Martin stopped and looked into each other's eyes. Without saying anything, they kissed each other on the cheek. They stepped out into the cold December morning air and hastened to the warm kitchen for breakfast.

# Late 1755: In a Thicket of Bushes

The morning quickly evaporated. There were formal farewells at the landing. Adam and Martin shook hands, but they also placed their left hands firmly on top of their clasped hands. Their eyes met, and they nodded at each other and smiled. Shortly, Captain McGaw's boat headed down stream.

Afterward Mr. Ashley and Adam spent the morning and much of the afternoon in the warehouse. Mr. Ashley was pleased with his business arrangements. Once again he thanked Adam for his careful management of the warehouse. "Once the ship begins to make its runs twice a year, you will be busier than ever," Mr. Ashley warned Adam. Adam replied that he was prepared for that.

In the two hours before the supper bell rang, Adam walked to the bend in the river. He stared across to the opposite side at the large tree with its overhanging branches. That was the turn-around point for his races with Lance. So much had happened since they made that first race. So much was yet to happen, he told himself, when Tim comes. "I wonder which of us will win the races across the river?" he asked the cold wind rippling the river. Since he heard no answer, he headed back to the kitchen for supper.

The kitchen was lively. The house servants and many of the black slaves from the dependencies were there. They were crowded around a young black girl with a baby in her arms. Adam shut the door behind him quietly and leaned back against the wall. He wanted to watch the celebration. With a large cup in her hand, Hannah went from person to person. Each took a long sip. Behind Hannah, Berta carried a platter of corn bread muffins soaked in molasses. The kitchen was filled with low cries of congratulations. The young mother sang her thanks. Just when the gathering seemed at its happiest, the kitchen door burst open to let in the cold wind and George.

doi:10.1300/5623_12

265

"What the hell is going on?" George grumbled as he elbowed his way to his seat at the table. "Where's supper?" he called to Hannah.

"Almost ready. We celebratin' a new baby." Hannah answered joyously. Then she saw Adam standing against the wall. She went to him and extended the cup. Adam smiled and took it from her and drank from it.

George's mouth dropped in disbelief. He turned his head away from Adam in disgust. But his disgust turned to anger when he saw Hannah approaching him. He shook his head violently and raised his hand at her. The merriment lowered to a murmur. At a nod from Hannah and Berta, the dependency slaves circled around the young woman and her baby and left the kitchen. The house servants whispered among themselves and then took their seats at the table at the end opposite from George. Except for the rattle of dishes by Hannah and her helpers, the kitchen was quiet.

"Well, Adam," George asked nastily, "which end of the table for you—or do you intend to eat standing against the wall?"

"Blind hatred," Adam said to himself. However, since he did not want to cause a disturbance, he left the wall and took his seat across from George. Hannah put filled plates before them.

"It was a celebration, George. They were happy about a baby. You should have taken a sip."

George glowered but did not answer. The two young men ate their meal in silence. When they had finished, George leaned across the table and said in a low voice, "Is there anything you won't do? Sipping from the same cup as them."

"There are many things I won't do," Adam said.

"But still you do some disgusting things," George quickly countered. "You drink with blacks. You share your bed with a redskin."

Adam said nothing.

Leaning forward across the table, George asked in a low voice, "You and that Indian. Did he prong you? Or did you prong him? Red meat, you might say."

Inwardly Adam exploded, but in a low, calm voice he said, "I told you last night to stop that kind of talk. I'm telling you again, George, don't you ever talk to me like that again."

Aware of the tension, Hannah looked over at the two men and walked to the table. "No trouble in my kitchen," she told them.

"Don't worry, Hannah. I'm sorry I got you upset." Adam said.

George snickered but said nothing.

In an attempt to calm matters, Hannah said, "I hears we gettin' a new shoemaker."

George cocked his head at the news and asked, "That so, Adam?"

"Yes. He comes from Williamsburg soon."

"Sharin' your quarters?" Hannah asked.

"I hope not, for his sake. Better he take over mine," George said.

Both Adam and Hannah looked at George in surprise. "You been so busy these days, Adam, that I guess Mr. Ashley never found time to tell you."

"Tell me what?"

"I'm going to Williamsburg. There's more need for good carpenters there than here. I hear Mr. Ashley got a good price for the rest of my indenture. I now belong—or soon will—to a builder in the capital."

"When do you go?" Adam asked, stunned, delighted, apprehensive—all at once.

"I don't know. Ask Mr. Ashley. But soon, I think. I'll be glad to leave here."

Slowly a great sense of relief settled over Adam. He cut the last chunk of cold pork and topped each piece on corn bread. He ate with deliberate slowness. Over seven years ago he had regretted seeing another George leave. The earl's coachman had introduced him into a world he wanted to enter but did not know how. But, here at Ashley Landing, Adam was glad to learn that this George was leaving.

As Adam chewed the last bite of pork and corn bread, he realized that he was being stared at.

"You feelin' right?" Hannah asked.

"I'm fine," Adam answered.

"A bit of red meat would do you good. Perhaps even a large piece of white meat might help," George said in a matter-of-fact way.

Adam had no idea what George meant by his remark. But he knew he needed to be on his guard after he left the kitchen. As he started to leave, Hannah called to him, "You been workin' too hard. Get you some rest tonight."

"I'll try. Good night, Hannah." When he realized that George was not going to leave, Adam said, "Good night, George." George nodded at Adam and smiled.

Outside it was cold. After a trip to the privy, Adam needed to get logs for a fire. At the woodshed he was startled and disturbed to find George there, just as he had the night before.

"We're making a habit of meeting here," George quipped.

"I'll be quick and be out of your way."

"Don't hurry, Adam. I want to talk with you."

"If it's more of your nasty talk, I don't want to hear it."

"Don't be unfriendly, Adam. True, you and me disagree about drinking from the same cup with blacks and sharing a bed with a redskin, so let's not talk about those things anymore. But, like I said in the kitchen, a bit of white meat might do you some good."

"What does that mean, George?"

"Simple. Why don't you just follow me back to my quarters and we lie in bed together for a spell. That would save you building a fire. And I think we could keep each other plenty warm."

Adam was stunned. He was speechless.

"Do I surprise you, Adam?"

"Yes. That is, if you mean what I think you're saying."

"Adam, I think you're playing a bit of the innocent. You can't tell me that, on occasion, when your ballocks really needed unloading that you and Lance did not have a bit of fun."

"We weren't . . ."

"Hold on. I'm not saying that you wouldn't rather have been with a woman. But with none around, a quick prong up another man's butt was a passable substitution."

Adam had to find a way to get control of the situation. He didn't want it to turn into another experience like that with Matt in the stable barn. There was no Lance this time to intervene.

"Well, am I right?" George asked.

Adam moved closer to George. "Is that what you and William did?"

George laughed. "Why, yes, when we were down here. When we were working with the overseers up river, it was different."

"How so?"

"Easy to find a willing black gal there."

"Mr. Ashley wouldn't like that. It's against your indenture agreement."

"He wasn't there though."

"What about the overseers?"

"Adam, you are an innocent. The overseers were the ones who told us which gals to go after."

"Well, I guess you wish you were back up there. Things don't go that way down here at the Landing."

"I know they don't. That's why Will and me did what we had to do when the need arose. That is, when our cocks arose and we didn't want to handle ourselves."

Adam could not believe he was hearing all he was.

"You haven't answered my questions, Adam."

"Which were?"

"Isn't that what you and Lance did once in a while?"

Somehow Adam knew a denial would get him nowhere. But he also knew that George would not understand the love Lance and he had for each other. What George and William experienced was quick sexual release, nothing more. "Yes, every once in a while," Adam finally said.

"Better than doing it by hand, wasn't it?"

"I guess. But every time we always felt ashamed after we were done."

"No need for that. Now answer my first question."

"You mean, about going to your quarters?"

"Yes."

"George, I just don't feel like it tonight. I'm tired, like Hannah said. Let's wait 'til another night."

"I might not be here that much longer."

"But you're not leaving tomorrow."

"I ready for action tonight, Adam."

"But I'm not."

"I think I could take you if I had a mind to."

"Yes, I suspect you could. You're stronger than I am. But, George, if you try that, I'll fight you for all I'm worth. I'll make it so that you don't have one damn bit of fun all the time you're trying to get inside me."

"Yes, I suspect you would put up a damn good fight," George said. He paused and then continued, "Adam, I know you don't like me. You don't like my way of thinking about people who aren't like me— a white man. It turns my stomach that you feel the way you do about those other kinds of people. But then, Adam, I also am honest enough with myself to know that most men would find my willingness to prong with Will—or you, if you'd let me—unnatural. To me, doing that is—just doing it, like I go about with a black girl."

"What are you trying to say, George?"

"Will you go to quarters with me?"

"No." Adam shook his head. Then he said, "But I hear your need. It's cold, but lower your breeches. It won't take long for me to unload your ballocks."

George didn't understand Adam's sudden willingness to take his sex. But it didn't matter. What he did enjoy was having Adam's warm mouth around his badly swollen cock. As Adam had promised, it didn't take long.

Shortly the two men loaded firewood in their arms and, without speaking, went to their separate quarters. Adam dropped his wood at the fireplace but didn't build a fire. Instead he was quickly out of his clothes and under the bedcovers. He pulled himself into the womb position and quivered. Soon he began to talk with himself.

"Why did I do that?

"It was the only way to avoid violence.

"If he had tried to take me, would I have fought with him?

"Probably. But I might just have let him take me.

"And enjoyed it?

"Probably.

"Did I like having his cock in my mouth?

"Yes. It was a large one. Like Matt's.

"Will I do it again before he leaves?

"I don't know. And I won't know until such encounter comes along, if it does.

"Does this mean that I'm not ready for Tim?

"No. I need Tim, and he needs me.

"Would Martin understand what I did?

"Understand, yes, but he would not have approved. Because, like Will, I just gave a few moments of sexual pleasure, without any affection. Just the need to do it and get done with it.

"Am I ashamed?

"No. Why lie to myself? I want the love of another man. A man like Tim. But I did enjoy the raw pleasure of the brief sex with a man like George. He will be gone soon, and with him the temptation to do it again. The man I need is Tim.

"Yes, the man I need is Tim. We shall learn to love each other."

Adam was soon asleep.

For the next week Adam and George ate at the kitchen table without saying much to each other and certainly not anything about the incident at the woodshed. Occasionally Adam stared at George, but usually George kept his face down toward his plate. It was as if he was ashamed to look up at Adam. After supper, each gathered logs from the woodshed—but without meeting each other.

Shortly after the middle of December snow fell. Adam joined young William Ashley and Joseph's oldest son in building three snow forts. Adam's fort was between the other two. He faced snowballs from two directions. Since he could throw in only one direction at a time, he soon waved his cap in surrender. He watched the two boys go at it until they tired and decided to declare a draw. They boasted, however, that they had beat Adam.

The boys headed away from the battlefield in opposite directions, but Adam could tell they were up to something. Suddenly they were snowballing each other in a frantic attempt to win the day. Adam watched out of their firing range. Finally he yelled to them, "You are both winners on a cold December afternoon. Now get home, both of you."

That night at supper, as she handed him his plate, Hannah commented to Adam, "Snowball fight this afternoon."

"Did you win?" George asked.

"No, I lost. They ganged up on me. They threw to a draw. I think they got hungry and cold, so, after one last brief battle, they stopped throwing and parted as friends."

"Speaking of parting," George said, "I leave tomorrow." His announcement attracted the attention of everyone at the table. "Mr. Ashley and I leave early. We are riding down the back trail. And, Adam, I heard Mr. Ashley say that the new cordwainer would ride my horse back the next day."

Adam was delighted to hear that Tim would be here the day after tomorrow. But, in a calm manner, he said, "I'll ask Mr. Ashley about that."

"Whether he's here or not is no concern of mine. All I know is I won't be here tomorrow night for supper," George replied.

After supper was over, Adam shook George's hand, wished him well in his new indenture, and started to leave the kitchen.

"Let's go together," George called to Adam. "I want a word with you."

Adam sucked in his breath. He had hoped to avoid seeing George outside. Reluctantly Adam waited, and the two men left the kitchen together.

The sky was clear. The snow on the ground sparkled. Adam took the lead and headed to the woodshed. He wanted to be one step ahead of anything George wanted to say or do this evening. "It's damn cold," he said. "I need an extra log tonight."

"The log you need is waiting for you," George said.

"Which one is that?" Adam asked, knowing full well that George was talking about his cock.

"Mine."

"I don't want that one. How about this one!" Adam exclaimed. He picked up the largest log he saw. He whirled around and shoved the log close to George's face.

George backed away from Adam. "I didn't think you'd go for it. I won't try to make you. As you said the other night, you'd put up a good fight."

"Yes, I would. And, if you were able to get your cock in my mouth, I'd bite the head off."

George laughed. "Well, I wouldn't want that."

Adam said nothing, but he held on to the large log.

"Tell me something, Adam."

"What?"

"The other night when you took my cock, you did that like an old hand. It was a damn good job you did. I think you and Lance must have been with each other more than just 'every once in a while.' It was a pretty steady thing, wasn't it?"

When Adam did not respond immediately, George said again, "Wasn't it?"

"Yes. Lance and I were lovers."

George snorted. "Always thought there was something unnatural about you and him."

"There was nothing unnatural about the love between Lance and me," Adam quickly countered.

"The law and the Bible say two men lying together is unnatural."

"Then they are wrong," Adam calmly declared.

"Does Mr. Ashley know about you?"

"Not that I am aware."

"Would you mind if I told him?" George asked sarcastically.

"If anyone tells him, I will."

"But you won't."

"Not unless he asks, and I don't think he will."

"Take my log, Adam, and I won't tell him."

Adam waited a moment, then said, "If you do, he'll want to know how you know, and he'll see through any lie you tell him. If you tell him the truth, you'll incriminate yourself. We would hang together. And I don't think you want a broken neck any more than I do. That's my answer, George. I won't take your log again."

"Looks like we reached a draw, just like the boys this afternoon in the snowball fight. Shall we part as friends like they did?"

"We are not friends, George. Still I wish you well."

George started to go but stopped and turned back. "You and that new young man be careful what you do. Someone might catch you doing it 'every once in a while.' That would be the two of you getting hung. Not you and me."

"I'll give you similar advice, George. If anyone catches you with a black woman, you'll be in trouble."

"I doubt either of us is going to pay too much attention to the advice we got."

Adam had nothing more to say. He added several logs to the large one he was still carrying and left for quarters. As he walked away, he thought to himself that George's advice about being careful was very much like that Martin had given him.

The next morning Adam delayed leaving quarters until he thought Mr. Ashley and George would be at the stable yard ready to leave. He wasn't anxious to see George again, but he did want to ask Mr. Ashley about Tim. He put on his heavy coat and stepped out into the cold. The sky was clear, but even with the sun not much snow would melt away today. He was right. There was activity at the stable. When Mr. Ashley saw Adam, he called to him and motioned for him to join them.

"George and I are ready to leave. I'll see Timothy this evening and tell him to prepare to ride back with me tomorrow. We should be here by late afternoon," Mr. Ashley said.

Adam looked up at the clear sky. "I doubt you'll have snow on either ride."

"I hope not. Any messages for your aunt, Adam?"

"Yes. I send her and Master Tisdale greetings for the holiday season. Tell her that all goes well with me, and I hope the same for her. And tell Tim that I expect him to share quarters with me and that I'll see him at supper in the kitchen tomorrow night."

"That I'll do. Let's be off, George. You ride ahead. I'll follow you. No time or reason to talk. Rest your horse when she needs it. But, other than that, just ride until we reach warm rooms in Williamsburg. It's a good day's ride."

As they started off, Adam waved to them both. As George passed Adam, he leaned down, grinned, and said, "Enjoy yourself, Adam— every once in a while." Then he put the mare into a fast walk.

Adam watched until the two riders were out of sight on the plantation trail that lead to the back trail. His relief at seeing George gone, his anticipation of Tim's coming, and his empty stomach sent Adam to good smells of the kitchen.

That day went by more quickly than Adam expected. But whatever he did or wherever he was, one thought kept repeating itself. *Be-*

*fore Tim arrives, I must finally let go of Lance.* His dream that night was a strange mixture of the back yard at Alan's shop in Williamsburg, the stable barn at Cromley Hall, the bend at the river with the sound of a broken branch, the small gravestone with Lance's name engraved on it, a navel button with light fuzz around it. Adam suddenly awakened. He was sweating despite the chill of the room. *Tomorrow I go to the cemetery. Tomorrow Tim comes. Tomorrow night we lie here together.*

The next afternoon was clear and sunny, but the breeze was chilly. There was still snow on the ground. As Adam walked to the cemetery where Lance was buried, he recalled the many experiences they had together. He shuddered when he heard Lance's cry of pain from Matt's bullet grazing his arm. He laughed when he thought about the many races across the river and about Lance's playful boasts at so often being the winner. What kept coming back in his mind though was the pleasure they experienced that afternoon in the woods when they first realized that they wanted each other. They had certainly tortured themselves lying naked in bed and desperately trying to avoid each other's body all those weeks before that afternoon in the woods. Adam chuckled. Well, Tim and I won't have that uncomfortable time, he told himself.

When he reached the cemetery, he brushed the snow off the small gravestone. He looked down at the inscription, LANCE MORLEY, 1730-1755, ASHLEY LANDING CORDWAINER. As he stood there, he felt he ought to be crying, but only a temporary light mist obscured his vision before he wiped it away.

Then clear-eyed, Adam silently said a final good-bye to his dead lover. "I know nothing is perfect, but our time together was about as perfect as anything can be. We were lovers. But you're gone now, Lance. I need to move on, and I'm ready. In the church you gave Tim and me your blessing as a couple. Tim's coming sometime today, and we start a life together. At the moment I have a strong affection for Tim, not the deep love I had for you. In time Tim and I will come to love each other, I am sure of that. It won't be exactly like the love you and I had, Lance. It shouldn't be. But in its own new way it will be another deep love. If you can hear me, Lance, which I doubt you can, give Tim and me your blessing again, as you did in the church."

The only sound Adam heard was that of a busy woodpecker. Adam smiled and hoped that the bird was finding something to eat that cold afternoon. He took a last look at the gravestone, pulled his coat tighter around himself, and started back the path to the great house. He was happy and at peace with himself. He whistled a tune he had learned as a boy at Cromley Hall. Suddenly he realized that his whistle was being repeated by someone concealed in the bushes down the path.

Adam whistled several bars of the tune and stopped.

The hidden whistler answered with the same bars.

Adam whistled a few more notes. Those, too, were answered.

"Tim!" Adam called with delight.

"Adam!" the whistler answered. "Come to me. I want to show you my navel and to get a look at yours."

Tim's whistle guided Adam down the path and into the thicket of bushes. The woods were silent for a long time until the woodpecker from the cemetery found another tree to his liking. It was at the thicket of bushes.

# ABOUT THE AUTHOR

**Gavin Morris** is an author who lives in the Pacific Northwest.

doi:10.1300/5623_13

## Order a copy of this book with this form or online at:
### http://www.haworthpress.com/store/product.asp?sku=5623

# VIRGINIA BEDFELLOWS

_____ in softbound at $16.95 (ISBN-13: 978-1-56023-588-0; ISBN-10: 1-56023-588-8)

Or order online and use special offer code HEC25 in the shopping cart.

COST OF BOOKS_____

☐ **BILL ME LATER:** (Bill-me option is good on US/Canada/Mexico orders only; not good to jobbers, wholesalers, or subscription agencies.)

☐ Check here if billing address is different from shipping address and attach purchase order and billing address information.

POSTAGE & HANDLING_____
*(US: $4.00 for first book & $1.50 for each additional book)*
*(Outside US: $5.00 for first book & $2.00 for each additional book)*

Signature_____

SUBTOTAL_____

☐ **PAYMENT ENCLOSED: $**_____

IN CANADA: ADD 7% GST_____

☐ **PLEASE CHARGE TO MY CREDIT CARD.**

STATE TAX_____
*(NJ, NY, OH, MN, CA, IL, IN, PA, & SD residents, add appropriate local sales tax)*

☐ Visa ☐ MasterCard ☐ AmEx ☐ Discover
☐ Diner's Club ☐ Eurocard ☐ JCB

Account # _____

**FINAL TOTAL_____**
*(If paying in Canadian funds, convert using the current exchange rate, UNESCO coupons welcome)*

Exp. Date_____

Signature_____

Prices in US dollars and subject to change without notice.

NAME_____

INSTITUTION_____

ADDRESS_____

CITY_____

STATE/ZIP_____

COUNTRY_____ COUNTY (NY residents only)_____

TEL_____ FAX_____

E-MAIL_____

May we use your e-mail address for confirmations and other types of information? ☐ Yes ☐ No We appreciate receiving your e-mail address and fax number. Haworth would like to e-mail or fax special discount offers to you, as a preferred customer. **We will never share, rent, or exchange your e-mail address or fax number.** We regard such actions as an invasion of your privacy.

*Order From Your Local Bookstore or Directly From*
**The Haworth Press, Inc.**
10 Alice Street, Binghamton, New York 13904-1580 • USA
TELEPHONE: 1-800-HAWORTH (1-800-429-6784) / Outside US/Canada: (607) 722-5857
FAX: 1-800-895-0582 / Outside US/Canada: (607) 771-0012
E-mail to: orders@haworthpress.com

**For orders outside US and Canada,** you may wish to order through your local sales representative, distributor, or bookseller.
For information, see http://haworthpress.com/distributors

*(Discounts are available for individual orders in US and Canada only, not booksellers/distributors.)*

PLEASE PHOTOCOPY THIS FORM FOR YOUR PERSONAL USE.
http://www.HaworthPress.com                                    BOF06